PLAYING WITH FIRE

ALSO BY CYNTHIA EDEN

Once Bitten, Twice Burned

Burn for Me

Angel of Darkness

Angel Betrayed

Angel in Chains

Avenging Angel

Immortal Danger

Never Cry Wolf

The Wolf Within

Eternal Hunter

I'll Be Slaying You

Eternal Flame

Hotter After Midnight

Midnight Sins

Midnight's Master

And read more from Cynthia Eden in these collections:

Howl for It

The Naughty List

Belong to the Night

When He Was Bad

Everlasting Bad Boys

PLAYING WITH FIRE

CYNTHIA EDEN

KENSINGTON PUBLISHING CORP.
www.kensingtonbooks.com

BRAVA BOOKS are published by

Kensington Publishing Corp.
119 West 40th Street
New York, NY 10018

All Kensington titles, imprints, and distributed lines are available at special quantity discounts for bulk purchases for sales promotions, premiums, fund-raising, educational, or institutional use.

Special book excerpts or customized printings can also be created to fit specific needs. For details, write or phone the office of the Kensington special sales manager: Kensington Publishing Corp., 119 West 40th Street, New York, NY 10018, attn: Special Sales Department; phone: 1-800-221-2647.

ISBN-13: 978-0-7582-8410-5
ISBN-10: 0-7582-8410-1

First Kensington Trade Paperback Printing: September 2014

10 9 8 7 6 5 4 3 2 1

Printed in the United States of America

First Electronic Edition: September 2014

ISBN-13: 978-0-7582-8412-9
ISBN-10: 0-7582-8412-8

ACKNOWLEDGMENTS

I need to offer a round of thanks to so many people.

First, my readers—thank you for all of the support that you have given to me. You are absolutely incredible.

To Eden's Agents—what would I do without you? You're all amazing!

For my fabulous editor, Esi Sogah—thank you for your wonderful editorial insight. Working with you has been a pleasure.

Happy reading!

PROLOGUE

"Please stop, Daddy. Please!" The little girl twisted and struggled desperately against the thick straps that held her down on the cold, metal table.

"Now, Cassie, be a good girl and don't fight." Her father loomed above her, wearing his white lab coat. He had a mask over his face, and all she could see were his glittering eyes. "This is going to make you stronger. Don't you want to be stronger?"

He was going to put the medicine in her again. She could see the needle. It glinted under the bright light. So long and sharp.

"I-I don't want to be stronger," she whispered. She wanted out of that room. Away from him.

Far, far away.

"There are monsters in the world, Cassie. We have to stop them." His voice had hardened. His voice was always hard and cold.

He looked like a monster. With the light all around him. With the white mask over his face. White gloves on his hands.

Tears leaked down her cheeks as he pushed the needle into her arm.

She screamed. It felt like fire was pouring into her veins. Her body started to thrash and jerk on the table.

He sighed. "That's why I had to use the straps. I couldn't have you hurting yourself."

Her screams grew louder.

"Don't worry. We only have a few more weeks of injections to go."

She kept screaming. She couldn't stop. She was *burning.* Her head banged against the table. Over and over. Black dots danced before her eyes.

"Once the transformation is complete, you'll be our weapon. So perfectly cloaked in a child's innocence."

Her screams stopped. She choked, trying to pull in a breath, but she couldn't get air. Her gaze flew around the small lab. Her daddy's lab. He usually made her stay out of the lab. But he'd brought her in today—even when she'd begged to go outside.

He was staring down at her. His eyes . . . looked worried. He never looked that way.

"Breathe, Cassie," his voice snapped.

She couldn't.

Machines started to beep around her.

"The dose was too high!" her father yelled.

The light seemed to be fading.

"Cassie?"

He'd injected her with something else. She had just made out the glint of a needle before it was shoved into her arm.

"Her heart has stopped beating." A woman's voice. A nurse. Mrs. May. She sometimes gave Cassie lollipops when her father wasn't looking. Mrs. May had always seemed so nice.

But she had strapped her down minutes before. Usually, one of the men would strap her down. Not sweet Mrs. May. Not . . .

"Cassie!"

She couldn't see her father anymore, but at least the fire

had stopped burning her body. She didn't feel the fire anymore. Didn't feel anything.

"She's flatlined!"

Cassie heard nothing more.

Cassie sucked in a desperate breath. Then she screamed because she *hurt*.

"She's back! Dammit, she's back!"

That was . . . Daddy's voice. She tried to see him, but the light above her was too bright. So Cassie looked down . . . and saw the blood that covered her body. "Dad . . . dy?"

Then he was there. Lowering his face toward hers. "It's going to be all right, sweetheart. I took care of you."

She'd never seen him smile like that before.

"You're going to be so strong now. So strong . . ."

She didn't feel strong.

"You'll change the world. You'll *change the world* . . ."

Cassie could only lay there and feel the wet warmth of her blood. The straps cut her, but they didn't hurt nearly as bad as . . . as the stitches that her father was putting into her skin.

But Cassie didn't cry out again. There was no point. Daddy wasn't going to let her go.

She turned her head. More nurses were around her. Mrs. May even brushed a soft, gloved hand over her cheek.

Cassie held her body as still as she could and wished, so very badly, that her father hadn't brought her back.

Because in those few moments, she'd enjoyed death.

Cassie crept quietly down the hallway. Someone new had been brought into the facility. She'd heard the raised voices. The thud of footsteps.

Her daddy had said that his program was growing.

Her daddy scared her.

When she saw him leaving the room at the end of the hall, she ducked back into the shadows. He passed her flanked by two big men with guns, and he never looked her way.

Her hands were shaking so she balled them into fists. Then, her bare feet making no sound, Cassie slipped down the hallway.

She opened the door to the last room, but no one was inside. Stairs were in the corner. Stairs leading down below.

Cassie bit her lip. She wasn't supposed to be there. Her daddy had said . . .

Daddy's bad. He hurt me.

She went down the stairs. Then she saw him.

Big, dark. In a . . . cage?

His head jerked up, and he spun toward her. "Who are you?" the man in the cage demanded. His voice scared her. It was like an animal's rumbling growl.

But she crept closer to him.

He stiffened as his dark gaze raked over her. "Why is there blood on you?"

"He killed me." She understood exactly what had happened. And what *would* happen. "He's going to kill you, too."

The man came toward the heavy bars that separated them. "Do you want to help me, little girl?"

She nodded.

"Go back upstairs. See if you can find a key to open the cage and—"

Her fisted hand opened. She'd already taken the key.

Sometimes, her daddy didn't realize how smart she really was.

She put the key in the lock. Heard the *snick*. "I don't want him to kill anyone else." Soft, sad.

The man came out of the cage. He bent before her. Stared into her eyes. "Who are you?" he asked again.

His eyes were so dark. Just like the darkness that had claimed her when she died.

"Cassie . . . Cassandra."

"Come with me, Cassandra. We're both getting out of here." His fingers wrapped around hers.

His hand felt too warm.

"I want to get out," she whispered, nodding quickly. "Please, help me."

His fingers tightened around hers. "I will."

She heard the thud of footsteps, coming down the stairs.

"Cassie!" Her father's shout. "Cassie . . . *what have you done*?" He was there. He wasn't alone. More men with guns. Always . . . the guns.

"Shoot him," her father ordered as he glared at the man beside Cassie.

"No!" she yelled.

But they didn't listen to her. They never did. Bullets flew by her. They thudded into the body of the man who'd been caged.

Hard hands reached for her and yanked her away from him even as his body fell.

"No!" She kicked and twisted and clawed, but she couldn't get back to him. "Stop!"

"Move away. The fire's coming . . ." Her father's words. Heavy with an edge that sounded like he was excited. His smile made her stomach twist.

Her eyes returned to the man—dead now. Just like she'd been on her daddy's table.

"Don't worry," her father told her, finally glancing her way. "He'll come back, too."

A few minutes later, the man's body began to burn right in front of her eyes. Fire raced across his skin.

"I told you, Cassie," her father said as he stroked her hair. "Monsters are real."

The man continued to burn.

"Y-yes, Daddy."

He was right. There was a monster in the room. But it wasn't the man who was starting to rise to his feet—even as he burned. No, Cassie knew the real monster was the man smiling and hugging her.

Her father.

And one day, she would stop him.

One day.

CHAPTER ONE

It was hard for Cassandra Armstrong to love a man who didn't remember her.

It was even harder to walk into the seediest paranormal bar that existed on the backstreets of Chicago and discover said man in the arms of some trashy vamp.

Cassie's eyes narrowed as she stared at Dante. He was in the back corner, probably trying to hide in the shadows, except the guy wasn't exactly the type to blend well.

Too big. Too dangerous. Too sexy.

And that vamp had her fangs way too close to his throat for Cassie's peace of mind.

Cassie shoved her way through the crowd, muttering apologies as she bumped into the various paranormal beings—and the humans—who filled Taboo. A few years ago, the paranormals had stopped pretending they didn't exist and gotten wild with their coming out party. Since then, clubs like Taboo had popped up in all the major cities in the U.S. and around the world.

Dante stood against the back wall. The vampire, a woman with long red hair and a way-too-short skirt, had her hands all over him. Blood-red nails, of course. Typical. The redhead was arching up on her toes and putting her mouth close to Dante's neck.

"Okay. You're just going to need to get away from him," Cassie snapped as she closed in on them.

The vampire froze.

Dante tilted his head to the side and glanced curiously over at Cassie. Was there any recognition in his dark gaze?

Of course not. To him, she could have been any stranger off the street.

Don't let it hurt. Don't. Dante couldn't help what he was.

But he could get the hell away from that trashy vamp.

The vampire spun toward Cassie and hissed.

Wait. Hissed, really? Cassie barely controlled an eye roll.

"Get lost," the vamp told her, baring her fangs. "He's mine."

Think again. Cassie's hands were clenched into fists, and it took all of her self-control not to swing out at the chick. "No, he's not." Said very definitely. She looked past the vampire. "Dante, we need to leave."

He stiffened.

That's right. I know your name. Why oh why can't you know something about me? Anything?

But that was the way it always was for them.

Cassie kept holding Dante's gaze. "Trust me on this. You don't want her sinking those fangs into you."

His blood was special, and rather addictive to vampires. If the redhead got one sip, she wouldn't be backing away from him anytime soon.

Then I'd have to stake her. Oh, what a pity.

"Dante, we can—" Cassie's words ended in a gasp.

The vampire had lunged forward and wrapped her hand around Cassie's throat. With that one hand, the vampire lifted her off her feet. "Maybe I'll just sink my fangs into you, bitch." Then she leaned her head in close to Cassie and whispered, "Because no one gets between me and my meal."

"Y-you . . . don't . . . want . . ." Cassie tried to choke out the words but it was hard to speak, um, what with the vamp actually *choking* her and all. She was trying to tell the redhead . . . *You don't want to put your fangs in me. That would be a huge mistake.*

But the vamp wasn't giving her the time to talk.

"Let her go." Dante's voice. Cold. Flat. And as deliciously deep as she remembered.

The vampire's eyes narrowed as she stared at Cassie with a mix of disgust and rage. "You're right. We don't need her. We don't—"

"I said . . . *let her go.*" The threat in Dante's voice had goose bumps rising on Cassie's arms. "And I meant do it *now.*"

The vamp dropped her.

Cassie landed on her ass.

Figured. She'd never been the graceful type.

The redhead turned toward Dante. "Ready to leave?" she purred to him.

Purring. Hissing. The vamp was so annoying.

"You leave." Dante sent her a look that could have frozen a desert. "I'm not done here."

"But—"

"And I'm not your fucking meal," he added, a touch of heat whipping through his words.

So he had heard that part. Cassie had thought his enhanced hearing would pick it up.

The redhead glared at Dante, then at Cassie. There was a promise of retribution in the vamp's eyes.

Ah, yes, another day, another enemy. Cassie swallowed and rose slowly to her feet.

"I'll see you again," the vampire murmured. The words were directed at Cassie, and they sure sounded like a threat.

Wonderful. As if she needed any more threats in her life.

Then the vampire was gone. Probably off to find another meal.

"Who are you?" His voice was a low rumble of sound, one that sent a few more shivers dancing over her skin. Maybe some people—okay, *most* people—would find that deep rumble scary.

To her, it was sexy. Because of Dante, she'd always had a thing for men with deep voices.

She squared her shoulders and stared up at him. "Did you burn again?" She'd seen him just a few months before in New Orleans.

He'd saved her life then. Had actually seemed to remember her . . .

But there was no recognition on his face now.

She stared up at him. Those high cheekbones, that square jaw. The firm lips that she'd never seen smile, despite all of her attempts to make him happy. His eyes were dark, so dark they appeared almost as black as the thick hair that hung a little too long and grazed the back of his shirt.

Those eyes were watchful, guarded, as they swept over her. "Burn?" Dante repeated carefully.

In the next second, he lunged forward—his move faster than the vamp's had been. His hand—big, strong, hot—wrapped around her arm and pulled her close against his chest. "Now just how the hell would you know about that?"

Cassie wasn't as tall as the redhead. Not even close. She was barely skirting five foot five, so she had to tilt her head back to hold his gaze. Dante was at least six foot three, and the guy was built along some very muscled dimensions.

His hold tightened. "Answer me."

His fingers seemed to heat even more, and she knew his power was coursing through his blood. If she wasn't careful, he might burn her. Just how much control would he have then?

"Please." Cassie kept her voice even with an extreme effort. "I'm not here to hurt you." No, she was there to beg for his help. If he'd remembered her, even a little, that begging would have gone over much better.

Since he seemed to not know her at all . . .

His gaze swept over face, then . . . narrowed on her mouth. His left hand lifted, and his index finger reached out and lightly touched her lower lip.

Cassie stopped breathing. Her body was far too tuned to his. The man had pretty much ruined her for any other guy.

Not that Dante was a man. He was much, much more.

The Immortal.

That was the name he'd been given during his captivity. A captivity that she had been a part of.

His finger lightly grazed across her bottom lip. Just that touch had her nipples tightening and her whole body aching for him. But it wasn't the time. Definitely not the place. She had a mission to complete.

His head bent toward her, and Cassie wondered if Dante was about to kiss her. She even arched up to meet him halfway.

But he shook his head, and his hand fell back to his side.

So much for the moment.

Cassie cleared her throat. "The burn must be fresh. Your memory usually comes back within a week or so after your rising."

His face seemed to turn to stone.

Usually was the keyword. Dante had been through so much in the last few years that his memory was a very brittle thing. So was his sanity, a situation that made him a walking, talking nightmare for many.

"You must have been attacked," she whispered. Attacked . . . and killed. Because death was the only way—

He lifted her up and tossed her over his shoulder.

Cassie yelped, totally not expecting that move. She shoved

her hands against his ass—um, a very nice ass—and pushed herself up so she could see around her.

Some of the club's patrons were looking at her, amusement on their faces. They weren't exactly the kind to help a lady in distress. The redheaded vampire was staring her way. *Glaring* her way, rather.

And Dante was stalking away with her, his grip on her legs unbreakable.

Okay, so that was one way to get his attention.

She heard the sound of shattering wood. Had he just smashed a door? Sounded like he had. Cassie tried to crane around and see where they were going. It looked like they were headed inside some kind of back room. Stacks of boxes and bottles of alcohol lined the shelves.

"Get the hell out of here!" Dante's snarled order.

Three bodies ran past her, fast.

The world spun a bit, and Cassie found herself sprawled on top of a wooden table. Dante held one of her wrists in each of his hands as he stood between her legs.

Oh, wow.

"Who are you?" he demanded.

"My name won't matter to you." She barely breathed the words. "If you rose recently—"

"Your name!"

"C-Cassie Armstrong. Cassandra . . ."

His eyelids flickered. "Cassandra." He said her name as if he were tasting it.

Please, remember me. There had been so many times over the years, when she was sure that he did remember her, but then the tortures would start again. Torture and death.

He'd lose the memory of her, and she'd have to try so hard to get close to him again. To *make* him remember.

An endless cycle that left her hurting inside.

"I've dreamed about you," he whispered. His hold was an unbreakable grip on her wrists.

At his confession, her heartbeat picked up and hope blossomed inside of her. Finally, finally, he'd—

"In my dreams"—a muscle flexed along his jaw—"you kill me, Cassie Armstrong."

Oh, hell. "I told you. I'm not here to hurt you."

"But you *have* killed me before, haven't you?"

Cassie knew she had to be careful. She wasn't like him. Dante could die, again and again, but he would just come back from each death.

He'd rise from the ashes and be born again.

While she would just—well, die. There would be no coming back for her.

With a thought, he could incinerate her. The heat that warmed her skin could turn into a blazing inferno at any second.

"Last night, I dreamed about you." His words were a low growl as he leaned closer to her.

The noise from the bar drifted into the room. The blaring beat of music. The scents of sex, blood, and booze.

"You stared right at me, then you stabbed me."

His bad memories weren't going to make things any easier.

"So maybe you should tell me why I shouldn't just pay you back for that right now." His breath blew lightly over the sensitive skin of her neck. "And end *you.*"

She shook her head, sending her long hair sliding over her shoulders. "Please . . ."

"Oh, I like it when you beg."

Actually, he did. But that was another story.

"So you've had dreams." Cassie started talking, fast, because she had seen him incinerate a man before. She didn't want that same fate. "Well, I'm your key. I know you.

Every dark spot in your mind? I can shine the light and show you—"

His mouth was just inches from hers. Inches? More like *an* inch. "What are you going to show me?"

"Everything," she whispered, promised. "I can tell you the secrets of your life. I can tell you *who* you are, if you'll just trust me."

His gaze searched hers. Some people thought that his eyes were just dark—mirroring his black soul, but they were wrong. There were flecks of gold hidden in his eyes. You just had to look hard and deep enough to see them.

"Why should I trust a woman who's killed me before?"

"Because I've saved you, too." She'd risked so much to save him. "Believe it or not, you actually *owe* me."

"I don't believe it."

Her lips trembled.

His gaze dropped once more to her mouth.

"Dante . . ."

He kissed her.

She hadn't been expecting the move, and when his lips closed over hers, shock froze her for a moment. Then she realized—*Dante.*

Her lips parted eagerly for him, and the wall that she'd built to hold back her need for him started to fracture. His tongue pushed into her mouth. Not sampling, but taking, and it was just like she remembered. He kissed her, she wanted. Lust tore through her, and her wrists twisted in his grip because she wanted to touch him.

She wanted—

His head lifted. His eyes blazed down at her, the gold starting to heat. "I remember . . . your mouth. Your taste."

She'd never been able to forget his kiss. He'd been the first man that she ever kissed. The first to make her feel like she belonged to someone.

A someone who sometimes seemed to hate her.

"You can trust me," she whispered, desperate to make him believe her.

He gave a hard shake of his head. "No, that's the last thing I can do." He moved away from her, leaping back.

For an instant, she didn't move. His eyes were on her, sweeping from the top of her hair down to her small sandals. He seemed confused. Yeah, well, so was she.

Don't kiss me and jerk away. She didn't have the damn plague.

"I woke up a week ago," he told her quietly, his voice still making her ache. "In an alley that had been scorched. I was naked, and there were ashes all around me."

Her heart beat faster as she straightened on the table.

"What happened to me?" he demanded.

"Dante, I—"

"Is that my name?"

The memory loss seemed more severe than it had been in the past. "Y-yes. That's what you told me to call you." But was it really his name? She wasn't sure. He'd never confessed too much about his life—at least, not his life before he'd come to be a prisoner.

"How did I get in that alley?"

She pushed away from the table. Her knees were trembling so she locked them as she faced him. "I don't know. The last time I saw you, you were down in New Orleans."

A faint furrow appeared between his brows. He appeared to be a man in his prime, maybe close to thirty-four or thirty-five, but the truth was that Dante was much, much older.

There was a reason he'd been called the Immortal at the facility.

"New Orleans?" He yanked a hand through his hair. "What was I doing down there?"

That was an easy answer. "Saving my life."

His hand fell. Suspicion was on his face as he asked, "Are you sure I wasn't trying to kill you?"

Actually, no, she wasn't. But she was still breathing, and if he had truly wanted her dead, she'd be ash.

His enemies had a way of ending up as ash drifting in the wind.

"What happened to me in the alley?"

Okay, if she was going to get his trust, she was obviously going to have to share with him. "I think you died."

He laughed. The sound was bitter and hard, just like the laughter she'd heard from him a dozen times. She'd tried for years to get a real laugh from him. That hadn't happened.

"If I died," he asked, "then how am I breathing now?"

That was the tricky-to-explain part. "Look, Dante—"

Shouts erupted from the other room. High-pitched, desperate screams that were immediately followed by the rat-a-tat of gunfire.

They found me. Cassie's heartbeat froze in her chest then she was the one leaping forward and grabbing Dante's hand. "We have to go. *Now.*"

She yanked him, hoping he'd follow with her.

He didn't move. Not even an inch. "I don't run from anyone."

Well, yes, that was true. He didn't.

She did. When you weren't a paranormal powerhouse, you learned to flee pretty quickly.

More screams. More blasts from guns. "If they catch me," Cassie said, voice soft, "they won't let me get away."

His gaze held hers.

"If they catch *you,* they're going to toss you back in a cage, and you won't see daylight again anytime soon." Her heartbeat seemed to thunder as loud as the gunshots. He had to believe her. "They'll keep you in that cage, and they'll torture you again and again."

"How do you know this?"

She licked her dry lips. "Because that's what they did to you before."

His jaw hardened. "Then I think it's time I faced these bastards."

Wait—what? Hadn't she been trying to sell the guy on running?

He pulled from her and rushed toward the broken door, heading right toward the sound of gunshots and screams.

As she watched him run away, her heart iced. She'd followed Dante to Chicago because she'd needed him. She'd hunted for him, searching desperately . . . and she'd led his enemies right to his side.

Dante, I'm sorry.

But he wouldn't believe that apology. He never did.

Men wearing black ski masks had rushed inside of Taboo. The drumming music had died away, and only the screams of those still trapped in the club remained.

Most of the patrons had run away. Those wounded on the floor appeared to be mostly vampires. It seemed they were fine with walking amongst the humans these days. There were shifters, too.

Dante hadn't felt even mild surprise when he'd seen a man shift into the form of a fox just the night before. Maybe it was because his memories were gone that he felt no surprise. It seemed that vampires and shifters were a normal part of the world.

Or at least, they felt normal to him.

"You there!" A male's voice called out. "Stop!"

A big, black gun was pointing at his chest.

Dante. She'd said my name was Dante. The name had felt

right in his mind. Just as the sexy brunette had felt right in his hands.

"Are you a human?" the voice snapped out from behind a mask. "Or a Para?"

He'd learned yesterday that *Para* was the slang for a paranormal being. He didn't quite know what he was, so he just stared back at the man, not particularly feeling the urge to answer him.

"What are you?" the man demanded as he came closer.

"I'm someone you don't want to piss off," Dante said. A fair warning.

"That's him," another masked man said, his voice breaking with excitement. "The one from the video feed. He's the one who torched that den of vampires in the alley!"

Dante stiffened.

"Holy hell," said the fool who still had his gun pointed at Dante. "It looks like we've got big game today."

"No," Dante said very definitely. "You don't." He let his gaze sweep the club. Men and women were cowering under the upturned tables . . . but Paras were supposed to be stronger than that.

No one makes me cower. The knowledge was there, pushing inside him. He feared no one and nothing.

I make others fear.

"Get out of here now," Dante told the men. "While you still have a chance at life." He counted a dozen men in the black clothing, complete with heavy, thick vests that covered their chests. They were all armed to the teeth. He didn't care about their weapons. He'd learned that he had a weapon of his own. One that always seemed to be at the ready.

He lifted his hands.

And he let the fire burn through him. The power started as a warm pool within him, then it heated, going molten, and seeming to spread through his veins. Soon the fire was bursting from his fingertips, rising right over his hands, swirling in a thick ball. Red, gold, and orange, those flames flared higher and brighter.

The men swore and jumped back. But they didn't flee. Fools. They lifted their weapons. Aimed at him.

He would incinerate them.

He would—

"No!"

It was her scream. His head whipped to the right, and Dante saw the woman with the thick, dark hair running toward him. Her face was paler than it had been before. Her green eyes seemed huge, her red lips were trembling and—

"Dante, get out of here! They'll drug you!"

The men fired their weapons. Except they didn't aim at him.

A bullet blasted and slammed into Cassie's shoulder. Her eyes widened as she stumbled back. But she didn't go down. "Run!" she yelled at him. "Get out of here!"

He wasn't running anywhere.

They'd shot her.

The fire raged hotter and fury had him snarling—and letting that fire go.

They'd shot her.

The flames flew from him and the fire raced right for the gunmen. They screamed—*yes, now it's your turn to scream*—and dropped their weapons.

Falling to the floor, the men rolled over and over as they tried to put out the flames that licked greedily along their clothing.

"Dante . . ." A whisper. Her whisper.

The woman who'd haunted him. Obsessed him.

Enraged him.

She was on her knees, struggling to get to him, and he . . . found himself running to her side.

"I-it's a drug," she whispered. "They were . . . trying to take us in . . . alive . . ."

The men weren't taking anyone in. They were running *out,* dragging their wounded with them. The other paranormals were rushing for safety, too.

"Go," Cassie told him. "Before they're back with . . . reinforcements." Her eyelids were sagging closed. The drug she'd spoken of was knocking her out. "Go," she whispered again.

What was he to do with her? Leave her there? She'd just said the men would come back with reinforcements. When they returned, they'd take her.

No. No one takes her from me.

The thought made him tense. It was—though he did not know why—the first thought he'd had when he'd looked up and seen her coming toward him in Taboo.

No one takes her from me.

He scooped her into his arms. Rose with her held tightly against his chest. He worried—too late—that the heat from his hands might burn her.

But there were no burn marks on her delicate skin.

Her head fell back against his shoulder, but her eyelashes were still flickering, and Dante knew that she was fighting to stay awake.

"What will they do if they take you?" he asked her.

"C-cage . . ."

An image flashed in his mind. Thick, metal bars. A flickering fluorescent light. A dirty, stone floor.

He could taste ash rising on his tongue. He didn't want to taste the ash. He wanted to taste her again. Sweet, light . . .

Temptation.

"You're not going in a cage," he promised.

His arms tightened around her. This woman . . . he'd thought she was a phantom from his mind, someone else to torment him. Not real. Then he'd looked up and seen her. She'd come to him.

Flesh and blood.

Real.

He strode from the wreckage of Taboo, hurrying into the night. Sirens wailed. Voices cried out.

He ran faster. Held her even tighter.

Cassie Armstrong was the key to his life. The key to finding out just who—what—he was.

And he had no plans to let her go.

No one takes her from me.

Lieutenant Colonel Jon Abrams marched into the wreckage of the paranormal club. Tables were overturned. Chairs smashed. The doorway still smoldered from the flames that had been unleashed on his men.

"You had him here?" Jon demanded, turning to the men who stood behind him. Burned, beaten, those men were so useless to him. "You had him, and you let the bastard just walk away?" What part of *priority containment* had they missed?

"He shot fire at us!" Kevin Lysand said, straightening his shoulders. "No one said the Paras could—"

"He's a phoenix. What did you think he was going to do, just stand there and let you drug him?" Jon spun away from the men, the fury nearly choking him. After all those months. To be so close . . . and have those idiots let his prey escape.

"I . . . it was the woman." Kevin's voice was softer.

Jon glanced over his shoulder. "What woman?"

Kevin's Adam's apple bobbed. "Th-the one from Genesis. Cassandra—"

Jon lunged and grabbed the guy's shoulders. He lifted him up, forcing Kevin to look him straight in the eyes. "Are you telling me that Cassandra Armstrong was actually here, in Taboo?" He'd been ripping the country apart looking for her.

A grim nod. "That's when the big guy attacked. When we shot at her."

They'd shot at her, but she wasn't there. Hell, *no one* was there anymore. Those who hadn't ran out before the infiltration had crawled out when his men had retreated.

"He went wild when we shot at her," Kevin told him with a quick nod.

Jon forced himself to release the other man. "Did he take her out?"

Kevin didn't speak.

Because he didn't know?

Fucking incompetence. Jon heaved out a sigh. "You didn't see them leave, did you?"

Kevin wet his lips. "I was on fire then, sir."

Like a little fire should have stopped him.

Jon whirled away. "Tell me that you had a tracker in that tranq you fired into Cassandra." A new little invention, one that Uncle Sam was rather proud of—a drug and tracking combination bullet all in one. Some paranormals could flee even after the drug hit them. They had the strength to run, for a time.

But sooner or later, the drug got to them.

And when it did, the tracker came into play. It would light up in their system and lead Jon and his men right back to their prey.

Easy.

"Tell me," he demanded without looking back. If the dumb bastard hadn't done his job and gotten a track on Cassandra, Jon might just shoot the fool himself.

"There was a track in there," Kevin said, his tone growing more confident. "She won't be getting away from us."

Hell, yes. But Jon didn't smile, not yet. The tip that he'd received about the phoenix—and Cassandra—had been right. He'd have to be sure and reward his informant. First, though . . . "Burn this place to the ground."

Taboo was far enough away from the hub of the city that most folks wouldn't have heard or seen the attack. Just in case, he was used to covering his tracks.

The paranormals might be out in the world, trying to blend with humans, but they were also still hunted. Still targets, especially the walking, talking nightmares that stalked the earth.

Nightmares like the phoenix.

Some beings were too dangerous to live.

Some needed to be stopped, by any means necessary.

In this instance, the means was one Cassandra Armstrong. A weapon had never looked so innocent.

"Burn it." The fire could always be blamed on the phoenix. "Then get me the track on Cassandra."

She'd led him on a chase for months, but he'd have her soon. She wasn't getting out of the program. She was too vital.

Too useful as a weapon.

He began to whistle as he walked out of the club.

Kevin and his men were pouring out alcohol and smashing the bottles, soaking the scene for one fine blaze. They wouldn't make a fire that burned as hot as a phoenix's flames, but they'd come close enough.

Close. Enough.

Jon kept whistling. *I'm coming for you, Cassandra.* She'd run from him, but their little cat and mouse game was almost at an end.

Cassandra should have known there would be no escape. Her father had brought her into the program years ago.

And once you were in, death was the only way out.

CHAPTER TWO

She was . . . not beautiful.

Dante told himself that even as he leaned toward her and let his fingers trail over the curve of her nose. A few freckles rested on the bridge of that nose. His finger slid to the side, tracing the curve of her cheekbone. Her face was oval, pale, and he didn't like the dark shadows under her eyes.

She wasn't beautiful.

He told himself that again . . . and realized he was such a liar. This woman, the woman who'd killed him in his dreams, had him staring at her like some kind of lovesick fool.

He pulled away from her and clenched his hands into fists so that he wouldn't touch her again. They were in some two-bit, pay-by-the-hour motel room. She was spread out on the bed and he was beside her.

She was still out cold, and he was far too distracted by her body.

Far too—

Her eyelids began to flicker. His stupid heart beat faster.

Who is she to me?

There was something between them. Death, *yes*. Hate? Betrayal? *Maybe*.

Something.

She moaned softly, and he didn't like the sound of pain on her lips. He found himself leaning forward and tucking the pillow beneath her head.

When he bent forward, she screamed. The sound was high and desperate and absolutely terrified. She tried to bolt from the bed.

He couldn't have that, so he caught her arms and—as gently as he could—pushed her back against the mattress. "Easy."

At his voice, her scream died away. Her eyes widened as she stared up at him. Her gaze wasn't clear as it had been before. Instead, her green gaze was hazy, a little lost.

"Dante?" Cassie whispered his name. Smiled. "I missed you."

His heartbeat seemed too loud. That smile of hers . . . yeah, she was fucking beautiful, all right. And dangerous.

She was also trying to lean up and kiss him.

What had been in that drug?

"You left me," she told him, voice husky, "and I thought you were supposed to—" Cassie broke off, blinking. Then she groaned and shook her head. "Where the hell am . . . I?" Her voice wasn't quite as husky, but he still found that he liked the sound.

"Not hell," he told her as he eased back a bit. "Just a cheap motel."

When he moved back, Cassie bolted upright, then winced. "My shoulder . . ." Her right hand lifted and touched the wound. "They shot me."

Yes, they had. And they'd almost died for that crime. He didn't know why the fury had blasted through him so hard, but it had.

"They shot me," she whispered again, then she shoved against his chest. "Get *away from me*!"

He rose slowly. "You're welcome. Maybe next time, I'll just leave you on the floor." The words were deliberately cold and brutal, but she didn't even seem to have heard him.

She was climbing from the bed, nearly falling on her face. He locked his body and refused to go to her. If she was so desperate to get away from him—

Wait. Why would she want to leave? She'd been the one to seek him out. He frowned.

"They're coming . . ."

He heard her whisper as she ran into the bathroom. Then there was the sound of drawers being opened. Slammed shut.

He glanced toward the motel room door. She'd told him to get away from her. There was no need for him to stay with her any longer.

Yes, there is. She knows about my past.

"I want answers," he said, raising his voice so that she'd have to hear him over her mutters—

And the sound of breaking glass.

What was happening in the bathroom? He hurried to it and saw that, no, it hadn't been glass shattering. It had been the mirror behind the sink. Cassie had driven her small fist into it. Blood dripped from the knuckles of her right hand.

"What are you doing?"

She didn't answer. Just picked up a big, triangular shaped chunk of the mirror—and shoved the sharp edge into her left shoulder.

"Cassie!" He grabbed her hand and yanked the chunk back out.

She whimpered at the pain and tried to fight him.

He just held her tighter. "Is it the drug they gave you? Is it making you do this?" The scent of her blood was driving him crazy. Pissing him off. "Dammit, *stop*."

Her breath heaved out. "They're coming."

Yeah, he'd heard her say that before.

"There's a tracking device in me. When they shot me"—she sucked in a deep, pain-filled breath—"it implanted. I have to get it out, or they'll get me."

"So you decide to do emergency surgery on yourself with a chunk of glass?"

"I don't . . . have a lot of options." Her lips trembled and twisted into a faint smile. "Don't worry, I'm a doctor."

That smile shouldn't have made his heartbeat kick up. It did.

He could only shake his head. "You're an insane woman who is bleeding all over the place." Grabbing a washcloth, he shoved it against her shoulder. "You're probably going to get an infection and—" He broke off. How did he know about infections? He knew how to drive a car, how to talk in French, how to beat the hell out of anyone who tried to give him a rough time.

But he had no actual memories of his life. Well, except for those dreams of her . . . *killing me.*

"D-don't worry. I never get infections. I can't."

Such a lie. Humans could catch anything. *They're weak.* The knowledge was there, inside him, coming from the man he'd been before that dirty alley.

She wasn't fighting him anymore. "Please." Her whisper. "I don't have much time. I need to get this thing out of me."

He understood now. "That's why you wanted me to leave you. Because you think they'll track you here."

A broken laugh came from her. "You're pretty big game to them. If they think you're with me, then, yes, they'll be coming for you, too. And I promised you that I'd never let them lock you up again."

I don't remember that promise.

"Too bad you don't remember that," she said, seeming to echo his thoughts. "Or me."

His hands fell away from her. The bloody cloth slid to the floor.

Cassie squared her shoulders and reached for the chunk of mirror once more. "You don't . . . you don't have to watch."

He was watching. Leaving her didn't seem like an option.

She stared at her reflection in what was left of the mirror and slowly made a deeper cut on her shoulder. Blood slid down her skin, soaking the shirt. Her breaths seemed loud in that small space, and he hated the pain that flashed across her delicate features.

But she didn't cry out.

Her finger slid into that wound.

His back teeth locked.

A tear leaked down her cheek. But she didn't cry out.

"G-got it . . ." Her bloody fingers slid from her wound and she dropped a tiny computer chip into the sink. It hit with a clatter. Then her hands curled around the edge of the sink, and she seemed to steady herself. "A tear or two would make this so much easier," she muttered.

He frowned at her bent head. She *was* crying. The woman realized that, didn't she?

She glanced over at him. "But I'm guessing you don't remember that part, either, do you?"

He just stared at her.

"Right." She took in another deep breath then ripped away the bottom of her T-shirt. He saw the smooth flesh of her stomach as she twisted and tied the fabric around her shoulder.

His hands lifted, taking over the task as he realized she was trying to bind the wound.

"Th-thank you."

A woman in a torn, blood-soaked top wouldn't exactly go unnoticed in the city. But at least she wasn't dripping blood everywhere anymore.

"I have to get back to my safe house," she said with a

nod. "I've got . . . supplies there. I can stitch the wound. Change. Regroup." Her gaze held his. "You haven't left me yet."

The woman was stating the obvious.

"You haven't killed me, either." Again, she seemed to enjoy the obvious.

"Why?"

He glanced down. Saw that her blood was on his hands. The sight seemed familiar.

Don't die, Cassandra. Don't leave me.

The words pushed through his mind. His words. Another time. Another place. An image came to him. Her body had been broken and bloody, and her eyes had gone glassy as she—

Died?

"Dante?"

He hunched his shoulders and jerked on the faucet, sending water surging into the sink. The blood on his hands washed away even as the hazy image faded from his mind. Surely he'd never held the woman and begged her to live.

He stared down at the red water and the bits of broken mirror in the sink. "You said you were my key."

"I—"

He turned off the water and glanced back at her. "You don't escape me until I get all of those secrets that I was promised."

She nodded.

He hated the smell of her blood.

"We should hurry," she told him as her gaze darted away from his. "They're fast trackers."

"Who are *they*?" That was the first secret he wanted.

But before Cassie could answer he heard . . .

The squeal of tires. Engines growling.

Cassie began, "They're—"

"Here." In the last week, he'd discovered that no one had senses quite like his, and he'd heard the approach long before she had. "They're here."

Her eyes widened.

Fine. If they wanted a battle, then he'd give them a war that would rip their lives apart.

"No." Her hand grabbed his. Her knuckles were still bleeding. "There are too many humans around here. Your fire . . . you can't always control it. We need to get the hell out of this place." She brushed by him and eyed the small window on the side of the bathroom. "Think you can fit?"

No. But he stepped forward and drove his fists into it. The whole window frame flew backward and slammed into the ground.

"Right. Super strength," she whispered. "Handy." Then she was jumping from that window, even though they were on the second floor. He tried to grab her, but it was too late. Her body curled in and she hit the ground with a thud.

Teeth locking, he leaped after her. His knees didn't even buckle when he landed on the ground.

The thunder of footsteps told him that their pursuers were rushing toward the front of the motel.

And he and Cassie were running toward the back parking lot. She jumped in the driver's seat of an old, beat-up Jeep and slid under the dash even as he climbed into the passenger seat. In the next second, the engine kicked to life, and Cassie shoved her foot down on the gas.

The Jeep rocketed out of that lot, heading into the waiting darkness.

Dante glanced back, but saw no sign of the men who'd been after them. The fools were probably going into the motel room. It would take them precious moments to realize that he and Cassie had vanished.

"They can't follow me without the chip," she said, raising her voice to be heard over the engine and the whip of the wind as it beat against the open Jeep. "We'll be safe." She paused. "For a while."

Maybe she hadn't meant for him to hear that last part.

If she knew him as well as she claimed, the woman would understand that he could hear even the faintest whisper from fifty yards away.

He'd clearly heard her words and the fear that trembled in her voice.

"Did he attack her?" Kevin asked as his gaze swept over the blood-stained bathroom. "I thought you said he wasn't a threat to the woman."

Jon shouldered his way into that closet of a bathroom. His gaze swept over the blood—and the two bloody handprints on the sink. "Get a team in to analyze the blood." But he already suspected he was staring at Cassie's blood, not Dante's.

Cassie wouldn't risk hurting Dante. She needed him too much.

"What did he do to her?" Kevin whispered.

Ah, Kevin was making a mistake. Most people did when they looked at Cassandra Armstrong. Small, delicate, *human*—they automatically thought that she was weak.

Jon knew she wasn't. Cassandra Armstrong was the most dangerous adversary that he'd ever faced.

She was also the woman he'd once wanted to marry. When he saw that much power, he wanted to possess it.

But Cassie had wanted someone else.

His fingers skimmed over the edge of the sink. He touched the miniature tracking device. She would have known to look for it, and she wouldn't have minded a bit of pain if it meant she kept her freedom.

Clever Cassie. Always so clever.

"She did it to herself." He inhaled. Cassie's blood smelled . . . different from most humans. It was a scent that he easily recognized. "We don't need the tracker to find her." Not while she was bleeding.

The blood would create a distinct trail of its own.

Either his team members would find her . . . or someone else—something else—would find her. Cassie's blood was too sweet, a lure designed by science. She should have known better than to run away with an open wound.

She was going to attract all manner of beasts.

Beasts who wanted only one thing—to drink that blood and drain her dry.

"This is your safe place?" Dante's voice was heavy with doubt.

Cassie glanced over at him with a frown. "Look, I didn't say I was hanging out at the Ritz." The rundown warehouse on the edge of town was the perfect crash spot for her. She tucked the Jeep behind the building, making sure it was out of sight, and led Dante toward what looked like a boarded-up door. The windows had that same, boarded-up look.

Appearances could be deceiving.

She pushed a panel, and the door slid open. Inside . . . the lights immediately flashed on, revealing an apartment. "Sometimes, this place can *almost* be as good as the Ritz."

She could tell by Dante's hanging jaw that she'd caught him by surprise. Score one for her.

"I have a friend," she said, though *friend* might be stretching things. *Patient?* Yes, that was a better description since they hadn't exactly had lots of meaningful conversations. "The guy's a computer genius. He's rich as all hell, and he's got a few of these . . . safe spots around the country." Since he couldn't currently use them, they were sure coming in handy for her.

She headed toward the bathroom. "Just give me a minute, okay?" A minute to stitch up her wound and get the blood off her skin.

Cassie didn't look back to see if Dante was waiting. If the guy had planned to ditch her, well, he would have left her butt back at Taboo. Since he was there, she knew he wouldn't leave. Not until he'd gotten what he wanted.

If only what he wanted was her.

The T-shirt bandage was soaked red with her blood. Great. Gritting her teeth, she peeled the wet cloth away, prepared to see the jagged sight of—

Healed skin.

Her breath rushed out and she angled her head down, trying to peer at what should have been a gaping wound. But she wasn't bleeding any longer. The skin had already sealed closed.

She hurriedly slammed the bathroom door shut behind her and barely managed to stop herself from sinking to the floor in shock. Unbelievable. Her skin was healing on its own. The wound just vanishing.

Her fingers slid over the skin. It was still a little pink, but there was *no* blood. "Amazing."

The door shook behind her. Dante's hand was pounding on the wood. "Cassie?"

She stripped away the remains of the bloody shirt. Tossed it to the floor. Her bra was stained red, too. Fabulous. "Give me a . . . ah . . . minute."

Silence, then almost grudging, "Do you need help?"

You've already helped me. He was the reason why her wound had closed. Why her whole life had changed.

A human didn't just magically heal herself.

He'd altered her down in New Orleans. Everything had changed for her in a blood-soaked instant of time.

When she'd opened her eyes, ready to thank her rescuer, Dante had been gone.

Her body wanted to shake at the memory, but Cassie stiffened her spine. She yanked on the shower's faucet and the water rushed out. Hurrying, she finished stripping.

She'd get the blood off, then she could deal with the mess that was her twisted relationship with Dante.

She'd put one foot in the shower when the door came crashing open behind her. Yelping, she tried to cover herself—one hand over her breasts and one hand over the juncture of her thighs.

His cheeks were flushed. His eyes—sweeping over her. Heating up. Burning not with the fire of the beast that he carried, but with desire. Lust.

"I-I told you to give me a minute." She backed away from him and went right into the path of the shooting shower spray.

His gaze was on her body. "Your shoulder's cut open."

She could feel that gaze of his like a hot touch.

He was heading toward her. Stalking her. "You shouldn't be in there. You need stitches."

Still keeping her hands in place—so not enough coverage—Cassie twisted her body so that he could see the wound. "All gone," she whispered. It was almost like a fantasy she'd had once. Dante had come in. He'd been desperate for her. He'd picked her up, put her against the shower wall. Licked her neck and—

He grabbed her hands and shoved her back against the shower wall. The breath rushed from her lungs. In her fantasy, he hadn't been that . . . rough. "Dante?"

"*What* are you?"

Naked. No coverage at all. "I-I'm human."

The water hit him, too, but he didn't seem to care. His shirt brushed over her breasts and her heart slammed into her chest.

"I might not remember everything," he said, "but even I know humans don't heal that fast."

Steam rose from the shower. From the hot water? Or from him? His touch was heating . . .

"I can explain." Her words tumbled out.

He didn't let her go. "You seem to say that a lot, but so far, I haven't heard any explanations."

She was naked and he was—just pissed.

It definitely wasn't like her fantasy anymore.

It was time for her to get pissed, too. She couldn't break away from his hold, but she lifted her chin and snapped, "Fine. You want to know why I'm this way? Why my wound just vanished?"

"Yes!"

"Because of you, okay? *You* did this to me. I nearly died about two months ago in New Orleans when some psychotic bastard vampire ripped into me. I would have died, but you saved me." And he had changed her, only she hadn't realized the full consequences of his actions at the time.

She *should* have realized it, though. Now she'd have to do more study and—

He lifted her up, putting their gazes on the same level. "How?"

"You cried for me." Whispered, but it was the truth. "You cried and you saved me."

She hadn't expected him to move so fast. One minute, he was holding her close, and in the next second, the guy was out of the shower. Actually, he was about five feet away from her.

He was laughing, but the sound was bitter and twisted. *What would his real laughter sound like?* She'd pretty much given up on ever hearing it.

"Bull," he snapped at her. "You're going to lie to me and say . . ."

She turned off the water and jumped out of the shower. Fumbling, Cassie grabbed a towel. Better protection, but still not perfect. Not that he'd exactly been overwhelmed by her charms. "I'm not lying to you, Dante. You want to know what secrets are locked up in your head? You want to know why you woke up in an alley, surrounded by ash?"

"Yes." Nearly a roar.

Right. She swallowed. "You're a phoenix shifter."

"A what?"

"A phoenix. Most people just think the phoenix was a myth, but they're wrong. You . . . you aren't a myth. When you die, you burn, and you come back." It probably wasn't the moment in which she should tell him that every time he died, he came back . . . broken. Darker. Even more dangerous.

"Stop lying to me!" His voice was a loud fury.

Hers was soft. "I'm not. Just like the mythical phoenix, your tears can heal. If you cry—just like you cried when I was dying in New Orleans—you can save a life." She stepped toward him. Held tight to her towel. "You saved my life. Gave me some of your power. Your magic."

He didn't speak. Did that mean he believed her words? She hoped so.

"That power must still be in me, and that's why I healed just now. *You* healed me. I really am just a human, but you're something far more." She wanted to reach out and touch him, but wasn't sure how he'd react. "That's why you woke up surrounded by ash in an alley. You must have died and burned . . . and you came back."

He lifted his hand. Fire was burning just above his fingertips. Touching him had definitely not been a good idea.

"A phoenix shifter can control fire," she said, still trying to keep her voice soft and soothing. He seemed to need soothing. But then, he'd always seemed to need that. "You're a very, very powerful paranormal being. Extremely rare and—"

"I'm a monster." Flat. Brittle.

She shook her head. "Paranormals are everywhere these days. You don't have to hide, you can—"

"No one should live forever." His head lifted, and he stared at her.

She could see the fire beginning to swirl in his gaze, lighting the darkness. It scared her. Truth be known, his fire had always scared her.

"You're saying I do keep living, don't I?"

She managed to nod.

"How old am I?"

"I-I don't know."

"How many times have I died?"

She had no answer.

"How many?"

"At least thirty times . . . that I know of." Pain rippled beneath her words. *Thirty times.*

"I was in a cage."

She swallowed. "Yes." She'd told him that before, right? Or was he remembering?

The flames flared brighter in his eyes. "You were there."

Oh, shit. He was *remembering.*

"You shoved a knife into my heart."

Um, once. Were they back to dwelling on that?

"You killed me. You were there when they cut into me. When they tortured me." His voice rose with every word, but he made no move to go near her. Or to touch her.

That was good because the flames burning in his eyes matched the fire swirling above his hand.

"You were in a white coat. In a lab." His jaw locked. *"You were one of them."*

"Let me explain—"

"I should have left you to die when I had the chance." The brutal words seemed to tear into her heart.

Cassie shook her head. "You don't remember everything yet. It's natural after a rising." She tried to smile. Failed. It hurt too much to smile. "When your memory comes back fully, you'll remember it all. You'll know that I didn't—"

He spun away from her. Stormed from the bathroom and headed for the exit.

"Dante!"

He didn't stop.

She raced forward—*don't burn, don't burn*—and grabbed his arm. He whirled back toward her, and the flames came right at her face.

Cassie screamed.

The flames froze above her, inches from her skin.

"You want to let me go now," he ordered. His voice had lowered to a lethal growl of sound.

She should let him go, she should. Instead, Cassie lifted her chin. "You're going to get those flames the hell away from me now because we both know you aren't about to burn me." She was impressed. Her words sounded much braver than she felt.

His brows climbed. "How do you know that?"

"Because you've never hurt me." Maybe that was his weakness. Others had said it was. "I don't know why, but you *can't* hurt me."

His flames sputtered away. "I think I can." He walked away. Out of the warehouse. Didn't look back. Just . . . left her.

She realized that he was right. He could hurt her. Not with flames or with fists, but by walking away. Leaving her behind.

"I need your help!" she shouted after him.

And heard, "Too fucking bad."

It wasn't the first time that he'd broken her heart, but dammit, it *would* be the last.

He stood outside the warehouse, sucking in deep gulps of air. The fire had been too close to her skin. Too damn close. If he'd burned her . . .

You've never hurt me. Her words rang in his ears. She'd sounded so sincere when she told him that. Staring up at him, her eyes so green and big—and reflecting the fire that he barely held in check.

Human . . . if he believed her story.

He did. Dammit, he *did*.

He had no business being around a human. Humans couldn't survive the touch of flames. They couldn't survive his strength. If he touched her, he could kill her.

He didn't want Cassandra Armstrong's death on him.

Dante wasn't sure why she'd sought him out in Chicago, but the *why* no longer mattered. He needed to get away from her. As far away as he could.

He took one step. Another. Didn't look back. Wouldn't. But he could still smell her. Still *feel* her silken skin beneath his hands.

He took another step.

She'd been naked in that bathroom. The water had glistened on her skin. He'd wanted to lick the droplets away. To lift her up against that shower wall and just feast on her.

Human.

He took another step.

His flames could have disfigured her. During the last week, he'd awoken from nightmares only to discover that he was burning the bed down around him. Over and over. The shrieking of smoke alarms had been what saved the people in the cheap motel rooms near him.

When he slept, he lost control.

When he was near Cassie, he *wanted* to lose control.

And if he did, she would burn.

Not her.

He took another step. Cassie wasn't following him. She was letting him go.

He wouldn't turn around. He would not go back to her.

Because he wanted her to keep living.

CHAPTER THREE

Cassie jerked on fresh clothes as quickly as she could. She'd thought about running right out after Dante, but running out stark naked wasn't her best plan ever, especially with the sun getting ready to rise. Luckily, Trace seemed to keep his safe houses stocked with clothing for both men and women. The guy must like to be prepared.

She had searched the drawers and found underwear. Jeans. T-shirt. Tennis shoes. And—

She heard the thud of a fist hitting the back door. Her head snapped up. *Dante? Coming back?* Hope had her rushing toward the door, but caution—the caution that had saved her life plenty of times over the last few years—had her glancing at the security feeds before she opened that door.

Trace Frost—the shifter and computer genius who actually owned the warehouse—had wired the safe house so that he could see just who came calling to his door. She inched carefully toward the bank of security cameras. *Hell.*

Dante wasn't on the other side of the door. Four men were—men with bared fangs.

Vampires.

Her eyes squeezed closed for an instant. *My blood.* She had been so intent on getting away from the motel room and putting some space between her and that damn tracking device that she'd forgotten all about the blood.

And the fact that her blood was like a homing beacon for vampires.

The door banged, nearly buckling inward, and the whole building actually seemed to shake.

Her eyes flew open and she jumped back. *Weapon.* She needed a weapon, fast. Those vampires weren't going away.

Another frantic glance at the monitor showed that the vampires were slamming their fists into the door. Since vampires had enhanced strength as one of their little bonus features, those were some very powerful fists.

Cassie rushed toward the dresser. When she'd been searching for clothes, she'd noticed a nice little surprise hidden in a drawer. She shoved the T-shirts aside and her fingers curled over the gun that had been stashed inside. A gun—and wooden bullets—all conveniently stored and ready for her. Her fingers fumbled a bit as she loaded the wooden bullets into the gun.

The door shook again.

She slid the last bullet home.

The pounding stopped. Silence, punctuated only by her heaving breaths. Carefully, Cassie crept over so that she could see the security feed once more. Trace had set up cameras all around the perimeter of the place. He wasn't a fan of being caught off guard.

Neither was Cassie. She kept the gun in her right hand. A few taps of the keyboard had the image on the screen splitting and then shifting focus so she could see from the four cameras that were positioned around the property.

Camera one—at her back door—showed nothing. *Where had the vampires gone?*

Camera two—the lens that should be focused on the street—showed . . . a vampire. *There you are.* His fangs came toward the camera and the image turned to static.

Her heart beat faster.

Camera three—on the front of the building. She didn't see any vampires there, but—

Wait. Yes she did she them. Their shadows were crawling along the warehouse's roof. She heard the scratches above her—from their claws?

Camera four . . . she leaned toward the screen. That camera was locked on the second floor of the warehouse, on the windows to the left.

The windows that were—

She heard the shatter of glass, and the scratches and rustles suddenly became much louder.

The vampires weren't outside any longer. They were inside. And they were coming for her.

She moved quickly, putting her back against the nearest wall. They were coming down the stairs, so she'd be ready for them.

"Get out of here!" Cassie yelled up to them. "I don't want to hurt you!" She didn't. Her job was to help, to cure.

Not to kill.

She'd left the killing to her father. The guy had pretty much made it his life's work. She was trying to pick up the pieces and mend the lives that he'd torn apart.

The vampires rushed down the stairs. Their fangs were out, fully extended, and hunger twisted their faces.

That was what her blood did. It made them desperate. Drunk.

Crazed.

Her blood soaked shirt was still in the bathroom, so she wasn't surprised when the first vampire ignored her entirely and ran in there.

But the second and the third? They locked their hungry gazes on her . . . and advanced.

"I don't want to hurt you," Cassie repeated again. "Please, leave."

The vampire closest to her, a man with blond hair who

looked like he was barely twenty, just laughed. “But I don’t want to leave.” He lifted his hands. The guy was sporting wickedly sharp claws. “And I *do* want to hurt you.” He leapt toward her.

She shot him.

Dante froze as the thunder of a gunshot echoed in his ear. He was in the middle of the warehouse district, walking through the night, trying not to look back—

But that gunshot had come from behind him.

Cassie?

He heard the roar of another gunshot. Another.

He didn’t think. Didn’t hesitate. He just turned and ran back to her.

No one takes her from me.

Even when he walked away from her.

I’m coming. Hold on, Cassie. Hold on.

As he ran, another image flashed through his mind. A memory. He’d had flashes before, like scenes straight from a movie that he watched instead of lived. And in this scene . . .

Blood covered Cassie’s chest. She stared up at him, emotion filling her beautiful eyes. An emotion that he didn’t want to face.

“It’s . . . okay . . .”

He could barely make out her words. But he knew she was lying. Cassie was such a terrible liar.

The wounds on her body were too deep. There was too much blood.

She would never survive.

He could save her. He had to save her. There was no way that Cassie could die.

Only . . .

The life drained from her eyes. He saw it vanish. “No!” His roar. He yanked her against him. Held her as close to his body as he could. Her blood soaked his shirt and his skin.

She wasn't breathing. She wasn't moving.

He was too late.

She was gone.

The image vanished as swiftly as it had appeared, leaving behind the bitter taste of fear in Dante's mouth. He wouldn't be too late. Couldn't be.

He pushed himself, desperate to rush back to the woman that he'd so foolishly left moments before.

He reached the back door. Tried to swipe his hand over the hidden keypad that Cassie had used before. But the damn door wouldn't open.

Another shot thundered.

"Cassie!" Dante yelled her name.

He heard snarls and shouts and . . .

"Help!" Her voice. She was still alive. She'd better stay that way.

He slammed into the door. The damn thing wouldn't give. It must have been reinforced.

Fine. If it wouldn't give, then he'd just burn it down.

Because he *was* getting to Cassie. "Hold on!" Dante shouted to her. "Just hold on!"

He wasn't up to having her die in his arms a second time.

She was out of bullets. She was also a terrible shot. Cassie hadn't hit even one of those vampires in the heart.

She'd just blasted them until her gun clicked. Two of the vampires—the blond and a bald guy—were on the floor. But the others were closing in on her.

Crap.

Smoke began to drift in the air. Her head whipped toward the door. Dante was out there. That was *his* smoke. She'd heard his shout. He wanted her to hold on—hold on to what? The vampires were right freaking there!

One grabbed for her. She slammed the gun into the side of his head and managed to break free of him. Then she raced for the wooden table in the corner. The vampire she'd hit grabbed her legs and she fell, face-first, onto the floor. She ignored the pain from that impact and grabbed out with her hands. She caught the side of the wooden chair and yanked it back.

The vampire was pulling her toward him even as the chair slammed into the floor—slammed and broke apart.

She grabbed for one of the broken pieces of wood.

"Got to taste . . . got to *taste* . . ." the vampire snarled.

"No. Trust me, you don't want a taste!"

He didn't listen.

His fangs came at her.

She drove the makeshift stake into his chest. That close, well, that close her aim was dead-on. He screamed, but the cry choked off as his body stiffened.

His blood pulsed out of his chest as she shoved him away from her. Cassie jumped to her feet.

And realized that she was surrounded.

Three vampires . . . including one that she recognized.

"Hello, bitch," said the redheaded female vamp that Cassie had last seen in Taboo. "Didn't think you'd get away from me, did you?"

Sometimes, Cassie truly thought that she had the worst luck in the world.

She bent and scooped up one of the chair's broken legs. "This is your last chance to walk away."

The smoke was thickening. Dante was outside, probably growing more pissed by the moment. The angrier he got, the more powerful he would become. She just needed to buy a little more time. Time for him to burn his way through the wall of the building.

"One of us will walk away," the vampire promised Cassie with a click of her too-sharp teeth. "But it won't be you." The redhead rushed toward her.

Cassie screamed and brought up her stake.

The redhead just ripped that stake out of her hand—and *laughed*. "Amateur hour is over, honey. Time for you to play with the big girls." The stake was thrown against the wall. The redhead grabbed hold of Cassie's hair and yanked back her head, baring her throat. "You should never have come between me and my snack."

That *snack* had just burned his way through the back side of the warehouse. As Cassie gasped, flames leaped around them, racing up the walls, burning hot and bright.

Over the female vampire's shoulder, Cassie saw Dante surging toward them. The flames were reflected in his eyes. "You should run," she whispered to the vamp.

"And you should die," the redhead snarled, then she sank her teeth into Cassie's throat.

Cassie cried out as the woman tore into her neck. The bite was brutal, and she felt the knife-slice of those teeth as they sank deep into her jugular. She tried to push the redhead away, but the vampire was too strong.

Cassie's eyes were still open, and her wild stare saw that the other vamps were rushing toward Dante. He sent balls of fire flying toward them. The flames hit the vampires, and they ignited.

"Get . . . off . . . me . . ." Cassie yelled as she twisted in the redhead's hold.

The redhead jerked her head up. Blood dripped down her lips. Her eyes widened with horror, even as a tendril of smoke rose from her mouth. "What . . . the hell . . . are . . . you?" She stumbled back.

Cassie had told her to run. "I warned you . . ." She put her hand to her throat, trying to stop that gushing flow of blood that she could feel on her neck.

Dante was rushing toward the female vampire, coming with his fire and fury, but there would be no time for his attack.

She hit the floor. The vamp was screaming. Every bit of color bleached from her skin, and her body stiffened, contorting, and she died . . . thirty seconds after tasting Cassie's blood.

What . . . the hell . . . are . . . you?

"Poison," Cassie whispered, then her knees buckled.

She didn't hit the floor, though. Dante was there. There with the fire in his eyes and a touch that should have scorched her, but didn't. His arms wrapped around her, and he lifted her high into his arms.

"Tell me that you'll heal," he ordered, voice thick.

He'd come back for her. She swallowed, but felt the pain of that small movement rock through her whole body. "I'll . . . heal." If that was what he wanted to hear, then she'd give him the words.

"You better not be lying to me."

She tried to smile. Then she realized that the fire was still burning. Seeming to rage out of control, the flames had raced up the walls and were rolling across the ceiling.

The fire surrounded them.

It had pretty much destroyed Trace's safe house.

"Dante . . ."

His hold tightened on her. "I've got you."

Even though the fire crackled around her and blood dripped down her neck, she felt safe. Her eyes closed. She didn't want to see the flames. She felt the heat lance over her skin, a hot wind, but there was no more pain.

A few moments later, she could taste fresh air again. They were outside, and Dante was running toward the Jeep. The faint light from dawn lit the sky.

He put her into the Jeep and started to rush around to the driver's side. "No." She grabbed his arm. "My blood—"

"When are you going to heal?"

She had no idea. "My blood . . . lured the vampires here. The men who are after me . . . after us . . . can use vampires to track us." Cassie shook her head. "The blood will lead them to me. As long as I bleed, I'll make you a target."

"If anyone comes after you, I'll turn them to ash."

Her breath caught.

He leaned in toward her. "Do I look like I'm afraid of vampires?"

"N-no."

He'd touched them. They'd burned. End of story. Vampires were particularly susceptible to the flames.

He started to walk away.

She grabbed his arm again. Yes, they needed to go. The flames currently stretching high into the sky would attract humans and paranormals, but first she had to know. "Why did you come back?"

Tell me it's because you needed me. That you couldn't stand the thought of something happening to me, that—

"Hell if I know."

She glared at him.

But he didn't even notice. He'd pulled away. Hurried around the front of the Jeep and jumped into the driver's seat.

They drove away with a squeal of tires.

Cassie wasn't bleeding anymore. The woman really could heal at an amazing speed. But Dante didn't know if he believed that her healing talent came from him.

Or from his tears.

He might not remember his life, but he didn't exactly think that he was the crying sort.

They'd stopped at a pharmacy earlier. She'd run inside, bought a cheap new T-shirt, changed, and ditched her bloody old one. She came back out with only a faint red mark on her neck.

At the moment, they were driving on the interstate. The wind whipped through the Jeep, the sun beat down on them, and—

She was sleeping.

He slanted a glance toward her. She'd yanked her long hair back into a ponytail, but tendrils had escaped with the wind and they blew lightly around her face.

In sleep, she looked innocent. Delicate.

But then, she'd looked delicate in his dreams, too. Right before she'd killed him.

Did she have dreams? Nightmares? He'd like to know.

"Stay on the interstate," she said, her voice barely rising over the whipping wind. "We need to head down south."

Huh. So she wasn't sleeping. "What's in the South?"

"People who are counting on me." She shifted in her seat, stretching a bit. When she stretched, that T-shirt pulled across the round curves of her breasts in the *best* way.

His fingers tightened around the steering wheel, and he forced himself to focus on the road. He had been driving for four hours already. He eased toward the nearest exit, thinking that they'd gas up, and head out again.

"You *are* coming with me, right? You aren't planning to ditch me at this exit?"

There was no missing the worried edge in her voice.

He hadn't thought about, uh, ditching her, but then, he didn't know why he was still with her. Why he felt the *need* to stay close to her.

Dante slowed down the Jeep as they turned toward the lone service station that sat at the top of the hill. He wasn't even sure what state they were in, but the Jeep's engine had started to sputter, and he was worried that sound meant the vehicle wouldn't make it much farther.

"How the hell do I know," he asked, not answering her question, "how to drive? How to tell that it sounds like the radiator *might* make it a few more hours? I didn't know my own damn name before you told me, but—"

"It's a type of source amnesia." Her words were soft. "That's what I figured, anyway. You can remember how to do things, like drive a car or—or kiss." She cleared her throat. "But you don't remember when or where you learned them. It's all the specific, explicit memories that you lose when you burn."

"They come back." Hadn't she said that?

"Usually. You never told me what it was like when you burned. You never told anyone for certain, so I don't know what happens to you. Where you go."

Hell.

"There have been times when you came back, and all of your memories were with you. It was rare, but it happened."

"And when it didn't?"

"They were usually back in a week."

Usually? He got the feeling the woman was being deliberately vague, and he sure wasn't in the mood for any games.

Dante waited until he'd braked the vehicle then turned his full attention to Cassie. No one else was around, so he figured he could be honest with her. "I don't know if I should help you or kill you."

Her eyes widened. "I . . . didn't realize that killing me was an option on the table."

It wasn't. He'd said the words to get some kind of response from her. Any response. Her words before had been too careful and quiet. Like the woman was hiding what she really felt.

She was *still* hiding. The slight flaring of her eyes wasn't good enough for him. "Who are the men hunting you?"

"Hunting *us*?" she corrected carefully. "That's what you meant, right? Because they're hunting both of us. Not just me."

He locked his back teeth.

"Those men work for the government. A very secret group that humans don't know about. The paranormals who know about them? Well, let's say they probably all wish they'd never heard of them, too." Her gaze darted behind him. There wasn't anything to see back there. Just a field of wheat.

"What do they want with you—us?" Dante asked.

Her gaze came back to him. "They want us to make them an army. An unstoppable army with your fire and immortality."

That said why they wanted him. "Why *you*?"

Her smile was broken. "Because I'm the mad scientist that they believe can create this army for them." She climbed from the Jeep.

He followed her. "Why the hell would they think that?"

"Because my father already made them one army of *enhanced*"—she stressed the word as she tried to shove back her loose tendrils of hair—"vampires. Of course, that turned into a freaking nightmare, but the guys in suits just don't learn, do they?"

Her *father*? Dante caught her arm and turned her toward him.

Her gaze lingered on his. "Every time you rose, I always wondered . . . will this be the time he remembers nothing? When the memories just don't return?" The mask was falling away.

He didn't speak.

"Maybe—maybe there are some things you'd rather not remember. There sure are things I'd prefer to forget." She smiled.

He knew it was a fake smile because her eyes didn't light up. So much for her mask sliding away.

"I'll go pay for the gas. Good thing you had some cash on you, huh?"

He'd stolen the money. Not such a "good" thing. But Dante was realizing he wasn't well acquainted with good.

He handed her the money. As soon as his fingers brushed hers, he felt the connection again. A surge of lust and need that seemed to pulse all the way through his veins.

She tried to pull away from him.

He didn't let her go.

"Do you think I don't remember that we were lovers?" He asked the question deliberately. Again, wanting to see her response.

But she shook her head. Her fake smile fell away. "We were never lovers, Dante."

Yet he knew her taste.

When she pulled away again, he let her go. He watched her walk away from him and toward the station. Enjoyed the sway of her ass, and then he called out, "Cassandra!"

She stopped. Looked back at him.

"We will be," he promised her.

He saw her swallow.

"You left me hours ago—just walked out. Now you think you'll sleep with me?" She shook her head. "You aren't that irresistible, no matter what you think."

She headed into the small station. His eyes narrowed. *We will be.*

The bell over the door jingled when Cassie entered the station. She glanced toward the counter and saw the clerk staring her way.

Older, balding, with a faded shirt and a grizzled jaw, he seemed to be studying her a bit too closely.

She gave him a smile, trying to put on her friendliest face. "Twenty dollars' worth of gas, please." She headed toward the counter. A glance to the upper right corner revealed the surveillance video that was currently showing Dante as he put gas in the Jeep.

She slid her cash across the counter and glanced up at the TV that had been mounted behind the counter. A sports show was on—a basketball game.

"Where you headed?" the clerk asked, taking the money and ringing up the sale real fast.

She kept her smile in place. "My boyfriend and I are going to visit some relatives in Georgia." She didn't actually have any relatives anymore. They were all dead.

"Maps are in the back," he told her, inclining his head. "You might want to pick up a few."

That wasn't such a bad idea. The old Jeep wasn't equipped with any GPS, and if they could find a short cut that would take them to Belle, Mississippi, in time . . . "Thanks. I'll do that." She turned away from him and headed toward the maps.

The basketball game kept playing behind her. She heard the rustle of footsteps.

"Authorities are still looking for the two suspects wanted in connection with an arson that killed four people in Chicago . . ."

That wasn't the basketball game. That was a newsflash that she'd rather be doing without. Cassie kept walking. It wasn't the time to panic. She glanced over at the maps and tried to act casual.

"Federal officials have identified one of the suspects as twenty-nine-year-old Cassandra Armstrong, an ex-doctoral student from Tulane who—"

Ex-doctoral? She'd gotten that doctorate—and an MD.

Cassie turned for the door and found her path blocked by the store clerk. He had a shotgun in his hands. "That same news story has been on every fifteen minutes for the last four hours. They've been running a picture of you every time it airs."

The gun was pointing right at her heart.

"Did you kill those four people in Chicago?"

They *were* dead, though they hadn't exactly been people.

Or, well, humans, anyway. "Does it matter that they were trying to kill me?"

The clerk was between her and the door. *Dammit.* She should have realized that her story would be fed to the media. It was a strategy that had been used before.

Give your prey no place to hide. Let everyone hunt them.

She was being hunted, all right.

"Cassandra Armstrong is considered armed and dangerous. She should not be confronted. If you see her, you should call . . ." The news reporter quickly rattled off a number that Cassie was sure was also flashing on the screen at that moment.

"You don't look dangerous to me," the clerk said, frowning.

Appearances can be deceiving. "This isn't your fight. Just step out of my way, and let me go."

His hold tightened on the gun.

She had a handy new healing technique, but would she heal from a gunshot wound to the chest? Cassie didn't think she wanted to find out.

Sweat beaded the man's brow. "You . . . killed those people."

The bell jingled behind him.

Oh, crap. If he swung at Dante with that gun—*Dante would burn him.*

"No!" Cassie cried out, then she slammed her body into the store clerk's. They tumbled onto the floor, but she got up faster than he did.

And she came up with the shotgun in her hands.

The man's eyes seemed to bulge out of his head. "I-I got a wife . . . kids . . ."

"Cassie?" Dante was behind her.

"You're gonna keep that wife and kids, sir. I'm not hurting you." She backed up and bumped into Dante. "You just stay on the floor. Count to one hundred, and forget you ever saw us." She would *not* have this man's death on her conscience.

Her conscience was already messed up enough.

"One . . . two . . . three . . ." The man closed his eyes as he started to count. He didn't get up off the floor.

Cassie shoved her elbow into Dante's rock-hard abs. "Let's go."

He was staring at her with a furrow between his brows. Another shove had him moving. When they were at the Jeep, she tossed the shotgun into the nearest trash can and jumped into the vehicle.

Cassie thought Dante would gun the engine and get them out of there. He didn't move. He was in the driver's seat, and the guy was just . . . staring at her.

"What?" Cassie snapped.

"You jumped on that man . . ."

That was obvious.

"You were . . . saving me?" He seemed stunned.

"Yes, well, when you die, it's not exactly pretty." And if he'd risen, he would have blown up that whole gas station. "Now can we *please* get out of here? I don't buy for a minute that the guy is counting all the way to one hundred before he springs to his feet." More likely, he was already calling the cops on them.

"You should have killed him."

"No." She grabbed for the key and cranked the ignition. "He was a human, one who was just trying to do the right thing." *Been there, done that.* "He didn't deserve to die." Her gaze sought Dante's. "Now come on. Get this thing moving."

He held her gaze a second longer. Then the Jeep jerked forward. Finally. They left that gas station with a squeal of their nearly bald tires. Left the shotgun.

She was very afraid that trouble would be following

close behind—trouble in the form of Lieutenant Colonel Jon Abrams. Jon was the leader of the group Uncle Sam had gunning for her—and Jon was also the man who'd once said he loved her.

She hadn't believed him. Despite the fact that he was a damn good liar.

Once upon a time, he'd been a would-be fiancé. Now, he was the man who wanted her to make him an unstoppable army.

Sorry, Jon, that's not going to happen.

Unfortunately, she knew from bitter experience that he didn't give up easily. Especially when he wanted something badly enough.

"And you're sure the woman you saw was Cassandra Armstrong?" Jon asked as he stared across the counter at the shaken store clerk.

The guy—Tommy Wells—gave a quick nod. "That was her. She—she jumped me. Took my gun before I could call the cops." His head hung a bit in shame as he gave the confession.

Jon lifted a brow. Considering that Cassie was all of five foot five and barely pushing past one hundred and thirty pounds, the confession couldn't be easy for the guy. If she was a paranormal, the defeat wouldn't have been quite so embarrassing, but since she was, in fact, mostly human . . .

Tommy's cheeks flushed an even deeper red and he muttered, "She had a guy with her. Big bastard who looked like he wanted to rip me to pieces."

"This bastard . . . describe him."

Tommy pointed to the height chart near the door. "Six foot three, freaking linebacker. Black hair, black eyes, a face that I don't ever want to see again . . ."

"Don't worry, if you see him again, it won't be for long." *Black hair, black eyes, the right size.*

Tommy frowned. "W-what do you mean it won't be for long?"

"If he comes back, the guy's here to kill you." But Jon didn't think the phoenix would be coming back. He was running with Cassie, sticking to her like glue.

The phoenix's obsession with Cassie hadn't lessened over the years. Jon would use that obsession. It would be what finally broke the phoenix known as Dante.

CHAPTER FOUR

"We can hide the Jeep in the back," Cassie said as the car eased to a stop at a cabin nestled in the mountains of Kentucky. Another safe house, courtesy of Trace. She'd stayed in it on her way up to Chicago, and it was the perfect place for them to rest up and regroup before the second leg of their journey.

Once the Jeep was covered—they would *not* be taking that rickety vehicle again because Trace had left backup transportation at his cabin—they went inside.

Trace did enjoy his luxury. Or he had, *before* his life had become a nightmare.

He was one of the patients that she had to get back to in Belle, Mississippi. He needed her. Cassie's assistant Charles would do his best to keep Trace stable until she got back, but time was of the essence, for Trace and for the other patient who needed her.

"Is this place yours?" Dante's voice was low, rumbling as he glanced around at the sleek lines of the cabin.

She shook her head, then realized he wasn't looking her way. "It belongs to a friend."

He touched the monitors that she'd activated minutes before. Monitors that showed the exterior of the cabin and the lone road leading up to it. *Trace sure seemed to love his security setups.*

"This the same friend who owned the warehouse?" Dante asked.

"Yes."

He looked at her with a hooded gaze. "Must be some friend if he lets you have access to all his homes."

Since Trace was incapable of using said homes at the moment, she wasn't sure that "letting" was involved so much. "We're both exhausted. We'll crash for a few hours, then hit the road again, and we should make it to Mississippi—"

"Is *he* waiting in Mississippi?" Dante stalked toward her, his head cocked. "The man who owns this cabin . . . is he waiting down there for you?"

She nodded.

"And he just let you walk away from him?" The back of his hand skated down her cheek.

She absolutely refused to tremble at his touch. She refused. She—

Trembled. *Dammit.*

"It wasn't a matter of me walking way. I told Trace that I'd be back."

"He's your lover."

"No." Cassie shook her head. "He's just someone who needs me." Actually, maybe it was time to lay her cards out for him. "He's the reason I came after you." Her breath whispered out as she pulled away from his touch. "Do you have any memory of your life before that alley? I mean, have the images started to come to you at all?"

His guarded expression told her that he did have some memories. It also told her he didn't trust her enough to tell her what he knew.

Fine. She'd tell him. "It was called Genesis." It had been her father's brainchild. "The media billed it as being a research facility. Everyone was told that all of the paranormals there had *volunteered* to be brought in. Our government was supposed to be developing a faster, stronger soldier at Genesis." Her hands fisted. "It was the next wave of mankind's development. Our evolution."

He just watched her with that dark gaze that could unnerve her too easily.

Just watched . . .

"Some of the paranormals *did* volunteer, but they didn't realize they were giving up their lives. The rest of them were taken. Abducted and forced into the program. Then the experiments started." She swallowed, remembering the screams that had haunted her for so long. "Most folks these days think that Genesis was a fairly new program. One that started a few years ago once the paranormals merged with society and stopped staying in the shadows."

"They think wrong."

Was he speaking from his own memories? He'd been in Genesis for far longer than a few years.

Before his *first* escape, anyway.

"My father started Genesis over thirty years ago. That was when he started to play God with the subjects in his labs." When she'd been seven, he'd started to play God *with her.*

"Where is your father now?" Anger. No, rage.

She could see it in the golden flames that had sparked to life in his eyes.

"In the ground." True. "He was killed a few months ago. Staked, then he lost his head." Maybe she should be sad, but she wasn't. "He experimented on himself. Hell, he experimented on everyone." *Don't, Daddy. Please.* "He was a vampire, but now he's just—*dead.*"

There would be no coming back for him.

"Trace . . . Trace Frost was infected." Because of her father. Because of her brother—though Richard was dead now, too. A whole family of Frankensteins, that was all they were. "Trace was given a drug that brought out his more . . . primal instincts."

"What is he?"

What . . . ah, so Dante did understand. "Trace is a wolf shifter. He used to have control of the beast, but thanks to Lycan-70, the beast has control of him now." If she couldn't reverse the effects of that drug, the man that Trace had been would never come back.

"You . . . care for him."

"I care for anyone who is tortured like that. From all accounts, Trace Frost was a good man before he was given the dosage. I want him to be that man again." Cassie squared her shoulders. "And I want you to help me."

A line of stubble coated Dante's jaw. He looked big and dark and dangerous. Normal for him.

She crept closer to him. "You're with me now. *Stay* with me. When we get to Mississippi, come with me to my lab—"

She had just said the *wrong* thing.

He grabbed her hand and yanked her right up against him. "I remember being in a *lab*." Snarled at her.

She didn't flinch.

"They cut me open. They shot me. They drugged me. They even drowned me a few times."

He had far more memories than she'd realized.

"I won't ever fucking go back in a lab again."

Her gaze held his. "Trace isn't the only one that is suffering down there. There are vampires. And there's an infection that's spreading faster than anything I've ever seen. The humans who get bit . . . can't think or reason any longer. All they do is hunger and kill—"

"Then they need to be put down."

"They have families. *Lives*. If I can cure them, they can go back to the way they were before."

Dante's eyes narrowed at that. "You think you can cure a vampire? Turn him human again? That's not possible."

"A man who dies and burns and rises from the ashes shouldn't be possible, either." She swiped her tongue over too dry lips and noticed that his gaze followed that small movement. Her heart slammed into her ribs. "Your tears can cure anything or anyone. If I can just get a sample from you . . ."

He pushed her away. "Is that what you want? For me to cry for you?" His face had twisted into lines that looked cruel. "They tried for years to get me to break. I never did." He spun away from her. Headed for the stairs.

"You did." The words slipped out. She shouldn't have said them. Big, big mistake.

But they were the truth.

He froze with his hand on the wooden bannister. "What?"

She knotted her fingers into fists. "You did break. The phoenix shed a tear."

He glanced back at her.

"If you hadn't cried, I wouldn't be here."

"Find another fucking phoenix!"

It wasn't like they were easy to find. "As far as I know, there are only three phoenixes in the United States."

He whirled toward her.

Right. Ahem . . . phoenixes had a tendency to kill each other. She probably shouldn't have mentioned that the others were actually in the U.S.

A phoenix was truly vulnerable only in that one moment of rising. When a phoenix's body regenerated and he rose from the flames, it was during that instant of time when he could truly die. A forever death—one from which he would *never* rise again.

Most enemies couldn't brave the heat of the fire long enough to kill a phoenix.

Another of your kind could do it. Phoenixes could—and had—killed each other before.

"You're the oldest phoenix that has ever been discovered," Cassie said, voice quiet. "According to my father's journals, you *are* the first."

Dante simply stared at her.

His stare made her nervous and shaky and so she kept talking. "I took a tear from one of the other phoenixes and tried to synthesize a cure. It didn't work." She stepped toward him. "*You* are the key to the cure. If you're the first, I can study your DNA. I can analyze your tears. They could be a more pure form than—"

"I'm not your damn experiment."

She flinched at his fury. "I didn't say that you were."

"But you want to put me in your lab, right? Want to run your tests . . . cut me open . . . just like they did."

"I'm not like them." She forced the words through numb lips.

"Aren't you?"

Damn him. She'd worked hard to save lives. To help those who'd been injured by her father and Genesis. "Why are you even here with me?" Cassie demanded. "If you don't trust me"—she closed the space between them and angrily grabbed on to *him* as she jumped up those bottom steps—"why are you here?"

"Because I can't walk away."

Her laugh was bitter. "You didn't seem to have that trouble in Chicago."

His nostrils flared. The banked flames in his eyes lit. "When I breathe in your scent, I ache."

Her lips parted in surprise.

"When I kissed you, your taste had me maddened."

"Dante . . ."

"I look at you, and I think . . . *mine.*"

Could he hear the drumbeat of her heart? It felt like it was about to race right out of her chest.

"You say we aren't lovers, but in my dreams, I've seen you naked."

She dropped his hands. He wasn't supposed to—

His hand rose. Touched her just over the curve of her right breast. "There's a freckle here. I've licked it. I've kissed it." His gaze swept down her body. "In my dreams, I've kissed you everywhere."

Her memory was absolutely fine and that had *not* happened. "Just dreams," she breathed out. "Not reality. That hasn't happened!"

"I'm not leaving you because I can still taste you. I'm not leaving you because I fucking want you under me. I want to be buried so far inside of you that I stop caring about what's real and what's a dream."

"Th-that's why you're with me? Sex?" He wanted her to sleep with him? Like that was some kind of hardship.

"Possession."

She didn't understand what that rough growl meant. "I don't—"

"I feel like you're mine. I'm here . . . fucking *here* . . . because I can't let you go." Then his mouth was on hers. He'd wrapped his arms around her. Lifted her up against him, and just taken her mouth.

He didn't kiss her softly. She was sure that he'd known little of softness in his long life. No tentative hunger. Just an avalanche of need that should have frightened her.

It didn't.

Cassie wrapped her arms around him and held on tight. Her lips parted beneath his, her tongue met his. The electric surge of lust seemed to pulse between their bodies wherever they touched.

She wanted to touch him everywhere.

There were no monitors to watch them. No guards. No fear of pain or retribution. For once, they were alone. They had a bed upstairs. They had time.

She could have him.

He could have anything he wanted from her.

His hands were trailing over her body. Curling around her hips. His fingers spanned her ass, and he pushed her up higher against the hard length of his cock.

Her phoenix was aroused. *Definitely* aroused.

"Why?" He pulled his mouth from hers, but he didn't let her go. He just started to kiss her neck, and, oh, the skin was so sensitive there.

She felt the rasp of his tongue on her, and quivered. Yes, *quivered*. She'd never done that in her whole life.

But then, she'd never been with Dante like that.

"Why do you want me?" He growled the words, and they seemed to vibrate against her skin. "You know what I am."

Didn't he realize that was *why* she wanted him?

"I've wanted you for a long time," Cassie confessed.

He'd been her first crush. The star of too many fantasies. He'd talked about dreams. She'd sure had her share of them.

Dante's hold tightened on her. Then he pulled back. Glared down at her. "You think if you fuck me, I'll do what you want."

Wow. Talk about being able to kill a mood. Her cheeks went ice cold, then she felt them heat with her embarrassment and fury. "No, I thought if I fucked you," she tossed right back at him, "then maybe the constant need I feel for you would go away." She pushed past him. "But right now, maybe we both just need to cool down."

No, she needed to get away from him before the jerk saw that he'd made her cry.

A phoenix didn't cry easily.

But she wasn't a phoenix. And she'd sure shed plenty of tears for him over the years.

"Cassie!"

She didn't stop. She stomped up the stairs. "Give me space, Dante. Just, dammit, give me some pride." She was swiping away her tears.

She'd forgotten how easily he could hurt her. Just a few careless words.

Cassie reached the landing and didn't glance back at him. She'd looked back at him before, other times just like this, when he'd wound up rejecting her in some way, and there had never been regret on his face.

He might lust for her—she'd felt the strength of that need—but Dante had never loved her.

Sometimes, she wondered if he could love anyone.

He dreamed of her again. Dreamed of a room with a silver ceiling, silver walls, and a silver floor.

A bright hell.

"You shouldn't have come back." Her voice.

His Cassandra.

He turned and realized . . . one of the walls was actually a mirror. When he focused just right, he could see through that mirror.

He could see her.

"You were safe. You should have stayed away." Her voice was sad.

He strode toward that mirror. He could see his own image staring back at him. But, through that image . . .

Her.

She had her hand on the glass. He put his above it. Could have sworn that he felt the silk of her touch.

He knew why he'd come back. Because he hadn't been able to leave her. He'd tried to stay away, but he'd needed her too much.

He'd had to get back to her.

Every step away from her had seemed to rip a hole into his chest.

Now he would have her.

Even if he had to burn that whole building down to claim her.

Dante stared out in the night. The cabin was quiet behind him, still. His dreams had tormented him for hours. No, not dreams. Memories, streaming through his mind.

Different times. Different places.

The thing that had always been the same? The fire.

Consuming.

Destroying.

Cassie was in the bedroom at the top of the stairs. Did she dream of him?

Something had been done to them, he knew that now. The attraction that he felt for her was unnatural. The ache to be close to her . . . the pain of being apart . . .

Another fucking experiment?

When he'd been in Chicago, he'd felt like part of him had been missing. At first, he'd thought that hole came from not having all his memories. That it was just the result of all the dark spots in his mind.

Then he'd looked up in Taboo and seen her and thought—

There you are.

Did she feel the same intense need that he did? Probably not. In his dreams . . . fucking memories . . . she'd been one of the people wearing the white lab coats. She'd been there to experiment on him.

She hadn't been part of the testing. Whatever had been done to make him need her so much, hell, maybe she'd even been a part of that manipulation.

He turned away from the window and its view of the

darkness. His gaze centered on the stairs. Had she known? Had she deliberately manipulated him so that he'd need her?

That way, I'd never truly be free. Because the lust for her compelled him to seek her out.

It was what he was doing even as he stalked up the stairs. They creaked beneath his feet, the only sound to penetrate the stillness of the cabin. He climbed slowly, heading for her, the need to see her driving him.

In front of her closed door, his fingers curled around the doorknob. He twisted.

And found the damn thing locked.

What the hell?

"Did you really think I'd just leave my door unlocked for you?" her voice called out.

Not asleep. For a second time, she'd fooled him with that sleeping trick. So he just shoved open the door, splintering the lock.

She jerked up in bed, gasping.

"No, what I *thought*"—he headed for the bed, for her—"was that if I fucked you, this constant need I have for you would go away." He tossed her own earlier words right back at her, but they were the truth. Maybe that was what he needed. Just one time with her. One long, hot time.

Cassie had a death grip on the covers as she clutched them to her chest. "You—you have a constant need for me?" She blinked. "Wait! That's what I told you." Her head shook, whipping her hair around her shoulders. "You're making fun of me now? Asshole! Get out of here! Just get—"

He was on the bed. On her. Crushing her down onto the mattress. His body caged hers. Held hers. His fingers twined with hers as he pushed them back against the pillow near her head. "I'm not making fun of you." Unbidden, the thought came . . . *I'll kick the ass of anyone who dared.*

"You don't even remember me," she whispered the words to him. "So don't act like—"

"I remember . . . flashes of you."

Her body tensed beneath him.

"In my first dream, you drove a knife into my chest."

Her lips trembled.

He bent his head and brushed his lips over hers. "But I realized soon enough that it wasn't really a dream, was it? That was a memory."

He knew she'd killed him, so why was he there, holding her so tightly?

Her scent surrounded him and made him nearly feel drunk.

"I had to do it," she told him, her voice a husky tremble that seemed to stroke right along his skin. "It was the way you escaped. Th—the other doctors thought we were just running new blood work on you. They hadn't planned for a containment with your fire. When I stabbed you and your fire broke free, you were able to get away."

"I got away, but lost my memories." His legs were on either side of hers, but he couldn't feel the smooth silk of her thighs. The sheet was between them.

He wanted nothing between them.

"For a time, you did forget. But then we met up again in New Orleans, and your memories seemed to be coming back."

He wished he had all of his memories.

"You wanted to forget." Sadness darkened her words. "You told me that you never wanted to remember Genesis."

Or me.

She didn't say those words, but they seemed to hang between them.

"There are some things you can't forget." He brought his lips to hers once more. He didn't trust her. The story about helping him escape could be pure bull, but the need for her overwhelmed everything else in that instant.

So why not take her?

They were alone. She was beneath him. His body was so hard for her that he ached.

Why not take her?

When he kissed her again, the kiss was harder. Deeper. His tongue swept inside, taking every bit of sweetness that he could. And she was sweet. Her taste made him heady, eager for more.

Her fingers curled around his, and she was shifting beneath the covers. Arching her hips against his.

He wanted those covers gone.

His mouth went to her neck. Her scent was stronger there, and he loved that light, sexy smell. He licked her skin, sucked the tender curve of her throat, then scored her with his teeth.

"Dante!"

The covers had to go.

He freed her hands. Yanked at the covers. When they got tangled up, he just ripped them away.

She was naked.

For some reason, he hadn't expected that.

"I-I . . . only had the one pair of clothes and when I got into bed . . ."

His fingers caressed the tip of her breast. Her nipple was tight and tempting.

"I didn't want to—" Cassie's words choked off in a moan.

And when he bent his head and took that nipple in his mouth, her whole body trembled.

Yes. This was what he'd wanted. Her. All of her. Spread before him. Her body was perfect to him. Smooth and sexy, making his cock grow heavier and harder.

He wanted to drive into her as deeply as he could go.

But he held himself back. His savage instincts screamed for him to—

Take.

But another part, a part somewhere deep inside whispered . . .

Savor.

So his fingers trailed over her skin. He licked her breasts. Kissed those nipples. Loved the sound of her gasps as her nails sank into his back.

I haven't had her before? He must have been insane.

More covers ripped as he pushed down between her legs. His finger slid up her thighs. Up, up . . .

"Dante?" There was a note of fear in her voice.

He didn't want her afraid.

His gaze held hers, even as his fingers slipped over her sex. "I won't hurt you." That was a vow.

Her lips parted on a sharp breath.

His fingers eased into her. Tight. So incredibly tight. Wet. Hot.

His fingers slid out.

Her eyes widened.

He pushed into her again, then slid out, letting his fingers trail over the center of her need.

Cassie's breath came faster and harder with her rising arousal. He could make her come, just like that, caressing her so slowly, he knew he could.

But he wanted more.

Savor.

Take.

He wanted to taste all of her. To put his mouth on her and mark her as his.

He'd been looking for something ever since he woke in that alley. Now he'd found her.

Once won't be enough. So much for the brilliant plan. Already, he was sure once wouldn't even begin to take the edge off his hunger.

He began to kiss a path down her stomach.

Then he heard the faint rumble of a car.

They'd taken a long, twisting drive to get to the cabin. There were no other homes near.

Just them.

He kissed her skin once more. He was so close to what he wanted most.

So damn close.

But that rumbling engine was getting louder. And it wasn't just one car.

He heard a *whoop-whoop-whoop*. His jaw locked and he glanced up at Cassie. In the dark, her eyes gleamed. Her breath panted out.

"Company." *Fucking company.* "Someone's coming, Cassie." Coming in fast, and, from the sound of things, by land and by air.

Hating it—*hating it*—he pulled away from her body. That *someone* was going to pay for denying him what he'd wanted most. Someone would burn.

Cassie blinked and shook her head. "What?"

Whoop. Whoop. Whoop.

Louder. Closer.

"A helicopter," she whispered as her eyes widened. "How? How did they find us?"

The how didn't matter. Getting away mattered.

Dante jumped from the bed, and Cassie rushed to dress in her jeans and T-shirt. A damn shame, that. He much preferred her naked. *I didn't get to taste all of her.*

But he would. Every single inch of her.

"Dante?" She stilled, staring at him. Probably because he looked like he was about to leap on her again.

He jerked a hand over his face. "The cabin's isolated," he

said as he paced to the window. The isolation would work against them now that they'd been found.

One road in.

One road out.

They wouldn't be able to use the Jeep to escape. And with a helicopter watching from above, it would be even harder to ditch their pursuers.

He turned toward Cassie. "They're closing us in."

She hurried toward him. "There's supposed to be a motorcycle hidden in the shed behind the cabin. We can get it, then cut across the mountain." She hesitated, then muttered, "Or we can *try* to. I don't actually know how to drive a motorcycle."

Didn't matter. They'd figure out the how—hell, maybe it would be one of those things that he "knew" how to do. The bike was an escape option. He caught her hand, and they flew down the stairs to the back door.

The beat of the helicopter's blades grew louder. The flash of lights lit up the cabin.

Dante yanked open the door and saw the helicopter touching down. Air rushed against him, blowing hard as the blades whipped around. It looked like half a dozen SUVs were driving into the area, too.

He ducked, held tight to Cassie, and ran as fast as he could. They hadn't been spotted. Not yet. Not—

Dante lifted his leg and kicked open the shed door. They hurried inside. Cassie grabbed a tarp and tossed it to the ground. He saw the long, hard lines of the motorcycle then, and climbed on. Cassie jumped on behind him.

They were pinned in the lights before he could even start the cycle. Lights that were too bright as they focused right on him and Cassie, nearly blinding him for a moment.

"Get off the motorcycle!" a voice shouted.

Dante felt Cassie tense behind him.

"Get off the bike and get away from the woman!" the same voice ordered.

Screw that. "Get out of my way." Dante had the motorcycle growling and lunging forward.

Huh, so he *did* know how to drive a motorcycle.

There were more shouts then a hail of bullets slammed into the motorcycle. It looked like those guys weren't in the mood to play nice.

Fine. He wasn't exactly in a nice mood, either.

As the motorcycle flew out of the shed, Dante let his rage build. The fire crackled through his veins and burst from his fingertips. It was a round swirling ball that grew and grew. He lifted his hand, ready to toss the flames at their attackers.

He got his first look at the line of men who'd come out to surround the shed. They were all wearing heavy, white uniforms and masks—they almost looked like they were astronauts as they lifted their weapons and took aim.

I'll take aim, too.

But he heard Cassie whisper, "Fireproof," right before his flames flew toward the men.

They didn't burn.

Hell.

He revved the engine. If his flames wouldn't push them back, he'd drive right over the jerks.

"If you don't stop, we'll shoot you both!" It was that same voice, calling out from the line of men in white. "You'll come back, but will the woman be so lucky?"

He counted a dozen guns aimed at him.

Cassie's hold tightened on him. "Go, Dante. Don't worry about me, just . . . *go.*"

Because she could heal? She *had* healed before, but what if a bullet hit her in the head? The heart? Would she—could she—heal from an injury like that?

"Go!" Cassie yelled. "They're not going to shoot me!"

But she was wrong. They were firing at them. He bent low and chose the weakest link he could find in that sea of white then drove forward fast and hard.

The man screamed as Dante bore down on him. Screamed and shot. A bullet drove into Dante's chest. One ricocheted off the motorcycle. Another sank into his shoulder.

Dirt flew up around the motorcycle. People were yelling. The helicopter's blades were spinning and sending the air rushing against him.

"Aim for the motorcycle!" It was that same shouting voice. The man who had to be in charge. The man that Dante wanted to rip apart.

Instead . . . he sent a ball of flames flying back at their attackers as the motorcycle raced toward the trees. They were close. Once they made it inside that sweeping band of trees, their pursuers would have a hard time catching up to them.

He tightened his hold on the handlebars, fighting to keep the bike steady.

A bullet sank into the front tire.

Then another hit the back.

The motorcycle spun out of control. Cassie's arms weren't around him anymore. He tried to grab for her, but was thrown from the bike, too. His body flew through the air even as Cassie's scream seemed to echo in his ears.

Then he hit a tree, slamming headfirst into the thick wood, and he didn't hear her scream anymore.

CHAPTER FIVE

"Dante?" Cassie ran toward him. Her ankle throbbed—she'd heard it crack—and the skin had been ripped from the side of her right arm when she'd slammed into the ground.

But Dante . . . he'd hit so much harder than she had.

Footsteps thundered toward them. Lights cut through the darkness.

She sank to her knees beside his still body. The moonlight spilled down onto him, and she could see the twisted angle of his neck. That very *unnatural* angle.

Her breath whispered out as her fingers lifted to his throat. No pulse.

The thud of approaching footsteps came closer. Ever closer.

She could run. There was time. She could leap to her feet and disappear into the forest. She might even get away.

She didn't run. She just eased closer to Dante. Her bruised fingers brushed back his hair. Blood was trickling down his forehead. When the motorcycle had started to spin, she'd tried to hold onto him, but she hadn't been strong enough.

The lights fell on her. Too bright and hot.

"Is he dead?" The voice came from behind the light. It was a voice she'd grown to hate over the years. Once she realized just what the man truly was.

"For the moment," Cassie said quietly. The words were the truth. She glanced down at Dante's still face, lit so well by the shine of flashlights. "While you can, you and your men need to get the hell out of here." Because when Dante rose, there would be no controlling him. In an environment like that, where there were so many trees and miles and miles of wilderness, a phoenix would be capable of doing an immense amount of damage.

"We'll be leaving," she was told. Then the leader of the group stepped forward, and Cassie glanced up to see the hard features of Lieutenant Colonel Jon Abrams. He stared down at her. "But you'll be coming with us."

Jon hadn't changed much since she'd last seen him. Same hard, handsome face. Same military short, blond hair. Those deceptive blue eyes. He could look so harmless with those eyes.

But when he wanted, those eyes could be lethal.

Dante's skin began to heat beneath her touch. Already, he was coming back to her. Sometimes, the risings were fast. Brutal.

So destructive.

What would this rising be like? Would he come back, full of fury and sending flames at everyone and everything in his path?

Would he know her? *Please, know me. Come back with the memories.* It could happen. She'd seen him come back with his memories . . . maybe . . . two times before. *Bring them back now.*

But she knew that, all too often, he came back only as a beast.

"I'd suggest that you step away from him, Cassie." Jon was actually trying to sound like he cared.

She had to give him credit. He'd always been a good actor. He'd convinced her once that he actually wanted to marry her.

"We've gone to a lot of trouble to find you," Jon continued, "and we're not eager to watch you burn."

Her lips twisted. She called the lie. "Aren't you?"

He lunged forward and caught her wrist. Yanked her up and away from Dante, his strength far more powerful than a human's should have been. She fought him, punching and kicking, but Jon wasn't letting her go. "You aren't"—he growled out the words as he twisted her hands behind her—"dying for him."

He would throw that up at her. Just because she'd almost died once before, while trying to save Dante, didn't mean she had some kind of death wish.

Jon bent over her, and his mouth brushed near her ear. "I want you to stand back and watch him rise. Watch the monster that you risked so much for."

Wait. He *wanted* Dante to rise? But Dante would just kill them all if—

Her gaze flew toward the men who'd swept onto the scene. Men in those heavy, fireproof suits.

"The guys in the government labs have been making some modifications," Jon told her softly. "When your phoenix burns, he's at his weakest, right? Well . . . we're about to have a little test."

No, it wasn't a test. It was an execution. If those fireproof suits were strong enough, the men could get close enough to kill Dante.

Then there would be no rising. Not if they destroyed him as he was regenerating. Not if they destroyed him in that one weak moment.

"No!" Desperate, she stopped fighting, knowing that if she was going to help Dante, she would have to catch Jon off guard. "Don't do this!"

"He's a monster that can't be controlled. The orders came from above."

She heard the smug pleasure in Jon's voice. He'd hated Dante since the moment he realized . . .

I love him.

"What can't be controlled must be killed," Jon told her. He jerked his head to the left, and, at that signal, two men in white began to advance toward Dante's prone body.

"Don't do this! He hasn't even started to burn yet!" Cassie cried out.

"He will soon enough."

She still wasn't fighting him. If she didn't fight, he might lower his guard and loosen his hold. The instant that hold loosened, she'd escape.

"I thought you wanted him alive. He's the most powerful of his kind! You need his DNA—"

"I don't need him at all. He's a threat that will be eliminated."

The men were close to Dante. Too close.

And . . . she could smell smoke. Could see the faint tendrils rising from his body in the bright light.

When he burned, they'd attack. There might be no more risings. No more Dante.

"Nothing is stronger than his fire." She hoped that was true. Prayed it was. But in the government's secret labs, anything could be created—and had been.

A suit to resist a phoenix's fire?

No, please, no.

"We're about to find out." Jon still held her.

"They'll die!"

He didn't respond. Did he care if those two men in white died?

No, he didn't. She'd seen beneath his mask too late. He wasn't concerned with collateral damage. He never had been.

But . . . but his hands weren't holding her as tight anymore. His attention was totally focused on his two men as they closed in on their prey. One man had his gun just inches from Dante's head.

"Wait for the flames!" Jon yelled. "If you attack too soon, it won't do anything. He can only be destroyed when he's actually rising! The regeneration isn't complete then!"

"That gun had better be phoenix fireproof, too," Cassie snapped. "Because if it isn't, your boys are going to die!"

The fire began to burn along Dante's body. Sweeping up, flaming higher and higher.

"Go to hell, shifter." Jon's rough snarl had nausea tightening her stomach.

But his grip on her eased even more as he moved a bit to the side in order to better watch the show.

Your mistake.

She drove back with her elbow. Slammed it into his stomach and jumped forward. *"Dante!"*

The man with the gun was leaning closer to him.

Jon tried to grab her. Not happening. A burst of speed and a wild lunge shot her forward, slamming her body into the man in white—the jerk who thought he'd shoot her phoenix.

They hit the ground. Rolled. When she looked up, that gun was pointed right between her eyes.

"Stand down!" Jon yelled. "Stand—"

The *whoosh* of fire cut through his words. She felt the heat lance her skin, and she glanced up in time to see flames rolling toward her.

The other man who'd approached Dante—the second man in the fireproof suit—was rolling on the ground. His suit was burning.

So much for being fireproof.

"Nothing is strong enough to resist a phoenix's burn," she said as she glared back at the man with the gun. "Instead of pointing that thing at me, you should be saying thanks. 'Cause I just saved your ass from the flames."

The guy's buddy was screaming. His teammates immediately started spraying a thick, heavy extinguisher fluid on him.

And Dante kept burning.

The man with the gun hadn't lowered his weapon. He also hadn't said thanks.

"We have to get her out of here." Jon's voice. He was no longer sounding so smug. He shoved the gun away and hauled Cassie back to her feet. "I'm getting her out in the chopper. Load up in the vehicles and clear out."

His hand was bruising her as he yanked her behind him. Her gaze flew around the area. The man who'd burned—he was out of his suit, looking unharmed, but shaken.

Another few moments, and he wouldn't have been so lucky.

"Dante!" She shouted his name as her gaze focused on the fire that surrounded him. She couldn't even see him over the flames. The fire was so high. Raging. Consuming.

She dug in her heels, fighting to stay back. She couldn't get on that helicopter with Jon. He'd make her disappear, just as Genesis had made so many others disappear over the years.

She had work to do. People who were counting on her down in Mississippi. Cassie knew that if she didn't get back to them, they'd die.

Or . . . they'd kill.

"Let me go!"

But Jon didn't let her go. "Couldn't do this the easy way, could you? Sorry, baby, but I don't have any drugs to give you."

Good. That would mean that she could keep fighting him. She punched him.

He punched her right back with a punch that had a whole lot more strength than hers. The blow staggered her. When she stumbled, Jon lifted her into his arms. "Get that chopper moving!" he yelled.

The wind beat against her. The *whoop-whoop-whoop* filled the air again.

But she still heard the roar of fury quite clearly. They all did. As that roar shook the night, everyone seemed to freeze for a moment.

She lifted her head, fighting to see Dante. She knew that roar had come from him.

She'd heard him make the same sound before. Or, rather, she'd heard the phoenix make that sound.

But Jon was shoving her into the helicopter. Holding her down.

"Get us out of here!" he snarled to the pilot.

Her gaze flew over his shoulder.

The flames had died down, fallen just enough for her to see that Dante was standing strong. His shoulders were bare—the fire always burned away his clothes—and he was striding forward.

He was looking at the helicopter.

At her.

"Dante!" She had to get to him. If she didn't stop him, he'd rage out of control.

But Jon's hold on her wasn't loosening.

"Dammit, he'll kill them!" Cassie cried.

Dante's fire was racing out and following the fleeing men in their not-so-phoenix-proof suits.

Jon frowned. "You're the mission, not them."

The helicopter was rising into the air.

Dante ran toward her. Faster.

"Don't kill them!" she screamed. "Dante, pull the fire back! Pull it back!"

He was still running. The flames were burning.

She had to get out of that helicopter.

"Hold her!" Jon snapped.

Hard hands grabbed her—one of his men? She was shoved against one of the helicopter's seats. Held down.

Jon lifted his gun and fired. Six shots. In fast succession. "That'll buy the men on the ground some time."

She knew what he'd done.

Six shots. Jon had always been such a damn fine shot.

"Three to the heart," Jon said. "Three to the head."

Her lips trembled, but she lifted her chin. "He'll come back."

"Doesn't he always?" Jon glanced down at her. "But he won't be able to find you. Hell, maybe we'll be lucky, and he won't remember you at all."

She was buckled into a seat then. Jon was beside her. Her body ached and throbbed, but that pain didn't matter.

The thing that hurt the worst?

Her heart seemed to have been carved right out of her chest.

She was afraid that he was right. Dante wouldn't find her. Despite her hopes, hell, he probably wouldn't remember her at all.

While she could never forget him.

The helicopter turned, circling around, and she stared down below. A circle of fire surrounded him, showing his splayed body. He'd fallen so that he stared straight up at the sky. He wasn't moving at all.

But she knew that, soon enough, he would be.

Please, please, remember me.

Without him, she wasn't sure she'd be able to escape.

The fire swept around him. The flames were like voices. Laughing. Mocking. Burning.

He felt claws dig into his skin. White-hot knives that cut and tore as he fought his way out of hell.

He couldn't stay in the fire. There was something he needed.

Something he had to have.

He shouted as the flames spun around him. Dante fought his way through that fire, determined to get to—

Her.

The flames flickered, and he rose to his feet. The fire was burning beneath his skin, clawing him from the inside, but he took a step forward.

Another.

He could hear the distant whir of a helicopter.

They'd taken her on the helicopter.

The memories were there. Strong and sharp. He could see her face. The delicate beauty. The stark fear that she'd felt as that bastard had taken her away.

A fatal mistake.

The man would die for that.

Dante looked up into the air and saw only the stars. The helicopter was gone.

His Cassandra was gone.

But every memory that he'd ever had—so many lifetimes—those memories were back.

He smiled and began to hunt.

No one takes her from me.

Cassie stared at the door of her cell, and wondered if Jon was planning to feed her any time soon. She wasn't exactly sure how much time had passed, but the gnawing in her stomach told her it had been at least a day since she'd left Dante.

When the helicopter had touched down, Jon had met up with more of his men and, of course, they'd immediately drugged her. The better for her not to see where the hell they were taking her.

She'd woken in her cell. And it was most definitely a cell

for prisoners, not some nice room for guests, no matter how Jon wanted to spin the place. All of eight feet wide and seven feet long, Cassie had been pacing that cell for hours. No windows. One door.

And lights that were too damn bright.

She heard the click of a lock and spun toward her door just as it swung open.

Jon stood there. He arched a brow as his blue gaze swept over her. His lips quirked in that mildly amused smile she detested. "Cassie, who would have thought we'd end up like this?"

She wanted to rip him apart. But she had to play it smart, so she didn't move at all. "Like this?" she repeated carefully as she raised a brow. "You mean with you being a kidnapper and a killer and me being your prisoner?" She shook her head. "Um, no, I didn't ever think we'd end up quite like this."

The first time she'd seen Jon, he'd been one of the new recruits brought in to Genesis. One of the actual volunteers—because he'd been human. A soldier who'd agreed to become part of an experimental unit for Uncle Sam.

Humans who had their bodies enhanced by science. He'd wanted to be a true super soldier.

She'd tried to warn him to leave then.

He hadn't.

Of course, back then, she'd just thought he was being misled. That he was clueless about what the government was doing to the paranormals.

Her gaze cut to her cell. *Not so clueless anymore.*

"Cassie . . ." He sighed out her name as he came closer to her. "You know it doesn't have to be like this. We need you—"

"We?" She shook her head. "In case you missed the dozens of news stories that have been running lately, Genesis is dead. My father? Gone. Public opinion is against you. No one wants the paranormals tortured—"

"I'm not torturing anyone."

Bull. "I'm about to collapse from hunger. You've held me here without—"

His fingers skimmed down her cheek. Goosebumps immediately rose on her flesh, and *not* the good kind of goose bumps.

"Baby, do you really think a little hunger equals torture?" His eyes hardened. "I could show you real torture. The kind that makes a man scream for hours."

Her throat went dry. "When did you become like this?" she whispered.

He smiled. "You were always so blind. But . . . hey, my timing was good, right? If your phoenix hadn't just broken out of the facility when I arrived for my therapy—"

Therapy? Was that what he was seriously calling it?

"Then we never would have gotten as . . . close . . . as we did."

She knew her cheeks had flushed. She'd been twenty-two when Dante escaped—the first time, anyway.

She'd been sure that he'd never come back. Jon had pursued her for months, and she'd been hesitant to trust him.

Should have stuck with my instincts.

But she'd been so lonely and she'd missed Dante so much. When the months had slipped into a year, she'd finally agreed to date Jon.

He'd wanted more from her and had made it clear. She just hadn't realized quite how much more he wanted, not until he started talking marriage.

I couldn't marry him. How could I marry one man when I wanted another? Even when that "other" had forgotten her.

"We have a chance to do something very special together, Cassie," Jon said as his gaze held hers. "With your brains and my resources, the world could be ours."

No. "I don't want the world. I just want away from you." Because she'd seen, after she'd turned down his proposal, the real Jon. The Jon that was cold and diabolical—and willing to do anything to get what he wanted.

His eyes narrowed. "Getting away isn't an option." His nostrils flared. "You know . . . you smell even better now than you did when I first met you. But that's part of what *he* did to you, isn't it?"

He . . . Jon wasn't talking about Dante. He was talking about her father.

"No one knows the full extent of my father's experiments," she said. "His files were destroyed when the two Genesis labs were—"

"Obliterated?"

They had been.

"I know what your blood can do." Jon was staring at her neck.

She could feel her heartbeat drumming madly and wondered if he saw the frantic movement of her pulse just beneath the skin.

With his enhancements, she bet he could.

"You're a weapon, Cassie, one that I intend to use."

He surprised her. "You—you brought me here for my blood?"

"Um, that's part of the reason. I'll take that blood, study it. Replicate the poison."

The poison that could take down a vampire in seconds. The poison that lived in her.

"But I want more, Cassie. I want you to work with me. You're the best researcher in paranormal genetics. You could create soldiers, design a fighting force that the world has never seen."

A force that the world wouldn't be able to handle. No, thank-you.

"I'm not making any more monsters." She shook her

head. "You can keep me locked up for as long as you want, but I'm not doing—"

He was laughing at her. "Cassie, Cassie . . . so brave, *now.* But as we discussed, you really don't know much about torture." He backed away from her. Looked mildly regretful. "That's about to change."

She knew more about torture than he realized.

The door opened behind him once more.

"This time, you get to see what it's like to be the test subject," Jon said as he tilted his head to study her. "And I'm afraid that this part will *hurt.*"

Guards came in then. They grabbed her. One lifted her upper body, one caught her thrashing legs. In less than a minute's time, they had her strapped down on a gurney. The wheels were squeaking as they rolled her down the hallway.

She screamed for help, but her screams were met with silence.

Jon brushed the hair off her forehead. "You should probably save your strength."

"And you're a sadistic bastard who *should* let me go!"

He just smiled. The smile that flashed his dimples. The smile that chilled her.

She was pushed into another room. A room with even brighter lighting. And men and women in lab coats came toward her. A hysterical bubble of laughter broke from her.

Jon thought he was so smart, trying to frighten her by making her the test subject. *I've been the test subject my whole life. Try again, jackass.*

"Remember times like this?" His hand was still on her forehead. "I was strapped down once."

He'd volunteered for it. Been eager to jump on that gurney. No one had taken him, kicking and screaming.

"But you still came in that day, and you tried to get me

out of there. Tried to get me to leave." His brows lowered. "What the hell were you thinking?"

That she could save him.

But he hadn't left. He had turned her in. If it hadn't been for her family connections, she would have been killed for her actions that day.

"We need to find out what dear old daddy did to you. That way, we can do the same thing to others."

And what? Eradicate the vampires with her poison blood?

"Should we sedate the patient?" one of the doctors asked.

"I'm not a patient!" Cassie screamed. Seriously, they saw that she was fighting.

"No sedation, but we should probably gag her." Jon did. The bastard actually tied a gag around her mouth.

The doctors just watched.

"Dr. Shaw, we're going to need extensive blood work, skin grafting, a spinal tap, a bone marrow sample . . ." Jon began to rattle off all the procedures. The doctor nodded quickly and pushed instrument trays closer to her.

Cassie shook her head.

"We'll keep her stationary for some of the procedures—temporary paralysis may be needed—but we want to make certain that Cassie is fully aware of everything that happens to her." He bent toward her face. Smiled again. "That way, the lesson will stay with her much, much longer." He put his mouth near her ear. "After this, you'll do anything to make sure you're not the one who winds up on the table."

Her gaze flew toward the men and women in lab coats Tears were leaking down her cheeks. *Please* . . . She knew her eyes said what she couldn't. *Help me. Don't let him do this. Don't you do this to me.*

But they wouldn't meet her gaze.

The first needle was driven into her vein, and at almost the exact same time, a scalpel sliced across her arm.

Jon eased away from her, but he didn't leave the room. He just stood back there and watched.

She didn't cry out. Like she could with the gag. But she wasn't going to give him the pleasure of watching her pain. Her gaze turned up to the light.

It isn't me. It isn't me. She just had to pretend that the pain was happening to someone else.

He thought it was her first time to be under the knife? How did he think her blood had come to be poison?

She stared up at that light. Focused only on it.

It isn't me.

The harder that she looked at the light, the more it looked like fire.

Dante.

She could almost see him there.

Dante stared at the low buildings sprawled across the land. From the outside, they looked like he was staring at an old ranch, one that had fallen into disrepair.

But the reinforced fencing around the ranch—that heavy barbed wire—and the dozens of vehicles that had gone toward the place told him the ranch was far from abandoned.

And the fact that there seemed to be no animals there?

Well, the barbed wire had to be an effort to keep someone in.

His gaze went to the left, to the right. Guards were out there, patrolling. He'd caught sight of them a few times.

They hadn't seen him yet. That was why they were still living.

His stare returned to the row of buildings.

Cassie was in one of those buildings. He knew she was. He'd followed the bastards who'd left him in that field. They'd been so busy running away that they hadn't bothered to look behind them as they sped off in the SUVs.

He'd been right there.

Another motorcycle had been hidden in that shed. Dante had jumped on it, and hauled ass after them as quickly as he could. The night had helped to cover his tracks. He hadn't bothered with headlights.

He'd kept the SUVs within sight. Followed them all the way.

The helicopter was behind the ranch. He'd spotted it earlier.

The trick was to get it. To get her.

He didn't plan to leave without Cassie.

"I didn't realize that the subject was incapable of feeling pain."

Jon glanced up at Dr. Shaw as she approached him. A faint frown was on her face. A pretty face—pretty but cold.

"You should have told us sooner," she said, her pale blue eyes showing her censure. "It would have made the others feel much less nervous about the procedures."

Cassie hadn't made a single sound—not a moan, not a whimper—while the doctors had been working on her.

"She feels pain." He knew she did. He'd seen her react to pain before.

He pushed away from the wall. Headed toward her. "Get back," he ordered the doctor with the graying hair.

The man immediately stumbled back. He didn't move fast or far enough, so Jon shoved him out of the way.

"Cassie."

She didn't respond. Didn't even blink. She was staring straight up at the light.

"Cassie!"

Still nothing.

Jon bent his head over hers, forcing her to see him. But she didn't. Her pupils were fixed. She was still staring straight ahead, and not appearing to see a damn thing.

He cut away the gag. They didn't need that. The woman's body was there, but her mind was somewhere far away.

Interesting trick. He hadn't realized that Cassie would be able to pull off something like that.

He'd underestimated her.

Again.

"I won't make that mistake again." He motioned toward Dr. Shaw. "Keep going."

"H-her heart rate seems to be dropping." This was from the guy he'd shoved back.

Jon glanced at the heart monitor. Yes, it was dropping. "We're not in the danger zone yet." He stepped away from Cassie. "Finish."

Dr. Shaw nodded quickly as she stepped forward.

"I . . . see . . ." That weak whisper was Cassie's voice.

Jon stiffened. "What do you see, Cassie?"

"Dante . . ." Her lips actually curled. "I see his fire."

An alarm began to sound, echoing through the facility.

"I see . . . his fire . . ."

Impossible.

But . . . Jon felt a surge of fear inside him as he whirled to race from the room.

CHAPTER SIX

When a guard saw him and shouted out a warning, Dante decided—

Screw the subtle approach.

—even as the shriek of an alarm blasted through the night.

He rose from the shadows. Lifted his hands—and sent fire flying toward the thick fence and its barbed wire. The flames blasted right through that flimsy protection, and he walked straight ahead, clearing a path with his flames as he went.

He kept the fire burning. When a guard tried to shoot him, Dante sent flames his way. The guard yelled and ducked for cover.

Humans. So predictable. Give them something to fear, and they always broke.

It had been that same way for centuries.

More guards came at him. What did they hope to accomplish? Did they think they'd take him down with the bullets long enough to subdue him? Not happening. It wasn't a weak, confused moment after a rising. He wasn't going to let those bullets hit him.

His flames were burning bright and hot, and he melted the guns in their hands.

More screams from the humans. They always screamed. He looked up and saw the lens of a security camera focusing on him. Dante stared into that lens. He knew the fire lit his face, probably made him look like the devil.

Like he hadn't been called the devil a time or twenty in his lifespan. "You have something I want!" he yelled. "Give her to me or"—he lifted his hands, let the flames dance—"I will burn this place down around you all."

"He's bluffing." Dr. Shaw peered over Jon's shoulder at the computer screen. "Isn't he?"

"No, he isn't." *The fire-throwing bastard.*

Dante had risen with his memories intact. And he'd also risen very, very pissed.

"I-I thought you left him—"

"I guess the phoenix didn't like to be left behind."

"But we just started the experiments on Cassandra. We need more time!"

More time. Jon leaned forward and pressed the intercom button. "If you burn us, you kill her, too." Had the phoenix's fury blinded him to that fact? "Do you really want her to die?"

Dante's face was a stark, intimidating mask of fury as the flames surrounded him. "I want Cassandra."

"Why is he fixated on her?" Dr. Shaw asked. "Are they lovers? Are they—"

"The phoenix would destroy any lover he took to his bed." Jon had read that tidbit in the research notes he'd acquired. "His fire is too dangerous."

"Five seconds, and I start burning down buildings!" Dante roared.

Jon flipped the switch that connected him to all the guards on a secure frequency. He knew his message would be sent to their transmitters. "Shoot him. Full force. Do *not* let that bastard—"

Before any bullets could fire, Dante swept out with his fire. It rose—and the security screen went blank.

Jon's gaze flew around the monitor bank. Every security screen had gone blank, and there were over fifteen cameras installed out there.

The facility was for research, not long-term containment. It sure couldn't hold off someone of the phoenix's strength.

"I don't think he's going to wait for her to come out." Dr. Shaw edged toward the door.

No, he wasn't. The phoenix was coming in, and Jon knew he'd burn anyone who got between him and Cassie.

Jon also knew he couldn't lose Cassie. She was vital to his mission goals. "Take him down!" he ordered once more then rushed from the room and ran back toward the lab. Toward Cassie.

He shoved open the door. She was still strapped on the table, and her gaze was still fixed on the light.

He grabbed the scalpel and sliced away the straps that held her down. He pulled her up, but her head sagged back weakly. "Cassie!"

She didn't respond.

"I'm going to destroy your phoenix, you know that, right?"

Still nothing.

"Lieutenant Colonel?" Dr. Shaw's voice shook. She'd been racing behind him in the hallway. "He won't get in . . . will he?"

Yes, he would. "He's going to smell her blood on your hands."

The other doctors were there, too. They'd backed away the instant Jon had grabbed the scalpel.

"He'll probably try to kill you all first."

There was a sharp gasp and two of the doctors immediately ran for the doors.

Fools. What had they thought would happen? That paranormal research would be a safe occupation?

"B-but we didn't—" Dr. Shaw began, sputtering as the faint color leeched from her cheeks.

Jon pulled Cassie into his arms. Wherever she'd gone in her mind, the lady wasn't even close to coming back yet. "You cut her open."

"You told us—"

"Get her blood off your hands, Shaw! Get the smell off you, or you'll be dead once he breeches the perimeter."

But the increasing shrieks of the alarm told him that the perimeter had already been breached.

Water immediately began to pour from the sprinklers positioned along the ceiling. Ah, right . . . the phoenix's flames had been detected. The spray of water wasn't going to do much to stop him, though.

Jon knew that he had to get Cassie out of there. They'd escaped on the helicopter before. They could do it again.

He just had to run fast enough. But he could do it. No problem. The others who smelled of Cassie's blood . . . the others who were running into the path of the phoenix would be his perfect distraction.

Sometimes, a leader had to lose a few soldiers in order to win a war.

Or, in this case . . . the doctors had to die so he could survive.

He lifted Cassie higher into his arms and ran from the room.

"My Cassandra . . ." Dante inhaled then stilled as he caught her very distinct scent. It had often drifted to him when he'd been held in that pit at Genesis.

She smelled of sunlight and flowers. Life. Hope.

Except . . . her scent was deeper and tinted with the faintest trace of copper.

Blood.

"Stop!" The barked order came from behind him. "We'll shoot—"

A bullet slammed into Dante's shoulder. They weren't *going to shoot*. The asshole was *already* shooting at him.

Too bad the guy had horrible aim.

Dante twisted and sent his flames racing toward the trigger happy fool. The man dropped his weapon. Ran away as fast as he could.

Dante turned to the right, following Cassie's scent. Someone had hurt her. Someone would *pay*.

Two men in white lab coats were running down the hallway. They stopped as soon as they saw him.

His eyes narrowed. They had Cassie's blood on their gloved hands.

"Please!" the man in front shouted. He was in his early fifties, with graying hair and a paunch. "She's alive! I swear, she's alive."

Dante grabbed him. Slammed the bastard against the wall and kept him there with one hand shoved against the guy's chest. Dante knew that hand would burn him—it *was* burning as smoke rose from the fellow's shirt. "What did you do?"

"Sh-she was just here for some research. We didn't know, we didn't—"

"We knew!" The shout came from the second man. He was tall, thin, balding. "But what choice did we have? The lieutenant colonel calls the shots. He made us—"

The rage in Dante was swelling ever higher. "You both hurt her."

The second man screamed then, a high, terrified cry. He yanked something out of his lab coat pocket and lunged for

Dante. The man drove a needle toward Dante's arm. "This'll stop you!"

Dante caught the syringe. Snapped it in half. "No," he said, slowly, definitely, "but I will stop you."

The man's jaw dropped. He spun around to flee.

Guards came around the corner then. Half a dozen of them. They took one look at Dante and opened fire.

He used the two men in lab coats as his shields. They fell, bodies riddled with bullets, even as he sent his flames out toward his attackers.

Her blood . . .

He kicked in the door nearest him. Found another hallway waiting.

Water poured from the ceiling, but it didn't stop his flames. Nothing was going to stop him.

Jon dropped Cassie into the chair in the back lab. She barely seemed to breathe, and that scared him.

He hurried toward the small cabinet on the right wall and used his private code to bypass the security system in place for the particular resource he wanted. A hum, then a beep, and the metal doors swung open. The dosages were there, just waiting for him.

He grabbed a syringe and drove the white-hot liquid right into his vein.

"What are you doing?"

He spun around to see Dr. Shaw standing in the doorway. She had never realized that he'd been one of the test subjects at Genesis for years. Her surprised gaze was on the needle he'd just shoved into his arm.

"I'm taking precautions." He hadn't been one of the dumb bastards who'd signed up to receive the modified vampire transformation. He hadn't wanted to spend his days and nights drinking blood.

He'd wanted power. Strength.

He'd gone into the Lycan program.

Until something better had come along.

His back teeth clenched as the dose burned through him. It was always a burn, one that seemed to be destroying him from the inside out.

But it didn't destroy him. It made him stronger.

"What was in that syringe?"

Ah . . . Dr. Shaw. She was one of the newer recruits. Someone that Uncle Sam had hoped would be able to match Cassie's wonderful brain.

There was no match.

The alarms kept shrieking.

"A brew that one of your predecessors created," Jon told her. Unfortunately, that predecessor was dead. Killed when the last main Genesis lab was torn to the ground.

Jon headed back toward Cassie.

Dr. Shaw blocked his path. The woman had been running and some of her blond hair fell from the sleek twist she usually kept at her nape. "I don't want to die."

"Then you need to get the hell out of here."

She sucked in a sharp breath. "You're going for the helicopter, aren't you?"

Yes, he was.

"Take me with you. You know I can help you—I understand the genetics of the werewolves and their mating characteristics so I can—"

He wasn't interested in the werewolves any longer, but the woman still might be helpful. He nodded. "But run fast, doctor. Run very damn fast."

She nodded, eyes wide. A woman with a strong instinct for self-preservation. He liked that.

He grabbed Cassie and lifted her over his shoulder. He—

Cassie drove a scalpel into his shoulder.

He yelled at the unexpected pain and his hold slipped on her. She fell, slamming into the floor.

Cassie shoved back her hair, and he saw that she was very much awake and aware and far, far from dying.

"Dante's here, isn't he?" She smiled up at him. "And you're terrified."

Jon would have been terrified if he hadn't been staring at his perfect weapon. He pulled that scalpel out of his shoulder and gripped it in his hand. "He's never tried to kill you, not in all those long years when you were with him at Genesis . . . so I'm betting he won't kill you now."

Actually, he didn't think the bastard *could* kill her.

"But I will," Jon told her quietly. "I will slice your throat open right here, right now, and I'll let you bleed out before your phoenix can get here."

Cassie stared up at him, and Jon knew she saw the truth in his eyes.

"Shaw already has your samples. I don't need you alive."

Cassie swallowed. Her gaze cut toward the blond doctor.

There was a soft click of sound. Jon looked over and saw that Dr. Shaw had a gun pointed at Cassie's head. Well, well, the doctor kept surprising him.

"I'm not dying for someone I don't even know," Dr. Shaw said, but the gun trembled in her hand. "So let's all just get out of here and get on that helicopter."

Cassie rose, but her knees buckled, and she hit the floor once more.

Ah, so she wasn't as strong as she wanted him to think. Jon caught her arms and lifted her toward him.

Her scent rose, filling his nose, and for an instant, he stilled. That scent . . . he'd always enjoyed her scent.

His eyes narrowed on her. "Do you want me to kill you right now?"

Cassie shook her head.

"Then do the fuck what you're told. Don't fight me, don't cry out, and I'll let you live." He scooped her into his arms because he didn't want her slowing him down. "Come on, Shaw," he barked to the other woman. Power and strength had flooded through him with that injection. He barely felt Cassie's weight. His steps were surer, faster, and he lifted his foot and kicked open the door that blocked him from the helipad.

The blackness of the night waited for him. The chopper . . . was less than fifty yards away.

Dante heard the helicopter's blades spinning. His head snapped up as that steady beat slipped past the blare of the alarm.

Cassie had been taken from him on that helicopter before.

He wouldn't let her go again.

He ran through the hallways, following the sound. No one tried to stop him. They turned and cowered when they saw him.

He didn't care about them.

Only her.

Outside once more, he raced toward the helicopter. Its lights cut across the clearing, flashing on him, then sweeping away.

The helicopter began to rise.

No. No, it can't leave.

He'd have to track her again, and Cassie was already hurt. The scent of her blood . . .

"No!" Dante yelled, and his flames flew out, hitting the whirling blades of the helicopter. Burning, the blades were spinning slower and slower. The chopper slammed back down to earth with a jarring crash.

He jumped toward it and ripped open the door. Saw Cassie slumped and strapped down in the backseat. Another woman was there—a woman with a gun that she lifted toward him. Her face was cloaked in the shadows.

He snatched the gun from her. Tossed it behind him and yanked Cassie out of the seat. Her eyes were closed. Her body was limp.

The chopper had fallen only ten feet—surely that wouldn't have been enough to . . . to . . .

"Cassie?" He put her down on the ground. Ran his hands over her, checking for injuries. And there were injuries. Cuts and scratches all over her. "Cassie. Cassie, open your eyes."

The beast that lived inside of him was clawing to be free. He could taste the ash rising on his tongue. The only thing holding that beast in check was Cassie.

Come back to me.

She'd been the only thing to ever hold him in check.

She'd been eight the first time she came to him. A little girl, big green eyes, trembling voice. *I don't want him to kill anyone else.*

She'd tried to save Dante then.

He'd died.

She wouldn't die now. He wouldn't let her.

Her eyelashes flickered.

Yes. "Cassie?"

Her breath whispered out and her eyes opened. "Knew . . . you were coming . . ."

Hell, yes. He pulled her against his chest. Held her tight right next to his racing heart.

Over her shoulder, Dante saw the blond female stumble out of the helicopter. She fell onto her knees, but pushed forward, all but crawling away.

The man who'd been piloting that helicopter shoved from the wreckage. He didn't try to crawl away. He stood there, glaring at Dante. "Do you remember *me,* bastard?" The man snarled.

Dante didn't let go of Cassie.

"I'm the one who took her from you. This time . . . all the times. I'm the one she was going to marry."

What the fuck?

"You think she's yours. You're wrong. She's been working you from the beginning. It's all part of an experiment. Every single moment." The man smiled and lifted his hands. "But you can't see her for what she is, can you? Because she's got you fooled."

"No . . . Dante . . ." Cassie whispered.

"Her injuries are from samples that *she* ordered us to take. She wanted to see how her body had changed since you were dumb enough to give up your tears to her in New Orleans."

Dante rose, making sure to put his body between Cassie's and— "What is your name?"

"Lieutenant Colonel Jon Abrams."

"You're a dead man, Lieutenant Colonel."

The man laughed. "You're already a wanted criminal. Thanks to me, your face is on every TV in the nation. You think you can walk away from here? Cassie won't go with you. She lured you here. Wanted to keep doing the tests on you."

"Dante, I *didn't.*" Cassie said, her voice growing stronger.

It sounded like she was backing away from him. He heard the rustle of her footsteps and realized that she was retreating.

Leaving him to face off against the other man.

"Do you know why she wants to study you so much?" Jon took a step toward him. "Because her lover is sick. Not sick so much as *transforming.* If she can't help her werewolf, she'll lose him, and Cassie doesn't want to lose Trace."

Trace. The name was familiar . . . Wait. The cabin and the warehouse—both had been owned by a man named Trace. Wasn't that what Cassie had told him?

"Cassie uses anyone she can, in order to get what she wants. She used you. She used me. She's not the damsel in distress that you seem to think."

The helicopter was burning behind Jon. The flames rose into the air, and Dante saw that men with weapons were spilling out of the ranch. Oh, so *now* they thought they were brave enough to fight?

Or were they just eager to die?

"Dante . . ." Cassie's voice called out quietly. "Get away from him."

What? "I'm not afraid of the human."

Jon took another step forward. "But I'm not just human." His hands lifted, moving in a fast blur, and knives slashed into Dante's chest.

No, not knives. *Claws*.

"I stopped being human long ago. I guess Cassie has a thing for monsters, huh?" Jon's teeth had elongated. He lifted his claws again—and came for Dante's neck.

Dante sidestepped, twisted, and came up ready to send his fire right into the man's heart.

A shot rang out, an explosion that ripped past the fire and the shouts from the approaching men.

Jon froze, then he looked down at his chest. A dark shadow bloomed in the middle of his shirt. Growing bigger, bigger. He lifted his head. "Cas . . . sie?"

Dante spun around and saw that Cassie had grabbed the gun that he'd tossed aside earlier. She still had that gun aimed at Jon.

"I told you, Jon . . . you should have left . . . the program."

It sure looked like he'd left the program right then.

More gunfire erupted—from the guards rushing toward them. Seeing their boss get shot down had driven them over the edge. A bullet sliced across Dante's arm as he leaped toward Cassie.

Using his body, he shielded her. "I'll stop them." A deadly promise.

There would be no more running.

No one would be left alive to hunt them.

"Dante, no!"

But he'd turned his back on her. Lifted his hands. It would be easy enough to send a wall of flames rushing toward their pursuers. They'd be dead in moments.

So simple.

He'd killed before like this. Taken out an army that came after him. A different life. The same beast inside.

The fire had raged and raged.

He'd eventually been captured, and later, accused of witchcraft. Of working with the devil.

"I am the devil," he whispered as his flames began to rise.

They'd hung him.

He'd come back, burning in front of them.

"I won't run," he said.

The shots stopped firing. Maybe the fools finally realized they were facing a creature they couldn't ever hope to defeat.

Good-bye.

Some were turning tail and running away. Dumb. They'd never be able to run fast enough.

"Dante, *no*!" Cassie jumped in front of him and grabbed his hands. "Don't do this!"

"They took you. They hurt—"

"They're people. Some of them might hate what they're doing, some don't even *know* what's really happening. You can't just . . . just kill them all!"

Of course, he could. With barely a thought. "Watch me."

"No!" Cassie held him tighter. "Let's get out of here. Let's just *go.*"

Running wouldn't work. "They'll come for you again."

"No, no, with Jon dead"—her head turned toward the downed Lieutenant Colonel—"they won't come for us. We can vanish."

Running wasn't his style. They'd hurt him by taking Cassie. Now they should hurt.

"Please," Cassie begged. "Let's get out of here." She drew in a ragged breath. "I don't . . . I *hurt,* Dante. Please just take me away from here."

Jaw clenching, he nodded. He'd take her away. Get her safe and secure, and when she wasn't watching—*when she can't see just how dark I truly am*—he would come back to finish the war these fools had started.

There would be nothing left but ash.

She smiled at him, the sight weak and trembling, but so beautiful.

He pressed his lips against hers. Sank his fingers into her hair. The beast wanted to be free to burn and destroy, but as he held her, she . . . soothed him.

She always had.

From the very first moment, when his cell door had opened and he'd looked up at a lost child.

She wasn't a child anymore.

But she was his.

He lifted her into his arms. Cradled her carefully. As they approached the thick wall and the barbed wire, he sent out a ball of fire to blast them an exit.

No one followed. No shouts or gunfire filled the night.

Those behind him were too scared to fight.

Good. But I'll return.

He wouldn't give his enemies a chance to come for him again.

He'd spared enemies before, only to see them come once more and attack when they thought he was weak. So much fire and death. So many centuries.

No wonder he had tried to push away the memories.

He found the motorcycle that he'd left behind. He put Cassie on her feet, and saw that she still gripped the gun in her right hand. He stared at the weapon. "I could have killed him." She hadn't needed the man's death on her.

I was going to marry her.

He'd *wanted* to kill the bastard.

"I tried to save him, tried to tell him to leave . . ." She shook her head. "It took me too long to realize that Jon didn't want to be saved."

Dante pulled the weapon from her hand and put it in one of the motorcycle's saddlebags. He climbed onto the bike and gripped the handlebars. "Will you be able to hold on to me?"

Cassie climbed on behind him. "Yes."

He wasn't sure he believed her. The lieutenant colonel's words replayed through his mind. *You think she's yours. You're wrong. She's been working you from the beginning.*

Her hands curled around Dante's stomach. Held tight.

He revved the motor. Rocks and dirt flew out behind him as the motorcycle sprang away from the patch of trees. He didn't bother with the headlights. He could see just fine as he raced ahead.

Cassie's body was warm and soft behind him. Alive.

Going after her—getting her back—had been his only thought when he'd risen from the flames. He'd always believed Cassie was his . . . his alone. But as the motorcycle pushed forward ever faster, a dark suspicion began to grow in his mind.

I was going to marry her.

Cassie hadn't said the man was lying.

Her lover is sick. Not sick so much as transforming. If she can't help her werewolf, she'll lose him, and Cassie doesn't want to lose Trace.

Cassie had said that she had to get to Mississippi. That there were those in that area who needed her.

Dante's left hand rose and curled around her. He held her as tightly as she held him.

He'd seen much in his years on the earth. Things he hated. Beings he wanted to destroy.

He'd only once ever found something that he craved.

And he'd vowed to himself . . . once he realized just how important she was . . . that he would never let her go.

If Cassie had been lying to him, if she'd been part of his torture, she would pay.

But she would not get away from him.

The fire came to him, consuming, burning, destroying. The white-hot flames burned from the inside out, and as he died, Jon saw hell.

Monsters were there. Beasts made of flame who struck out at him. Hitting and slicing. He tried to fight—

Only to find that the flames surrounded him. Suffocated him.

He tried to open his mouth to scream.

But had no voice.

Only flames.

So many flames.

Rising and rising . . . burning . . . but not destroying. Not anymore.

Creating.

"Lieutenant Colonel!" A woman's voice. Shouting. Shocked.

His eyes opened. At first, everything seemed tinted by red. By the fire.

He blinked, trying to clear his vision.

"What have you done?" the woman whispered. "Y-you were dead . . ."

He was standing, his body naked, a circle of flame around him.

He looked past the flames and saw a woman standing

there. A woman with disheveled blond hair. Fear covered the delicate curves of her face. "You're like him," she said as she stumbled back a step.

Jon could only stare at her.

"The injection. *What* were you putting into your veins?"

He lifted his hand.

"Do you . . ." She took another quick step back. "Do you even know who I am?"

His skin was unmarred. No blisters. No burns. He glanced down at his chest.

No bullet hole.

"Yes," he said, speaking slowly, "I do know who you are."

Even more, he knew *what* he was. The serum that he'd taken—so many of those painful doses—had actually worked.

He'd become like Dante. Only . . . better.

When Dante rose, his memory was often gone.

"I remember everything," Jon whispered. The flames were still around him. He waved his hands. More fire appeared.

Beautiful fire. Red and gold and orange.

He heard voices shouting in the distance. The fear in those voices carried in the wind.

"It's your men. They were running—"

Running away, instead of trying to stop Dante? "Where is . . . Cassandra?"

"He took her."

While my men had cowered.

He started walking toward the sound of those shouts.

"Lieutenant Colonel?"

The blonde . . . Dr. Shaw. He could still use her. "Stay back," Jon ordered. Things were about to get hot. If he accidentally killed the doctor, well, that would be unfortunate.

She froze.

He swept by her and let his fire grow.

"What are you doing?" Her horrified question followed him.

He didn't respond. He just let the fire loose. Let it race toward the old base.

As the fire grew, the flush of power filled him. He could feel . . . something . . . inside himself. Something different from the beast he'd carried since his first experiment at Genesis.

This new creature was clawing at him with fire. Struggling to get out.

"You want out?" Jon asked as he lifted his hands. "Let's see what you can do."

He stopped fighting the beast and let it take him. The flames leaped from him as he surrendered. The buildings caught fire, an inferno that lit up the sky. Booms burst in the air, screams echoed.

Those who'd run and left him to his fate . . . had their own fiery fate waiting for them. But they wouldn't rise.

He'd make sure of it.

CHAPTER SEVEN

Cassie held onto Dante as tightly as she could. Her memory of escaping from Jon was hazy. In order to block the pain, she'd had to go far into her mind, into the shadows that she'd first found when she'd been a child.

When her father had strapped her to the table in his lab.

He hadn't experimented on just the paranormals. He'd wanted to create stronger, better humans.

He'd planned for her and her brother to be the first "better" humans.

That hadn't worked out. But their father hadn't given up easily. He'd just ignored their screams and tears.

The motorcycle braked. She couldn't see anything in front of her. Just the darkness.

As they'd driven, she'd smelled smoke, a heavy, thick blast of smoke that had followed them on the wind. It was gone now. It was just them. And darkness.

"No one's here," Dante said. "You can go inside and rest." He turned off the bike.

Right. She was supposed to stop holding so tightly to him.

Her body still ached, but not as badly as it had. She climbed off the motorcycle slowly, then stood for a moment, making sure that she wasn't about to fall on her face.

Dante reached out and steadied her. At his touch, her

breath caught. She looked up and found his gaze just inches from hers. The gold in the depths of his eyes was burning once more.

"The place isn't as nice as the one your *friend* Trace had for you, but it's got a bed inside, four walls and a roof, so I figure it will do for now."

Had she just imagined the emphasis he'd placed on *friend*? She wasn't sure. She was so tired she just wanted to crash in bed—crash and not worry about someone coming at her with a needle or a scalpel.

But I did that. I was the monster with the needle, too. For so long.

Some would say she'd gotten her fitting punishment that night.

At least . . . at least the doctors had stopped before getting the bone marrow and the spinal tap. She rubbed her forehead. *Or had they?* Cassie wasn't sure just how long she'd been in that lab.

"Come on." Dante's hand curled around her shoulder.

She flinched. That area was still sore.

He immediately dropped his hand before she could explain about the samples they'd taken.

Cassie knew she was healing, but she still ached.

His breath eased out on a sigh. "Let's go in."

She noticed that the front lock looked as if it had been melted. Interesting lock picking technique. She would have questioned him on that, but just didn't have the energy.

A few moments later, Cassie realized that he'd told her the truth. A bed waited inside. An old table. Some chairs. Not much, but it sure looked like paradise to her.

She crawled in the bed, then she drew her legs up as she turned on her side, wrapping her arms around herself.

"Cassie?" He was behind her. She should look at him, but she felt . . . frozen.

She'd killed Jon.

"Cassie, I have to leave for a few minutes."

What? They'd just gotten there.

"You'll be safe here, and I'll be back soon."

The floor creaked. He was actually going to leave her.

Her shoulders hunched. "Don't."

Tension seemed to fill the air.

"Please don't leave me right now." She couldn't look at him. She had her eyes squeezed shut so she wouldn't have to look at anything, but in her mind, she could see Jon. The dark shadow that had been blood as it spread over his chest. He'd looked so surprised.

Cassie, will you marry me?

He'd asked her that . . . what seemed like a lifetime ago, but it had been just two years ago.

And yes, once, she'd thought about walking down the aisle with him. Maybe having a child.

Tonight, she'd killed him.

Dante wasn't speaking.

She knew what he wanted to do. Go back. Make sure that he destroyed that facility. He wanted to burn the place to the ground. If he did that, if he hurt the humans inside, wouldn't he be a monster, too?

Weren't they already monsters?

"I can't stop seeing him," she whispered.

Then it wasn't the floor that creaked. It was the bed. The mattress dipped, and she realized that Dante had crawled into the bed with her.

Her breath stilled in her lungs.

His hand came up and lightly trailed over her arm. The warmth of his touch seemed to banish some of her chill.

"What did he do to you?"

The usual. Strapped her to a table. Took her blood. Her DNA. Samples from her bones and— "What they always do to the people that Genesis wants to experiment on."

"You aren't an experiment."

Yes, she was. There was a reason her blood was poison to vampires. "I've been an experiment since I was eight years old." Her father had never seen her as a child.

He'd seen her as a weapon.

"I had a brother once," she whispered. He was dead, too . . . though she'd discovered his death only recently. Before he'd died, she'd learned that he'd become . . . twisted . . . just like their father.

Would she become that way, too? Was she already?

"My father gave him the . . . same injections that he'd given to me." At first, anyway. Later, she'd been given separate treatments.

Because she'd died during one of those experiments, they'd had to change up her dosage levels.

"I remember . . ." Her voice came out quiet and husky. "We were tossed into a pit with vampires once. My father wanted to see if they'd come after us, or if our poison blood would keep them away."

Dante's arm curled around her, and he pulled her back against the cradle of his body. His warmth surrounded her. Made her feel safe. . . . when she knew safety was a lie.

"Did they bite you?"

"One did, but when he died, no one else touched me. They didn't bite my brother. The vampires . . . were different, *enhanced*." How she hated that word. They'd been soldiers. Volunteers who'd been given a trip to hell.

Dante's hold tightened around her.

"That was the first time I ever killed anyone." The first time, not the last, despite her efforts to be careful. She'd always tried to stay away from the vampires. One sip of her poisoned blood would kill most of them. "I didn't want to kill Jon."

"You should have let me burn him. I *wanted* to kill him."

She knew that. It was part of their problem. "There's so much darkness in you." Her words were hushed. "It scares me sometimes." Maybe she shouldn't have said those words, but she was long past the point of a filter. Too tired. Too broken. Too everything.

In the morning, she could pretend to be strong again.

"If you're so afraid"—his words rumbled behind her—"then why are you in my arms now?"

"Because you're the only one who's ever made me feel whole."

Her eyes were still closed. Hiding in the dark, that was her way.

Silence filled the small cabin.

She became aware of his steady breathing behind her. In. Out. In . . .

Her own faster breaths slowed to match his.

Dante didn't speak again.

"Thank you," she finally told him.

"You shouldn't thank me." The words seemed to be a warning.

She shook her head slightly against the pillow. "You saved me."

"No, I just didn't let you get away."

Her heartbeat wasn't racing any longer. He was behind her, around her, and nothing could hurt her while her phoenix was close.

Cassie stopped fighting the lethargy that wanted to pull her down into a deep sleep. She stopped fighting and just let go.

She wondered if she'd see Dante in her dreams . . . or if she'd see Jon's ghost haunting her.

Cassie was asleep. He could leave her, slip away, and be back before she awoke.

She'd curled into herself, like a frightened child. Her voice had trembled with fear and pain, and she'd *thanked* him.

The woman should have been running from him.

He glanced toward the door. He could go back to that ranch. Burn the place with a thought.

There's so much darkness in you. It scares me sometimes.

She had asked him to spare the humans at that ranch. He leaned closer to her, and his lips pressed lightly against her cool cheek.

She whimpered in her sleep, and the fear in that small sound tore at him.

Cassie still needed him. Someone had to keep her nightmares at bay.

Carefully, he turned her so that she faced him. He pulled her closer, lowering her head over his heart and threading his fingers through her hair.

The humans at that ranch were lucky. The battered angel in his arms had given them a reprieve. If they were smart, they'd run fast and hard, and they would never cross his path again.

As for Cassie . . . her body was a slight weight against his. His beast was quiet, as close to calm as it ever was, and he realized that he could just hold her like that, all night long.

So he did.

"How long have you been here?" Cassie's voice was quiet as she stood behind the two-way mirror.

He knew that she'd realized—months ago—that he could see past the reinforced glass.

She stood less than a foot behind the mirror, her eyes up and clear—and on his.

"Too many years," he said softly as he headed toward the glass and to her.

"I remember you," she told him. "When I was a kid . . ."

She was little more than a kid. Nineteen, twenty?

"When you do get out, please don't ever come back. Just run and run."

His lips tightened. "What makes you think they'll ever let me out?" He was their prized specimen. They tortured him, they killed him, but they weren't letting him go.

She smiled, and the sight stopped his breath for a moment. "I know you'll get out . . . because I'll help you."

Her hand lifted. Touched the glass.

His hand lifted too, as if pulled by her.

But then the guards came in . . .

And Cassie left him.

Dante climbed from the bed as the moonlight streamed through the old blinds. So many memories were in his head, fighting to get to the surface and break free.

He hated some of the memories.

Treasured others.

Her hand, rising against the glass.

He never would have thought to find a glimpse of gold in that hell, but he had.

His gaze fell back on the bed. On Cassie. He'd known just what she was the first minute he'd seen her. When she'd only been eight, the promise had been there.

He could have broken out of Genesis sooner, but he'd needed to wait. He'd had to see for sure if she would become—

"Dante!" She screamed his name as she jerked up in bed.

He crossed to her instantly. "I'm here."

A shudder shook her slender frame and then her hands were around him, holding tight. "I was afraid it was a dream . . . that I was back there. They were going to keep hurting me."

I should have gone back and finished them.

"It wasn't a dream," he said as he shoved down his fury. "You're safe."

Her mouth pressed over his shoulder. Her lips were soft and silken. Her breath blew lightly over his skin.

Then she pulled away. Looked up at him. Her gaze searched his and her green eyes widened. "Dante."

She seemed to finally be seeing him.

No, she wasn't *seeing* him, but rather seeing *in* to him.

"You remember, don't you? You remember me?"

"I wouldn't have been able to track you if I hadn't." His voice had roughened because . . . she wasn't hurt any longer. No scratches or bruises on her skin. Completely healed.

She was in bed. Alone with him.

He'd wanted her for so long.

He'd been close to having what he wanted.

He *would* have what he wanted.

"What all do you remember?" Her voice was husky. Hopeful?

His fingers lifted and brushed back her hair. "Every damn thing."

I was going to marry her.

Dante's jaw locked.

Once, she'd been a virgin. She'd come to him, sneaking past the security, offering him heaven.

He'd been a fool to refuse.

I knew what she was. I should have held on tight.

Her lips lifted into a smile. "You know me?"

He didn't return her smile. "I'm going to devour you." *Fair warning.*

Her smile dimmed. "Dante?"

He pushed her back onto the bed. The control he'd held so effortlessly while she slept—cradled in his arms—was shredding with each passing second. She wasn't hurt. She wasn't trapped in a nightmare.

Cassie was in his arms, and he meant to have her.

"Are you afraid?" Dante asked her.

"The fire . . . what if . . . ?"

He knew what the idiots at Genesis had said—in moments of extreme passion, his fire would rage out of control. That he would hurt—kill—a lover.

That wouldn't happen with her.

Couldn't.

Because the phoenix wasn't allowed to hurt her.

I knew what she was . . .

"I'll keep you safe," he promised her.

His lips pressed to hers. He *had* to kiss her. He wanted her to forget the man she'd shot and any other bastard out there. The others would no longer have a place in her mind or heart.

There would only be room for him.

Her mouth opened beneath his . . . eager and sweet. He thrust his tongue past her lips and savored her.

So good. She'd always tasted of innocence and sin, a combination that had made him crazy so many times.

Every time he got his hands on her.

He should go carefully. Use finesse and charm.

But Dante had never been one for charm, and if he didn't get inside Cassie, he thought he might just go insane.

Been there . . .

And he'd left the flames behind to prove his descent into madness.

His hand slid between them. She was wearing some kind of little gown—like a hospital gown?—and when he shoved it up, he touched the smooth silk of her panties.

He'd come so close to tasting her there.

Mine.

His head lifted. Their eyes met.

De-fucking-vour.

Her breath caught as he pushed down her body. "Dante, you don't—"

He put his mouth on her, right through the panties. He pressed down, kissing that silk, then blowing lightly against her.

Cassie's moan filled his ears, and he knew that her nightmare was gone.

That wasn't good enough. He wanted her thinking only about him and the pleasure that he could give to her.

Because she was all that he could think about.

His fingers grabbed the edge of her panties and yanked them down. The underwear was shredded before he tossed the garment away. He put his mouth directly on that sweet flesh.

She tasted so damn good. He licked her. Kissed. Slid his fingers into her tight, hot core.

Cassie's breaths came faster, harder. Her nails sank into his shoulders.

It still wasn't good enough.

He licked her hard. Sucked the center of her need. Thrust two fingers into her. Kept up the friction, enjoying every single taste of her—and becoming desperate for more. Always, *more.*

She stiffened beneath him, her whole body tensing, and he knew that her climax was close.

He wanted that first climax to be when he was in her. As deep as he could go. He lifted up and positioned his heavy cock at the entrance to her body.

Cassie's gaze found his and her breath caught. "Your eyes . . ."

He wondered what she saw in his gaze, but whatever it was, it didn't seem to be scaring her. She reached for him. Her arms curled around his shoulders.

He stroked her once more, then drove deep into her. His thrust sent the headboard thudding against the wall. "Cassie?"

She'd tensed beneath him once more, but the tension was different, and . . . she was so tight.

So amazingly tight.

He had to pull back, had to thrust deeper. Again and again.

Her lashes had lowered, and he couldn't see her gaze. That wasn't the way he wanted it. He needed to see her. All of her.

"Look at me."

Her lashes flew up.

Was that pain in her eyes? Cassie couldn't know pain. Only pleasure.

His hand eased between their bodies, found her clit, and stroked her. He choked back his own need as he brought her to a feverish pitch once more. He'd take no pleasure until she found her release.

Her hips started to arch against him, and her nails dug into his back.

Yes, yes, this was what he wanted. What he needed.

Cassie climaxed beneath him, and he felt the strong contractions of her inner muscles along the length of his cock. Her gasp filled his ears—the sexiest thing he'd ever heard, sighing with pleasure—and he thrust harder, faster into her.

The headboard kept thudding against the wall.

The pleasure hit him, crashing over him, into him, and her name roared from his lips as the climax seemed to rip him apart.

His hands fisted on the covers. His hips pistoned against her, and the pleasure consumed him.

His breath heaved from his lungs and his mouth took hers. He kissed her, tasting the pleasure on her lips, and Dante knew that nothing had ever been this good.

No other lovers. Only her.

The woman had just ruined him for anyone else. But he'd known that truth about her for a very long time.

Right from the moment he'd realized she had the potential to be a phoenix's mate. One of the few who could handle the fire and fury that was within him.

His lips gentled on hers even as he still thrust lightly into her. He didn't want to leave her body. After so many years of wanting, he was finally where he needed to be.

He licked her lower lip, then slowly raised his head. Her cheeks were flushed. Her eyes sparkling. And she smiled at him.

Lethal.

His breath stilled in his chest.

"That was"—her smile widened—"worth waiting for."

He shook his head.

Her smile instantly dimmed.

"No," he told her, his voice a growl because that was all he could manage, "that was just the beginning."

His thrusts became stronger. Harder.

Her eyes widened.

Her smile returned.

So did the pleasure. So much pleasure. Enough to make a man lose his mind.

His fingers twined with hers. Her legs lifted and curled around his hips. When he thrust, she arched into him. Her sex was slick and—judging by those sweet moans—sensitive from her release.

It didn't take long until she was coming for him again. Her sex contracted, squeezing him. Slick and eager. He pumped into her, driving as deep as he could possibly go.

The second orgasm left him feeling hollowed out, sated, and more at peace than he'd ever felt.

He knew it wasn't the orgasm that had truly done that for him. It was her.

In the aftermath, he pulled her closer against him. Pressed a kiss to her cheek.

And slept for the first time in centuries with a woman in his arms. He'd never been able to hold another while he slept. He'd feared that his nightmares would bring fire—and that he'd wake to see death and hell.

But the fire wouldn't come with Cassie. It couldn't.

She brought peace.

The faint light of dawn pressed onto Cassie, and she blinked, slowly opening her eyes. Something was on top of her—something warm and strong and heavy.

Dante.

He was sprawled half on top of her, with his arm wrapped around her stomach. His eyes were closed. His face relaxed.

He'd always looked so fierce. So dangerous. Now, he just looked . . . handsome.

Her hand lifted. Her fingers were trembling. After last night, how could she still feel nervous around him? But her fingers shook as she brushed back a lock of hair that had fallen over his forehead.

At her touch, his eyes immediately opened. There was no grogginess in his gaze. Too alert, far too aware, that gaze locked on her.

Since it was her first official morning after, Cassie wasn't 100 percent sure what she was supposed to say. Actually, she wasn't even 10 percent sure, so she offered him a smile.

Dante didn't smile. But then, he never did.

One day, he will.

"There's no going back," he said.

No, they'd crossed a line last night.

"We'll leave this town," he continued and his fingers stroked over her shoulder. "Head north. I had a place in Canada once that I think—"

Wait. She stiffened beneath him. "I still have to get to Mississippi. I have people there who are counting on me." *He knew that.*

A furrow appeared between his brows. He sat up, pulling the covers with him.

She was naked. That fact hadn't embarrassed her at all last night. But it wasn't last night, and right then, her face flamed as she yanked the sheets away from him.

Dante frowned at her. "Those people . . . want to use you. If you go back, Genesis—what's left of it—will keep hunting you."

Yes, he was right. They would.

"I can't leave the people in Belle. They need me." She was the only one who could help them. "The other phoenixes are going to meet me there and—"

Dante's hands locked around her wrists. "Other phoenixes?"

"I-I thought that your memory was back." Surely he remembered the female phoenix in New Orleans. He'd gone to New Orleans to find that woman because—*Oh, crap. Because phoenixes have a history of killing each other.*

Since phoenixes could come back from nearly any death, they didn't have many natural enemies.

Just their own kind.

In order for a phoenix to truly die, he had to be killed during the moment of his regeneration, the moment when the flames burned at their brightest—a moment when only another phoenix could get through the fire. Those fireproof suits that Jon's men had worn certainly hadn't been strong enough to get the job done.

"Sabine doesn't want to hurt you," Cassie said, referring to the only female phoenix she'd ever met. Cassie clutched the sheet closer to her body. "Don't you remember? She just wanted—"

"I remember Sabine." Flat. Cold. "Her vampire tried to transform her."

Cassie nodded. Sabine's lover, a vampire, had tried to

turn the phoenix, but the results hadn't been quite what Ryder had anticipated.

"Sabine never wanted to hurt you." Cassie tried to make her voice sound soothing. "You don't have to worry about a threat from her."

"And her vampire? You think he will want me to keep living, knowing that I can kill his woman?"

Cassie's heart was pounding too fast. Her death grip was about to rip the sheets. "Are you planning to kill her?" Before Dante could answer, she grabbed for his hand and dropped her sheet. "Sabine wants to help us! She's working with me to try and find a cure for Trace—"

Dante's eyes glinted, the fire simmering.

Uh-oh. What was that about?

But he said, "Phoenixes. Plural." His head tilted. "You know of another phoenix? Not just Sabine?"

She swallowed. "I do. Another male, not as old as you, but he's still strong. Cain has agreed to—"

"Cain O'Connor?"

Dante's voice had gone lethal.

"Yes."

His hand twisted, and he was holding onto her. "You are not to get near Cain O'Connor."

"He's going to meet me in Belle, Mississippi. Sabine is going there, too." *Once she gets back in the U.S.*

Her vampire had taken her away for a while—a honeymoon time, of sorts.

Cassie straightened her shoulders and tried to pretend that she wasn't naked in front of Dante. "I *am* going. I wanted—I wanted you to come, too. That's why I came after you in Chicago. I'm so close to making a breakthrough, so close. With your help, I know I can do it."

He stared back at her. The golden flames in his eyes seemed to be growing brighter. So not good.

Cassie pressed her lips together. Then, unable to help herself, she asked, "You're the oldest, aren't you?"

He nodded.

I knew it. Excitement had her feeling a little giddy. "You're the key! If Trace can be cured, if the primal vampires can be reverted—"

"Primal vampires?"

Ah, yes. Another confession. "Genesis made monsters—real monsters that have no control. They exist only to feed and kill. Their virus is spreading like wildfire, and if I can't stop them . . ." She didn't even want to think about what could happen. "If I can't stop them, the primal vampires could take over the world as we know it."

No hint of worry or fear flickered over his face.

Okay. "This isn't about me," Cassie said. "It's about fixing the mess that Genesis created. About saving lives. I have to go back to Belle. And the phoenixes—*you*—are the only hope that we have."

His jaw locked. "Then you have no hope. You get the phoenixes together, and we *will* kill each other." His gaze swept over her face. "If Cain O'Connor gets anywhere near you, I'll send him to hell myself."

Cassie decided not to mention the fact that she'd already been around Cain a few times. He'd been the first one to seek her out because he'd wanted her to help Trace.

"Leave them all. They can sort out their own lives. Or they can die." Dante shrugged. "You and I will go north. We will—"

"How can you not care?" She pulled away from him and jumped to her feet. "I'm talking about people—innocent people! If they can be saved, we have to try!"

He shook his head. "I don't care about them at all." He climbed from the bed and stretched to his full length.

She backed up a step. *Damn.* Naked, the guy was intimidating.

Rippling muscles. Hot flesh.

Intimidating and sexy.

Her tongue swiped over her lower lip. *Focus.*

"I saved you," he said, the words falling heavily into the room. "You are what matters to me. The others can—"

"Die?" she finished, hating that a chill had slipped over her skin.

"If they don't stay away from me"—he gave a slow nod—"that is exactly what will happen."

He wasn't going to help her. The realization was staggering, and it hurt. "You know what it's like to be trapped, to be an experiment, and you'd still walk away from them?"

"I *cannot* cure them, Cassie."

"You're wrong! Your tears cured me in New Orleans!" That was the part she'd clung to for so long. Her one instant of hope. He'd saved her, so that meant he cared about her. Maybe not as much as she cared about him, but he'd cried, actually shed a tear. *He cared*. "Your tears must be the most powerful, since you are the strongest phoenix and—"

"I did not cry for you."

She shook her head. "Of course, you did." He'd felt some of the same emotion that she did. She was alive—her life was proof of that. "I'm alive because of you."

Dante stared back at her, his face an implacable mask.

"I'm alive because of you," she said again, her voice rising as fear spiked in her heart. "I was dying in New Orleans! You were there. You took me out of that horrible room and you—"

"I was watching you die." Brutal words that drove her fear higher.

"Then you saved me," she said stubbornly. "Because your tears—"

"I did *not* cry for you."

She spun away from him. She wasn't about to put on

that damn exam gown so she started yanking open closets and drawers and—

"I . . . got you clothing. I wanted you to have everything you might need. It's there." He pointed to a bag near the old table.

She grabbed for the bag and hurriedly dressed. Jeans. Underwear. T-shirt. Even shoes. All a perfect fit.

"You remembered everything." She knew he truly had. Once dressed, she turned toward him. "So why are you acting like you don't remember what happened in New Orleans?" Why was he trying to rip her world away? "You had to save me. I'd be dead if you hadn't—"

"I thought you were dying." He was still naked.

Damn it. The guy didn't even seem aware of his nudity. She was aware of everything about him.

"You were in my arms, and your blood was all over me. You were staring up at me, trying to talk, but you were too far gone."

Goosebumps had risen on her flesh. "That's when you saved me."

He shook his head.

She grabbed his arms. "Why are you lying to me?" He'd never lied to her before. "Sabine didn't save me. I know the wounds I had—would have killed me. The only way I could have survived was if a phoenix saved me." Cassie wanted to shake him. "Why can't you just admit that you actually care enough about me that you cried? After everything we've been through together, the feelings aren't just mine. You have to—"

"I did not cry."

Her heart was breaking.

Dante spoke softly. "You . . . healed yourself."

Her nails dug into his arms, then she was pushing away from him. "That's not possible."

He laughed, and the sound was rough and bitter.

"You're talking to a myth, and you want to tell me about possible?"

Cassie wrapped her arms around herself. They'd made love. He'd held her through her fear.

I did not cry.

If he hadn't saved her, if he hadn't shed a tear to spare her life in those last desperate moments, then what did that mean for them?

He doesn't care. The cold seemed to deepen around her. His fire had never been farther away.

"Your father experimented on you. The first time we met"—Dante's eyes seemed to cloud with the memory—"you were only eight. And you told me . . . you told me that he'd killed you."

She didn't want to think about that memory. She'd shoved it so far back into her mind.

"He'd killed you, but you were there, walking around, talking, trying to save *me.*"

"I was a child, confused—"

"You were an experiment." The faint lines deepened around Dante's eyes. "Just like the rest of us. Your father made your blood into poison, but he did something else, too. He gave your body the ability to regenerate. To heal."

"I was *dying* in New Orleans." Choking on her own blood. Her last memory had been of his face, then . . . darkness. When she'd opened her eyes again, he'd been gone.

I was alive. She'd been so sure her survival had been because of him.

"Your heart stopped. You did die, but you came back." His body was so still. "Not the way I do. There were no flames and no tears. You returned on your own. Your skin mended before my eyes, and then you took your first breath once more."

Her world was splintering apart. If Dante hadn't saved her—

Then he doesn't love me.

And she . . . was truly nothing more than an experiment.

"That was why Jon came after me," she said, voice weak. "He must have found some files . . . something that told him what I could do." He'd wanted to replicate her healing, not just her poison.

A body that could survive anything, minus the trip to hell that the phoenixes took with each of their risings.

An experiment.

Nausea rolled in her stomach.

"Cassie—"

"I-I need a moment. I need—" *what he can't give me.*

What he'd never be able to give. If he'd just watched her die and felt nothing . . . She'd been so sure that her future was tied with Dante. That when his memory came back, he'd realize they were linked.

But he didn't care.

And she . . . Cassie didn't even know what she was anymore.

He didn't stop her as she hurried into the bathroom. Didn't stop her as she slammed the door and clutched desperately for the bathroom sink so that she wouldn't fall to the floor.

She'd been so ridiculously sure of Dante. Even with his memory gone, she'd thought that the emotions that connected them were still there, right beneath the surface.

She stared at her ashen reflection in the mirror. There was no connection between them. Dante felt nothing for her.

Her world seemed to be crumbling around her.

Dante's hands clenched into fists. He wanted to run after her, to kick in that door—and what?

He'd given her the truth, one that was long overdue.

Cassie saw herself as a human, but she was something far more than that.

Death hadn't been able to take her.

In New Orleans, he'd been frozen, mute, so desperate when she died—but then she'd opened her eyes and seen him again.

No fire. Just life.

The water was running in the bathroom. He was very much afraid that she'd turned on the water to drown out the sound of crying. He didn't want her to cry.

Dante jerked on his jeans. Pulled on a white T-shirt he'd stashed in the cabin when he'd made a fast run for her clothing. Even took the time to put his boots back on.

Cassie didn't come out of the bathroom.

His breath exhaled in a hard rush. They had more talking to do. As much as Cassie wanted to head back to Mississippi, he couldn't let her go. Another male phoenix would recognize her for what she was.

And Dante couldn't allow that.

The others would have to fend for themselves. He'd crossed a line with Cassie last night, and there would be no other for her.

They'd head north. To Canada. Hell, maybe they'd even cross an ocean soon. He'd been away from his home in France for far too long.

Cassie still hadn't come from the bathroom.

He walked toward that closed door. He rapped lightly. "Cassie?"

He heard only the running of the water.

"You can't stay in there forever." *And you can't hide from me.* He knew that was exactly what she was trying to do. Not happening. He'd seen all of her last night. She'd seen all of him. "Cassie?"

He heard nothing but—

The revving of an engine.

Dante kicked in the door. The bathroom was empty. The window—a damn tiny window—had been left open.

"Cassie!" He bellowed her name then he was spinning around. Running back through the cabin and outside. He saw the whip of her hair as she raced away from him, riding hell-fast on the motorcycle.

And leaving him behind.

For a moment, he just stared at her in shock. She hadn't left him. He'd *saved* her at that ranch. He'd taken her in that bed. She *wouldn't* just leave him.

Dust drifted in the motorcycle's path.

She'd fucking just left him.

He whirled around and stomped back into the cabin. The water was still running. He yanked it off. *Left. Me.* He knew where she was going—to Mississippi. To meet up with the other phoenixes and with the werewolf who seemed to matter far too much to her.

Inside the cabin, he smelled her. That light, seductive scent. The scent that had nearly driven him out of his mind so many times.

She ran from me.

Because she'd known what he wanted? Her . . . far away from any others.

He inhaled deeper and stalked toward the bed. The sheets were tangled, and her scent was deeper there. More lush.

He grabbed the sheets. Yanked them from the bed. Hadn't she realized what was happening between them? There was no escape. There was—

Blood, on the sheets. Her blood.

From a wound that she'd received at the ranch? But, no, she hadn't been bleeding by the time they'd gotten to the cabin. Her healing ability had kicked in.

His fingers clenched around the sheets as he remembered the slick, incredibly tight feel of her.

Mine.

His breath came harder and the sheets—burned in his hands. Ashes drifted to the wooden floor.

"You're not getting away."

She could be afraid, she could run, but there would be no escape.

His gaze swept the cabin, making sure they'd left nothing of import behind. Then, just to be safe, because he didn't want any others following them, he let his flames take the old cabin. He walked out as the crackling fire rose up the walls.

There was no other motorcycle. No other transportation. He'd have to run up to the main road, then hitchhike. Dante knew that he didn't look like the kind of guy most folks would want to pick up.

People just didn't jump at the chance to give the devil a ride.

No matter. He would *make* someone pick him up. He had to stop Cassie before she reached Mississippi.

The flames devoured the cabin, and he watched it burn. Watched until only embers remained. Then he waved his hands, quieting the fire.

Only the most powerful of the phoenixes could stir *and* soothe the fire.

Cain O'Connor wouldn't have power to match his. If the two of them came face-to-face, Cain would be the one to die.

Phoenixes had a drive to seek dominance. One of their flaws. To dominate was to survive.

When phoenixes got close, they fought.

Until one was dead.

Dante strode toward the narrow highway. He didn't hear the rumble of the motorcycle's engine any longer. Cassie was long gone. Riding with no helmet. Even though he knew firsthand just how little damage death could truly do to her, he wanted her to be safe.

She'd been driving far too fast.

He stepped onto the old, broken highway. Cassie shouldn't drive when she was so upset. It wasn't good for her.

An engine growled in the distance behind him. The sound was deeper, rougher, than the motorcycle's had been. Dante paused and looked over his shoulder. In the rising morning light, he could just make out the shape of a big rig, heading steadily toward him. His eyes narrowed, and he headed into the middle of the road.

Then he waited.

The big rig ate up the highway. Its horn blared a warning for him to move.

He wasn't moving. That big rig *was* stopping.

Dante held his ground and the big rig came ever closer.

CHAPTER EIGHT

"Authorities are investigatng what appears to be an arson out on Piersview Road. A late night blaze at the ranch there claimed the lives of two dozen people." The camera zoomed in close on the reporter's tense face. But, behind him, Cassie could see the body bags being wheeled away from the blackened remains of the ranch.

The ranch that *she'd* been at last night.

Her eyes squeezed shut.

"Miss? Miss, are you all right?"

It was the waitress's voice. Cassie had pulled in at the first pit stop she found—a little diner in the middle of nowhere. She'd scavenged in the motorcycle's saddlebags and found a few bucks. Since she hadn't eaten in—jeez, she couldn't even remember when—she'd been desperate for food.

Except the pancakes weren't exactly sitting well with her.

"Hon, are you sick?"

Heartsick, yes. That blaze . . . all those people . . . had Dante done that?

Her eyes opened, and she forced a false smile for the waitress. "I'm fine, thank you."

The woman, who looked like she was close to Cassie's own twenty-nine years, gave her one more worried glance before heading off to refill coffee at the next table.

Cassie's gaze returned to the TV and to the reporter who was going over the harrowing tale of death and arson.

Two dozen dead.

She'd woken up during the night. Dante hadn't been beside her. His spot on the bed had been empty. When she'd called out to him, he'd come to her side fast enough but . . .

How long had he been gone from that bed? Long enough to go back to the ranch and let his fire loose?

Maybe she didn't really know him well at all.

She tossed her precious dollars down on the table and rose on legs that still weren't quite steady. She eased down the narrow aisle between the tables and pushed against the door, ignoring the little jingle as she hurried outside.

She'd parked the motorcycle on the side of the building, trying to keep it out of sight.

She hadn't been mentioned on the newscast. Neither had Dante. With Jon dead, no one would be pointing the finger at them, at least, not until his bosses figured out what was happening. That should buy her enough time to cross back into Mississippi.

She rounded the side of the little diner.

"Hello, sweetheart."

Dante was sitting on the motorcycle.

Cassie shook her head.

He lifted a brow. "It wasn't very nice to run, was it? To just leave without a word, after all I did for you."

Two dozen dead.

She didn't think. Just spun away and leaped forward, hoping to get back around to the diner's entrance so that she could get help.

But there was never a chance for help. Dante grabbed her, locked one arm around her waist, and he put his other hand over her mouth. "You're not getting away again."

She shoved her elbow into his ribs, and the jerk just laughed at her.

She'd actually thought he was the good guy? The one who'd help her save people?

Talk about being delusional. At least her blinders were finally off. Shattered, somewhere in the dirt of the Texas road because yep, they were in Texas. It hadn't taken her long to figure that one out.

She heard voices. Men. Talking. Coming toward them.

Dante spun her toward him. "If you try to get them to help you, it won't end well for them."

Who the hell was this man? She seemed to be looking at a stranger.

"Don't call out." With that last warning, he moved his hand from her mouth, and, of course, she wasn't about to risk any humans. Humans would never be any match for him.

His arms wrapped around her, and he pulled her flush against his body.

His lips took hers.

She was so surprised that she didn't even move at first. His mouth pressed against hers, and his tongue swept over her lower lip. A shudder went through her, and as much as she wanted to say that shudder was from fear—

It wasn't.

Her body was far too attuned to his.

He licked her lower lip once more, and her mouth opened for him.

I'm biding my time. I'll run when I can.

A wolf whistle sounded in the air behind them. The humans. And they were seeing exactly what Dante wanted them to see. An amorous couple. Not a woman in fear for her life.

Two could play at this game.

Her hands rose—when had he let them go?—and her fingers tunneled in his hair. She pulled him down, closer, harder against her, and she was the one who took over that kiss. He'd thought to seduce her? Well, just because she didn't have a long history of lovers didn't mean that she didn't know a few tricks.

She bit his lower lip, a light sting, then she was the one licking him. Sucking his tongue. Tasting him and making him groan as he clutched her ever closer.

If he hadn't been a walking, talking disappointment to her, she would have blown his mind in the next bout of lovemaking.

Your loss, jerk.

The footsteps shuffled past them as the men kept heading toward their cars. A few moments later, she heard their vehicles pull away.

That was her cue to pull away from Dante, only he wasn't letting her go. His arousal stretched against the front of her body. Long and hard and thick. His hands were on her hips, and he was holding tight.

She kneed him in the groin.

Cassie didn't know if she hurt him or shocked him, but Dante let her go as he swore. She stumbled back, raising her hand to her lips. She could still taste him.

Dammit. I want more of that taste.

She would *not* be having more.

"I didn't realize . . . you liked things rough," Dante growled.

Her heart skipped a beat at that. Images flew through her mind—*no.* "Why?" she demanded.

"Because I can give you anything you like," Dante said as he straightened.

No, she hadn't hurt him. Figured.

"All you have to do is ask." He stepped toward her.

Cassie threw up her hands. "Why did you kill them?"

His unblinking gaze stared back at her. "I've killed a lot of people, sweetheart, so you're going to have to be far more specific."

"The people at the ranch—the guards, the researchers," she gritted out. *The ones who hurt me.* "I asked you to let them live."

A shrug rolled his shoulders. "So you did."

"And you lied to me!" *What about him isn't a lie?* "You waited until I slept, then you went back and burned the place to the ground."

That same furrow—a thin line—appeared between his brows. "What makes you think I did such a thing?"

"Uh, because you're a phoenix? The only one in the area. And because I *saw* the destruction on the TV in that diner not five minutes ago." Her breath heaved out as she dropped her hand. "Two dozen people were killed in that blaze, Dante. Two dozen. They weren't perfect, but did they all deserve to die like that?"

"I have no idea what they deserved. I'm not their judge."

"Just their executioner?"

A muscle jerked in his jaw. "I did not kill them."

"I saw the wreckage! The place was destroyed. It wasn't—"

"If I had burned it, I wouldn't have left any bodies behind. There would have only been ash left."

The nausea rolled through her again.

He frowned. "Cassie, are you all right?"

"No, I'm talking to an insane phoenix, and I just found out that I'm some kind of freak experiment." She huffed out a breath. "Why are you here? *How* are you here?"

His gaze—that couldn't be real worry in his dark stare—swept over her face.

"I'm here because this is where you are." He took another step toward her. "I can follow you anywhere."

She retreated automatically, and her back hit the diner's brick wall. *Great.* Bricks to her back, a phoenix to her front. "How? How did you find me here? How did you find me at the ranch? And how did—"

"I guess you could say that I'm . . . tuned to you. There is no place you could go on this earth that I could not follow."

"Provided you wanted to follow me." The words just snapped from her. "You were too busy with the vamp in Chicago to—"

"My memories of you hadn't crystalized by then. In time, I would have found you." His words, so very certain, sent a tendril of unease through her.

But since she was walking on a big old knife-edge of fear, she didn't let the extra unease stop her. "Did you kill those people at the ranch?"

He shook his head. "I swear to you, I let them live." His lips thinned. "Though I'll confess, I did entertain the thought of going back to finish them off."

He'd *entertained* the thought?

"Why are you looking so shocked? You knew what I was all the time I was caged at Genesis, but you still let me out of my prison."

A monster . . . a killer . . . that was what the guards had always said. Dante belonged in maximum security because of the threat he posed to the world.

She'd never believed those whispers. She'd looked into his eyes and thought she'd seen a man who needed her.

But then, she'd also thought Jon had needed her.

She had to get a freaking clue.

"How are you tuned to me?" Cassie wanted to know. If she was ever going to get away from him, she'd have to be sure he didn't follow.

His lips twisted. Almost a smile. As close as she'd ever seen. She hadn't expected it to look so cruel.

"Ah, Cassie. If I tell you that, you'll just try to escape, and that's not on the agenda for us."

"What is on the agenda?" Though she probably didn't want to know.

He stared back at her.

"I'll tell you what's on *my* agenda," Cassie snapped. "I'm going to Mississippi. People there are counting on me." Without Dante's cooperation, she wasn't sure how to begin helping them.

"You're going to the other phoenixes."

"Yes."

His gaze studied her face. "Then I will come with you."

Wait. What?

He shook his head as he read her expression. "What did you think I would do? Hunt you down, force you to come with me?"

"I didn't think you'd hunt me at all. I thought . . . I thought you'd be free of me."

His hands flattened against the bricks behind her, and she was caged between his body and the wall. The wonderful, enticing heat of his flesh seemed to wrap around her.

"What makes you think I want to be free?" Dante asked.

Maybe because he didn't love her? Maybe because he'd been spouting about Canada?

"While I hunted you—I mean, while I followed you . . ."

Her eyes narrowed.

"I realized that I had been too hasty. Perhaps it would be good to meet my own kind. There have been too many battles between us over the years—the centuries. It's time to move past that. When I meet the others, I won't be alone any longer."

"No, you won't." Hope was trying to stir within her again. If she got him to Mississippi with the other phoenixes, maybe they could all convince Dante to join the research. She could find a cure and undo the nightmares her father had caused.

"So you will take me to them." His mouth was just inches from her own. "And you won't try to leave me again."

Her gaze searched his. "Promise me," Cassie demanded.

His brows rose.

"Promise me," she said again, "that you didn't have anything to do with that fire at the ranch. That those people—that you *didn't* hurt them."

"And you'd believe my word?"

"I don't think you've ever lied to me." Even though there were times she would have preferred his lies.

Maybe a lie of love over the years wouldn't have made her heart feel so battered.

His head moved in a small nod. "I promise you, I didn't kill those people. I spent my night with you." A slight pause. His gaze warmed. "In you."

Her sex clenched as the hot memory pierced through her. *Damn him.*

"And"—his mouth came closer, but instead of kissing her lips, his mouth pressed lightly to her cheek—"I'm the only one who has enjoyed that pleasure."

Her cheeks flushed.

"Why is that?" Dante asked even as he pressed one more kiss to the curve of her jaw. "Why me?"

Because I love you.

He hadn't lied to her, but she couldn't give him the truth. Besides, wasn't it a truth he should already know?

Clueless phoenix.

There hadn't been any other lovers because she couldn't sleep with one man while loving another. She just wasn't made that way. Hell, at this point, she was wondering just how she *was* made.

"No answer?" Dante chided, his mouth over her neck. Over the pulse that raced so frantically. "That's not like you. Usually you have an answer for everything." He licked her skin. Nipped her.

Her panties were getting wet. She was angry, afraid, and aroused. All because of him. Always . . . *him*.

Her hands flattened on his chest. "We need to go." There were a whole lot of miles to cover between there and Belle.

He didn't stop kissing her neck.

Her legs wanted to become jelly. So she stiffened her knees. Pushed harder against him. "Dante!"

His head lifted. "I love the way you say my name."

What?

"Husky and rough, trembling a little with that faint Georgia accent you never quite lost." His gaze swept over her face. "When you call my name, it makes me want to fuck you."

A car horn echoed in the distance.

He gave a little laugh. Not the bitter sound from before, but softer, rougher. Nearly a real laugh. "Don't worry, I'm not fucking you here."

Her spine snapped straight up. "No, I'm not fucking *you* here."

"But you will be fucking me again . . . very soon."

He wished.

And, so did she. "Get me to Mississippi." She wasn't entering that battle with him.

He nodded. "Then I'll have you." Not a question.

It should have been. Wasn't someone being overconfident?

"Then I'll do my job." The job she'd taken on—fixing her father's mistakes.

I didn't realize I was one of those mistakes. She should have known though, as soon as she realized what her blood could do. *I should have known that he'd made more changes to me.*

Her father had been a real-life Frankenstein—and she'd been his monster.

Dante backed away. Finally.

She sucked in a deep breath then hurried past him and

climbed onto the motorcycle. Was it better for her to drive? She wouldn't have to be plastered to him if she was controlling the bike. And for someone who'd never driven a motorcycle before, she'd done a pretty good job for her first time. Good thing she was a quick learner.

I got this.

He climbed on behind her.

His arousal immediately pushed into her ass.

Crap. She should have let him drive. *I don't got this.*

His body curled around hers. His fingers covered hers as they rested on the handlebars. "One thing . . ."

Something else? They were burning daylight, they were—

"Don't *ever* run from me again."

She wasn't about to make him a promise that she couldn't keep.

"Cassie . . . "

"Don't give me a reason to run, and I won't."

She kick-started the motorcycle and it pushed forward. Dante didn't say anything else, and she tried not to think about all of the reasons a woman had to run from a phoenix.

And the only reason she had to stay with him.

Because she still loved him.

"I need to do blood work on you," Dr. Shaw said. Her clothes were covered in ash, the white lab coat pretty much black.

Jon had taken her to a backup facility in the area, one that had been a satellite office for Genesis at one point.

The small office was empty. Abandoned. Perfect for his purposes.

He hadn't called his bosses. Hadn't let them know that he was alive.

If they know, they'll shove me in a cage and try to replicate my success.

That wasn't happening. It was *his* success. His transformation. He was the most powerful being on earth. Even death couldn't stop him.

Jon could feel the power flowing through his veins, hot and intense. Pulsating within him.

"What was in that injection?" Dr. Shaw asked nervously. "Did it make you . . . what you are?"

He turned his head and stared at her. She was afraid of him. *Good. She should be.* She would also prove to be useful. Because he had such plans . . . "Yes, it did." He'd hoped for that result—several now dead scientists had worked toward that goal for a very long time, but he hadn't been sure of the transformation.

Not until he'd died.

During the course of the dosages, they hadn't exactly had the chance to experiment and see if the injections were working. The only way to experiment and see if he could rise like a phoenix—was death.

Jon hadn't been particularly eager for that phase of the project. If the injections hadn't worked . . . *that would have been the end of me.*

"A young phoenix was held in Genesis a while back," Jon shared with her. There was no one for her to tell. "Sabine was easier to break than the males, because she didn't realize what she was." Not until the first fire had consumed her.

He'd watched the videos of Sabine Acadia's deaths. Seen her terror. Each time, she'd been so afraid.

But she'd kept coming back.

"Her tears were collected and used to create the serum. It was believed that if someone with shifter DNA received enough dosages of that serum, he would change."

"You were a shifter?"

"Thanks to Genesis, I was." The first stage of their experiments. He glanced down at his hands. Since the fire, his claws hadn't come out. Were they gone for good?

He would miss them. It had been enjoyable to slash the throats of his enemies.

It had been even better to watch men burn before him.

"Is it a . . . permanent change?" Shaw asked carefully. "I heard that the soldiers who went through the shifter program had to undergo continuous injections in order to keep their beasts."

They hadn't been born with the animal in them. Without those injections, the beast died.

"You took your injection right before Cassandra shot you," Shaw continued, frowning. "If you die again, is that it? Or will you rise again?"

He wasn't sure of that. *That's why you're still living, Shaw.* "We're going to need more tears to keep creating the serum." More tears. More dosages. He wanted to be *certain*.

"How are we going to get them?" Shaw asked, nervously shoving back some of her hair.

He smiled at her. "We're going to hunt phoenixes, of course." He knew exactly where to start.

The strongest phoenix. Dante. The bastard who actually thought he'd escaped with Cassie. "You *did* insert the tracking device on Cassie, correct?"

A grim nod. "I slipped it into her vein. If she tries to take it out, she could bleed to death."

Shaw was appealing to Jon more and more. A strong mind and, seemingly, a very weak conscience. She'd be the perfect tool for him.

"I wish you hadn't destroyed all of my samples," she said, the words snapping a bit.

His eyes narrowed. He hadn't meant to do that—the fire had just gotten a little beyond his control.

And I liked it.

"But . . . ah . . . I am sure that we'll get more samples from Cassandra soon."

Yes, they would.

"You *must* find Cassandra Armstrong," Shaw said. "We need her."

His temples began to throb. "Cassie's mine."

Shaw nodded. "We can't let her escape."

Cassie's scent had seduced him for years. He'd been drawn to her even before his enhancement program had started. But *after* that enhancement, he'd wanted her even more. Her voice—her scent—everything seemed to call to him.

"She won't get away." He needed her for the genetics knowledge she would bring to him, but more than that . . . he just needed her.

Shaw was still talking. Saying something else about Cassie. The throbbing in his temples was worse, and all he could see—wasn't Shaw. It was Cassie.

Cassie was the key to everything he wanted. *Cassie.* Once they captured her and Dante, they'd take as many samples as they wanted.

They would *do* what they wanted.

The power of hell was in Jon's veins. There was no stopping him now. And those who tried . . .

They'd die.

"I have men I can contact to help us. An army at my beck and call," he snapped, suddenly realizing that a heavy silence had hit the room. An army that wouldn't realize he wasn't taking orders from Uncle Sam anymore. They would follow his orders, never thinking that he would mislead them. *Fools.* He'd been waiting for this, planning.

By the time the suits upstairs in the government offices figured out what was happening, it would be too late.

The world would be his.

And so would Cassie Armstrong.

* * *

They were in Louisiana. Progress. Cassie's legs definitely felt like Jell-O . If she didn't get off that motorcycle soon, she was pretty sure that she might collapse.

She braked at a gas station. Well, gas station/casino. It was one of those weird combos that she saw only in Louisiana.

There was a small motel behind that station, and then—nothing but swamp. Twisting trees. Thick green water. And, she was sure, plenty of alligators.

"Why are we stopping here?" Dante's voice rumbled from behind her.

She shoved down the kickstand. "Because while you might be superman, I'm not." *Not even close.* "I need to rest." Before she fell on her face. Just a few hours of sleep, then they could keep going on the road.

If they weren't on the motorcycle, they could take turns—one driving while the other slept.

But unless she stole a vehicle . . . *and that would just attract attention we don't want* . . . she needed to crash in that no-tell-motel.

"Please tell me you have some money," Cassie muttered as she pushed away from the motorcycle. If he didn't have money, she might just sleep right there on the ground.

"I have money."

She could have kissed him. Except, well, she knew where the kissing would lead.

Dante glanced around the dark station and then toward the motel. "No one seems to be here."

"Because it's close to one a.m., and sane people are sleeping." She took his hand and started dragging him toward the motel's office. "Let's go be sane, too."

The door to the office was locked. Fabulous. Cassie lifted her fist. Banged. "Hello!" *Oh, please, come answer. Please.*

"Someone's coming," Dante said as he stiffened beside her.

Great. Perfect. She was going to crash into that bed and—

His fingers curled around her hand, stopping her banging. "Not from inside."

Uh, what?

He turned his head and stared out at the swamp. "Someone is coming from out there."

He stepped in front of her, putting his body between hers and whoever it was that was venturing out of the swamp.

"Put your hands up!" The roar broke the night.

Dante didn't raise his hands.

"I said . . ."

She was pretty sure that was the sound of a shotgun being cocked.

"Put your hands up!"

Cassie poked Dante in the back. "Don't burn him."

Not yet. She knew Dante tended to have instincts that demanded he attack first and think later.

It wasn't one of those instances.

Dante lifted his hands.

"Tell the woman to step around you! I want to see her!"

She started to ease around him, but Dante moved at the same time, blocking her.

"You put down that shotgun," he snapped, "and then you can see her."

A stark pause. "You humans?"

Dante wasn't. She . . . Well, Cassie didn't know where she fell on that score.

"Yes," Dante said, his voice clear and calm.

A flashlight was shone on them. More footsteps came toward them. A lot of footsteps. And a lot more flashlights.

"Show us your fingers and your teeth!"

Wait. Fingers and teeth?

Fear twisted in her stomach. She didn't like where this was going at all.

"He looks normal!" a new voice called out.

"Drop the shotgun," Dante snarled.

She was afraid he was about to fire up.

"Thought you were one of 'em . . . always come up at night . . ."

That fear in her stomach was twisting into an ever bigger knot. She lifted her hand and clutched Dante's broad shoulder. "One of what?" She was on her toes and could see that the shotgun was pointed at the ground.

"Vampire." The man holding the shotgun—she couldn't see much of him, just a dark shadow—said the word like it was a curse. "Only them vampires are different . . . black claws, every tooth's a fang, and they just want to feed and feed."

Primal vampires. "You've seen some of them? Here?"

"We staked five last night."

The infection was spreading. She'd thought all of the primals in Louisiana had been stopped, but it was so easy for their virus to spread. One bite, and the human was infected.

Her gaze swept the circle of flashlights. "Were any of the people here bitten?"

"Jamison . . . he ran into the woods before we could—" The man broke off, but she knew what he'd been about to say.

Take him down.

Cassie flinched. "This is why I have to get to Mississippi," she whispered to Dante, guilt pushing through her. She'd been tired so she'd wanted to stop and rest, but people were dying. "We can find a cure."

"Ain't no cure for them," the man with the shotgun

called out. "Only death. If we want to keep livin', we have to take out all the vampires."

But not all vampires spread the primal virus. The virus had been man-made, generated in Genesis.

"Now get back on that motorcycle," the man shouted to her. "And you drive as fast as you can through the bayou. Don't stop for anyone or you'll be dead."

Dante wasn't moving. Cassie tugged on his arm. "Come on, Dante."

"They're lying."

Her heart slammed into her ribs. "What?"

"Get out of here!" the man yelled at the same time.

"More were bitten. I can smell it, like rot in their blood."

Oh, crap.

Dante pointed straight ahead. At the man with the shotgun. "He's infected."

The shotgun blast broke the night, but Dante had moved in an instant. He'd grabbed Cassie and shoved her back against the glass window of the motel.

"I think Jamison might be the only one *not* infected," Dante muttered. "I can smell the rot on all of them."

But . . . but they were talking. The primals she'd seen had been barely able to do more than growl and snap with their teeth.

Is the virus still mutating? That was a terrifying thought. But . . . it had to be. *Mutating,* changing, as it was transferred from host to host.

This was so bad. Very, very bad.

"Why did they tell us to run?" Cassie whispered. She didn't get that. Why not just spring up and attack them?

Crap—those thudding footsteps were closing in.

"Get away from the woman!" The shout came from the darkness. "Or we'll kill you."

"They wanted to see what I was before they attacked,"

Dante whispered. "I can smell them, and they could smell just enough about me to tell them I was different."

The motorcycle was about ten feet away. They could run for it, but . . .

What would happen the next time someone stopped for gas or a motel room? It was the perfect place to pick up prey.

The shotgun blasted again. It blew out the glass in the motel's window.

Cassie gasped as a heavy shard of glass embedded in her arm. By habit, she immediately clamped her lips together, holding back any other cries.

Her cries didn't matter. The blood did. And that scent was in the air. As if things weren't bad enough.

"Sweet . . . so fuckin' sweet . . ."

"Blood . . ."

"Mine!"

The voices were wild, frenzied, and suddenly, at least four men were charging for her. As they rushed closer, Cassie saw that their mouths were full of gaping fangs.

"She's not yours." Dante's voice was flat. "So go to hell." He opened his hand and sent a ball of fire rolling right toward them.

Cassie grabbed the chunk of glass, yanked it from her arm, and backed away. That fire he'd just sent out— *"The gasoline!"* Had Dante forgotten they were near a *gas* station?

The explosion ripped through the buildings, and the force of the blast sent her flying back through the air. She didn't know where Dante was, couldn't see him at all and—

"Got you." His voice. The man who'd been talking before. The man who'd shot at them. He grabbed her injured arm.

She felt the slide of his claws over her skin. Then his mouth was on her, and he was drinking her blood. Guzzling it.

"No!" Cassie screamed as she punched at him.

Her punches weren't having any effect.

But . . . her blood was.

He stiffened. Shuddered. Fell onto the ground as he convulsed. His head jerked and twisted and then—he stopped moving entirely.

The virus might be mutating, but her poison still worked.

Her arm throbbed where he'd bitten her.

"Cassie!" Dante was there, hauling her to her feet and running his hands all over her as he searched for injuries. When he touched the blood on her arm, he froze. "Did he—"

"He bit me." His teeth had torn into her, digging deep. "But I won't turn." She couldn't. Though the first time a primal had bitten her, she'd been terrified that she'd spout fangs and claws.

But her poison destroyed the virus—and the vampires.

"What the hell are they? I've never seen vampires like them."

"Genesis made them. They were supposed to be super soldiers." Her gaze was on that still vampire. The fire that Dante had sent out—burning so bright and hard—lit the scene. The man was definitely dead. Pity. He looked to be so young, barely twenty. "But Genesis just made a virus that took over its host. The progression is fast, so fast . . . all the host soon knows is bloodlust and hunger."

A bloodlust that could never be fully slaked.

"One bite," she whispered, "that's all it takes."

Dante's hold on her tightened. "Are you sure you won't turn?"

She tilted her head to study him. He'd destroyed the other vampires so easily. "Would you kill me, if I did?"

"Will you turn?" He shook her once, and she could see a stark expression of—was that fear?—in his eyes.

"I can't," she said softly. "I've been bitten by primals before." Her head shook. "I don't turn."

Her blood was poison to them. Not a cure.

"This is why I need you," she whispered. "These men were probably normal humans until recently. If we can find a cure, we can stop this. But if we don't, I'm scared the primals will take over." Especially if they were mutating on their own, getting even stronger.

The primals should never have been allowed out of Genesis. But when the facility had fallen in the mountains, some had escaped and gone on a feeding frenzy.

Dante's gaze locked with hers.

"We have to stop them," she said again.

He gave a grim nod. But then he stiffened and whirled from her.

"Dante!"

He was running away from the fire. Toward the swamp. Toward the man who was staggering toward them.

Cassie rushed after him.

But then he stilled, stopping just a few feet from the man.

He wasn't a man. A boy. Maybe thirteen. Fourteen. Covered in scratches and bruises. His eyes were wide and desperate. "Please," he whispered, "please kill me."

Cassie shook her head.

Dante said, "Show me your teeth. Show me your hands."

Those were nearly the same words that had been given to them.

She could already see the boy's hands. They weren't lined with claws. And his teeth—the boy opened his mouth.

No fangs.

"I don't want to be . . . like them. . . ." His breath panted out. "I saw—saw what you did." He lunged forward, caught Dante's hand, and put it right over his chest. "Kill me," he begged again.

"Dante, don't!" She grabbed for the boy.

He started to cry. "My . . . brother was the one with the shotgun. I don't want to be—"

"You're not infected!" Cassie said, then she looked up at Dante's face. He'd said that he smelled the . . . rot . . . from the others. "Is he?"

Dante shook his head. "You shouldn't beg for death."

The boy shuddered. "It has to be . . . better . . ."

"No, it doesn't. Not if hell waits for you."

She thought the boy might faint. He was sure weaving. "Are you Jamison?" The guy had said that Jamison ran into the swamp.

A weak nod. "J-Jamie . . ."

"Jamie, what happened?"

"Vampires . . . attacked everyone. W-we staked as many as we could . . . then . . . the others started to change."

And he'd run. She looked back up at Dante.

His face could have been carved from stone.

"We can't leave him out here alone."

Dante jerked his hand away from the boy. "He isn't my concern." Dante caught Cassie's hand in his. Tried to pull her away.

She wasn't in the mood to be pulled. "More primals could be in the area. We can't just leave him to die."

"Why not?" Dante shrugged. "It's what he wanted to do."

Cassie wanted to slug him.

"And what of the others?" Dante asked. "The *more* that you talk about so much, Cassie. Are we supposed to go out and save every human in the area?"

"Th-they killed all those vampires who came," Jamie whispered.

"You want to save the world," Dante said, eyes seeming to gleam in the dark. "I don't."

"I'm not asking for the world." Not right at that particular moment, anyway. She glanced over at Jamie. "I'm asking for him."

She was pretty sure that Dante growled.

Then he said, "We can't fit him on the motorcycle."

"Th-there's a truck, my brother's truck, a few feet back there." Jamie threw his thumb over his shoulder.

Dante swore.

Cassie glanced at Jamie. "Do you have any other family?"

"N-no, ma'am. It was . . . just me and Tim."

And she'd killed Tim. She couldn't let the boy die, too. "You're coming with us."

Even in the faint light cast from the moon and stars, the hope that lit his face was painful to see.

Dante was still swearing.

"Is he . . . *What* is he?" Jamie asked as he wiped his hands over his cheeks. She suspected that the boy was wiping away tears.

"I'm not a hero," Dante said flatly.

No, he isn't. "He's the man who'll keep us safe."

Dante glanced at her but was silent. After a moment, he gave a grim nod.

Jamie's breath rushed out then he was running and leading them toward the old pick-up.

He climbed into the bed of the truck.

Cassie slid into the front with Dante.

He caught her hand. "Why?"

She frowned at him.

"Why do you care about saving people?"

When your family business was wrecking lives, you have a whole lot to make up for. "I didn't save those vampires."

"The only way to save them was death."

She flinched. "There has to be more than that, even for vampires."

His hold tightened. *"Why?"*

"Because I don't want my family to have only been monsters, okay?" *Is that so crazy?* "I want to help, not destroy everything I touch."

His touch was warm against her flesh. Heating with the

phoenix's power. "Why not?" His voice had hardened. "It's what I do." His hand pulled away from hers. "After a while, you might even start to like the destruction."

No, she wouldn't.

And she didn't think he did, either.

"How the hell am I supposed to start this thing?" Dante snarled. "There's no key."

She leaned forward. Pushed under the dash. Her cheek pressed against his thigh.

Dante stilled.

Her fingers fumbled with the wires, and, in a few seconds, she had the engine sparking to life.

She pulled back, aware that his thigh felt rock-hard.

"How'd you do that?" His voice was low.

Cassie swallowed. "I've got a few tricks you don't know about."

His hand rose to her arm. She flinched. She was still bleeding.

"Yes," he said softly, consideringly, "you do."

Cassie scooted as far away from him as she could.

But she could feel the heat of his gaze sweeping over her.

"Get back on the highway, keep driving straight until I tell you to turn." They could sleep in shifts, and make it back to her base sooner.

Silently, he followed her orders. The black pavement started to disappear beneath the truck's wheels.

She tore part of her shirt away and wrapped up her arm. It seemed like a trend for her—using clothing to bind her wounds. But hey, it worked. When she had the wound covered, Cassie leaned her head against the window's glass, staring out at the night that waited.

So much for an easy pit stop.

The boy was behind them, silent in the bed of the truck. Why hadn't he tried to get up in the front with them?

Because he's probably terrified of us. Right. She didn't blame him for that. Especially since he'd no doubt watched her kill his brother.

Lately, she'd started to scare herself.

"What will you do if you can't save them?"

She jerked at Dante's voice.

"The shifter that waits for you . . . what if you can't save him?"

"I will save him."

Dante shook his head. "That's not an answer, you know."

No, it wasn't. Because she didn't have an answer.

"Will you be able to put him down? Sometimes, death is the only cure."

She didn't want to think about that, but . . . Dante was right. She looked down at her injured arm. *Death is the only cure.*

CHAPTER NINE

It didn't look like much of a lab to Dante.

He braked the truck. Checked the scrawled directions that Cassie had given to him before she'd passed out. Yes, it was the place.

It looked like a hole-in-the-wall.

His head turned, and he glanced down at Cassie. She was beside him, her head sagging on his shoulder. The boy had finally asked to come up front when the sun rose, and they'd all crammed in together.

The boy hadn't slept though.

Not that Dante blamed the kid. When you watched your family die, it didn't usually put you in the mood for sleep.

"What did she do to him?" Jamie asked, his voice a whisper. It was the first time the kid had talked to him since he'd joined their little road trip from hell.

Dante glanced over at him, and found Jamie's eyes on his.

"My brother. She killed him, didn't she?"

"He killed himself." The minute he'd taken her blood, he'd been dead.

Jamie shook his head. "I saw . . . he was convulsing after he drank her blood." His gaze darted to Cassie even as he kept his voice whisper quiet. "What did she do?"

"She lived." Dante wanted to brush aside the hair that had fallen over her face, but the kid was watching him far too closely.

"What are you?" An even softer whisper.

Dante held his stare. "I'm the man you don't ever want to cross, because if you do . . . if you do anything to hurt me or to hurt her, you won't have to beg me for death." The boy needed to get this message. Clearly. "I'll kill you before you can even scream."

Jamie's eyes widened, nearly filling his face, and his Adam's apple bobbed. "You don't scare me."

"Yes, I do." Dante scared everyone. Even Cassie, though he knew she tried to act like she didn't fear him. He'd caught glimpses of the fear in her eyes. "She wanted you to come with us, so you did. If it had been up to me . . ."

"You would have left me alone out there."

Damn straight. Dante gazed steadily back at him. "Don't ever give me reason to regret hauling you out of that swamp."

"Dante?" Cassie's husky voice asked. "We aren't moving. We're—" She sat up, snapping to attention. "We're here!"

Yes, wherever *here* was.

She shoved against him, trying to get out. Dante slid over and when she hurried toward the ramshackle buildings, he followed her.

Jamie was on his heels.

"This is your lab?" Dante asked, voice doubtful. It looked like they were in the middle of an old corn field, and the buildings that surrounded them looked like abandoned barns.

"Don't let appearances fool you." Her voice was actually perky. "This place was set up by the government back in the fifties. They forgot about it." She pushed aside some wood that was near the door of the barn and quickly punched in a code on a security screen. "My father didn't. *I* didn't."

"Identify yourself," a computer voice demanded.

"Doctor Cassandra Armstrong," she said at once.

The barn door opened—but they didn't head into a *real* barn.

The door slid open to reveal an elevator.

"Told you," Cassie said, sounding pretty satisfied with herself. "Appearances can deceive you."

"That is freakin' cool," Jamie said.

Dante frowned at him.

"Now, we're heading down to the lab." She bit her lip. "I'll send Charles back up to hide the truck."

They were descending, a fast descent that Dante thought took them down two floors. When the door opened again, a thin man with curly hair was standing in front of them.

"Cassie!" He rushed toward her. "I was afraid you weren't coming back!"

The man was hugging her far too tightly.

Dante decided that he didn't like him.

"I'm sorry, Charles. It took a bit . . . longer than I'd thought for the retrieval mission."

Charles glanced over at Dante. His gray eyes doubled in size. "It's *him*."

The *him* could hear.

"Is he going to kill us?" Charles whispered as he edged behind Cassie. "It looks like he wants to. It looks like he wants to fry us both!"

Cassie laughed, and the light sound caught Dante off guard. Her laugh was so sweet he wanted to hear it again.

"No, he's not going to kill us," she said. "He's here to help us."

Not really, but they'd get around to the true reason for his visit later.

"And the boy?" Charles asked with a questioning glance toward Jamie.

"We need to keep him safe . . . and use our ties to find some of his family who can take care of him."

Jamie's chin jutted up in the air. "I told you, my family is—"

"There was a primal attack," Cassie said quietly. "His brother didn't survive."

Charles's gaze dropped to the bloody shirt that was still wrapped around her arm.

Jamie's shoulders hunched.

"Can you . . . can you put him in one of the unoccupied rooms?" Cassie asked softly. "Give him something to eat?"

Charles nodded. "As long as he doesn't mind the locks on the doors."

Jamie backed up, edging toward the elevator.

"It's okay!" Cassie quickly reassured him. "Some of the . . . patients here can't be let out." Her voice was soothing. "You won't be locked in, Jamie. You're free to go anytime you want. I was just offering you a safe place to stay while we looked for your family."

"I told you, I *have* no family." The kid was pretty vehement on that point. "Tim and I were in the foster system till he turned eighteen, then he got me out." Jamie's hands had fisted in front of him. "He said we weren't ever going back."

And now Tim was dead.

No, there would be no going back for him.

"If you decide to leave"—Cassie kept talking in that same soothing voice—"I just ask that you tell no one about us. Forget this lab. Forget me. Forget Dante."

Damn if she wasn't soothing Dante, too, and he hadn't even realized he'd needed soothing.

The kid's eyes were like saucers. "Are you making monsters down here? Like I saw on the news—that Genesis place that got blown up—"

"We're healing the monsters," Cassie said carefully. "Not making them."

Did she believe that lie? It sure seemed as if she did.

But Jamie was nodding. *Ah, he bought the lie, too.* "I-I'll stay, for now."

"Good."

Charles hurried forward. "Come with me, uh—what's your name?"

"Jamie."

"Come with me, Jamie."

Dante noticed that Charles gave him a particularly wide berth as the man took the boy down the hallway.

And just like that, he was alone with Cassie again.

"I need to check on Trace." She turned away from him.

Hold the hell up. He caught her arm and turned her right back around. "We've been traveling non-stop." For more hours than he wanted to think about. "You were captured by some military assholes, you were bitten by vampires—and the first thing you want to do is go and check on *him*?" Jealousy was there, clawing at him.

"I have to see if Trace's condition is still stable."

Screw that. "Cassie . . ."

She pulled away from him. "I have a room down at the end of the hall." Her hand rose, and she pointed to the left. "You can go rest in there. I'll see you in a little bit, okay?"

No, that isn't okay.

But the woman didn't wait for an answer. She just spun on her heel and went down the hallway that branched to the right. Did she think that he was Charles? About to jump at her every little command?

She needed to rethink that.

He began to stalk after her. He wanted to see this Trace that she talked about so often. The man that she was desperate to save.

The man that was in his way.

Dante needed Cassie to have ties only to him. In the life that he would have with her, there would be room for no others.

She needed to leave everything behind. Everyone else.

She would. It was just a matter of time.

He headed down the hallway, his steps silent. Cassie was up ahead of him. He could see her as she tapped on a control panel before one of the rooms.

The place might have been built in the fifties, but it had undergone some serious upgrades. Just who had made those improvements? Suspicion swelled in him.

Cassie entered the room.

A wolf's howl seemed to shake the lab, echoing up that hallway.

That was no man. That was a beast.

A fully transformed werewolf.

Shit. Bellowing Cassie's name, Dante raced down the hallway.

Jon wasn't following a trail of breadcrumbs. His eyes narrowed on the wreckage. He was following a path of fire.

The phoenix had been there. And he'd left a dead vampire in his wake.

"I've never seen a vampire like him," Shaw whispered as she stared at the man's claws. "Did you see his teeth?" Fear whispered through her words.

Jon's gaze left her. Slid around what remained of the lot. The motorcycle was there, tossed on its side. Cassie and Dante must have switched to a different vehicle. They wouldn't have gone into the swamp on foot.

"What is he?" Shaw asked.

"He's a primal," Jon told her, the words coming quickly. "Trust me, it's a good thing he's dead." But a very bad thing that he'd been out in the open. Someone needed to alert Uncle Sam to the fact that more of those freaks were out and infecting others.

That someone wouldn't be Jon. He still needed to stay off the grid.

"Cassie's tracking signal led us here."

He glanced over and saw Shaw frowning down at the phone in her hand—and at the tracking screen that had appeared on that phone.

"She *should* be here." Shaw seemed confused.

Jon headed toward the primal vampire. "You put the tracker in her arm?"

"Yes, I—"

"Is the signal still transmitting?"

Shaw pointed to the vampire. "It says that she's right there."

Dammit. "She isn't, but the asshole who fed on her is here." That was why the vamp was frozen. "Got a taste of her poison, didn't you, dumbass?" Jon muttered to the dead man.

"Wait, you're saying he—"

"When the vamp fed on her, he ate the tracker, and Cassie is long gone." *Fucking hell.*

Fury flooded through his body. He'd thought that he was close, that he would have her back by now—

But she was gone.

Gone.

He whirled and grabbed Shaw, yanking her up against him. "You said you could find her!"

Fear rolled off Shaw in waves that he could smell. Then she was gasping, twisting in his hold as she tried to break free.

Smoke rose from her arm—from the touch of his fingers.

He was blistering her flesh. In a few more moments, he'd give the bitch third degree burns.

"I'm sorry!" she yelled. "Stop! Please, stop!"

He didn't want to stop, but he stepped back. *For the moment.* "I need Cassie."

Tears leaked down Shaw's cheeks. "I know. You *have* to find her."

He did. The throbbing was back, nearly ripping through his temples. "She's gone. There's no tracker." Fire burst from his fingertips. It would be so easy to put that fire against Shaw's skin. "I have no fucking clue what kind of car she is in or where she went."

"Please! Keep the fire away!"

The fire wasn't touching her. He had control. For now. "She's with the phoenix. Dante isn't going to let her go. He'll keep her close and—"

Shaw stumbled back.

He smiled. "A phoenix's weakness."

She had fallen to the ground. "What?"

"Do you know why there aren't many phoenixes around?" His voice was mild.

Shaw shook her head.

"Because they can kill each other. They have, actually, over and over again." He glanced at the wreckage. All of that wonderful fire. "They don't know I'm alive." A huge advantage for him. "When I start to burn, they'll think it's another phoenix."

"Burn? Burn what?"

He glanced over at her. "Everything."

Every damn thing that Cassie had ever held dear. Good thing he knew her well. "I'll light up Cassie's world until Dante has to come for me, and when he comes, she'll be there."

If he couldn't find Cassie, then he'd smoke her out—literally.

She'd come to him, and he'd get exactly what he wanted.

I need her.

Something inside Jon was pushing him to find her. Clawing to get out and get to her. Was it the phoenix? Dante's beast had recognized Cassie as a mate. Jon knew that from the Genesis reports he'd read. During one of Dante's desperate risings, that confession had broken from him. He'd claimed Cassie only once, but that slip-up had been noted by Genesis.

Maybe Jon's own, newly developed phoenix was experiencing that same instinctive recognition.

"Why did Dante come for her at the ranch?" he asked.

Shaw shook her head. "I don't know."

Dante had risked himself to go and rescue Cassie. Now . . . Jon was finding himself obsessed by her.

Cassie's blood was poison to vampires, a little tweak that her father had performed on her.

But what if there was something . . . else . . . that had also been done to sweet little Cassie?

Something that was drawing him to her. Something that was making him think . . .

Mine.

"We light up her world," Jon said again. "And we bring her to *me*." He'd find out what was happening *and* he'd get the tears that he needed.

Failure wasn't an option.

Shaw rose slowly to her feet once more and nodded.

"Cassie!"

Dante grabbed her and yanked her away from the—*what the hell*? The howl had sounded as if it had come from a fully shifted werewolf, but Dante wasn't staring at a beast.

He also wasn't staring at a man. Not really.

But rather, he was looking at a combination of both.

This was Trace?

Trace saw him, and his lips peeled away from his teeth, revealing fully extended fangs. He jumped toward Dante, but the silver chains that were locked around his wrists and ankles jerked Trace back.

Claws burst from the man's fingers—long claws, easily as sharp as knives. Trace was big—too tall, too wide—with muscles bulging over his body. His eyes were wild, feral, glowing. Currently looking at Dante with a bright hatred.

Trace's features were sharp, hard, very much like a wolf's, but he *wasn't* a wolf.

Was he?

"Trace, please. Calm down!" Cassie said as she pushed Dante back. "I'm a friend, remember? *Friend.*"

Those glowing eyes slid to her. The man-beast's muscles bulged, and Dante was afraid that the guy was about to rip those chains right from the wall.

He sure looked strong enough to do it.

"I'm Cassie, remember? I help you."

"Help." That guttural growl was no human's voice. If a wolf could talk—*that one could*—Dante figured it would sound just like that snarling sound.

Cassie nodded. "That's right. Dante and I are both here to help you."

The glowing stare came back to Dante once more.

Then the man-beast gave a sharp shake of his head. "Kill," he growled as he looked straight at Dante.

Dante's eyes narrowed. *Come on and try, beast. I'll fry that fur right off you.*

Cassie hurried toward a cabinet on the right. She pressed her thumb against the screen on a small locking pad, and the lock hissed open. "I need to give him his dosage. He's due for one now, and Charles always gets nervous when he has to come inside and do it."

Charles was afraid the wolf would eat him.

The glowing stare followed Cassie's movements. The beast looked like he wanted to make a meal of her.

Not happening.

"How much of him is man?" Dante demanded. He wanted to know just what he was dealing with in that room.

"All of him," Cassie snapped as she pulled out a needle from the cabinet. "Trace is in there, and from what I've determined, he understands everything we say."

Dante realized the beast was staring at him. He bared his own teeth. "Screw off."

The beast heaved against his chains.

So he *did* understand.

"Dante! Don't! Don't antagonize him in any way. Trace is inside, but the Lycan-70 dosage that he was given put his beast in charge. He can't change back to his normal form, and he can't shift fully. He's"—her breath exhaled on a rush—"trapped like this."

In a form somewhere between man and beast.

She headed toward Trace, acting like she didn't see the claws and fangs that would rip her apart.

Dante grabbed her.

The man-beast snarled.

Dante snarled right back then told Cassie, "You aren't injecting him! Get Charles and his cowardly ass back in here to do the job!"

She shook her head, sending her hair brushing over his arm. "Trace isn't going to hurt me."

Dante wasn't in the mood to test that theory.

"He won't," Cassie said, sounding so sure. "I've given him dozens of injections, and he's never attacked me."

"There's a first time for everything." Dante didn't let her go. "If his beast is in control, he could attack at any moment."

Her fingers tightened around the syringe. "He won't. Just . . . give me a minute to do this, all right? Once he gets the dosage, he'll be calmer. He always is."

Dante wasn't sure he bought that bullshit. The thing he

was sure of? He didn't want Cassie getting any closer to Trace.

"Give it to me," Dante gritted because he knew what he had to do.

She blinked.

Dante smothered a sigh. "Give me the damn syringe. If anyone's getting close to the guy, it sure won't be you." He could handle himself if the wolf got wild. He'd just burn the beast.

But Cassie was hesitating. "I don't want you killing him."

Dante took the syringe from her. "Then he'd better not attack me."

Sure enough, as he stepped toward that man-beast, the guy tried to lunge for him.

"You don't want to piss me off," Dante told him, voice flat. "You won't like it when the anger burns through me. No one ever does."

The man-beast snapped his teeth together.

And Dante drove that syringe into the fellow's throat in one fast, hard hit.

A loud, echoing howl broke from Trace, and he sagged in his restraints, falling down to his knees.

Dante carefully eased back, watching the guy closely.

The claws didn't vanish. Those bulging muscles didn't change. So far, that injection wasn't doing anything. How long was it supposed to take before—

The guy's head tilted back. His eyes weren't quite so wild. The beast still glowed there, but Dante could have sworn he saw a hint of the man, too.

"Thank . . . you . . ." Trace gasped as his shoulders sagged forward.

Cassie took the syringe from Dante. Disposed of it. Then she was back, sliding toward the kneeling werewolf. "I told you," she said as she glanced back at Dante. "He's calmer after the dose."

Calmer, and far more human.

Dante frowned, but he didn't try to stop Cassie when she approached Trace.

Cassie reached out and slid her hand against the werewolf's arm.

Trace looked at her. "You . . . came . . . back . . ." Each word seemed to be a struggle for him.

Cassie nodded and smiled at the guy.

Yes, the werewolf was calmer, but Dante wasn't. With that touch and smile, the tension in his body deepened.

"I told you that I'd be back. And Dante over there? He's here to help you."

The werewolf's eyes turned to him. Weighed him. "How?" Trace rasped.

How indeed.

"Let me work on that part," Cassie said. "But first, I need to check you out. So let's just keep those claws away." She started to check the werewolf. Putting a stethoscope against his heart. Drawing his blood.

Running her hands over his back.

Dante's back teeth clenched.

It was a clinical exam. Nothing sexual there at all, but—

He remembered the lieutenant colonel's words. *Her lover is sick. Not sick so much as transforming. If she can't help her werewolf, she'll lose him, and Cassie doesn't want to lose Trace.*

Cassie wasn't Trace's lover. Dante knew that. Cassie had never been anyone's lover.

But mine.

He stayed close during the exam, not trusting those knife-like claws, but Trace made no move to attack Cassie. By the end of the exam, he was sitting in a metal chair, the chains pulling against him.

"Okay, that's all for now." Cassie rose to her feet. "I'll run the blood work and see where we are—"

"Cure . . ." Trace growled.

Cassie nodded. "I think we're close, Trace. I do. With Dante here—"

But Trace gave a hard shake of his head. "Cure . . . or kill . . ."

Dante eased closer to Cassie. The werewolf had better not be threatening her.

"Cure . . ." Trace said again, his face locked in desperate lines as he struggled to speak. "Or . . . kill . . . me."

Dante felt the ripple of shock go through Cassie's body. "We're not to that point, Trace! There's hope. You just need to give me more time."

Dante wasn't seeing hope in Trace's gaze. And that gaze swung to him. The same plea the werewolf had just voiced to Cassie was in that stare.

"Why the hell is everyone asking me to kill them?" Dante muttered. He didn't like the pain that he could suddenly feel emanating from Cassie. She shouldn't know pain.

"You." He pointed at the werewolf. "Save the death wish for later. Dying is easy. I know—I've done it more times than I can count. Use the power of your beast and live."

Anger flared in Trace's eyes. He surged to his feet, but the chains stopped him from advancing.

Dante smiled at him. "Maybe one day those chains won't be on you. Maybe . . . if you stop asking folks to *kill* your mangy ass . . . you can be free."

The anger made the glow deepen in Trace's eyes.

Good. Anger was far better than desperation.

Better than hopelessness.

Dante pushed Cassie toward the door. She had her tests to run, and, well, now that the wolf was getting amped again, Dante didn't want her close to him any longer.

Cassie slipped from the room.

"Her . . . smell . . ."

Dante looked back at the werewolf's rough words.

"Mate . . ." Trace growled.

Anger pumped through Dante. "No, she's not yours, so don't even think—"

"Dangerous . . . protect her . . ."

"I'll keep her safe, because she's *mine.*" Had been, for longer than Cassie even realized.

Dante left the room. Cassie sealed Trace back inside. Had she heard what the wolf said? What he'd said?

A tear slid down her cheek. Dante bent and wiped that tear away.

"He didn't deserve this. Trace was just trying to help his friends. He was helping them when *my* brother—"

She had a brother?

"My brother injected him with Lycan-70. Richard knew how dangerous that mix was, but he didn't care." Her hand raked through her hair. "That's always been my family's problem. They just don't *care* who they hurt."

She cared. Cared so much that she was risking her life for a werewolf who could choose to *take* his own life at any moment.

"You aren't like them." Her tear was cool on his finger. "You were never like them."

She swallowed and gave a slow nod. Then she exhaled. "You should get some rest. I need to run these tests."

She pulled away, straightened her shoulders, and headed back down the hallway.

Dante didn't move. His gaze followed her until she turned the corner.

He had two choices. He could destroy the lab and everything that linked her to it. Then he could take her. She would know only him.

Or . . . he could help her. Help her save the werewolf. Help her try to stop the primal virus from spreading.

He'd never been one to help.

He just took what he wanted. Let the rest of the world save or destroy itself.

No, that wasn't exactly true. Centuries before, he had tried to help.

Madness had swept through his village. Turning all those of his kind against one another. He'd tried to fight the madness, tried to save his brother.

But there were some who couldn't be saved. No matter how hard he'd tried, he couldn't save them. He'd been forced to fight Wren.

And, in the end, he'd sent his brother to hell.

Dante glanced at the closed door.

Help or destroy . . .

For Cassie, maybe he'd do a bit of both.

CHAPTER TEN

When the alarm rang, shrieking through the lab, Cassie jumped to her feet. She'd been working with her samples for hours, and silence had been her only companion.

Until then.

Her gaze flew to the monitors. The alarm was coming from room eight.

Not Trace's room.

Oh, crap. Room eight. It was for the only primal vampire she had in the facility.

She grabbed a wooden stake from her desk drawer, even as she prayed that she wouldn't have to use the weapon. That primal—she'd promised his father that she would do everything possible to save him.

But if he was loose and tried to attack someone, she'd have to stop him.

Charles was in the underground lab. Jamie was there, too. He wouldn't make it through another attack.

Cassie grabbed for a dosage of tranqs, then hurried forward. She shoved open the sliding doors that led from her work area and raced toward room eight. Her shoes slapped against the tile even as her heart thundered in her chest.

The door to room eight was open.

No, no, it shouldn't *be—*

She sprang into the room.

Vaughn Adams, the vampire, had his arms wrapped around Jamie. The primal's teeth were inches from the boy's throat.

One bite, and Jamie would be infected too.

"Stop!" Cassie yelled.

Vaughn's head jerked toward her. His nostrils widened.

"Let him go, Vaughn." She'd had no treatment success with Vaughn so far. All of the serums, the drugs—nothing could give him back even a hint of his humanity.

Jamie whimpered.

Cassie's fingers curled around the stake. She'd agreed to help Vaughn, but she would not let him hurt the boy.

She stepped forward, and her right foot kicked against—another stake? Her gaze followed the stake as it rolled a few inches away, then her eyes whipped back up when Vaughn hissed.

"Tasting . . . you . . . soon . . ."

So he'd told her before. Once upon a time, Vaughn Adams had been a New Orleans cop, a guy torn between the paranormal and normal world. A bite from a primal vampire had sent him into a walking nightmare. One that, after months, he still hadn't been able to wake from.

"Why wait?" She lifted the sharp point of the stake and slid it over her wrist, drawing forth some blood. "Come and get it now."

"No!" Jamie shouted, his eyes bulging.

Vaughn shoved him aside and came right at her, all those terrible fangs in his mouth snapping.

"Cassie!" Dante's roar. The alarm had drawn him to their little party.

She didn't look back at Dante. She couldn't take her eyes off Vaughn. One taste of her blood, and he'd be dead.

She wasn't ready to give up on him yet.

When he came at her, she yanked up her left hand—the hand that had been in the front pocket of her lab coat. Her fingers were curled around a syringe—one full of enough tranqs to knock the guy out for a week.

She drove that syringe into his heart.

But he didn't stop. His hands locked around her shoulders and he yanked her up against him.

No, no. He should have been on the floor. He should have . . .

"Bad mistake, vampire." Dante's voice was lethal and cold, so at odds with the sudden heat in the room.

Vaughn's mouth was inches from Cassie's throat.

But . . . he wasn't biting her.

Cassie lifted her lashes. She stared into Vaughn's eyes. Bloodlust stared back at her.

But he wasn't biting her.

In the next instant, he *couldn't* bite her. Dante had yanked her away from the vampire then turned, putting his body between her and Vaughn. Dante's hand was suddenly lit by fire as he reached for the primal.

Vaughn fell to the floor before Dante could touch him.

"He dies," Dante said. "He *dies*."

Cassie couldn't let that happen. "No! Don't touch him!" She pulled Dante back. "He's not a threat now."

"He wanted to *bite* you." Dante stared at her as if she were crazy.

Only a little.

"He could have killed you!" Dante charged.

"You know that's not true." Her words were quiet. "My blood would have killed him in an instant."

Dante's eyes blazed at her. "And what about the kid?" He jabbed a finger toward the cowering Jamie. "Do you want him to become like his brother? Like this bastard here?"

She flinched. "You know I don't! I'm trying to help—"

"Some beings are too dangerous to help! Some only need to be put down."

She'd heard those same words before. They'd come from her father. "My father said the same thing about you once."

Dante's hands fell to his sides. "He was right."

She shook her head.

"Why is he here?" Dante's gaze was on Vaughn's prone form.

"I need a test subject if I'm going to find a cure." She hated those cold words, but they were true. "I have to see if I can reverse the primal state with the vampires, and Vaughn—Vaughn's father begged me to try and help him."

"Helping . . . him?" Jamie's voice was shaky as he rose to his feet. "You didn't help my brother."

"He took my blood," she whispered. "There wasn't a chance for me to help—"

"You let my brother die, when there could be some kind of—of cure?" Jamie's face darkened. *"There's a cure?"*

They needed to get out of that room. She wanted to make sure Jamie was safe, and if she was wrong about the drug's effects on Vaughn, she didn't want the boy getting attacked again.

She reached for Jamie's hand.

He jerked away from her. "I saw him die"—his voice thickened with pain and fury—"when there was a *cure*?"

Dante grabbed the boy and hauled him from the room.

"Wait, jerk! Let me go! You need to let—"

Dante dropped Jamie in the hallway.

Cassie secured the door shut once more. How had it even opened? How had Jamie gotten in there?

"There's no cure yet," she said, trying to keep her voice calm. "I'm working on it, hoping—"

"Tim didn't have to die!"

He had. The instant he took her blood his fate had been sealed. "There's something different about me," she confessed to Jamie. "Vampires—all vampires—have a terrible reaction to my blood."

Jamie had stomped toward the right wall. "Reaction?"

"It kills them," Dante said bluntly. "Your brother was dead the instant he put his mouth on her."

The bright color leached from Jamie's face.

"What were you doing in there?" Cassie asked, shaking her head. "*How* did you get in there?"

Jamie opened his fist. She saw Charles's access card in his hand. One swipe of that card, and Jamie would have been able to get inside any room in the place.

"Charles . . ." Jamie rasped. "He asked how I hooked up with you. I told him about my brother . . ."

"And Charles told you about the primal here." *Dammit.* She'd been so rushed to get back to her research that she hadn't taken time for detailed instructions. She should have been more clear with Charles about the boy.

"He told me . . . to stay away from this room because of the guy in there."

So Charles had been trying to protect Jamie.

It looked like Jamie hadn't wanted protecting. She remembered the stake that had rolled across the floor.

"I swiped the access card after I saw Charles open a few doors with it."

"And you came inside to kill the primal."

"My brother is *dead*! All of them should be dead, too!" Jamie swiped a hand over his eyes. "Tim was all I had! We were going out to LA! Going to start a life . . . His life is *gone*! It's all gone! Because of those fanged freaks."

No, it was gone because of her father and his experiments. More lives destroyed, all in the name of science.

"I'm sorry," Cassie whispered.

"If you're really sorry, you'll go back in there and stake that bastard." Jamie spun on his heel and stalked away. "Send him to rot with my brother."

Cassie watched him storm out of sight.

"Are there . . ." Dante began quietly, "any more . . . experiments . . . here that the boy needs to watch out for? I'd sure hate for him to stumble onto something that might feel the urge to eat him."

Cassie shook her head. "Only Trace and Vaughn are here. The rest of the place is empty." Cassie tried to brush by Dante. "I need to get back to work—"

He caught her, caged her between his body and the wall. "What happens if you can't cure them?"

Cure . . . or kill . . .

She didn't want to think about Trace's words then. "I told you, I will cure them."

"If you *can't*? Will you kill the werewolf?"

Her chest ached. "Why does it always have to be about killing? Can't I save someone?" She pushed against Dante's chest.

He didn't back away. "Still trying to atone for the sins of others, aren't you?"

"No. It's my own sins I'm atoning for."

Trying to, anyway.

Failing.

"Fine." He bit out the word, and finally—thank you!—backed away. "You want to cure 'em? You want your shot at this? Then let's go."

What?

The guy was half-dragging her down the hallway and back toward her office. Apparently, they *were* going.

"You think a phoenix is the key, then go ahead, slice me. See if you can find the key in me."

They were in her workroom. He walked to a tray of instruments near the left wall and picked up a scalpel.

She tried not to remember the feel of a scalpel slicing into her own skin.

"Where should I get?" Dante sat on the gurney in the office. "Will this work? And don't worry about strapping me down. I won't fight."

As he'd fought before, when the Genesis scientists had spent years slicing him open. Dissecting him while he'd still been alive.

"Dante . . ."

"That was the point of me coming here, right? So you could use me? To save them?"

Cassie swallowed. Took the scalpel from him. Put it away.

"You're gonna have a hard time getting your samples with your bare hands," he muttered.

Her lips wanted to tremble. How had everything gotten so messed up? "I just want to help."

"No, sweetheart, you're trying to take the stains off your hands. But that blood isn't there because of you." He was definite.

"Yes, it is!" *Why doesn't he see that?* "I was there, Dante. For years. I should have stopped it. I should have helped those people."

But she'd been afraid.

Trapped.

"You helped me."

He was still on the table.

As he'd been so many times.

As I was.

Cassie pulled in a deep breath. "You escaped when I was twenty-two . . . because I killed you."

A death that the guards and doctors at Genesis hadn't been expecting, so they hadn't been prepared to deal with him as he rose.

She'd cleared the exits. Even drugged a few of the men on patrol outside so Dante could get away scot free.

He'd come back. Years later, but . . . *he came back.*

"I thought about burning the building to the ground that night."

His confession.

"Why didn't you?"

"Because something important was inside."

Her gaze searched his. "Is that why you came back?" She knew he hadn't just been captured. The crazy phoenix had actually let himself be caught by Genesis.

And she'd had to work to free him again.

"I came back for you."

How many times had she wished to hear words like that? At first, hell, she actually thought she was imagining them.

"I'd waited long enough for you, and I was there to claim you."

But he hadn't. He'd escaped again when Genesis was destroyed, and, according to him, she'd *died* in New Orleans.

"The first time I left . . . you stayed behind to help the others, didn't you?" Dante asked.

Cassie nodded. She'd worked, slowly but surely, to free others trapped in Genesis. She'd tried sending data to the media, had tried to get someone to see what was happening in the research facility, but the madness hadn't stopped until a reporter named Eve Bradley had gone to work—undercover—at Genesis.

"Why do you keep bleeding for them?"

"Someone has to do it."

His gaze fell on the scalpel. "All of those years and Genesis never figured out a way to use me. *And you think you can do it now?*"

"Cain O'Connor should arrive tomorrow." The only other male phoenix she'd ever met. The phoenix who'd fallen in love with Eve Bradley when she'd been undercover at Genesis. "I want to look at DNA from both of you and see—"

"Then you'd better get to cutting."

She didn't want to cut him.

She didn't want to hurt him at all. "Did you truly come back for me?" Cassie whispered.

His eyes swept over her face. "You've been mine for years. Did you really think I'd ever let you go?"

Her breath caught. *Mine.* It was all about possession and need for him. Was it even possible for Dante to love?

"I thought you'd leave Genesis and seek me out."

Cassie shook her head. "How would I have ever found you?"

His hand lifted. Pressed over her heart. "The same way you found me in Chicago. The same link."

Okay, now she was starting to get nervous. "Link?"

"Have you studied your own blood, Cassie?"

She'd done tests on herself, yes, and not just blood work. She knew that her DNA had been mutated when she'd been a child.

"You were different even before you father started his work." Dante paused. "Maybe that's why he started."

Cassie gave a hard, negative shake of her head. She didn't want to hear this.

"You've mentioned a brother. Your father. What about your mother, Cassie? Where is she?" Dante was sitting on the gurney, and she was standing between his spread legs. She hadn't felt trapped until that moment.

"My mother died just a few months after I was born."

"How." No question. A demand.

"A . . . a car accident." So she'd been told.

Dante was the one to shake his head. "I doubt that."

Her heart was beating faster.

"I think your father wanted to create very special children, and he found a woman who could provide him with those children."

Her skin felt icy.

"Nothing too dangerous, not if he was going to have it in the family, but something powerful nevertheless."

Some*thing*?

"You're not supposed to exist, sweetheart, but then, neither am I."

His words were starting to scare her. She'd been born human. Her blood had changed only because of her father's experiments.

Right?

"And maybe . . . maybe your father couldn't resist your mother. That would have been part of her charm, after all."

Her charm? He was losing her. "You're wrong, Dante. I'm just—"

"A siren."

Cassie laughed. She couldn't help it. Laughter was her first response. "There is no way—"

"Sirens are real, you know. As real as any other paranormal that walks the earth."

Her mouth suddenly felt very, very dry. "Sirens lure sailors to their deaths." She knew the myth. Beautiful women, or at least, they appeared beautiful at first, but they were really monsters. "In Greek mythology, they'd sung to lure in their prey. When the boats crashed on the rocks near the sirens, the sirens had fed on the wounded."

"That's the myth . . ."

She was adamant. "That's *not* me."

"Humans only know part of the sirens' story." His hand lifted, brushed back her hair. "In truth, there were so many ways for them to lure in the men they wanted. Except sirens weren't interested in mortal men."

Her heart was going to burst out of her chest.

"They wanted paranormals—because sirens craved power. Magic."

How many times was she going to have to say it? "I am not—"

"Vampires are lured to you by the sweet scent of your blood. It's different from anything else they've ever experienced. They can scent the poison, too, but your blood is too strong for them to resist."

Cassie put her hands on his chest. "My father made my blood that way. A lure and a poison."

"He made it poison. Nature made it a lure."

Her breath rushed out.

"Werewolves will be drawn by your voice. It soothes their beast. That's why the one called Trace is calmer when you're near. I realized that when I watched you with him. He hasn't attacked you yet because your voice puts his beast at ease."

"Sirens sing, I don't—"

"The lure is different for every paranormal. I *know* what you are. I've met your kind before."

She had a kind?

"The magic isn't as strong in you, probably because of the brews that your father gave you, but it's there. I've known it from the time you were eight years old."

Her world was spinning. He was solid beneath her hand. "Then why didn't you tell me?"

"Because you wouldn't have believed me."

"My mother—"

"She probably tried to get away from your father. But the thing is . . . once a man has a siren, he becomes obsessed with her."

A chill skated down Cassie's spine. Dante's dark eyes were so intense, so focused on her.

"Once they mate, the siren can walk away, the ties won't bind her, but her prey . . . is trapped. The only way he can escape her hold is death."

Cassie didn't like what he was saying. Didn't want to hear another word.

I'm no siren. I'm Cassie Armstrong. I'm a doctor. I'm twenty-nine. I'm—

"Don't you want to know how you lure me to you?"

No. "Yes." Soft, scared. She would *not* be scared.

Hell, she was so scared.

"Part of it is your scent." He inhaled deeply, and his fingers tunneled in her hair, pulling her close to him. "Shifters can usually catch a siren's scent, even if they don't necessarily realize what that scent means."

"But you know what it means . . ."

"I've dealt with sirens before."

It didn't sound like he'd dealt with them in a positive way.

He bent his head and his lips pressed against her throat. Her heartbeat spiked.

"It's not just your scent, though," Dante rasped, "it's your taste that draws me, too. So sweet and light . . . tempting me to gobble you up."

He scored her flesh with his teeth.

"I had to be careful. I tried not to kiss you for a long time, but the first time I tasted your lips, the lure was set."

"You left after our first kiss." Cassie had kissed him right before she'd killed him at Genesis. Stupidly, desperately, she'd hoped that the kiss would make him remember her.

His head lifted, but her neck tingled, as if she still felt the heat of his mouth. "I thought I could break the link. I tried . . ."

That hurt.

"I couldn't. You kept pulling me back to you."

He was wrong. She'd wanted him to be free. "No, I didn't do anything—"

The gold deep within his eyes began to burn. "Did you dream of me, Cassie?"

She had. So many dreams. But what was wrong with a dream? Cassie nodded.

"A siren can lure through her dreams. The link was between us, and you used it. Every time you dreamed, every time you longed, you sent that longing to me. Made me feel it."

He sounded almost angry.

But she hadn't meant to do anything like that. "I'm not a siren." Her desperate whisper. He was wrong. He had to be.

"A phoenix can't mate with just anyone. Our fire burns too hot. We'd kill human lovers." His lips twisted. "I know phoenixes who have—and they couldn't even take their own lives when the guilt ate at them."

She couldn't speak.

"A male phoenix can mate with a female of our kind, but it's rare. We just don't fucking trust each other enough. Our killer instinct is stronger than our mating instinct."

That would be why phoenixes weren't populating the world.

"Dragon shifters work as potential mates. They can handle any fire. But, because of that, they're also threats to us."

Any being that could handle the fire could also attack a phoenix during his weakest moment—the rising.

"But there's one more that can mate with us. One who can soothe our fire, with her siren's song."

Cassie shook her head.

His eyes narrowed. "You're my mate, Cassie. There's no denying it. I took you, I claimed you, and now, you *are* mine."

Jamie ran through the lab and slammed the door of his "room" shut. His hands were shaking and his stomach twisted with fear.

He'd wanted to kill that vampire—that freak was just like the one who'd turned Tim.

But when he'd gone in there with the chunk of broken wood he'd taken from the chair he smashed in his room, the vampire had been too strong for him.

The guy's fangs had been at his throat. If Cassie hadn't come in . . .

I would be dead.

Or, even worse, he'd be a vampire.

He didn't know what was happening. Didn't understand anything, not anymore. When they'd first come out to the world, vampires had told everyone that they could get along with humans. They'd been all friendly on the TV shows.

Then those fanged freaks had attacked.

And Jamie's world had ended.

He sucked in a deep breath. One. Two. The breaths didn't calm him down any. Tim used to tell him . . .

Don't get so angry, man. Breathe. Relax.

Tim wasn't there anymore.

Jamie wasn't going to let that vampire keep living in that room down the hall. Tim was dead, and that guy deserved to die, too.

Jamie just had to find a way to get to the vamp again—get to him, and take him out.

When he'd hidden for all those hours in that swamp, he had made one vow. Just one. If he survived . . .

He'd kill every vampire that ever crossed his path.

That vampire—Vaughn—was going to hell.

CHAPTER ELEVEN

Cassie was afraid.

Dante could see the fear on her face in the widening of her eyes, and hear it in the rapid breaths that slipped from her parted lips.

"You truly had no idea of just what you are." He'd wondered for a long time. She'd seemed so unaware of her power—when she could have used it to her advantage numerous times.

If she wanted, she could soothe any shifter with just the sound of her voice.

But she hadn't tried. Had never used that soft, seductive whisper that sirens loved so much.

Actually, she *had* used that voice—when she'd been naked with him.

And his phoenix had stayed buried so the man could claim her.

"Your voice is your power. When you inject it with the magic that's deep inside you, Cassie, you can command anyone."

"I-I don't want to command."

No, she wouldn't.

"Remember, that's where your power is." If she needed that strength, he damn sure wanted her to use it. "When you sing your siren's song, when you do it right, no one can hurt you."

She still had doubt in her eyes.

"You're not going to age anymore. At least, the sirens I've met stopped aging in their late twenties." Dante shrugged. They stayed young and attractive—the better to keep luring in their prey.

Even though Cassie was only half-siren, he suspected the same aging rule would hold true for her. All the other siren traits were there—buried, but there— so it stood to reason she had that perk, too.

"How many sirens have you met?"

"Three." He wouldn't mention that he'd killed the first one. She'd been his brother's lover, and they'd both been bent on Dante's death.

The siren and his brother had burned.

He'd risen.

"And you're sure . . . absolutely sure . . . that I'm—"

"I know what you are. If the werewolf could manage more than one word at a time, he'd tell you, too."

She looked shattered. "My mother . . . ?"

"Sirens don't usually bear children with nonparanormals. They find humans too"—*How to put this?*—"weak for breeding."

Cassie flinched. "Uh, did you just say *breeding*?"

"Your father experimented on you. I suspect he experimented on himself, as well. He could have changed his body enough to fool her, but once she found out the truth . . ." *The siren would have left him.*

A siren's prey wouldn't have allowed that. Without her, Cassie's father would have gone insane.

Maybe he had.

"He killed her." Cassie's voice was whisper-soft.

Dante wanted to kiss Cassie again. She looked so lost, so hurt. But she needed the truth.

He would give her that from now on. "I think he did."

Her lips trembled. "If I were truly a siren, wouldn't I have used my power on you before?" Pain pushed through her words. "When you came back to me, when you rose, wouldn't I have made you remember me?"

Not if she hadn't realized her power. "The next time I rise, just kiss me."

She shook her head. "Through the fire? Yeah, right. I'll just go through the flames and put my mouth on yours."

"You might be surprised at what happens when you put that sexy mouth of yours against mine."

She opened her mouth to speak—

And he kissed her. Dante *had* to kiss her. She was so close, and though she didn't realize it, everything about her was pulling him in. Making him want, making him need, and driving him to the very edge of control.

His hand rose, sank into her thick hair, and he brought his lips down on hers. Her mouth was open, so he pushed his tongue inside, tasting all of the sweetness that waited for him.

Luring me in.

Her taste was addictive. *She* was addictive. He didn't think he'd ever be able to let her go. He wanted her naked. Wanted *in* her.

And what a phoenix wanted . . .

A moan built in her throat. The sound was sexy, driving up the heat of his arousal.

She can handle my fire.

The phoenix didn't want to consume her. He just . . . *wanted* her.

He rose from the table. Still kissing her. Then he was stripping her. Shoving down her jeans. Tossing away her shirt.

"Dante?"

She stared up at him, need bright in her green eyes. Her cheeks were flushed. Her lips red from his mouth.

He kissed her again.

He couldn't stop.

Couldn't.

He put her on the table. Licked her breast and loved the way she gasped his name. He should go slow with her.

Slow wasn't an option for him.

He pushed between her legs. Found her wet, hot. His fingers thrust into her. Withdrew. Thrust. Even as he kept licking her tight little nipples. So sweet.

She arched up against him, damn near jumping off that table. "Want . . . you!"

And there it was. That hard push of power in her voice. The siren's call that she didn't even realize she'd given.

Lust exploded through him, burning hot and wild, and nothing—no fucking thing—could have made him leave her then.

His siren called.

He answered.

Dante thrust deep into her. He withdrew, then angled his body so that each drive into her took him over the sensitive core of her flesh.

Her nails sank into his shoulders, and he loved that bite of pain.

"You feel so good," she whispered.

She felt like the best dream he'd ever had.

And her voice . . . sex and pleasure . . . temptation. Lust.

Her voice drove him on as she whispered his name.

She was coming. He felt the ripples of her release around him and couldn't hold back any longer. He exploded within her, the fire burning inside him but never—*never*—touching her.

The phoenix couldn't hurt the one he wanted as a mate.

Nothing could hurt Cassie.

He held her tight, his mouth against her neck, his arms locked around her, as the release pumped through him.

He wanted to keep her there, right in his arms.

He *would* be keeping Cassie. Could almost understand his brother's obsession.

Almost.

Would he kill for her?

Yes.

In an instant.

He'd kill to protect her. He'd destroy anyone who sought to hurt her.

Her fingers were on his back, sliding over his skin in the softest of caresses. Her heartbeat drummed at a frantic rate—he could feel the wild thunder—and her breath panted out softly.

"I used to wonder . . . what it would be like with you," Cassie whispered.

Dante forced his head to lift. His gaze held hers.

"It's better than I thought." Her smile was so wide and beautiful.

He stared at her a moment, feeling lost.

Was it her siren's song? Was she still pushing power through her words?

No, he realized. It was just . . . Cassie.

Her hands kept caressing his back. "You always feel so warm."

The fire always burned within him.

Her gaze held his. "Should I ever worry about your flames?"

No, not her.

But before he could speak, a loud alarm pierced the air, echoing around them.

"Not again!" Cassie cried.

Yes, fucking again. But at least he'd had her before more chaos came calling.

Adrenaline flooded through Dante as he carefully pulled away from Cassie. Who had found them—or who was being attacked *this* time?

Cassie yanked on her clothes and rushed toward a series of monitors. She tapped on a keyboard and the images on those screens sharpened.

Dante stared at the image of a tall, muscled man. A man who had his arms wrapped round the shoulders of a dark-haired woman. Dante had never seen the man before, but, as he stared at that screen, tension gripped him. An instinctive, battle-ready edge that could only mean one thing.

Another of my kind.

"They're here early," Cassie said as she frowned at the screen. "I didn't expect Cain and Eve to arrive until—" Her words ended in a startled gasp as Dante picked her up and carried her toward the small supply closet.

"Dante? Dante, what the hell are you doing? Put me down!"

Red began to coat his vision.

Another phoenix, a male, near his siren.

No.

He put her down—inside the closet. She stared at him with disbelief in her green eyes, looking for all the world like she thought he'd just gone insane.

Maybe he had. "Stay here."

Her jaw dropped. "Those are my friends out there! Hell, no, I'm not going to—"

He slammed the door. Locked it. Cassie would not be getting in the middle of his battle.

"What the hell are you doing?"

He heard the sound of her small fists pummeling the door. More thuds—was she kicking it, too? It sure sounded that way.

"We just had sex!" she cried. "You can't do this to me! You *can't* lock me in here!"

He could. He had. And the sex had been phenomenal.

"Let me out of here!"

"I will," he promised. "Once the threat is gone."

Dead silence. Then she said, "That's why you came. Not to help me. You wanted me to lead you to the other phoenixes!"

His hand pressed against the door. "We're a dangerous lot. Not to be trusted."

"Yeah, tell me something I didn't just figure out when you *locked me in the closet*!"

His hand dropped. "He would have turned on you. With your siren blood, it would have been only a short time before he realized what you were. I'm protecting you." Dante spun away from the closet.

It had been so long since he'd battled another phoenix. He didn't know how old Cain O'Connor was, but the guy couldn't be as old as he was.

So Cain wouldn't be as strong.

More pounding came from the closet. "Dante, *no*! Don't do this! Cain and Eve are here to help! Dammit, don't!"

Dante would do anything to keep her safe.

Killing had always been easy for him.

When he'd watched his brother die, he had sworn to never be fooled by another of his kind. Cassie wouldn't understand just how deceptive a phoenix could be.

He knew.

"Dante!"

He left her.

The sound of his footsteps faded away. Cassie had her left ear flattened against the wood of the door and knew when he left her. Actually left her locked in the closet.

Damn him!

The only light she had spilled beneath the door, showing her pretty much nothing. She spun around, fumbling in the darkness as her heart raced. She didn't have much time. Dante was going after Cain, and she would *not* let Cain die.

He used me.

She'd thought—so foolishly—that Dante had wanted to help her, but all along, she'd just been a means to an end for him.

A siren? Total BS. Another line he'd spewed so that she'd trust him.

The absolute worst part was that she could still feel the jerk inside her. Her sex was flushed and sensitive—from him.

And he'd just locked my ass in a supply closet.

She'd gone from having an absolutely mind-numbing orgasm one minute to being shoved into a dirty supply closet. Dante's after-sex technique sucked on so many levels.

Her fingers closed around the wooden pole of a mop. She tried ramming it into the door.

The thuds were louder than they'd been when she'd used her fists, but the door didn't open.

"Help!" Cassie screamed. *This can't be happening. I can't actually be trapped like this.*

Eve was her friend. Cain had been nothing but good to her.

And Dante . . .

The two phoenixes couldn't battle. When they did, only one survived.

"Help!" Cassie screamed again.

She was very much afraid that no one was coming to her aid.

"Help!"

The cry reached Trace's ears and his beast tensed. He knew he was more beast than man. He knew that his control was gone, and . . . some days, he almost wished for death.

Almost?

The cry pierced through the rage his beast carried,

reaching the man inside. There was something about that voice. Something that spoke to the beast and the man.

Cassie.

Her image appeared in his mind. Her dark hair. Her soft hands. She'd never hurt him. Always promised to help. And when she whispered to him, things *did* seem better. The rage cooled within him.

But something was wrong.

He opened his mouth and howled.

Cassie shouldn't be crying for help. Cassie couldn't be hurt. She was his last hope.

He howled again and jerked at the chains that bound him. The silver burned, cutting deep into him, but he didn't care.

Help her.

The beast snarled and his muscles burned. He pulled and pulled . . . and the chains began to snap.

Dante wasn't going to bring the battle down to Cassie. She would be safe in the little underground lair that she'd made for herself.

Silently, he rode the elevator up to the ground level. The other phoenix would not know that he was coming. His guard would be lowered.

The better for me to attack.

Cassie had been calling for help when he'd left her. Her cries had twisted his guts, but he hadn't stopped. He remembered, too well, what it was like when another phoenix came for you.

Brother . . . why? I meant you no harm.

But his brother had just laughed. *As long as you live, you're a threat. Didn't you learn anything from the others?*

Once, there had been a dozen phoenixes in their village. They'd been the power . . . until they turned on one another.

The fire led to bloodlust. Fury. The need to dominate and control.

For days, their village had been turned black with ash.

Others—humans down the mountainside—had started to spread rumors of dragons attacking.

There had been no dragons.

Dante stared down at his hands. Saw fire.

Only us.

He hadn't wanted to kill his brother. Wren had given him no choice. Dante had been burning. Wren and his siren had come at him as he rose, come for his head and his heart.

They'd almost taken his head.

But his phoenix hadn't been ready for death.

The phoenix who stands last is the only one with power. Wren's panting words to him. *I will stand last. I will have the power. You, brother, will have hell.*

Dante squared his shoulders. The elevator doors opened. Cain had his back to him—such a mistake. He saw the man's dark hair, a shade very similar to Dante's own.

Cain spun toward him.

His eyes widened. "You're not—where's Cassie?" He grabbed the woman with him and shoved her behind his back.

Dante's nostrils flared. The woman's scent . . . *speaking of dragons.* He hadn't caught that particular scent in centuries. Those two were even more of a threat than he'd first thought.

Dante stepped forward. The elevator closed behind him. His gaze slid to the woman as she peered over her man's shoulder. "I'm sorry," Dante told her. "I didn't want to kill you." He shook his head. "Leave now, and I will spare you." Even though he knew *what* she was.

"Who are you?" the woman whispered.

Dante lifted his hands. The fire was burning so brightly now. Spinning. Flaming. "I'm death."

Cain gave a rough laugh. "Am I supposed to be impressed by that shit? I can conjure, too." In an instant, he had fire flaring in his own hands.

Dante smiled. He hadn't expected much of a challenge from this one. He'd been wrong. "What have you had? Maybe fifty risings? And probably all during your captivity at Genesis."

Cain's dark eyes narrowed—*his eyes look like mine*—as he glared at Dante. "Did Cassie tell you about me?"

"I can smell the risings. Hell leaves its own stamp on us."

"That why I can smell brimstone on you?"

"I've risen more times than you can imagine." Maybe that was why he had to fight so hard to cling to his sanity. "And I will be the one who rises again. You will be the one to stay in hell this time."

"No!" The woman yelled from behind Cain. She tried to lunge forward, but he pushed her back. The fire didn't burn her. Of course, it didn't. One sniff, and Dante knew that the woman had dragon shifter blood in her body—there was no mistaking that scent. Fire wouldn't harm her.

There were still plenty of other ways for her to die.

"She doesn't belong in this battle," Dante said softly. "Send her away. Face me on your own."

"Why the hell are you doing this?" the woman yelled. Eve. Cassie had called her Eve.

Cassie . . .

Help!

Was she still crying for help?

"It's what we do." The answer came from Cain. His voice was grim. "Our kind—we kill. I told you that before."

"We're here to help Trace!" Eve shouted. "This isn't supposed to be about killing!"

She almost reminded Dante of Cassie.

"Step back," he warned her.

"Swear that she will stay unharmed," Cain demanded.

Dante inclined his head. "When I kill you, I will let her live."

"No!" Eve's voice was nearly a shriek.

Cain laughed again. The flames died above his hands. "No, dumbass. I meant don't hurt her during our battle. While I'm killing *you*." He reached under his jacket, yanking out a gun.

He lifted the gun and fired at Dante.

The closet door swung open. Because Cassie was aiming again with her mop, she tumbled forward, and the mop clipped Charles on the side of his head.

"Ow!" He frowned at her. "See if I rush to your rescue again." He hurriedly stepped back, adjusting his lab coat. "You don't *attack* your rescuer, Cass. You know that, right? It's bad form."

She shoved him out of her way and rushed toward the security screens. "He's got a gun." Of course Cain would have come armed. The man wasn't the type to take chances. That gun was aimed at Dante.

Hands slick with sweat and body tight with fear, Cassie whirled away from the monitors and ran for the door.

"You're welcome!" Charles called out behind her.

"Thank you!" she yelled and flew for the elevator. She had to get up to the ground level. If Cain shot Dante, she didn't even want to think about what would happen next.

Fire.

Rising.

Death.

Not Dante's. She didn't actually think anything was

strong enough to kill him permanently, not after all she'd seen during his years of captivity at Genesis.

She didn't want Cain to die. He'd been a captive at Genesis, too. Tortured, hurt. The man had just found happiness with Eve. Neither one of them deserved to have that happiness snatched away.

Cassie jumped into the elevator. "Hurry, hurry," she whispered under her breath. She realized that she was still clutching the mop. As weapons went, it wasn't exactly a major threat.

Not that she had a whole lot of options.

She sucked in a deep breath and hoped that when those elevator doors opened, fire didn't greet her.

Charles watched Cassie vanish. He wasn't sure how the woman had wound up in the closet. When she stopped running, he'd be sure to get that story from her.

He glanced over at the monitors. Oh, hell, that looked like a situation he didn't want to—

The door crashed open behind him. Charles spun around, his hand automatically rising to his chest.

He's out. Fuck, fuck. He's out!

The werewolf stood before him. If possible, the man's features had become more twisted in the form of a beast. He was bigger than before. Charles was sure of that. And the werewolf's claws were much sharper now, too.

Bad. So very bad.

As Charles stared at him in horror, the beast dropped down onto all fours and let out a deep, rumbling growl. When those glowing eyes locked on him, Charles was pretty sure that he saw his own death reflected in that gaze.

"No," Charles whispered. "Please, I tried to help you. Don't you remember that?"

The beast snarled.

Charles ran forward and dove into the closet. He yanked the door shut behind him just as claws drove through the wood, coming through about two inches away from his head.

So damn bad.

The bullet exploded from the gun, rushing right at Dante. He couldn't help it. He smiled as he pushed his flames hotter. Higher.

The bullet melted before it could ever touch him.

Above the crackle of the flames, he heard the woman's shocked gasp.

"When you're as old as I am, the power is so much greater," Dante murmured. He let his flames flicker away so that he could meet Cain's stare once more. "Want to try again? Feel free to shoot every bullet in your gun."

Cain's hold tightened on the weapon.

"But you should know, they won't hurt me." Dante tilted his head. "Though they will piss me off."

Eve's hands fisted in the material of Cain's shirt. "Cain . . ." Fear threaded his name.

Dante heard the grind of a motor. The elevator. Lifting up once more.

He couldn't have an enemy at his back and one at his front. He leaped to the side, not sure who he would see when the doors slid open. Cassie was safe in the closet—

The doors parted to reveal Cassie's worried face.

"Cassie!" Dante roared. He tried to leap toward her.

Too late. His roar had revealed far too much.

Cain had rushed toward her, too. Cain reached her first. Cain wrapped his arms around Cassie and pulled her close against him.

Dante hadn't intended to make the phoenix shifter's death particularly brutal. In that moment, he changed his mind.

The woman—Eve—had frozen, but Cain hurried back to her, pulling Cassie in front of him like the shield that she was.

"You want to let her go," Dante snapped.

Cain shook his head and put his gun to Cassie's head.

The fool.

"What are you doing?" Eve demanded. "That's *Cassie*! She's helping Trace!"

The elevator doors closed.

Cain shook his head again. "She set us up, don't you see that? Lured us out here so *he* could attack."

Cassie's wild-eyed stare landed on Dante. "I didn't," she whispered. "I didn't know what he'd planned."

Dante saw betrayal in her stare, and that look made him feel strange. His chest ached.

"Move the gun away from her head," he ordered.

The gun didn't move.

"Cain!" Eve snapped.

"Don't move the gun," Cassie said in the same instant.

What?

"Eve, call up the elevator," Cassie said softly. "You, Cain, and I will go inside it. Dante won't— He won't hurt us as long as I'm in front of you two."

She was choosing to protect them? Even as that jackass pressed a gun to her head?

Cassie held Dante's gaze. "I'll lock the system down once we're inside. He won't be able to follow us."

No, no. That would not happen.

"Cassie . . ." Her name was a warning growl from Dante.

Cain slowly backed them toward the elevator.

"You don't follow us," Cassie whispered to Dante. "You just . . . get the hell out of here. Don't look for us, and we won't look for you."

He didn't think Cain was going to agree to that plan. The expression on the guy's face promised retribution.

Dante wasn't leaving him alive. "That's not happening," he vowed.

"You used me," Cassie said, shaking her head.

Had her voice broken? *It had*. Broken with pain.

"I trusted you, but you just wanted to hurt them."

"No," Dante said. "I wanted to kill the phoenix." It was what he'd been taught to do. The only way he'd survived.

The phoenixes in his village had turned on one another, battling in a fury of bloodlust and fire.

Until only one remained . . .

Because of the siren.

Cassie didn't realize that she was the danger that would destroy so many. He knew what powers she held inside. He'd known from the beginning.

Maybe he should have just killed her, but that act had always been beyond him. She made him weak.

Just as Zura had made his brother weak.

It doesn't have to be this way! We can be strong together.

Hadn't he tried to stop his brother? Hadn't he tried to use reason before fire?

Until there had been no reason left.

Just flames.

Wren hadn't wanted them both to live. He hadn't wanted them both to be stronger.

I'll be stronger on my own. Wren had told him those cold words, even as his fire burned hell-hot. *And I'll never fear you turning on me.*

The elevator's doors opened. Eve stepped toward those doors then stopped. "Trace?"

The wild scent of the wolf hit Dante. *Impossible. The werewolf is chained below. He is—*

The werewolf shoved something, someone—the human, Charles, a very bloody Charles—onto the ground and leaped out of that elevator. He looked different, far more savage and animal-like, as he lunged for Cassie.

"No!" The bellow was Dante's. But he was too far away.

The werewolf hit Cassie and Cain, sending both tumbling to the ground. Cain's weapon fired, the bullet exploding, and Eve screamed.

The wolf didn't stop. He grabbed Cassie and yanked her back.

Dante attacked. He lifted his hands, conjuring the most powerful fire he had within him. The werewolf wouldn't survive the blast. Cassie had thought to save this beast? There was no saving a being that thought to hurt her.

No saving . . .

Dante's fire launched out.

The beast dropped Cassie and rushed toward Cain, moving so fast—incredibly fast—as he dodged the flames. The fire barely singed him. The werewolf's claws swiped over the other phoenix, cutting him deep. Cain swore and fire swirled over his fingers.

Eve grabbed his arm. "That's Trace!"

"That's a fucking dead wolf," Dante shouted. Cassie was bleeding. The wolf's claws had cut her and the wolf was—

"Help . . ." That cry was more beast than man. Far more. "Help . . . Cass . . ." the werewolf growled. Then he was curling his powerful body around hers.

Dante stepped toward them.

The werewolf bared his teeth. "Kill . . ."

His claws weren't near her throat. He had wrapped his arms around Cassie's stomach.

"The change is . . . even worse," Eve whispered. "I thought he was getting better."

The wolf *had* looked better. Before.

He seemed to be turning more into the beast as Dante watched. Thick, dark fur burst from his skin, and the werewolf opened his mouth to snarl with the pain of his change.

"Trace." Cassie tried to push free of his hold. "Trace, you're hurting me."

The phoenix within Dante began to attack with his flaming claws. Wanting *out*.

Trace stiffened.

"Let me go, Trace. Please."

Trace shook his head. The transformation seemed to have halted with Cassie's words.

The siren's song is controlling him. Dante stalked toward Trace.

"Help"—Trace growled—"Cass . . ."

Dante took another step.

Trace's head snapped up and his glowing eyes locked on Dante. *"Kill."* The werewolf's teeth snapped together.

"Come on and try," Dante invited. "Let's just see what you've got."

Trace freed Cassie.

Yes.

Then the beast was running for him.

Dante lifted his hand and sent flames right at the beast.

"No!" Cassie screamed as she ran *after* Trace.

The man-beast fell, rolling on the ground and howling as he tried to put out the flames that flared over his body.

"Stop!" Cassie shoved at Dante, sending him stumbling back in surprise. "Don't hurt him! Don't you see? He's protecting me!"

He was—what?

Cassie shoved Dante again. "Stay away from him! From me!"

He couldn't. He couldn't ever stay away from her.

She fell to her knees beside the werewolf. Smoke drifted from him and dark burns covered his arms. "Trace?" she whispered.

His head turned toward her. "Help . . ." he whispered.

She put her hand on his bulging shoulder. "You did help me. Now just relax. Please relax, and let me help you."

The werewolf's claws were too close to her. Dante stepped toward her.

Cassie's head immediately turned toward him. Tears glistened in her eyes. "Stay away! Haven't you done enough hurting for one day?"

She stared at him as if—as if he were the monster.

He was, but Cassie had never looked at him that way before.

"Cain, help me," Cassie said.

Cain, still bleeding, hurried toward her.

"We need to get Trace downstairs. I have to treat him. He's . . . changing. I can *feel* it."

Transformation was the way werewolves healed from injuries. It was instinctive for them. The wounds Trace had received from Dante's fire were pushing that change.

"If he changes fully," Cassie said, shaking her head, "I don't—I don't know if we will be able to get him back. I have to give him some tranqs to get him calm and stable."

The werewolf wasn't fighting. His head was tilted toward Cassie, and the beast seemed to hang onto her every word.

Siren.

"It's okay," Cassie soothed him. "I'll take care of you."

Dante heard the special, almost lyrical notes in her voice that a siren got only when she charmed.

The werewolf's breathing eased.

Cain was close to them. He frowned down at Cassie and blinked a few times.

Yeah, you heard it, too.

"Will he make it?" Eve wanted to know. She'd helped Charles to his feet. The human was pale, scratched, but suffering no mortal wound.

Dante knew her question was about Trace.

"I hope so," Cassie said, still using that same tone. The tone that calmed Dante's phoenix, that had Cain looking confused . . . and had the wolf lying still beneath Cassie's probing touch.

And the woman claimed she wasn't a siren?

She had them all under her power.

Once she realized just how strong she truly was, Cassie could prove to be incredibly dangerous.

As dangerous as Zura, when she'd gone mad with her power.

She turned us on each other. Made us fight until only ash was left.

All with the power of her voice.

The phoenixes had learned a lesson that day . . . stay away from their own kind. They weren't immortal when their own were close enough to kill.

It had taken just the whisper from a siren to start that war.

"We have to get him to the lab," Cassie said.

Cain bent to reach for the werewolf's shoulders.

Trace snapped at him, biting the phoenix and drawing a curse from Cain.

"Trace, *no*!" Cassie commanded. "We're helping you!"

He stilled instantly.

Cain frowned down at the beast. "If he bites me again, I'm kicking his ass."

"Cain." Eve's voice was worried.

Dante grabbed the wolf before Cain could reach for him again. He slung Trace over his shoulder and ignored the claws that sliced into his skin.

Cassie stared up at Dante with shocked eyes.

"You want him back in his cell?"

He was actually tossing another paranormal in a cell? After what he'd been through?

But . . . yes, he was.

"Then lead the way," Dante said.

Cassie just stared blankly at him then shook her head. "Give him to Cain. I can't trust you."

That ache was back in Dante's chest. Worse.

But he gave her a grim smile. "You have it wrong, sweetheart. We're the ones who can't trust you." Not once she started to use her power. Not once she realized . . .

She could control and kill with a word.

Cain frowned at Cassie but his stare wasn't exactly believing. He glanced back at Dante. "You going to try to kill me as soon as the elevator touches down?"

"No. I'll wait till we drop off the wolf." Dante stared down Cain. "Then you and I will leave the others. There's no sense in harming them."

"No!" Eve immediately yelled.

Cain gave a grim nod.

Cassie pushed her way on the elevator. "The hell you will. Dante, you aren't hurting Cain. You aren't hurting anyone." She jabbed his arm.

No, she jabbed a *needle* into his arm.

An icy liquid shot through his body, chilling him, quenching the fire of the phoenix that always seemed to burn so brightly within him.

The werewolf fell from his arms. Dante sagged back, hitting the elevator wall.

"I won't let you hurt anyone," Cassie said, her voice breaking with pain.

Pain that he had caused her?

"I never wanted it to be this way." Cassie's voice was so soft and sad.

He tried to turn his head and look at her, but couldn't. His body slid down and crashed onto the floor of the elevator beside Trace.

"You didn't give me a choice."

"Damn." Cain's impressed drawl. "I didn't expect you to be so cold, Cassie."

"Neither did he. And that was Dante's mistake."

Deep inside, the flames of the phoenix died away.

CHAPTER TWELVE

"He's gonna be pissed when he wakes up." Cain dropped Dante's body in the cell—a reinforced cell that Cassie had never used before.

"I'll deal with his anger," Cassie said. *And he could deal with hers.* He'd been using her—all along. He'd never intended to help. He'd only wanted to kill.

It felt like the jerk had carved out her heart. Or maybe he'd just burned it out of her chest with his damn fire.

Cain glanced toward the chains. She saw his face tighten and knew he was remembering his own time with Genesis.

"You putting him in those?" he asked, voice flat.

"No." She'd never thought she would actually be the one locking Dante up. But she'd thought wrong. "The room will be secure enough. It's fireproof. He won't be getting out unless we let him out."

Cain nodded.

Cassie glanced down at Dante once more. His eyelashes cast dark shadows beneath his eyes. His face was still tense and hard, even when he was unconscious. As if he never let down his guard.

Why? Why did you do this, Dante?

She'd trusted him. In just a few moments time, he'd destroyed that trust. From sex to betrayal in five minutes flat. What girl was supposed to handle that?

"We need to get back to Trace," she said, squaring her shoulders. She'd drugged him already, dosing him with tranqs that had stopped his shift, but she still needed to treat the wounds on his body.

She noticed that Cain made sure she exited and *then* he came out after her, swinging the heavy metal door shut behind them.

And sealing Dante inside.

Cassie lifted her chin and tried to act like Dante hadn't just killed a part of her.

If only she were a better actress.

They went back to her lab. Eve was helping to patch up Charles. Poor Charles. The man looked shell-shocked.

"Are you going to leave?" she asked him quietly.

Charles had been Cassie's assistant for so long. His half-sister had been a shifter, one who'd been taken into the Genesis program on a very much *not* voluntary basis. By the time Charles had found her, it had been too late. She'd been broken by what Genesis had done to her.

Kerri had taken her own life.

He'd wanted to work with Cassie, to help others like Kerri, but there was fear in his eyes now.

"I think this is all too much for me," Charles muttered. "I thought I could handle it, but the ones here are just too strong. Too dangerous."

Wasn't that what Cassie's father had told her? That some of the paranormals were too strong and dangerous? That they had to be put down for the protection of the humans? She hadn't wanted to believe he could be right.

And she hadn't wanted to believe that Dante would betray her, either.

"If you want to leave," Cassie said, holding Charles's gaze, "I understand."

Charles nodded. His gaze drifted away from hers, and she knew . . . Charles *would* be leaving soon. There was too much fear in his posture.

And too much blood on his clothes.

He'd come close to dying, and she knew that he didn't want to join Kerri in death.

Cassie glanced toward her operating table. Heavy metal strips closed over Trace's arms, legs, and chest. A mask was over his face, and the drug that he was being given was designed to keep him out.

Stable, comfortable, and definitely *out*.

Charles shuffled out of the room. Cassie bit her lip and didn't stop him. He had been her confidant, and because she liked him so much, she couldn't stop him.

If he wanted to walk away and forget monsters for a time, didn't he deserve that chance?

When the doors slid closed behind him, her shoulders hunched a bit.

"What happened?" Eve asked as she crept closer to Cassie. "The last report that you sent said Trace was getting better."

"He was . . . "

"You also didn't mention in that report," Cain said, voice hard, "that you had a homicidal phoenix waiting to kill me."

She flinched. "I didn't know. Dante said he would help me."

"He lied."

Yes, he had.

"He's the oldest phoenix I've ever met," Cassie said as she rolled her shoulders, trying to push some of her tension away. "I thought his DNA would be the key I needed in order to find a cure—"

Eve brushed her fingers across Trace's forehead. "He's not going to ever be the same, is he?"

The same? "No, but that doesn't mean he can't still have a good life."

Eve nodded and kept caressing his forehead. A tear slid down her cheek.

"I don't understand how he got out." Cassie glanced around the room and her gaze lit on the smashed remains of the closet.

She'd been in that closet, calling for help. *Screaming* for help.

The memory of Trace's rough voice slipped through her mind. *Help . . . Cass . . .* She stilled. Was it even possible? No, no. Surely he hadn't heard her—

But his whole body had been enhanced by the Lycan-70 drug. That enhancement had made him bigger, stronger. Had it given him enhanced hearing and vision? Possible. So very possible.

It had been hard to fully gauge his enhancements because his beast side had been so powerful.

"He didn't hurt me," Cassie said softly. He'd tackled Cain because Cain had been holding the gun to her head. She frowned at Cain.

He blinked. "What?"

"Thanks for shoving the gun at me."

He flushed. "I was trying to do *something* to keep your attack phoenix off me!"

But he hadn't been able to stop Trace from attacking. Trace had sliced him and then Trace had come back and tried to shield Cassie.

"How are your wounds?" Cassie asked Cain.

"Hurting like a bitch," he replied instantly. "But don't worry. It's nothing that will kill me." His smile was bitter. "I've felt death coming too many times. The bastard isn't here now."

Eve had already taken out some bandages for Cain.

Once upon a time, she had done a stint in med school. The woman would be able to patch up her lover, no problem.

Patching up Trace? That would take much more of an effort.

"He calmed down when you talked to him," Eve said, nodding toward Trace. "Whatever was happening to him, he remembered your voice."

Your voice is your power. That was what Dante had told her. *When you sing your siren's song.*

She backed away from Trace. Turned slowly to face Cain. "Do you hear anything . . . odd . . . when I talk to you?"

He frowned at her. Eve was cutting away his shirt.

"Um, do I sound normal to you? Do I smell normal?" *How bizarre is this conversation?*

Speaking of bizarre . . . she'd just broken up a fight between two phoenixes and a werewolf. Her world was nothing but a bizarre bonanza.

Cain leaned toward her and inhaled deeply. "You smell . . . sweet." He winced when Eve applied a bit too much pressure to his wound. "Not like you," he hurried to reassure her. "Love, you know you smell like paradise and temptation. Every damn dream I've ever had."

She smiled at him.

Cassie glanced away, feeling like an intruder just to have seen that intimate smile. "I-I knew it wasn't true. I don't know why he said—"

"But . . . there *is* something about your voice," Cain muttered.

She tensed.

"It makes me feel . . . calm."

Calm was the last thing she was feeling.

Cain shrugged. "Maybe that's what is supposed to happen, though, right? You're a doctor. You soothe your patients."

Not all of them, she didn't.

Some, like Trace—she seemed to push to attack others.

Swallowing back her growing fear, Cassie focused on Trace. She had to do the best she could to heal him and to stabilize his beast.

Dante slowly opened his eyes. He was on his back on the hard floor, and a shining, silver ceiling waited above him.

She drugged me.

He surged to his feet, disbelief coursing through him as his gaze flew around the room. No, not a room. A holding cell. He recognized the silver metal that surrounded him. He'd seen it plenty in Genesis.

Cassie had thrown him in a special, fire-proof cell. Just like the ones he'd been held in before.

Not her.

"Cassie!" He bellowed her name.

He knew she was there.

To the right, a two-way mirror waited. The rest of the pricks at Genesis had thought they were safe behind that mirror. Fools. He'd always been able to hear them. And, when he focused his gaze just right, he could see them, too.

At first, as he headed toward that mirror, Dante saw his own glowering reflection. But when he focused his eyes, he saw Cassie standing there. Staring back at him.

For an instant, the past and the present merged for him.

She did this to me.

"Why?" Dante snapped.

She had her hands crossed over her chest. "That's just what I was going to ask you." Her voice was soft. She knew that she didn't need to shout. "Why did you lie to me? Why did you make me think I could trust you?"

"Cain is a threat! If I don't eliminate him, he'll come for me." Dante had been protecting himself, and her.

She shook her head. "Cain had no plans to kill you *be-*

fore you attacked him." Her breath whispered out, and he picked up even that small sound. "Now, yes, I'm sure you're on his hit list."

Bring it on. He didn't fear the other phoenix. He feared no one.

"You lied to me," Cassie said, her voice hardening. "Dante, I trusted you."

"You caged me!" he threw back at her.

"Because you're dangerous. I was told that, so many times, but I was so sure you were good inside." She sounded sad and lost—and that just pissed him off.

"I've never been a threat to you," he told her. He'd *saved* her from that jerk at the ranch. Had the woman already forgotten that? He'd been the one to rescue her from the lieutenant colonel jackass.

"No, you're just a threat to what *matters* to me."

Her words stopped him. He frowned at her.

"I want to help Vaughn. I want to help Trace. I want to cure all the primals out there—I want to undo what my family has done! How many times do I have to tell you this?" Her voice was rising. "But you . . . you nearly destroyed everything I wanted. Everything that I've been working toward. You shoved me in a closet and walked away."

"I wanted you safe!" *Was that so wrong?* He hadn't wanted her caught in the crossfire.

"You wanted to fight a battle that didn't exist. This bullshit about phoenixes going after their own . . . there's no need for that. Whatever war you *think* is happening, is over."

"I don't *think*," Dane told her, suddenly desperate for her to understand. "I know. I was there. You weren't. I watched them all die as they turned on each other. I saw the fire, I saw the death. I saw it all."

She stared back at him, only that glass separating them.

He wanted to punch through it and touch her, but knew it wasn't normal glass. It wouldn't break.

The glass at Genesis had never broken. No matter how many times he'd punched it, and he'd punched until his knuckles were bloody and broken.

"When?" Cassie asked him as her hands fell to her sides. "When was this battle?"

"When I became immortal." That's what he was. There was a reason he'd been given that name at Genesis. "You ever wonder where the phoenixes came from? They came from my village. My blood. We were powerful—unstoppable. We burned and we rose and our enemies fell beneath us."

Until her.

"What happened?"

"All creatures of myth start somewhere. We started in the mountains near Greece. Rumors and whispers about us spread. No one wanted to face an unstoppable army."

She wasn't speaking.

"Back then, the paranormals didn't have to stay in the shadows. And there were more paranormals than you can imagine. So many different monsters, even monsters that hid under a beautiful woman's smile."

She crept closer to the glass. "You're talking about a siren."

He nodded.

"Someone . . . like me."

Dante frowned at that. She was nothing like Zura had been.

"Zura fell in love with my brother, and he . . . Wren would do anything that she asked." Dante's voice was bitter. "When a siren sings her song and asks you to do her bidding, you cannot refuse."

Cassie took another step toward the glass.

"She learned of our weaknesses. She knew that another phoenix could reach through the fire and kill at the time of the rising." Memories were as bitter as ash on his tongue. "She didn't want any threat to my brother. Zura wanted to live with him forever, and never be threatened again."

"What did she do?"

"She called all of the phoenixes. She sang her song . . . and she commanded us to kill each other." All but his brother. Wren hadn't been there for the summoning.

He'd been far away, locked up by Zura for his protection. At first, Dante hadn't thought that his brother even knew the wickedness that she had unleashed.

He'd thought wrong.

"How did you survive?"

"I drove spikes into my ears, so I wouldn't hear her voice."

Through the glass, he saw Cassie flinch.

"I tried to stop the others, tried to get them to do the same. We just had to turn off her voice, but they were beyond listening. Once the bloodlust hit them, there was no stopping the phoenixes they carried."

He lifted his hand and touched the glass.

She did not lift her hand.

"The phoenix is always with us, but in those moments, when it felt the blood of its own kind . . . a new hunger hit me. Hit us all. And the fight for dominance began." Dante swallowed the ash. "When the fire died away, I was left standing. I thought it was over, but then my brother came for me. Wren cut my head from my body."

Her hand rose then. Pressed against the glass over his. "Dante . . ."

"The fire started. I began to rise, and, through the flames, I saw him coming at me again. I knew Wren was going to kill me. My hearing was coming back, and Zura's words were ringing in my ears, even over the crackle of flames. *'Kill him . . . kill him . . . let us be free!'* "

His brother had tried his best to kill him.

"What happened?"

Dante forced a shrug. "I didn't die. They did." Zura should have been more specific with her words. She'd never named him, so Dante had risen, and a siren had ordered him to kill—and he had.

His fire had exploded—going for Wren and Zura. When Zura had begun to burn, Wren had lost his last hold on sanity.

I'm sorry, brother. Dante had wished again and again for a different ending.

"Because of what happened then, you think every phoenix will come after you now?"

He shoved away the image of his brother. "It's what we do. That wasn't the only attack. Word spread after that—a phoenix's weakness is his own kind."

"So it's better to be the *only* one, than to have a threat out there? That's crazy!"

"That's the way of the phoenix," he told her quietly.

"That's the way of the insane. Cain isn't a threat to you. He isn't—"

"He'll realize what you are."

"No, he doesn't think I'm *anything* but human. I asked him if I sounded different. If I smelled different. You know what he said? That his Eve smelled like paradise and temptation. Like every dream he'd ever had."

There was an odd note in her voice. Almost . . . envy?

"He's not hearing any siren song from me, and I'm—I'm starting to wonder why you're lying to me."

"He's mated," Dante said, understanding at once. *Smelled like paradise and temptation.* That was the way a mate smelled to a phoenix. The way that Cassie smelled to—

"He's in love with Eve, yes, but that shouldn't affect the man's ability to smell a difference in me." Cassie turned away. "Get some sleep, Dante, we can talk tomorrow."

"You're . . . leaving me?"

She glanced over her shoulder. "Sucks, doesn't it? Now you know how I felt when you locked me in that closet."

"I was protecting you." *The woman should understand that.*

"No." A sad shake of her head. "You were protecting yourself. From a threat that doesn't even exist. Wake up, Dante. This isn't a world full of sirens and phoenixes any longer. You don't have to battle your own kind. But you *do* have to learn to trust them."

And she truly did just leave him.

The door closed behind her with a soft click.

But she didn't leave him alone.

Dante had known that another was there, even if Cassie hadn't realized it. Another had been standing just outside his cell door the whole time they were talking. Listening to them. Waiting for the moment when Cassie left.

The lock turned slowly, disengaging.

Cain stalked inside. The phoenix pulled the door shut behind him.

No Cassie. No Eve.

"I think we have some business to finish," he murmured.

Yes, they did.

"Why are you crying?"

Cassie stiffened at Jamie's voice. She'd thought that he was asleep, safe and secure for the night.

But there he was, standing at the front of the small makeshift bedroom she'd claimed for herself.

Cassie was sitting in a wobbly, wooden chair, and it trembled a bit as she hurriedly swiped her hands over her cheeks. "I'm not crying," she immediately denied.

He lifted a brow and looked far too old for his fourteen years.

"Fine. I was crying. A little." She sniffed.

He crept toward her. "Because of what I did?"

"No, because of something I did. Something that I wanted to make right. I'm not sure I can anymore." She'd clung to hope for so long, but it was vanishing.

Jamie came closer. Hesitated, then awkwardly patted her shoulder.

Cassie almost started crying again. "We . . . we're still looking for your family, Jamie. The foster family that you were with has moved and—"

"I don't want to go back to them." His voice had chilled.

Frowning, she looked up at him.

"I told you that. Not ever. When I was there, they didn't want me." His shoulders straightened. "They got a check for having me, and that's all they needed."

"Jamie . . ."

"Did your father . . . Did he really make the primals?"

She swallowed the lump that wanted to choke her. Jamie had a right to know. "My father was a scientist. He . . . worked with the paranormals. He was supposed to be making a stronger soldier . . . to help protect the country."

Jamie frowned. "Did he?"

She shook her head. "He got lost." That was the way she'd always thought of him, even as a child. "He stopped noticing the danger of what he was doing. He took humans, tried to give them the strength of vampires, but none of the weaknesses."

Jamie's eyes widened.

"He made the primal vampire virus, then he tried to keep the vampires he'd created contained, but you just can't—" She had to swallow again because that damn lump was choking her. "You just can't hide some things in the dark." Like she'd tried to hide her true identity. Her name wasn't just Cassandra Armstrong. It was Cassandra Armstrong Wyatt.

Jamie studied her a moment, then said, "If you can't cure them, then we have to kill them. Every single one."

Vaughn.

"Not yet," she whispered. "There's still—"

"How many humans are you gonna let die before you realize those primals *all* have to be stopped? Not cured? Just wiped away from the earth." Jamie's hands had fisted at his sides. "We need the freaking marines in here! It's a war—and we have to fight them." He gave a hard shake of his head. "Not cry over them. Not *them.*" He rushed from the room.

She didn't blame him, not for his anger and not for running away. How many times over the years had she wanted to turn and run away?

More than she could count.

But it was her mess. One she'd inherited. One she had to fix.

Her steps were slow but certain as she made her way to the lab.

Eve was there, keeping vigil over Trace, when Cassie entered the room.

Eve glanced up. "Do you think," she began quietly, "that we'll ever cure him?"

"Yes." It was what Cassie had to believe.

And she knew what she had to do.

Dante had said that his tears hadn't healed her in New Orleans. If the tears of a phoenix weren't what she needed, then maybe . . . just maybe . . . she already had the cure.

Inside of her.

"During your research on Genesis, did you come across any information on a Lieutenant Colonel Jon Abrams?" Cassie asked her curiously.

Eve gave a slow nod. She might have attended med

school, but she'd dropped out of the program to pursue her true passion—journalism. Cassie had leaked information about Genesis to her, and then Eve had gone undercover at the facility in order to see firsthand just what was happening.

It was because of Eve that Genesis had been destroyed.

"He was one of the recruits in the shifter program," Eve said slowly. "A success, from all accounts. Enhanced hearing, vision—"

"Strength and speed," Cassie finished. "And he got the bonus of having ready-made weapons in the form of his claws."

"Why are we talking about him?" Eve wanted to know.

Cassie walked toward her instrument tray. "Because Genesis isn't fully dead. Uncle Sam is still conducting experiments, and Jon Abrams was the man handpicked to carry on the work started in my father's labs." Her fingers curled around a scalpel. The sharp blade gleamed. "Jon tracked me when I went to Chicago. He caught me, locked me in an exam room, and then he started . . . taking samples from me."

Eve's chair squeaked as she rose. "What kind of samples?"

Cassie's hold tightened on the scalpel. "The same kind that you're going to help me take now." She couldn't do it on her own. And Charles was gone. She'd seen him slip away earlier. He hadn't stopped to tell her good-bye.

She didn't blame him.

But it still hurt.

"Why did he want samples from you?" Eve asked as she crept closer.

Cassie gave her a sad smile. "You knew my brother."

Eve stilled.

"You had to notice the resemblance," Cassie said. "I've been told that we have the same eyes."

"You do." Quiet. Careful. "But other than your eyes, you

are *nothing* like Richard Wyatt." There was anger there, rage.

Hate.

Most people hated Richard. He'd been as determined to carry through on his twisted experiments as her father had been.

But Cassie didn't hate him. She still remembered a boy who had rushed to her bedside just before her father put her under yet again.

Daddy. Daddy, no! Don't hurt Cass anymore. Use me. Use me, Daddy!

And their father had. He'd started to use them both in his experiments.

Her brother had tried to save her.

Until he'd become twisted, too. From the experiments? She thought so.

"I don't like to remember him the way he was at Genesis," Cassie whispered. "I like to remember the boy he was—when we were both too young to see the monsters."

She looked up and read the pity in Eve's stare. Cassie handed the other woman the scalpel. "My father experimented on me and Richard. He made us different."

"Is your blood poison, too?"

Eve had always been resourceful. Cassie wasn't surprised that the reporter knew Richard's secret.

"To vampires, yes, but I think there's more that is . . . different with me." Cassie stumbled over the words. She had almost said . . . *I think there's more that's wrong with me.* "In New Orleans, I-I think I died when I was attacked by a vampire."

Eve sucked in a sharp breath. "And your Dante saved you?"

Cassie's laugh held a touch of bitterness. "No, I thought . . . He said I healed myself."

Eve blinked.

"So let's find out how I did it, okay? We're going to take samples and we're going to see just what my father may have done to me."

"Uh, fair warning. I never finished med school. That was just a cover, you know that, right?"

"Don't worry. I'll guide you through it."

Eve's breath rushed out on a relieved sigh. "So I'm just taking your blood. Nothing major—"

"No, it will be quite major, but we have to get it done." The secrets that Cassie needed, the cures, could be within her own body. "Just lock the doors. Dante is secure, but I don't want to take any chances on being interrupted."

"Cassie . . ."

"People need our help. Vaughn, Trace. Let's see just what my father did. Maybe we can use it." *Use me.* "And some of the nightmares can end."

Eve gave a grim nod, and they went to work.

"I don't want to kill you," Cain said.

Dante very much doubted that. "Have you killed others of our kind?"

"Have you?" Cain tossed right back.

"Yes."

Cain's hands clenched into fists. "You're the one they kept in the other lab at Genesis, aren't you? The one they called the Immortal."

Dante nodded.

Cain's gaze raked over him. "Were you the first?"

"No."

"Then you don't know, either. You don't know where the hell we came from."

Hell was a pretty apt description. "Our home was on an old volcano. One that was dormant by the time I lived there, but . . . according to the stories, our village was born of that ash. Born from the fire and brimstone and hell that exploded onto earth." Dante had first heard those stories when he'd been a child, running around the countryside with Wren at his back. *Wren.* "From that fire, the phoenix came to be."

Cain just stared at him.

"There were so many of us in the village," Dante said, shaking his head as he remembered what it had been like *before.*

"Until you turned on each other."

"Kill or be killed," Dante murmured. In his mind, he saw the rain of ash that had hit during the deadly battle. A battle started by one woman's whispered word.

"It doesn't have to be that way."

"Are you sure?" Dante pushed him. "Even now, don't you want to go for my throat? Your mate is in this lab. I know exactly what she is. I know her weaknesses, I know—"

"And I know exactly what *your* mate is," Cain snapped out, temper biting in the words. "I know Cassie's weaknesses, but I've never hurt her. I *won't* hurt her. We may have a battle between us, but I don't pull in the innocent."

Dante could respect the other phoenix. He nodded.

"So don't threaten Eve. Don't even look at her sideways."

Dante's brows lifted. "Does your Eve know that you're in here now?" he asked, curious despite himself. The phoenix across from him was not at all what he had expected.

But then, he'd made sure to stay away from other phoenixes, except for the young female in New Orleans that he'd foolishly tried to save a few months back. Too late, he'd realized that she hadn't wanted to be saved from her vampire lover.

"No," Cain said. "Eve is in the lab."

With Cassie and the werewolf. "Why would you let her be near the wolf?"

"Because that wolf was her best friend once, and I owe him. I'll do anything I can in order to make him better."

Again, surprising Dante.

"Would you even give up a phoenix's tears?"

"I'd give up anything to make Eve happy." Said simply and without any hesitation.

Dante frowned at him.

"Now, are we going to rip each other to pieces or what?" Cain asked, sounding bored. "Because I need to get back to Eve's side."

Dante wanted to get back to Cassie's side. Except, she'd imprisoned him.

Cain slanted him an accessing gaze. "You hurt her, you know."

"I did not touch your Eve—"

"No, not Eve. Your Cassie. You hurt her." Cain gave a quick shake of his head. "Not physically, but inside, maybe where the pain can be the worst. Especially for someone like her."

Despite what Cassie had said earlier, Dante realized that Cain knew *exactly* what she was. "Do you hear her song? When she speaks, do you—"

"The power rarely slips into her voice. It's like she's not aware of it."

Because she wasn't.

"When she gets stressed or nervous, it comes through." Cain paused. "It was damn powerful when she was up on the surface and trying to soothe Trace."

Yes, it had been.

"I'd heard stories about her kind," Cain said, "but I'd never met one, not until her. It took me a while to realize what was happening."

That was a siren's power. Before you knew what she was doing, you were already under the spell of her song.

"Is it true that a siren can make you feel the same emotion she feels? When she's happy, her words make you happy, and when she's sad . . . she can gut you?" Cain asked.

"Yes." The word sighed from Dante.

Cassie was sad. That would explain why Dante felt like someone had shoved a knife into his stomach, and twisted it.

"You aren't going for my throat," Cain pointed out as he rolled his shoulders. "Are you waiting for me to make the first move?"

"I killed my own brother," Dante began.

"Uh, yeah. I heard rumors about that bit . . ."

Dante's jaw tightened. "But only after he came at *me*. I will do you . . . the same courtesy." *For Cassie. Because the phoenix held value to her. Because I broke her trust*. He'd acted on instinct and was afraid that act might have cost him something precious. "You can live, until the moment you come at me with death in your eyes."

Surprise flickered over Cain's face. "I don't want your death. We work for the cure, then we go our own separate ways. You won't see me again, and I *won't* see you."

Cain also understood how dangerous phoenixes were to their own kind.

"You've killed other phoenixes," Dante said.

"Some don't want to listen to reason. They attack first, without waiting to see if an enemy is really at their door."

Ah, yes, he saw that hit for exactly what it was.

"Some let their beasts rule them." Cain's stare was hard. "Do you rule your beast? Or does he rule you?"

"It depends on the day."

Cain blinked.

Dante strolled by him. He was ready to ditch that cell. He needed to find Cassie. They had to talk. Had to clear the air between them.

I might have to grovel some. Humiliating, but he'd try it, for her.

Cain had conveniently left the door unlocked. Another point in the fellow's favor. If Dante weren't so worried about dying by the man's hand, he might—

Cassie's blood.

There was no mistaking the scent. No mistaking *her.* He whirled back around to face the other phoenix. *"What have you done?"* Tricked him, kept him busy—while Cassie suffered?

Cain shook his head. "I didn't—"

Dante locked him in the cell and raced toward that scent. With every frantic footstep, the scent deepened.

He shoved open the doors to the lab.

Eve jumped up, yelping. She had on latex gloves—gloves that were stained with Cassie's blood.

"You . . ." Dante began as he closed in on her.

"Stop." Cassie's voice. Weak but steady. "I . . . asked her to do it."

She was on the exam table. So pale.

"You said . . . I cured myself. Have to find out . . . *how.*"

Eve had backed up a step. "She wanted me to do this. I didn't like the plan, but Cassie said—"

"It has to . . . be done."

He crossed to Cassie. Took her hand. Held tight.

"How are you . . . here?" She didn't pull away from him.

Maybe she was in too much pain to pull away. Maybe he was using a weak moment for her. Dante didn't care. He was touching her again. Holding tight to her.

"How are you . . . here?" Cassie asked again as she blinked up at him.

"Cain let me out."

Uh, yeah, and Dante had locked Cain *in*. They'd cover that part, later.

Eve inhaled sharply.

"He's . . . alive?" Cassie asked.

"We came to an agreement." Dante frowned down at her. "How much more has to be done?"

Her smile was weak. "Don't watch, if you . . . don't want."

"I thought you were going to use me. I thought I was the cure you needed."

"Have to hurry . . . every day that passes . . . someone else . . ."

Someone else could be transformed into a primal. Someone else could die, like Jamie's brother.

"Testing me, testing . . . you . . ." Cassie whispered. "Maybe together—"

"We can find a cure," Eve said quietly. She bit her lip. "Should I wait? Should I—"

"Finish," Cassie said quietly. "Please."

He *hated* seeing her like that. But if it was what she needed to do . . .

He held tight to her hand. "Look at me."

Her gaze found his.

"I won't let you down again."

"No more . . . closets?"

He shook his head.

"Don't . . . believe you . . ."

The ache was back in his chest. "Then I'll just have to prove myself to you." He could.

He *would*.

Eve went back to work, and Dante never took his gaze off Cassie's face.

Charles Trenton hurried away from the lab that he'd called home for the last six months of his life. He'd wanted to help Cassie. To make the world safer. Better.

So that no one would end up like Kerri.

Only . . .

He hadn't counted on monsters who could conjure fire or werewolves that tore down doors to get to him.

It was too much.

He was too weak.

He'd always known that Kerri was the strong one. Always Kerri. But she'd been broken . . . and had taken her own life when the experiments got to be too much for her.

I told Genesis about her. That was his secret shame. He'd been the one to first alert Genesis to his half-sister's condition.

Because he'd known that Kerri had always wanted to be normal.

He'd given up his own sister to that hell.

When he'd lost her, he'd wanted to atone. He and Cassie had that in common. The sins of the past often choked them.

He gunned his car's engine and shot out into the night. The car had been hidden in the old shack down the road, out of sight. Safe and secure.

He hadn't told Cassie that he was leaving. He hadn't been able to look her in the eyes—

Not the strong one.

Maybe . . . maybe he'd be able to go back after a few days. Maybe he'd be able to face what waited in Cassie's lab.

His headlights cut through the dark.

Maybe not.

For now, he was just going home. A little town that waited just across the state line in Louisiana. A speck on the map that didn't have monsters or nightmares.

He hoped.

CHAPTER THIRTEEN

When Cassie opened her eyes, the first thing she saw was . . . Dante. He was leaning over her, frowning.

"What have you . . . done now?" Hopefully not attacked Cain again. Or, jeez, not Eve.

"I've stayed by your bedside." His words were soft. "Waiting for you to wake up."

That wasn't what she'd thought to hear. Cassie slowly sat up. "Cain? Eve? They're both still—"

"Alive, yes. Eve, ah, freed her lover, and they're resting somewhere in the lab." Dante's fingers slid over her body. "And you're all healed. Quite amazing."

She didn't feel so amazing. Actually, she felt like she'd been hit by a truck. But there was work to do. "I need to start analyzing the results."

He brought her hand to his lips. Kissed her knuckles.

Her heart beat a little faster.

"I'm sorry for attacking your friend."

She was suspicious. "Is this the part where you think we're gonna kiss and make up?" *Not happening, buddy.*

One brow rose. "That sounds like a good option."

She shoved against his chest. "Think again. You *used* me." She was on her feet. Her first step was a bit wobbly, but by her third, she was in charge of her knees again. "I'm not going to forget that. You knew I trusted you, and you used that trust against me. You—"

"You're the only person who has truly trusted me in centuries." Dante had risen to his feet, too. "I didn't realize . . . what it would be like when your trust was gone."

"Yes, well, realize it now." Her heart was doing a double-time beat then. "I have to work, okay, Dante? We almost lost Trace last night because *you* attacked him. He's stuck now in worse shape than he was before, and I have to figure out a way to heal him."

Dante stared at her. Then he gave a grim nod. "You had your samples taken."

"Yes." She needed to analyze them and—

"Now take mine. Learn all my secrets." He walked closer to her. "I offer them to you."

Wait—*now* he was all about helping?

"Take my blood, my DNA, whatever you need. Take it." He shook his head. "The others experimented on me for years, and they could not replicate my cure. If you cannot succeed in helping the werewolf—"

She couldn't think about failing. Couldn't.

"Then I will help you to . . . ease his suffering."

Cassie stabbed her finger into his chest. "You are *not* killing Trace!" Why was everyone else so fast on the trigger when it came to killing? There were actually other options in the world.

"Sometimes killing is the kinder thing to do."

"No! Give me time, dammit! Give. Me. Time." Her breath huffed out of her chilled lungs. "I can do this." She had to do this.

He headed toward the exam table. Sat on it as he had the night before. But he seemed different. "Run your tests," he ordered. "Do whatever you have to do."

He was . . . helping?

"And in the end, if you need me to do what I must, I will."

Kill Trace.

"We're not at that point yet," she whispered . . . and prayed that they never would be.

Evansville, Louisiana, was a speck on the map. If you blinked, you'd miss it.

That was why Charles loved the place. No crowds. No fast pace. Just the spot to vanish for a while.

He slowly drove down the old highway that led to his grandfather's farm. All of his family members were gone now, but the memories waited there for him and—

The farm was burning. He could see the thick, black smoke drifting in the air.

No!

Charles shoved the accelerator down to the floorboard and gunned the car. The little vehicle jumped and bumped its way down the old road until he brought it to a screeching stop before the farmhouse.

Or what was left of the place.

He climbed from the car and stared at the twisting flames. They'd gutted the farmhouse, and were reaching up for the sky, stretching and destroying *everything.*

The only link he'd still had to his family. To Kerri.

Gone.

With shaking hands, Charles yanked out his cell phone. He had to get the fire department. Had to get some help—

"Well, well . . ."

The voice came from right behind him and had Charles stiffening. He hadn't heard any approaching footsteps. Just the crackle of those flames.

"I had hoped to find you inside, Charles, but when you weren't home, I got a little angry."

He *knew* that voice. Carefully, Charles turned to face the man he'd once worked for.

Lieutenant Colonel Jon Abrams.

"What have you done, Jon?"

The man looked different. His smile was cold and hard and—

Charles crept toward him, then froze when he got a good look at Jon's eyes. There was a fire burning in Jon's eyes. *The gaze of a phoenix.*

"You were always so tight like dear Cassie. Such good friends." Jon took a long, stalking step toward him. "That friendship used to piss me off, just so you know." He drove his fist into Charles's stomach, and Charles howled at the burning pain—and he burned. His shirt burned away and blisters sprang up on his stomach.

Charles staggered away. "J-Jon? What the hell?"

"Did Cassie know about your work with the female phoenix? Did you tell her about our little experiments?"

Charles shook his head. He'd barely worked on those experiments at all, just been backup to the others. He had *hated* the work, and he'd just wanted to help that poor woman escape from her prison.

"Guess what?" Jon came at him again, punching him in the face with that fist of fire. "The experiments worked."

Charles screamed at the pain and hit the ground. There was nowhere for him to go. The flames were behind him. Jon stood in front of his car.

"Cassie was always so fond of you," Jon said again. Then he knelt in front of Charles. "You know where she is, don't you?"

Charles didn't speak. He wouldn't risk Cassie. He could stay quiet. He could stay—

"I plan to burn my way to Cassie. I will destroy everyone and everything in my path." Jon smiled at him.

The smile was that of a monster.

"You can either work with me, Charles, or you can burn right here."

Terror nearly choked him The thought of holding back vanished. He'd never been the strong one.

"You know where Cassie is," Jon muttered. "I *need* her."

Cassie wasn't alone. She had two phoenixes with her—and a freaking werewolf. If Jon went after her . . .

They'll kill you, asshole.

Charles lowered his eyes. It would be okay to give Jon the information. Jon wouldn't hurt him anymore, and Cassie would be plenty safe with all of her monster guards. "I-I know . . ."

"Good. Because you're going to take me to her."

Charles nodded.

And they'll destroy you, Jon. Charles hoped he had a front row seat for the show. The guy had always been a prick.

Her DNA was . . . wrong.

Cassie stared down at the test results. She'd known that her father had altered her, but this—

"Seeing what you are?" Dante asked softly from behind her.

She jumped, then swiveled her chair to face him. "I—there must be some mistake. I'll run the tests again."

"There's no mistake." He was adamant. "You aren't human, and you never were." He wore only a pair of low-slung jeans. He'd ditched his shirt when she took her samples. He stalked slowly toward her. "You're a siren. Deal with it."

Her eyes narrowed. "I don't see how—"

"Conjuring fire is instinctive for me." His head tilted as he studied her. "I figured using your siren's song would be instinctive for you, but it isn't, is it?"

She licked her lips. "No, it isn't."

Siren.

"You used the power in your voice when Trace was attacking up on the surface. You calmed him."

"Is that what my voice does? It calms?"

Dante shook his head. "It can do a hell of a lot more. Get your pitch right. Use the power just right and—"

"You said that you couldn't trust me." The words tumbled from her.

Dante stilled.

"Is it because of what my voice can do? If I use the pitch just right, do you think I'll get you to kill, the way the other siren did?"

"I think you're not like anyone I've ever met before."

Cassie shook her head. "Dante, that's not—"

"A siren can compel. If she sings the right song, if she's strong enough, she can make anyone do anything she wants."

"Do you think I'm strong enough?" She barely breathed the words.

He hesitated.

He doesn't.

"I've been thinking about this," Dante said slowly. "You *should* know how to use your power, but you're a half-breed, so maybe it's not as strong with you. Maybe you can only pull up the power when you're scared or stressed."

Wasn't that her usual way of life, twenty-four seven? She should be bursting with power.

"There's one more time it comes out." He was close enough to touch her.

He did.

His hand lifted. His fingers brushed down her cheek. "It comes out when you're aroused. When the passion heats within you."

Oh. Ah, okay.

"I felt your power when I was with you," he whispered.

His head bent, and his lips brushed lightly over hers. "I want to feel it—*you*—again."

The hunger for him, the lust that he could stir so effortlessly, wanted to rise once more within her. Wanting Dante had always been easy for her.

Pretty much as easy as breathing.

Loving him? So much harder.

He kissed her once more, his tongue licking lightly over her lips. He seemed to enjoy that little lick across her bottom lip.

She sure enjoyed it, too.

Then he pulled away.

"Do your work. Finish your tests. When you're ready for me"—his gaze heated—"come to me."

He turned and walked away.

When the doors closed behind him, Cassie finally sucked in a deep breath.

"There aren't any antibodies," Cassie whispered as she stared at the samples before her. When the primal virus was spread, the host didn't create any antibodies to fight off the disease.

Except . . .

She glanced at her own results. Her breath heaved out. "I *have* the antibodies!" Cassie jumped to her feet. She had to synthesize them. That was going to be tricky. Her blood was poison to the vampires—both a poison and a cure. She had to get the poison out, but still use the antibodies that would help those who'd been infected.

All along, the cure had been right there. Right freaking there. She'd been bitten by a primal, and she hadn't changed. She'd thought the poison in her blood stopped the change. But no, it was so much more than that.

She was the cure.

Jon had actually been right. *It's me.*

She might not be able to help Trace yet, but she could help Vaughn . . . soon. So very soon.

She just had to get the poison out first. Get the poison out, and then she'd have the cure they needed.

Hope grew inside her, and it felt so good. Incredible. No more lives lost to the primal virus. No. *More.*

The doors to the lab flew open.

She spun around, heart racing. "I've almost got—"

Eve was there, looking grim.

"What's wrong?"

"I was watching the security monitors in the outer room. We've got company coming."

Company? "The last phoenix? Is she already—"

"No, it's not Sabine."

Cassie knew Eve had become well acquainted with Sabine's story, especially since Sabine had once come after Cain.

Those phoenixes . . . always trying to kill each other.

"It looks like it's Charles," Eve said, "but he isn't coming back alone."

Cassie headed for her own security monitors. Pulled up the feed.

There was Charles—she saw him climb from a black SUV. There was Charles and—

"Impossible," she whispered.

That could *not* be Jon Abrams exiting the vehicle and coming to stand next to him.

She leaned closer.

The same blond hair. The same hard jaw. The same hawkish nose.

She was staring at a ghost. "He's dead. I saw Jon Abrams die!"

"The guy doesn't look dead to me," Eve muttered.

"I shot him." He'd fallen. He'd been *dead,* hadn't he? It wasn't like she could have mistaken a living man and a dead guy.

Jon shoved Charles toward the hidden entrance, except it wasn't an entrance that was hidden any longer. Charles was walking the guy right up to the supposed-to-be-secret facility.

"Charles knows the code to get inside," Cassie whispered. She counted at least ten armed men with Jon.

If those men got inside . . .

She slammed down the button for the alarm before Charles could reach the key pad. When the alarm was activated, the whole security system went into high alert.

Normal codes were ignored. *I'm sorry, Charles. I can't let them in.*

She knew what Jon would do.

Her fingers frantically flew over the keyboard as she typed in her password, making damn sure that no one would be able to override the system. As long as the alarm mode was set, Jon wouldn't get in.

But those inside also wouldn't get out.

The doors banged again. "What the hell is happening?" Dante demanded.

Cassie glanced over her shoulder. Dante and Cain were both there, looking grim. Behind them, Jamie strained to see over their shoulders.

Fear was bright in his eyes.

"Cassie says a dead man is trying to break into the lab," Eve told them, voice tight. "And that guy Charles led him here."

"I don't think Charles had much of a choice." Cassie could see the side of his face now that he was closer to the security camera. It looked like he'd been . . .

Burned?

Her heart beat faster.

Dante rushed across the room. His shoulders brushed hers as he bent to stare at the screen. "That's the bastard we left at the ranch."

The bastard was up and walking around just fine.

She pushed a few more buttons on the keyboard. Another security feed popped up, and she saw that Charles was trying to input his code.

When the code didn't work, there was no mistaking the look of terror on his face.

Then Charles glanced up. He would know where the small security camera was hidden. He stared right at that camera and mouthed, *please.*

"What happened to his face?" Jamie demanded. He'd crept up beside Dante. "Who is that guy with him?"

"Someone very dangerous," Cassie said as she tried to keep her voice calm. "Jamie, will you go back to your room? Lock the door and stay there."

His eyes widened. "Are they—vampires?" His main fear.

She knew that would always be his fear.

Cassie shook her head. "They're the people who make the monsters."

His eyes hardened. "Then they're like you."

The words hurt, but they were true. She nodded. "Yes."

Dante growled. "Watch it, kid."

She glanced at Dante. "Please, take Jamie to his room. Make sure he's safe."

He nodded, but still gave her a good glare as he ordered, "You stay here until I get back."

Where was she going to go? Their main exit was currently blocked by a group of armed men.

Her gaze slid back to the security feed as Dante took Jamie away.

"Is there a way to get sound on that thing?" Cain asked.

She tapped the audio.

Heard nothing.

Then Jon's gaze rose to the camera. He'd found it, too. "Hello, Cassie."

Chill bumps rose on her arms. The audio was working just fine.

"That bastard sounds familiar to me," Cain said as his gaze turned to Cassie. "Was he at Genesis?"

"Yes," Cassie whispered. "Jon was a . . . successful experiment." *So they'd all claimed.*

"Cassie, open the door and come out to me." Jon's voice was mild. And he kept *smiling.*

"He's insane if he thinks you're going out there," Cain snapped.

Yes, he was insane. She could see that quite clearly.

"If you don't come to me," Jon continued in that same, almost relaxed, voice, "I'm afraid I'll have to hurt your friend here, while you watch. You *are* watching, aren't you, Cassie?"

She couldn't look away. Her eyes were glued to the screen as—as flames flickered over Jon's hand.

Flames?

"What the hell?" Cain was leaning over the screen. "Is he a dragon shifter?"

"No," Cassie whispered. The flames were so close to Charles.

"He's a phoenix?"

"No," she said. At least, he hadn't been. "He was human when he entered the Genesis Program. He was given a splice of shifter DNA, but he *wasn't* a phoenix."

"I'll give him a little burn," Jon said, "just to show you how serious I am."

He put those flames against Charles's right arm.

Charles screamed.

So did Cassie. Her hand slammed down onto the intercom. *"Stop!"*

The flames died away in an instant. "Ah, Cassie, I knew you were there." Jon stared up at the camera. At her. "Now be a good girl . . . *and let me the fuck in.*"

"What's happening?" Jamie demanded, huffing out fast breaths.

Dante knew the kid was rushing to keep up with his footsteps, but there was no way they could slow down. He wanted the boy safe and secure, and he wanted to be back at Cassie's side.

"Who was that guy with Charles? Is he—"

"He's someone who should be dead." Dante planned to correct that problem at the very first opportunity. He pushed open the door to Jamie's room. "Stay here. Keep the door bolted, and no matter what you hear, don't come out until I come back for you."

Jamie's eyes filled his face. "What are you going to do?"

"I'm gonna get rid of the unwelcome company at the door." Dante turned away.

But Jamie grabbed his arm. "You won't . . . die will you?" There was fear in the boy's voice.

He had known fear too much in his short life.

"Death doesn't stop me."

Jamie's lashes dropped. "You're not scared of anything. I-I want to be like you."

"No, trust me. You don't." When Jamie's gaze lifted once more, Dante pointed at him. "Stay here. I'll come back for you."

Jamie stumbled back with a quick nod. Dante hurried out, but he heard the lock engage behind him.

He'd be back for the kid as soon as he dealt with that ass Jon Abrams. The man had followed them all the way to Mississippi? Talk about a fucking thorn in their sides.

The lieutenant colonel was overdue for his trip to hell.

* * *

Jamie stared at the closed door. Whoever that man was outside, he was dangerous. Cassie had been afraid of him.

Dante hadn't.

But then, Dante feared nothing.

He just faced whatever threat was there. Eliminated it.

Fear didn't control him.

Jamie glanced toward the broken wooden chair in his room. Charles was outside. No one would be in his room. Before he'd cut out, had he left his keycard behind again? Before, it had just been tossed onto the small desk in his room.

Dante feared nothing.

Jamie wanted to be like Dante. He didn't want to fear the monsters anymore.

Everyone else . . . was busy with that guy—had Cassie called him Jon? They wouldn't be paying any attention to the vampire that was locked up.

No attention at all.

Jamie grabbed a few of those broken chunks of wood. He'd just see if Charles had left his keycard behind.

And if he had . . .

I will be like Dante.

He wouldn't fear anyone.

Or anything.

"Let him in," Cain said as his fist hit the table. "We'll give the bastard a welcome that he won't soon forget."

Cassie shook her head. "He died, I know he did." He'd died—and now the guy was conjuring fire. "He's . . . he's become a phoenix." It should have been impossible.

But these days, *nothing* seemed impossible. Not with science and magic at play.

"You don't *become* a phoenix," Cain immediately argued. "You're born one. You—"

More fire was spinning out there.

"Maybe you don't have to let me in," Jon snarled. That calm veneer was cracking with every second that passed. "Maybe I'll just kill him in front of you, and then I'll set the building on fire until you have no choice but to flee."

"He's a dead man," Cain said. The words sounded like a vow. Probably were.

Eve wrapped her hand around his arm. "Jon Abrams has some very powerful allies in the government." Her gaze slid to Cassie. "Genesis isn't ever going to be truly dead, is it?"

No, it wasn't. As for being dead, Jon obviously wasn't, either.

"I can't let him kill Charles." Cassie *couldn't* let him die. Charles was her friend.

Two men in black—one carrying a small briefcase—rushed toward the sealed door upstairs.

"They'll get through sooner or later," Jon said as his gaze cut to the security camera. "The longer it takes, the angrier I become."

Charles was trembling beside him.

"Let me in," Jon snarled.

Cassie's mind raced. She'd been so close to the cure. So close. She needed more time. Time that Jon wasn't going to give her.

She focused on Eve. "You have to get out of here."

Eve blinked at her. "Don't you mean *we* have to get out?" she asked carefully.

Cassie shook her head. "Jon might not even know you're here. He's after me. You can take my test results—and go. There's an emergency tunnel that will spit you out half a mile from here. Jon won't look for you there—"

"Unless Charles has told him about it," Cain cut in, his voice tight. "The way that poor bastard is hurting, I think he's telling everything he knows."

I can't let him hurt anymore.

Cassie spun away from the screen. She grabbed samples of her blood. Dante's. Got her results. She was racing as she secured them all in a container that would keep them safe. "Here." She shoved the container at Eve. "Take these. *Go.*"

Cassie couldn't open the door upstairs until they'd gotten a solid head start.

"You really think your Dante is gonna let you go out there and face that guy?" Cain demanded. His big body had tensed. "I can go ahead and tell you, that's *not* happening."

Dante isn't going to have a choice. "Charles isn't dying," Cassie stated forcefully.

"I'm waiting, Cassie!" Jon shouted. Oh, yes, that calm mask had shattered.

She knew he wouldn't wait much longer. Quickly, Cassie pressed the intercom button. "It takes a while to dis . . . disengage the security system. I'm working as fast as I can!"

He stilled. "You're lying. I can hear it in your voice."

Cassie glanced at Eve. "Go, please. Take the tunnel. I'll meet you in New Orleans. We can meet up at Vaughn's dad's place." It was the safest rendezvous point that Cassie could think of. "Midnight tomorrow. I will be there."

Or she'd be dead.

Eve nodded. She knew all about Vaughn and his father—they'd also been tied to Genesis.

After a grim moment, Cain took Eve's hand, and they ran for the door.

Cassie sucked in a couple of deep, hard breaths. *Think, think!* She had to keep Jon out of the lab. Had to keep Vaughn and Trace and Jamie safe.

And Dante . . .

If she went out there to Jon, would he leave the lab alone? There was a chance he might just take a deal. A big *might*. Her fingers trembled, but she pressed the intercom once more. "I come to you, and that's it. You let Charles go. You leave."

"You're hardly in the position to bargain!"

"Fine, then I don't come to you, and I stay in here and I shove a knife into my chest." Totally bullshitting. Would he be able to hear that lie, too? *Please, don't.* "Then you can get the samples from my dead body—how about that? Will that work for you?"

His eyes widened. "Don't!"

Maybe she did have some power.

Jon hesitated, then spat out, "Fine. You come up to me. When I've got you, I'll send good old Charles here down." His smile was dark and twisted. "But get your ass up here now, Cassie. *Now.*"

She jumped back and whirled for the door.

She found her path blocked by one very enraged phoenix shifter.

CHAPTER FOURTEEN

Jamie had found Charles's keycard tossed away. His fingers were slick with sweat as he slid it across the panel that secured the vampire's room. The vampire—Vaughn—would be in there, waiting.

The door opened soundlessly. Jamie had his stake in his hand. He wouldn't hesitate this time. Not even for a second. He'd go in, and he'd make the kill.

I won't be afraid.

He'd be just like Dante.

Jamie stepped into the room. His gaze scanned to the left. To the right.

He didn't see the vampire. But, the guy had to be there, right? He had to be.

"Hellooo . . ." the vampire whispered. He lunged at Jamie.

The guy had been on the freaking *ceiling.*

"Heard you . . . coming . . ." His teeth went for Jamie's throat.

"You are not going out there." There was no way Dante was letting Cassie risk her life.

"I can't let Charles die!"

"He won't. I'll go drag his ass back inside." Easy enough. There was no need for Cassie to be at risk.

But she was shaking her head at him, sending her dark hair tumbling over her shoulders. "Jon will attack you—"

Uh, yeah. Dante was a phoenix. Was that supposed to scare him?

"Let him try."

"He's controlling fire. He *died*. He's like you," she said, voice rising. "And if he's like you—"

She thought that jerk was strong enough to send him to hell, for good?

Dante pulled her into his arms. Kissed her. Hard. Demanding. "He's another experiment." He knew that had to be the case. He just didn't understand how the hell it had come to be. A phoenix made, not born? "He's new, and I've got plenty of age on my side." Like vampires, a phoenix's power increased with age. "I can defeat him."

"Dante, I won't let—"

"Sweetheart, don't make me shove you in a closet again."

Her eyes slit. "Try it and you won't like where I shove you back."

He kissed her again. "Let me fight this one. You keep working on your cure."

He did not want her facing Jon again. That man had hurt her, tracked her—that guy deserved a beat down.

Or a burn down.

But then Dante heard a scream. A long, terror and pain filled cry.

Cassie's breath caught. "Is that . . . Jamie?"

He'd left the kid in his room. He'd made sure he was safe.

Cassie ran for the doors.

"I'm done waiting!" Jon shouted at the same instant. "Charlie boy is dying now, and that death is on you!"

Dante caught Cassie's shoulders. "Find Jamie," he told her as he felt a tremble ripple through her body. "Make sure he's all right. I've got the bastard upstairs."

She nodded quickly, then she was running down the hallway.

Dante waited until she vanished then he headed for the elevator. He'd heard the deal that Cassie had made with Jon. She'd been going to exchange her life for Charles's.

He wondered just what kind of deal Jon would offer him. Not that it mattered.

Death was all the bastard would get.

Vaughn was loose.

Cassie stared at the open door to the vampire's cell, her heart thundering in her chest. The door should have been sealed.

A keycard had been tossed on the floor. *Charles's keycard.* And that had been Jamie's scream. It had come from that room, she was sure of it.

Jamie had gone after the vampire again.

"Help . . ."

Cassie rushed inside. She didn't have any weapons with her, no drugs at all, but she couldn't leave Jamie in there alone, because that was *his* voice whispering for help.

And there he was. Curled into a fetal position near the far wall, with blood around him. Jamie was hunched, rocking back and forth, whispering, "Help . . ."

Her heart ached as she ran to him. "Jamie. Jamie, I'm here!"

But where was Vaughn? She didn't see him anywhere. Had he gotten out after attacking Jamie?

When she touched Jamie, he screamed and tried to leap back. "Get away! Get away! I'll kill you!"

"No, it's not Vaughn. It's me." She tried to make her voice soothing. Dante kept saying she had power with her voice, she could sure use some of that power right then. "It's Cassie. I'm here to help you."

Tears leaked down his cheeks. "There's no way to help me." His breath sawed from his lungs. "H-he bit me."

The primal virus.

She grabbed Jamie's arm. "Come with me to the lab, *now.*"

"I'm dead! I'm *dead*!" He jerked away from her and bent to grab a chunk of wood. Then he was back, his hands shaking, as he grabbed her fingers and curled them around the wood. "Don't let me change." He brought her fingers—and the stake—up over his heart. "I don't wanna change. I don't wanna be . . . like that."

He was surprisingly strong, and she had to yank with all her might to get that stake away from him. *"No!"* Cassie yelled because he wasn't listening to her. He was trying to die right in front of her.

But at her yell, Jamie stilled.

"There's time." Those words were a lie. He already had the virus in him. "Come to my lab." She'd never had a sample from someone so newly exposed. Maybe there was something she could do. Maybe. *Please.* "Come with me."

"Promise . . . first. Kill me if . . ."

She wasn't making that promise. *"Come with me."*

He nodded.

She didn't drop the stake. Vaughn was out there. Somewhere. Cassie didn't know what he might do, and she had to keep some kind of weapon ready.

They raced down the hallways, their footsteps pounding as the alarm kept blasting. Jamie's blood made a trail behind them.

There was no sign of Vaughn. Yet.

At the lab, she pushed open the doors and they ran inside. Cassie grabbed a syringe and took some of Jamie's blood.

Then she got to work, checking the sample, using her microscope—

The cells were already changing. Mutating so quickly.

"How is it?" Jamie whispered.

"It's going to be fine," she told him, her voice wooden. "Just . . . give me a few minutes."

The cure was in her blood, but she didn't know how to get out the poison. He was changing into a vampire right then, and her blood was poison to vampires—

Cassie stilled.

He hadn't changed fully, not yet.

Jamie was still human. Primarily. But every second that passed would change that fact.

Her blood wouldn't kill him as long as he was human. But when the change was complete . . .

Cassie whirled toward him. "Jamie, I want you to trust me."

His eyes were wild and desperate. "I . . . feel it . . . inside . . ."

"*Trust me,* Jamie."

He gave her a slow nod. "What do I have to do?"

"Take my blood." If she was right on this, her blood would either cure him.

Or it would kill him.

Dante was ready when the elevator doors slid open. Jon had whirled toward him in surprise. Had the fool really expected Cassie to come up?

Dante didn't waste time. He lunged forward and snapped Jon's neck before the man could do more than send tendrils of smoke from his fingertips.

Jon's eyes were wide with shock as he fell to the ground.

Jon's men immediately started shouting and aimed their guns at him. Yes, it was what he'd expected, too.

The bullets sank into Dante's chest.

One bullet hit Charles. Sent the man's blood spattering into the air. Charles was yelling, trying to grab for Dante.

It all happened in just a few seconds' time. The elevator doors hadn't even shut yet . . .

Not yet.

Dante grabbed Charles and threw him past those open elevator doors.

More bullets hit then, driving into Dante's back. His legs stopped working, and he fell to the ground.

The doors shut.

He knew death was close. "Get the fuck . . . back . . ." Dante snarled, and he sent his fire racing toward the men with guns.

Their weapons melted. They got the fuck back.

He lifted his hand. Tried to reach for the elevator.

His blood smeared the panel.

His heart began to slow.

His body sagged. His gaze slid to Jon. Jon had died first. Would the bastard rise first, too? The phoenix who rose first would have the killing advantage. If Jon got to his feet, if the man got his power back first . . .

Dante's breath stilled in his lungs.

"What just happened?" Jamie whispered. The boy was shaking from head to toe. He'd taken her blood. He'd been so scared, but he *had* taken it, and then his gaze had fallen on the security feeds.

She'd been caught by those feeds, too. Dante had killed Jon, but then . . .

Dante.

"Stay here!" Cassie ordered Jamie. He wasn't stable, not by a long shot. She didn't know what effect, if any, her blood was going to have on him. He hadn't died right after taking it. That was a good sign, right?

As long as he didn't have some kind of delayed reaction, he just might be all right.

Please, be all right.

She quickly disengaged the security system for the elevator. She needed it to rise and open easily from the inside and outside—in case she and Dante got stuck out there. A few more clicks on the keyboard . . . *There.*

Her shoes slapped against the tile as she ran for the elevator. The doors had already opened. Charles stood there, eyes glassy, blood dripping down his arm. "C-Cassie?"

She grabbed him. Pulled him out of that elevator even as she jumped on it. "Get to the lab! Watch out for Jamie!"

Charles shook his head. "What?"

"He was bitten. I gave him my blood—"

The doors shut on her before she could explain any more. Hopefully, there would be time for a full explanation later. *Hurry. Hurry.* The elevator seemed to take forever to move. And then . . .

The doors opened.

At first, she couldn't even see through the smoke. It was too thick. Dark and heavy, it choked her as she jumped out of the elevator. "Dante!"

Where were the men with guns? Dante's fire had blasted them back, but she knew they weren't gone for good.

She tripped over something. Something heavy and still. She reached down, searching, and felt the strong curve of a man's shoulder. "Dante?" she whispered.

Over to the right, she finally saw something through the smoke.

She saw fresh flames quivering to life.

Jon was rising.

He was rising, but Dante was . . . still beneath her touch.

No. She grabbed Dante's arms and started dragging him back toward that elevator. They'd get down to the lower floor, then he could heal. All she had to do was buy him some time. Just a little time.

When he rose, would he even remember her?

Coughing, choking on that smoke, she made it to the elevator. Dante weighed a ton, but she wasn't about to let him go.

The flames were burning brighter, and Dante's arms . . . had started to feel warmer beneath her hands.

He was coming back to her.

He just needed to hurry the hell up. Or rather, hurry *out* of hell. She punched in her code at the elevator's security panel. The elevator door slid open and she started to drag Dante inside.

"Shoot her! Don't let her leave!" A woman's voice, cutting through the smoke.

More gunfire erupted. Blasting. A bullet whipped right by Cassie, burning her cheek. But then—

Something lunged out of those open elevator doors.

No, not quite something . . .

Someone.

She caught the wild, woodsy scent. *Trace*. He'd gotten loose—everyone was loose—and he was attacking.

Snarls and growls filled the air.

The woman screamed, a high-pitched, desperate sound.

More gunfire. *Rat-a-tat*.

Cassie kept the elevator door open. "Trace! Come back!"

Flames began to flicker over Dante's body. She realized that if Trace came into that elevator with them . . . *he'll die.* Dante might not hurt her when he rose, but Cassie had no clue what he'd do to a werewolf.

Heart racing, she looked up. She saw Trace's glowing eyes. "Run," she told him, focusing completely on the werewolf. "Get out of here. Don't stop for anyone or anything. You find Eve's scent. You follow it. You *follow it*!"

Did he even understand her at all? In that instant, with such wildness and fury in his stare, she wasn't sure.

But then the werewolf leaped away. The elevator's doors closed.

And the fire spread along Dante's body.

She inched back, trying to flatten herself against the right wall. Dante was in the middle of the elevator, sprawled on the floor, and the flames were rising. Rising . . .

The doors opened, and she jumped out. The fire lanced over her skin. The flames crackled. Cassie opened up the control pad and did a fast and frantic override of the system. Now that they were back down below, she didn't want that elevator going anywhere. And if the guys upstairs couldn't get down through the elevator . . .

It will buy us time.

Time that she desperately needed.

She stared at Dante. Watched those flames burn. He'd be back to her soon. She just hoped he came back sane.

She'd seen a few of his risings during his time at Genesis when he hadn't come back sane. She'd gotten lucky the last time he rose. He'd remembered her. If he didn't remember her this time . . .

He could kill us all.

The first moments after a rising were the most dangerous.

She wanted to stay with him, but there were others in that place who needed her.

Cassie spun on her heel and rushed back to Jamie and Charles. She shoved against the doors to her work room, but the doors wouldn't open. Her fist banged against them. "Charles! Charles, it's me! Let me in!"

"Is the phoenix with you?" His voice broke with fear.

"No." *Not yet.* "Hurry, open the door!"

She heard the slide of a bolt—the very large bolt that she'd never used but Charles sure seemed familiar with—and then the doors were opening. Breath heaving, she hurried into the lab. "How's Jamie, is he—"

He was strapped to a table. Convulsing.

Her heart stopped. Her blood hadn't worked.

It was killing him.

He knew only the fire. Consuming. Burning. Twisting. He could hear screams, but there were always screams in hell.

The fire of the phoenix came from the bowels of hell.

He felt hands on him, claws that tried to hold him back and stop him from rising.

But he had to rise.

Someone waited on him.

An enemy?

A lover?

Both.

The memories were there, just out of his grasp, burned by the fire that whispered to him. The fire that told him . . . he was strong. The others were weak.

He could destroy.

He could take.

He could do anything he wanted.

And still the fire burned. Burned and burned even as his eyes opened.

The flames had spread from him, scorching the floor beneath him and rising to lick at the walls and ceiling.

He climbed to his feet as his gaze swept around the area. No one else was there.

An alarm was shrieking—a loud cry that annoyed him. And water was shooting from the ceiling.

The water didn't stop his fire. Nothing could stop it.

Then he looked down, past his flames. On the floor, he saw drops of blood.

He inhaled, caught the scent, and the phoenix that he was—the beast that had taken over—knew the hunt was starting.

The flames followed him as he went after his prey.

* * *

"His blood pressure is skyrocketing!" Cassie tried to hold Jamie down.

Poor Jamie—he was so young. So terribly young. His eyes were rolling back into his head, and a keening cry broke from his lips.

"I'm sorry," she whispered.

But sorry wasn't going to save him.

"What happened to the phoenix?" Charles asked. He was still by the door, seemingly frozen.

"He's burning, rising." She couldn't deal with that, too. She gave Jamie an injection. "Come on. Don't do this. *Stay with me.*"

"Rising?" Charles's voice had sure, ah, risen too.

Then she heard him swearing.

The giant bolt—one that was the length of the swinging lab doors, slid into place. Locking them in.

Her gaze flew to him. Charles was shaking his head. "He's not getting in. He's *not*!"

Unfortunately for them, Cassie didn't think that metal bar would be providing them with a whole lot of protection. When faced with a phoenix's fire, the metal would melt.

Dante *would* get in.

One crisis at a time. She sucked in a deep breath and focused on Jamie once more. He wasn't shaking anymore, and his blood pressure was slowly getting back within the normal range.

Hope began to whisper in her heart. *Live.*

Sweat coated his body as if a fever had just broken. She picked up his hands. Studied his nails. No claws. She opened his mouth. Regular teeth. No fangs.

She took some of his blood and rushed to her microscope. Eyes narrowing, Cassie stared down at the specimen.

His blood cells were—not normal, but . . .

Not primal.

The cells weren't mutating into the primal form. In fact, they looked very similar to her own.

"Without the poison," she whispered, prayed. If his blood was clear, if he could make antibodies for the virus that didn't contain the poison of her blood, then they'd just found the cure.

She was the one shaking.

"Do— do you smell smoke?" Charles asked as he hurried away from the door.

Yes, she did. Had been smelling it ever since she'd left Dante in that elevator.

"Jamie?" Cassie whispered. "Jamie, can you open your eyes for me?"

His breath sighed out.

"I-I can't see anything on the monitors outside," Charles said. "The smoke and fire are too thick."

"Jamie?" Cassie fought to keep her own voice calm. "I need you to open your eyes. Look at me." She'd seen other primal transformations, and, by this point, the victims already had their fangs and claws. The treatment *was* working.

Jamie's lashes flickered. When his lashes lifted, she saw that his gaze was blurry. Lost. "Am I . . . dead?"

She threw her arms around him and hugged him tight. "No, you're very much alive." Tears stung her eyes.

He stiffened and tried to shove her away. "No, he bit me, I—"

Cassie didn't let him go. "You're the same. No fangs. No claws."

He shuddered against her. She eased back just a bit and hurriedly got the straps off him so he could sit up. Jamie stared down at his hands with stunned eyes, and then he reached up to touch his teeth. "How . . ."

"You did it," she told him, unable to stop smiling. "Your blood—mixed with mine—*you* made the cure."

He shook his head.

"We can stop the spread of the virus." And, maybe, with a little more work, she might even be able to revert those who were already primals.

"Th-that smoke is getting thicker. *It's coming under the doors*!"

Cassie's head jerked up at Charles's shout. He was right. Smoke was coming under the doors.

Where don't you want to be when a brutal fire is coming toward you? *Trapped underground, with no windows.*

There was only one way out of her lab room—through that barred door.

She could hear the crackle of flames coming closer and closer.

Charles turned to her. "What are we going to do?"

Sweat trickled over her skin. It was getting so hot in that room. Too hot. The smoke was making Jamie cough. "We have to get out. The tunnel . . . It's the only way." They couldn't go back up in that elevator. Fire waited in the elevator, above the elevator—and Jon had to be up there some place, too.

I can't face him now.

She already had one phoenix to deal with.

"We have to get out." Cassie was coughing, but she rushed toward the door. She reached for the bar—and it scorched her fingers. The heat near the door was blistering. Gasping, she jumped back.

Her gaze flew around the lab. She'd have to find something to use for prying up that bar. If she used her hands, she'd get second or third degree burns. Her gaze locked on the closet and the trusty mop she'd used before. She rushed for the closet.

The doors flew in behind her, bringing in more smoke and flames. Cassie slipped, hitting the floor. She rolled over and looked up—and stared into the burning stare of a phoenix shifter.

"We are so dead," came the frightened rasp from Charles.

Cassie shook her head. No way. They weren't dead yet. And she didn't plan on any of them dying soon.

She rose on knees that wanted to shake, but forced herself to hold steady. "Dante." If he remembered her, then this part would be a piece of cake. He'd kill his flames, and they'd all get out of there, no problem.

Easy.

His burning stare locked on her—with no recognition whatsoever.

It wasn't going to be a piece of cake.

"Dante!" She said his name, louder, harder. "Stop the flames!"

He didn't stop them. So much for that siren power.

"You're going to kill us!"

No response. Despite the blistering heat, her skin was chilled.

Cassie crept toward Charles and Jamie. Charles had gotten the boy off the table and was trying to shield Jamie with his body. Cassie lightly touched Charles on the shoulder.

The flames seemed to surge higher.

He doesn't remember me.

Which meant she had to be very, very careful.

"I'm going to distract him," Cassie whispered to Charles. "When I do, you and Jamie run like hell to the tunnel. Don't stop until you have fresh air in your lungs. And then . . . suck in that air and keep running."

Charles grabbed her hand. "Are you *crazy*?"

The flames definitely surged higher again. Dante's fire-filled stare centered solely on Cassie.

"Quite possibly," she confessed. "Get out of here, head to Vaughn's father in New Orleans. We'll meet you there at midnight." The same thing she'd told to Eve. "Tell him . . . tell him that I think Jamie is the cure."

Charles's fingers clenched around hers. "And *tell me* that you'll be right behind us."

"I'll be right behind you," she whispered.

His eyes were sad. "Cassie, you always were such a terrible liar."

She stepped in front of Charles and Jamie. "Dante!"

No flicker of recognition.

But he'd told her that a siren could soothe a phoenix's beast. She was supposed to be a siren, so she could do this, right?

She moved toward Dante. Fire was eating at the walls of her lab, and the smoke was going to choke her if she wasn't careful. But she *had* to get Dante away from the exit.

Then she could focus on living and breathing.

"Dante, come to me." She raised her hand. Tried to tamper down her fear and just project—hell—she wasn't even sure what she was projecting. But she was scared and most definitely stressed, and he'd told her that he thought her power came out at times like that.

He was advancing toward her.

Charles and Jamie began to edge to the side. *Yes, yes. Keep going.*

"Your fire will burn me," Cassie said, locking her gaze on Dante. "Do you want that? Do you want to hurt me?"

An expression of confusion crossed his face.

"Do you know me at all?" She eased a bit to the right.

He followed her.

Cassie took another two cautious steps to the right, then back.

Again, he followed . . . and opened up the escape path for Charles and Jamie.

They ran for the doors.

Dante never looked their way.

"Please remember me," Cassie said as she stood there, trapped by the fire and by him. "Dante, tell me that you know I'm—"

"Mine," he growled as he reached for her.

She tensed up, expecting to feel the scorch of the fire, but she just felt his warm, strong fingers curl around her shoulders.

She stared into his eyes. The beast he carried was right there, glaring back at her. She wanted to see the man he was—the man that his rising had made him forget.

She'd never asked him what it was like each time he died. She'd heard the whispers at Genesis. The stories that said a phoenix actually went to hell, that it was the hellfire itself that brought him back.

The fire had to come from somewhere, didn't it?

Just what did Dante see when he died?

"Mine," he said again, as if claiming her. His hold tightened.

When they'd talked before . . . when she'd told him that she wished there was a way for him to always remember her, he'd said that a siren could lure and control with her voice—and her kiss.

Just kiss me, he'd said, but no smile had lifted his lips.

Yeah, right, I'll just go through the flames and put my mouth on yours. She'd been mocking at the time.

Cassie swallowed. She wasn't exactly flush with options. "Remember me," she whispered, then she closed the distance between them. She wrapped her arms around his shoulders and rose onto her tiptoes. Her lips pressed to his.

CHAPTER FIFTEEN

She tasted of sweetness and sin. Her lips were soft and open beneath his, and her tongue pushed lightly into his mouth.

Mine. It was the thought he'd had when he'd first seen her, surrounded by his flames.

And it was the same thought he had as he tasted her.

His hands were around her, holding her tight, pressing her harder against him. She wore clothes. He didn't. His had been—burned away?

He tried to grab for the memories, but they were just out of reach. All he could remember was fury and fire and—

My need for her.

He deepened the kiss, taking more from her, desperate for that sweet sin. He lifted her up against him so he could control the kiss.

Control her.

She was important, this woman with the dark hair and the green eyes that had shone with her fear, even as she called out to him.

Dante.

His name. He'd known it when it came from her lips.

He thrust his tongue into her mouth. Wanted to thrust into *her.*

But that alarm was still shrieking, and water was shooting down on them in *this* room, too.

He lifted his head. Didn't let her go.

The water soaked her, him, but the cool liquid didn't stop his fire. Only he could stop that.

"If . . . if you don't put out the flames, I could die," she told him, her voice husky.

He killed the flames.

The water continued to pour down on them.

"Th-thank you." Her voice was . . . soothing.

The phoenix liked it. Wanted to hear more.

"We need to get out of here. We have . . . enemies close by. We have to run, Dante. Do you understand that? We *have* to run."

He didn't want to run. He wanted to fuck. Her.

Her gaze searched his. "Tell me that you're starting to remember."

Fire. Screams. Hell.

"Not yet, huh?" She exhaled and rolled her shoulders back. "Okay. At least I'm still alive and the fire's out. We'll just do this one step at a time."

She tried to pull away.

He yanked her right back against him and kissed her again. Harder. Deeper.

He wanted more of the sin.

She kissed him back, her tongue sliding against his, and the lust burned through him as powerfully as the flames. He would take her there. Learn all of her, experience—

Her hands shoved against him. "We can't! We're in danger here!"

She's in danger?

"Our enemies will find a way to get to us if we don't move. I told you, we have got to get out of here."

He wasn't worried about enemies, but he didn't want her afraid.

"We have to go now," she said, her voice seeming to echo with desperation, and he was powerless to refuse her.

She took his hand and rushed toward the smoldering doors. "There's a secret tunnel." She stopped and coughed. The smoke was thick. "We need to get to that tunnel, but—" She spun back toward Dante, eyes wide. "Vaughn!"

She was pushing Dante aside. Typing on a computer and staring at the screens around her, even as the water continued to soak her clothes and skin. "He's not here," she whispered, shaking her head. "He has to be . . . *the tunnel.*"

Dante saw what she was viewing. A man with dark hair was running through a small opening in the wall.

"He got out, but we've got to stop him! We can't let him bite anyone."

Bite?

"Let's go!" She grabbed Dante's arm again. Trying to pull him.

He frowned at her. "Mine."

She slapped her chest. "Cassie, okay? Just call me Cassie and let's get out of here."

He'd rather call her his.

But he ran with her through the doors and down the hallway. Her wet clothes clung tightly to her body, and his gaze fell on her ass.

"Focus!" she called back to him. "Dante—here." She tossed him a pair of jeans that she'd just jerked from some type of storage locker.

He pulled on the jeans. She stared at him a moment, and he saw the same fear lurking in her gaze once more.

He didn't want her to be afraid. Not ever.

"Stay with me." Her stare held his.

Always.

They ran, twisting through the halls, and he soon found

himself in front of the same narrow entrance that he'd seen on her computer screen.

I remember computers. I remember alarms. He knew what all of those things were. *Why not her?*

But he did remember her . . . Cassie's taste had been familiar to him.

She slipped into the tunnel first, and he followed right behind her. Though it took a bit more maneuvering for him to slide through that narrow entrance.

"Charles and Jamie left the door open," she murmured. "That's how Vaughn saw it. He's in here somewhere, so stay on guard."

She yanked the tunnel door closed behind them.

Instantly, they were in darkness.

He could see perfectly.

He heard her sharp gasp.

"Your eyes are still burning."

His beast was very much in control. He wanted to burn and destroy everything in sight but she was keeping him in check.

"You can see, can't you?" she whispered. She'd put her hands on the left wall and was carefully walking forward in the dark.

"Yes."

"Good. Because if you see a very hungry vampire coming toward us, give a warning shout, okay?"

Dante saw no point in bothering with such a shout. "I'll just burn him."

"Ah . . . he's kind of a friend. So focus on the shout." She stumbled, righted herself, and kept going. "The tunnel is half a mile in length. Once we get clear, we'll hit the woods and try to find some transportation."

Transportation, in the woods?

Her breathing seemed loud in the tunnel. Fear still rode

her heavily, and he didn't want that. He reached out for her, curling his fingers over her shoulder.

He heard a loud boom from behind them—and the whole tunnel started to shake.

"Was that an explosion?" Cassie whispered. Debris began to rain down on them.

From the sound of things, yes, it had been an explosion, and the tunnel was collapsing. Giant chunks of the ceiling hit the ground.

"Dante . . ." The fear had thickened in her voice.

He didn't waste time telling her to run. She couldn't see in the dark like he could. He picked her up, held her slight body tightly in his arms, and raced through the falling tunnel.

The air became thicker the farther he went. He could discern no light up ahead. He said nothing to Cassie, not wanting her to know what he worried—

That they were trapped in the darkness.

More explosions seemed to rock the building behind them. The enemies that Cassie had spoken of—it seemed as if they were trying to blast their way to her.

Dante inhaled deeply, trying to catch a scent past the smoke and dirt. He needed fresh air. Needed an escape for them.

Got it. He pushed forward, moving even faster, and then he saw it. Not in front of him, but above him. A thin stream of light coming from the ceiling.

There was a ladder to the left, one built into the wall. Cassie climbed up first, and he saw her hand punch out at the ceiling, only it wasn't really a ceiling. The wood above them swung open—a trapdoor. And more light shone down on them. She jumped off the ladder, and he rushed up after her.

They were in a cabin, an old, musty cabin. Someone had left a lantern on the floor, and that was where the light had come from.

"We did it," Cassie whispered.

Dante wasn't so sure that they'd done anything, not yet. "This place isn't safe." His body was taut, on edge with tension. Because he could *feel* danger lurking close by.

He went to the door, yanked it open, and stared into the night.

"We'll have to meet the others," Cassie whispered behind him. "But first we have to find Vaughn. He's a primal vampire and I can't let him stay loose on—"

A loud scream split the night.

Dante tensed.

That scream had come from the right . . . about thirty yards away. In those thick woods.

He stalked forward. The scent of blood teased his nose.

The scream came again, but was abruptly choked off. Dante kept gazing into the darkness.

Cassie ran by him, rushing toward the right and that scream. Her move made no sense to him. Why? Why would she rush *to* danger?

But if Cassie was going that way, so was he. Dante lunged after her.

Gone.

Jon watched the flames consume what was left of Cassie's secret lab. Oh, but she'd thought she was clever.

She was wrong.

The flames were crackling as they shot higher into the sky. The explosions had started moments before. Destroying. There would be only rubble and ash left when he was done.

"Was she in there?" Shaw asked as she crept toward him. She wasn't the only one giving him a wide berth. Most of his men looked at him with fear in their eyes.

He'd just risen before them.

They were right to fear him.

"The phoenix wouldn't let her die." He was certain of that. "He got her out." The question was . . . how.

Jon turned away from the fire. "Every Genesis lab that I've ever been in has an emergency exit. Cassie would have made sure that her lab had one, too."

Shaw's eyes widened.

"Get a map of the area. I want to search every building, every cabin, every damn shack within a two mile radius." An emergency escape had to lead somewhere. When he found that place, he'd find Cassie.

"Are you . . . are you all right?" Shaw asked him carefully.

"Of course. I'm fine, I—"

She pointed to his arms. His face. "You have blisters on you. From the fire."

He stilled. He hadn't even felt the pain, but as he lifted his arms, he saw the marks that ran from his wrists to his elbows.

Phoenixes weren't supposed to be hurt by the fire.

But then, he hadn't been born a phoenix.

Shit. I need more injections.

More tears from a phoenix.

"Get that search going!" Jon snarled. He'd get his tears, either from Dante or . . .

The female phoenix.

The weak, nearly broken phoenix who had family in New Orleans. Jon hadn't forgotten about her. If he couldn't get to Dante, then he would get to her. In New Orleans, that phoenix had a foster family that he could use in order to get to her.

He would use anyone or anything if it suited his purposes.

And he would *kill* anyone or anything.

He stormed away from the others. He stared into the night. Cassie was out there, he knew it. With Dante.

Jon inhaled deeply, trying to pull in their scents. One of his first enhancements with Genesis had been his sense of smell. It was even better than a full-blooded wolf shifter's.

Fucking better.

He inhaled and caught the coppery scent of blood.

Jon smiled. *I've got you.*

"Follow me!" he yelled to his men—those still alive, anyway. His fire had taken out five of them.

"Vaughn!"

Cassie broke through the clearing and saw the vampire on the ground. He was moaning, twisting. She rushed toward him—

And found herself jerked back by her phoenix.

"Vampire," Dante said in her ear. "Don't get close to him."

But Vaughn seemed hurt. He wasn't talking, just making a faint, moaning sound in his throat.

"Did he get burned?" Cassie whispered. She *had* to get a better look at him.

"I don't smell burns on him." Dante pulled her closer against his body. "Just blood. The vampire fed recently."

Oh, no. Vaughn had gone into that tunnel right after Jamie and Charles. And it wasn't like there were a whole lot of people running out in the night.

Footsteps pounded. Voices shouted.

"Men are coming," Dante said. "We either kill them or we run."

Okay, so there *were* a lot of people running out there.

"Vaughn. Vaughn, *look at me,*" Cassie commanded as desperation flooded through her.

Dante's hold tightened. *"Your voice. Sin . . . sweet . . ."*

Cassie cleared her throat. Now probably wasn't the best time to have a little chat about her voice. "Vaughn, look at me."

His head lifted. The moonlight fell over him, revealing the deep lines of anguish on his face. "H-help . . . *burns* . . ."

There was blood on his mouth. Dripping down his chin. "Vaughn, who did you bite?"

"B-boy . . ."

Jamie?

Jamie's blood had the antibodies in it. "I need to get closer to him." She fought against Dante's too-tight hold.

Dante's mouth was near her ear. "That's not happening. And those men are coming closer. Are they our enemies?"

"Yes."

"Then I kill them." He made it sound so simple. Absolute.

She frantically shook her head. Nothing was simple. *"No."* There had been too much killing. The men with Jon, did they even understand what was happening? "They're just following orders!"

"Then they need to think for themselves."

Vaughn sank his fingers into the ground, trying to crawl toward her.

Dante sent a line of flame at him, blocking his path. "You *don't* come near her."

That fire lit Vaughn's face and she saw—Cassie's breath choked out. He didn't have a mouthful of fangs. Not anymore. His canines were still too sharp, but his other teeth actually looked . . . normal.

"Burning . . . inside . . ." Vaughn muttered. He shook his head and lifted his hands to wrap around his stomach. "Hurts so much."

His knife-like, black claws were gone. His fingers were normal again.

"It's working," Cassie said, the words heavy with excitement. The cure could revert the primal vampires. It. Was. Working.

"Fire!" The shout came from behind them.

"Let me kill them." Dante's breath blew lightly over her ear.

Cassie shook her head once more. There was another way. They could—

"There! Get her!"

She whirled and saw Jon breaking through the line of trees. His face was twisted, not with fear or pain but with what looked like heavy burns.

"Kill him!" Jon ordered his men.

Kill him . . .

The men all began to lift their weapons without a moment's hesitation.

They need to think for themselves.

Only they weren't. They were getting ready to fire.

And she was standing between Dante and those bullets.

Horror flashed across Jon's face. "No! Not her, don't hit—"

The bullets were already exploding from their guns. Cassie braced herself. Whatever magic mojo she had inside of herself, she sure hoped it kept working.

Flames ignited in front of her. A giant, white-hot wall that lanced her skin even as the flames stretched high, covering her head, and wide, completely shielding her body.

The bullets never made it through the fire.

"You won't let me kill them, so we *run*." Dante didn't give her a chance to respond. He yanked her with him, and they rushed toward the waiting woods. The wall of fire he'd made protected their backs.

Cassie glanced over her shoulder, frantic. "Vaughn! *Come with us!*"

He stumbled to his feet. Tried to dodge the fire. His body was trembling, but he was coming toward her.

"You will come back to me, Cassie!" Jon's voice. Thundering after her.

He was near Vaughn. Too close to the vampire.

He was—

Jon grabbed a wooden stake from one of his men and shoved it into Vaughn's back.

Cassie screamed and jerked free of Dante's grip. *I'm coming back, you bastard, I'm—*

Fire flashed in front of her. Dante's fire. Blocking her.

"Leave him." Dante's order. His hand locked around her wrist. "He's already dead."

Vaughn had fallen to the ground. He wasn't moving.

"But he was cured," Cassie could only whisper brokenly. "He was . . . going to be normal again."

Through the flames, she saw Jon kick Vaughn in the ribs. The fire seemed to be everywhere. Raging so bright.

"Jon!" Her fury broke from her in the scream of his name.

"You will come back to me!" Jon shouted to her.

Dante's arms curled around her stomach. He lifted her off her feet. Didn't let her go.

"Cassie!" Jon's shout blasted over the flames.

But Dante wasn't letting her go.

Vaughn was dead.

And she wanted Jon to be.

They'd stolen a truck. An ancient pickup with faded paint and a clutch that didn't want to work. Sunrise was upon them, the faint trickles of light sliding across the sky.

Dante glanced over at Cassie. She looked pale, and her knuckles were white around the steering wheel. "The vampire . . . he mattered to you?"

Her lips trembled. "Yes."

Her pain seemed to fill the truck's interior.

Dante rubbed his chest. It kept aching, but no wound was there.

"Thank you," she whispered, and her gaze cut quickly to him. "I mean, you don't even remember me, and you still got me out of there. You could have just left me to die."

"No." That wasn't happening. She would not die. "I know your smell. Your taste. I know you are *mine.*" An instinctive awareness he'd had since the first instant he'd seen her.

Even when she'd looked at him with terror in her eyes, he'd known that she was his.

Her breath whispered out on a soft sigh. "We're almost to New Orleans. Jon will keep looking for us, but I-I know a place we can use as a safe house there."

Jon. The man with the burns. The man that I will be killing.

Dante had just needed to get Cassie away last night. To make sure that she was safe.

He hadn't wanted his fire to hurt her.

"We can stop soon," she said, and he wondered if the words were to reassure him or her.

Silence filled the vehicle as they came toward the city. Cassie's body was tense, and she seemed far too breakable. So fragile.

An image appeared in his mind. A little girl with dark hair. Cassie's frightened eyes. She walked toward him.

Her little gown had been soaked with blood.

"Why is there blood on you?"

"He killed me." She shook her head. *"He's going to kill you, too."*

"You're *not* dying!" His hand slammed into the dashboard, sending a crack streaking across the old, brittle surface.

Cassie jumped and glanced at him. "That is the plan, okay? Relax. I'm no immortal phoenix like you. I don't know how many repeats are left in me."

She turned the vehicle onto a narrow road. He saw the tops of—angels? Stone angels. Tombstones. They drove past a cemetery and under the interstate.

"The house isn't much," Cassie told him, "but we're not trying to attract attention."

The steering wheel was shaking in her hand. That truck didn't have many more miles in it.

A few more moments, then she was turning in front of an old, plantation style home. One that had burglar bars across its windows and spray paint on the walls. "Most of the locals think that this place is cursed," Cassie said as she pulled the truck around to the back. "So no one comes here much."

The truck's driver side door groaned when she shoved it open. Dante climbed from the vehicle and followed her up the old steps that led into the house.

Heavy boards crisscrossed the back door. She bit her lip, then glanced at him. "Ah, you think you could . . . ?"

With a yank, he had both boards falling onto the old broken steps.

"Thanks."

They went inside. Judging by the way the house looked on the outside, he'd expected to see dust, spider webs—anything but the too tidy space that waited him.

"From the front, no one can see any lights on in here." She'd turned on several lights already. "The windows are tinted, and thick curtains also help to block the interior light. If anyone glances this way, the place will keep looking abandoned."

Even though it wasn't.

"I told Charles we'd regroup at midnight, so we just need to lay low until then." She headed for the spiral staircase. It had probably once been the talk of the town. Now the steps squeaked beneath her feet. "There are a few habitable rooms upstairs. Take the one that you want."

She wasn't even looking at him. Just heading up those stairs.

No.

He rushed across the room and caught her hand, stilling her on the fifth step.

"Dante?"

His gaze raked over her. "I saw your eyes . . . in the face of a child. You said—you said someone had killed you."

She shook her head. "I don't know what you're talking about."

Wrong. She knew exactly.

"You sound different when you lie."

Cassie stilled.

He leaned toward her. His fingers brushed over her cheek. "I like the way your skin feels. Like silk." He inhaled, drinking in her scent. "And I fucking love the way you smell."

And the way she tasted.

Cassie's hands flew up and caught his. *"Stop."*

He frowned at her.

"You don't know how much it rips my heart out every time this happens. You die and you burn and you come back—and you don't remember me." Her laugh was too bitter and rough.

That wasn't the way her laugh should sound. He knew that, even if he couldn't recall the actual sound of her laughter.

"I got lucky when Jon took me to the ranch. You actually remembered, but it still didn't change the way you felt about me, did it?"

Dante could only stare at her as a dark tension swept through him.

"I don't think you do feel." She swallowed and pulled in a ragged breath. "I think you want and you lust and maybe it is because of what I am." Her lips twisted. "Siren." Said like a curse.

His muscles hardened.

"You look at me and see a stranger."

No, he saw a woman that he knew belonged to him.

As he belonged to her.

"I look at you and see the man who keeps breaking my heart." She dropped his hand as if he burned her.

He'd burned plenty of people.

Not her. Never—

"Why do I love someone who doesn't even know me?"

It was his turn to pull in that ragged breath.

Even softer, she said, "Someone who can't ever love me back."

She straightened her shoulders and carefully eased up a few steps. Putting distance between them. "I can't handle you right now. I'm too . . . raw. And you make me feel too much."

His hands clenched into fists so that he wouldn't reach out to her.

"Dammit, *remember me*!" Cassie suddenly yelled. "I don't want to be so forgettable to you! I *never* forget you! I never gave up on you! I just—" She broke off, and there was more of the bitter laughter that sounded so very wrong coming from her. "You can't help it. Just like I can't help loving you." She spun away. "But I've got to learn how to try."

Dammit, remember me!

Those had been the only words he clearly heard. Those words and her bitter laughter.

He stayed on those stairs as she raced away from him, and images began to flood through his mind.

Cassie had said . . . she was a siren.

Sirens are dangerous. So dangerous . . .

A whispered warning that came from within.

He squeezed his eyes shut and saw images of her.

They were in a crowded bar. Her eyes were wide and scared. He leaned close to her. "I've dreamed about you," he whispered. His hold had tightened on her wrists. "In my dreams . . . you kill me, Cassie Armstrong."

Another image. Another time. Another place.

Cassie stood in front of a broken mirror. Blood dripped down her arm. "They're coming. I have to get it out, or they'll get me." She drove a shard of glass into her shoulder and his phoenix roared inside.

Cassie and blood. They were bound in his mind. The blood . . .

"I'm not your fucking experiment."

She flinched before him. "I didn't say that you were."

"But you want to put me in your lab, right? Want to run your tests . . . cut me open . . . just like they did."

"I'm not like them."

"Aren't you?"

The images kept coming, rolling through his mind until all he could see was—

"You killed me. You were there when they cut into me. When they tortured me . . ." She'd stood before him, eyes so wide. "You were in a white coat. In a lab. You were one of them."

"Let me explain—"

There was nothing to explain. "I should have left you to die when I had the chance."

Dante glanced to the top of the stairs. The pipes were moaning. Cassie must have turned on the shower.

He began to climb those steps.

I should have left you to die when I had the chance.

His words.

They were alone. All alone . . .

You killed me . . .

Cassie wasn't getting away.

CHAPTER SIXTEEN

The water beat down on Cassie, and it was really freaking cold. Ice cold. But that was fine. She needed the chill to freeze the heat that Dante had stirred within her.

Just from his touch.

She squeezed her eyes shut and turned into the blasting water. She'd told him she loved him. Why? *Why?* She'd kept that secret to herself for so many years, and bam, give her some grief and desperation, and she started to over share.

He barely even knew her name.

Of course, he didn't love her back. How could he love a stranger?

There was still ash on her skin. She scrubbed harder, needing it gone. The smoke, the flames, the memory of Vaughn's desperate face. She just needed it—*gone.*

A whisper of warm air slid over her. Her heart began to beat faster. She'd heard no sound, but that heat shouldn't have been there. "Dante?" Slowly, she opened her eyes and turned around.

He stood in the doorway.

The water worked in the shower, but there was no curtain or door to shield her from his gaze. *No protection.*

If he could only remember . . . they'd been like this once

before. Though it wasn't like that scene had ended well—certainly not like the ending in her fantasies.

She yanked off the water. Fumbled for the towel that she'd found in the closet before getting into the shower. Didn't waste time drying off. She just wrapped the towel around her body and hurried out of the shower. "What's wrong? Has something happened?"

He gave a grim nod. His gaze swept over her.

There was something about his stare . . .

Her hold tightened on the towel.

His eyes met hers. "I remember you."

The whole room seemed to be getting warmer, and all of that heat was coming right from him.

"Please tell me that you remember the good stuff," she whispered.

"You killed me." Flat.

Crap. "That's not the good stuff." Cassie wanted to back away, but there was no place to go. The shower was behind her, and once again, Dante was between her and the only exit.

"I remembered . . . saying I should let you die . . ."

Still not good. "Okay, look, you might not believe this, but there are actually good memories that we share." It hadn't all been death and pain and fire.

Had it?

He stalked toward her. His hands reached out. Caught the edge of the towel.

"Dante?"

"I have *all* my memories of you. And some are so good"—the towel dropped to the floor—"that I want to have them again and again."

She needed to hop back in that icy water.

"Siren." His lips curled.

Wait. He was *smiling*.

"I remember the first time I had you naked." His fingers stroked over her breasts. Her nipples were already tightening, aching, so sensitive. "I remember the little moan that you gave. It sounded just like—"

The moan broke from her. His hands were so warm and strong.

"That," he finished in satisfaction. His head bent and he was kissing her. Driving his tongue into her mouth and making the lust that she'd tried to control grow so much stronger.

His fingers kept stroking her. Sliding over her flesh and warming her with every caress. Down, down his hand went, until those strong fingers were between her thighs.

His head lifted. "I remembered what you tasted like, everywhere."

His fingers thrust into her.

She rose onto her toes and her fingers flew out, locking around his shoulders.

"I'd never had anything so good. I want it again." His fingers were sliding into her, withdrawing, sliding in. "I want you again."

His thumb pushed over her clit. That moan—oh, yes, it slipped from her again.

Part of Cassie hated that she needed him so much. Hated that she didn't seem to have any power with him.

But, oh, she loved the way he could make her feel.

She'd shut her eyes. When had she done that? Her eyes flew open, and she stared at him. His cheeks were flushed, and she saw the phoenix lurking in his gaze.

"I remember . . ." he whispered.

She gathered her strength and pulled away from him. "I think it's t-time to make new memories."

Surprise flickered over his face. Surprise and uncertainty?

"Cassie . . ."

"New memories." She wanted to make him lose his precious control. Maybe he didn't feel the same emotions that she did, but he could feel the same reckless need that seemed to consume everything.

She eased to her knees in front of him, barely feeling the press of the tile against her flesh. Her hands reached out to him. She yanked open his jeans. His cock was heavy and full, completely erect, and warm, just like the rest of him. Always so warm.

"You don't have—"

"I want to make you wild." She would make him that way. She wouldn't be the only one lost to this need. Cassie put her mouth on him, hesitant at first, because she was uncertain.

But . . . he growled out her name and she heard the rough need in his voice.

Her mouth opened wider as she took more of him. Deeper. Her tongue licked over his shaft, then over the head of his cock.

She licked him again, savoring the taste of him that she could feel on her tongue.

His hands rose and locked around her shoulders. A shudder rippled over his body.

That was a good sign, right?

She tasted more of him. Her hand curved around his shaft, and she began to pump him even as her mouth slid over his cock. She could taste more of him, slightly salty, and she liked that. She liked him. Liked the way his fingers were curling ever tighter around her, and she liked the way—

"Cassie!" He roared her name.

Then he was lifting her up, swinging her high into his arms. His mouth crashed on hers. She sank her hands into his hair. She was wet and aching and wanted him *in* her.

He pulled his mouth from hers and began to kiss her neck.

Oh, yes, that was good.

"The bed," she managed. "Get us to the—"

He pushed her against the tiled wall. And drove into her.

Not making it to the bed. That was fine.

Her nails raked over him as she let her own control rip away.

His hands slammed down behind her, and she heard glass shatter. Was that the mirror? Tiles?

Screw it.

She arched toward him.

The heat thickened in the bathroom. So did he. His cock swelled inside her, and she pushed down eagerly, trying to take more of him.

Then he withdrew and slammed deep again.

"Dante!"

Her release was close, she could feel it bearing down on her. He lifted her higher, positioning her to take and take, and every thrust sent him pushing right over her clit.

She came, gasping for breath. Holding tight to him. But . . .

Dante wasn't done.

"Not . . . enough . . ." His words were growled.

She couldn't get a deep breath. She could only gasp and feel the pulses of her release coursing through her.

He was still in her. So deep and full. And he was carrying her out of the bathroom.

Finally, they were making it to the bed.

He lowered her onto the mattress. Caught her legs and lifted them up, opening her even more to him. "Need . . . *everything* . . ."

Her gaze was caught by the fire in his eyes. She'd wanted his control to shatter. It had. The beast was there, in his gaze, as desperate for release as the man.

He thrust into her.

The need built once more within Cassie. She was too sensitive and every stroke—

"Dante!" Her nails dug into him.

He growled. "Yes . . . *yes* . . ."

She came again.

And he exploded within her. His hands held her so tightly, the heat in the room built, and she almost expected to see flames shooting along the old bedspread.

Instead of fire, she saw him. Dante kissed her. She tasted his need and his lust and his pleasure.

So much pleasure.

It was sweeping over her and she could only shudder at the release that wouldn't end.

She never wanted it to end.

Slowly, so slowly, he lowered her legs. Slid out of her.

Dammit. She hadn't been ready for him to go.

He pulled up the covers, wrapping her carefully, and tucking her gently to his side.

"I like my new memories," he said, voice deep.

That was the *last* thing she'd expected him to say. A laugh slipped from her, one that was real and happy. In that moment, she was happy.

She was with Dante. Her whole body was blissed out.

And her phoenix liked his memories. He laughed then, too. It was deep and rumbly and wonderful.

Her own laughter stilled.

He *laughed.*

Her lips began to tremble.

Dante's laughter stopped. Worry chased across his face. "Cassie, what is it?"

I love you. I've loved you since I was eight years old. In all of those years, this is the first time you ever laughed—real laughter. Not the bitter sound of mockery that she'd heard in Genesis.

"I just got my wish," she told him softly.

He frowned at her.

No, her words would make no sense to him. She didn't care.

Cassie bent and kissed him and hoped that he hadn't noticed the tears in her eyes.

Dante was happy, and so was she.

He *hurt.*

Vaughn Adams cracked open his eyes and glanced around. He had no damn idea where he was, but he felt pretty sure that he was about to vomit.

"You're awake." A woman's voice. A voice he didn't know.

He turned his head to the right and saw her. A woman with blond hair, wearing a white lab coat.

Not the same woman. It wasn't the woman who'd come to him again and again, with the voice that soothed and made the bloodlust still within him, even as the scent of her blood had tempted him.

"Jon didn't intend to kill you. If he had, he would have made sure not to miss your heart." Her voice was very matter-of-fact. "Or he would have burned you."

"You . . ." Vaughn's voice was raspy, too rough. "You . . . talkin' about that bastard who . . . staked me?"

"Lieutenant Colonel Jon Abrams." She gave a quick nod and glanced back over her shoulder. Like she was nervous.

Or scared.

"He didn't want you dead," she told him quickly. "We can't . . . learn as much from the dead."

Vaughn tried to move and realized that he was strapped down on a table.

Not good.

"Let me up," he said, his voice gaining strength with his rising fury. "Your boss is crazy! He tried to kill me." *And when I find him, I'll offer some serious payback.* "But you haven't hurt me, so lady, I don't have any grudge against you."

She wasn't moving to let him up.

He strained against the metal straps.

"Those straps keep werewolves contained without any problem." Still that matter-of-fact voice that he didn't like. "So I think they'll manage to hold you just fine." She crept closer and studied him with a detached, clinical gaze. "Though I'll confess, I'm not exactly sure what you are."

"I'm a detective with the New Orleans Police Department, and trust me on this, you do not want to screw with the NOPD!"

"Until a few hours ago, I believe you were a primal vampire. I doubt that you've even spoken in full sentences like this since your . . . infection." Her gaze swept over him. "But now your claws are gone and you only have fangs on your canine teeth."

She acted like she'd missed the whole NOPD part.

But . . . her words were giving him pause. *Claws are gone.*

His heart started to race faster in his chest. *Cassie.* Her name slipped through his mind. The woman with the soothing voice, and the blood that had begged for him to drink it. She had cured him. She'd said she would.

She'd done it.

"I need to understand what she did to you."

Wow. Hold up. His gaze dropped to her right hand. That woman needed to put down the scalpel and step back from him.

"I have to replicate it. I have to see . . . Are you human again?" She shook her head. "I don't think you completely are, not with those fangs."

His tongue ran over said fangs. The two sharp canines were much better than the mouthful he'd had before.

"Do you want blood?"

She came closer with that scalpel.

"Keep it away from me!" He wasn't in the mood to get sliced.

The blonde blinked. "I'm not going to hurt you." She took the scalpel and sliced it over her skin.

Her blood trickled over her arm.

"I'm just going to see if you're hungry."

The blood glistened, dark red. And Vaughn realized that he was . . . He *was hungry.*

She held her arm over his face, and he opened his mouth, suddenly desperate for that blood.

"Vampires usually need a lot of blood after an injury. You still haven't healed fully yet."

He hadn't even felt an injury.

"But maybe that will change with a little blood." Drops of her blood fell into his mouth.

So damn good.

"Interesting."

After those few precious drops, she stepped back and began wrapping her injured arm in long, white strips of cloth. "You sure act like a vampire, but you don't look primal."

"I'm not," he gritted out. When he'd been in that primal haze of bloodlust and endless hunger, speech had been all but impossible. The longer he'd been primal, the harder it had been to pull up speech. As if . . . as if with each passing day, he'd become more of an animal.

And, sure, that woman's blood was like honey on his tongue, but he wasn't foaming at the mouth to have more.

I have control.

He wasn't planning on losing it anytime soon.

"Since I'm not primal, I'm not a threat." Vaughn tried to keep his voice calm and reasonable. Reason might work with this lady. "You can let me go."

She shook her head.

He heard the squeak of a door opening behind her. Footsteps came toward him, and he smelled smoke.

Vaughn glanced to the left and saw the same SOB who'd shoved a stake into him. He hadn't seen the man's face until he fell into the dirt—and nearly died.

"Cassie cured you," the man said.

What is his name? Jon—and he is a lieutenant colonel.

"He's still a vampire," the blonde said quickly. Her wound was completely wrapped now. "Just not primal."

The SOB came closer. "How'd she do it?" he demanded of Vaughn.

"Hell if I know." That was true. All he remembered was the hunger and . . .

Fuck, did I bite a kid?

He thought that he might have, and shame burned through him. Vaughn *never* wanted to be like that again.

Death would be better than being primal.

Jon's blue eyes locked on his. "We're going to cut you up and find out. I'll let Shaw slice you open, and then she can piece you back together."

Isn't he a cold-blooded prick?

Vaughn glared at him.

"Or maybe I'll let her take an . . . easier approach," Jon said with a chilling smile. "You help me, and I don't torture you as much."

Was Vaughn supposed to believe anything the guy who'd staked him said?

Jon stepped ever closer. His face had been burned so badly. But he acted like he didn't feel the pain as he demanded, "Where would Cassie go? She ran from her lab. *Where did she run to*?"

"No clue," Vaughn muttered. He wasn't telling this guy anything.

Jon shook his head and sighed. "That's the wrong answer." He glanced at the woman. "Shaw, cut open his chest."

Shaw didn't move.

Neither did Vaughn.

"Shaw!" Jon snapped.

"He's a cured primal," she whispered with a nervous glance at Vaughn. "Don't you see what Cassie has done? We need him alive. We have to replicate—"

"Do I look like I give a shit about curing the primals?" Jon snarled. "I can kill them all with a thought."

Vaughn's gaze swept over the man's face. "Those look like some pretty bad burns." On his face and his arms.

Jon stiffened.

Vaughn smiled. "Someone pissed off a phoenix, huh?" He knew about the phoenixes. Down in New Orleans, his best friend had a phoenix for a sister.

Sabine. He hadn't seen her in so long, not since she'd come to town with her vampire lover and—

"Ahh!" Vaughn cried out.

Jon had just shoved his burning hand onto Vaughn's chest.

"I'm the phoenix," Jon shouted at him, spittle flying from his mouth. "And if you say one more thing to piss me off, you'll just be the latest vampire that I burned to ash."

Vaughn's flesh began to melt away. He clenched his teeth and refused to cry out again.

"Please!" Shaw said, voice breaking. "He's the cure."

Jon let his hand linger. Let the fire burn deeper, scorching muscles.

"Let him go," Shaw cried.

With a grim smile, Jon lifted his hand. "He doesn't have to stay alive. Cassie's the cure. Cassie can replicate it. Cassie and that fucking fantastic mind of hers. I just need *Cassie.*" There was something in his voice—a desperation that pushed the edge of sanity.

Right, like that dude was sane. The pyro looked like he'd lost touch with sanity long ago.

Just like I had.

"Where did she go?" Jon demanded.

"I know where you can go," Vaughn yelled right back.

Jon's jaw clenched. "Let's see just how much pain he can handle."

Shaw was so pale. Pale and shaking, but she lifted her scalpel and came toward Vaughn.

"Lady, don't! That's the last damn thing you want to be doin'," he bit out, trying to reach her.

But she raised the scalpel.

Jon's hand flew out and wrapped around her wrist. She gasped, and Vaughn knew she'd just gotten burned.

"Did I just hear . . ." Jon asked, smiling, "the South in your voice?" That smile stretched as his gaze settled on Vaughn's face. "If I'm not wrong, that's . . . New Orleans."

Fuck.

"I've always been good with voices, and that was just a little bit of Creole there." He dropped the woman's hand. "I know who you are, vampire."

Good for you.

"Vaughn Adams. Your father Keith contacted me a while back about a female phoenix he wanted to cure." Jon shook his head. "Everyone is always so stuck on cures."

Sabine. Vaughn tried to keep his expression blank but his whole body went on high alert.

"You father knew the little phoenix well, just like you did."

Vaughn didn't like the way the guy's eyes had lit up.

"I need her," Jon gritted.

"And I need the hell off this table!" Vaughn cried.

"Cassie went to her, didn't she? New Orleans is close. She has friends there, probably a safe house. She ran there."

Vaughn hoped that she hadn't. But he suspected—*yes.*

Jon's gaze bored into his. "You are going to help me draw her out."

"No, no, I'm—"

"Or I'll kill your father. I'll kill your mother. Your aunts, uncles. Every one."

Shaw dropped the scalpel and scurried back.

"But . . ." Jon lifted a brow. "You help me find Cassie and that female phoenix, and I'll let you go."

Did Vaughn look like a dumbass? The guy was *not* going to let him get away.

"Your choice," Jon said. "You help me, or you burn."

It was going to hurt, so Vaughn braced himself. "Bring on the fire, bastard."

And he did.

Cassie paced the length of the den, her hands nervously fisted at her sides. They still had an hour until midnight. Would the others be at the rendezvous point?

If they weren't, she had no idea how to find them.

"Are you sure that you can trust Keith Adams?" Dante asked her.

She jumped at the rumble of his voice. She'd thought that he was still in the kitchen. Cassie turned and saw that he was leaning up against the mantel, his arms crossed over his chest and his eyes on her.

"I think so, yes." She gave a nod, just to try and emphasize that point. She sure hoped she could trust the man. At this stage, it wasn't like she had a whole lot of choice in the matter. She'd told Dante a bit about Vaughn earlier and thought to tell him more. "Once he found out what Genesis was really doing, Keith wanted to help the paranormals. He . . ."

Okay, she should probably be careful with this reveal.

"He's the one who sent Sabine to us." She paused and searched Dante's gaze. "Do you remember her?"

"I remember everything."

Her breath rushed out. "That's a relief. It seems like your memories are coming back faster. Maybe you're getting even—"

He shook his head. "My memories are back because of you."

She wasn't sure how to respond.

"You used the power of the siren and you ordered me to remember." A little shrug. "So I did."

"I thought we'd agreed I couldn't use that power." Her voice had dropped. A big knot had also formed in her stomach.

"No, we said when you were stressed or scared, that power comes out."

Yes, he was definitely remembering a whole lot.

"I'm guessing you were feeling pretty stressed"—his gaze drifted from hers and slid to the staircase—"when we were up there."

When she'd confessed that she loved him. Cassie knew her cheeks had to be flaming.

She'd confessed, he'd gotten his memory back, and, no, there had been no claims of undying love from him.

Obviously, they were back to business as usual.

She spun on her heel so he wouldn't see her face. "S-Sabine is the only female phoenix I've ever encountered. While at Genesis, she fell in love with a vampire—"

"Ryder."

Right. Cassie tried not to shiver at his name. He was very, very powerful, and he scared the hell out of her.

"I've dealt with Ryder before." No fear in Dante's words.

Figures.

She could fear enough for both of them. She ran a hand through her hair. "Keith has a place in the Quarter. If Charles and Jamie made it to the city, they'll be there tonight. Charles . . . and I have been communicating privately with Keith while we worked on a cure for Vaughn."

How was she supposed to tell Keith that his only son was dead?

"What about Cain?"

"He should be in New Orleans, too. He'll be with Eve and . . ." *What had happened to Trace?* "I hope Trace hasn't killed anyone," Cassie whispered. "Maybe Eve was able to keep Trace in check."

"I'm sure Cain has him under control." Dante didn't sound the least bit worried. "If not, then he probably killed the werewolf."

Cassie's control snapped and she spun toward him. "Why is death so easy for you?"

A shrug. "Because I've died hundreds of times."

She flinched. "Most of us don't get the luxury of coming back. Death is permanent for us. We live, we love, and many of us don't *want* to die. Death rips us away too soon from the people that we love!"

He pushed away from the mantel and walked toward her. "You came back. When you were hurt before, in this very city—"

"Because of something my father did to me! Because I'm a walking experiment! But how long does it last? I'm *not* like you. One of these days, I'll die, and I won't come back." Her breath heaved out. "So don't talk about killing like it's nothing. All the lives—they matter to someone. Trace has friends. Eve is his friend. I'm his friend." Cassie's shoulders slumped. "We all matter."

Dante was staring down at her with confusion on his face.

Did he truly not understand?

"Someone had to matter to you," she whispered. "At some point, at some time, it couldn't have always been so easy for you to kill."

"I kill so that others can survive." Hard words.

Maybe no one had mattered. Her hand lifted. She touched his chest.

He immediately stilled beneath her hand.

"I can feel your heart beating," Cassie whispered. Beating at a fast and strong rate. "You have a heart, but do you love?"

His eyes were carefully guarded.

I guess that's my answer.

She tried to pull her hand back, but his hand rose and curled around hers, holding it in place. "I loved my brother, and I still killed him."

The way of the phoenix.

"We do what we must in order to survive."

But if they all became monsters, what was that survival worth?

"I will do *anything*"—his hold tightened on her—"to ensure your survival."

Pushed too far, she had to ask, "Would you cry for me, Dante?"

His dark eyes held hers.

"If I couldn't heal myself, if I were dying right in front of you, would you cry for me?"

A phoenix's tears had to be shed willingly. They couldn't be harvested from the tear ducts. Their power came from the pain of the phoenix.

Dante wasn't answering.

That *was* an answer.

She forced herself to smile. "Not that you have to. I'm an indestructible girl, right? No need to ever cry over me."

He let her go. "I would kill in an instant to keep you safe."

"Again with the killing." She hoped her smile didn't look as sad as she felt. "Sometimes, it's not about killing. It's about sacrificing. Putting someone *else's* life first." Cassie tried to straighten her shoulders. "Look, how about we both just stay alive tonight, okay?" She glanced at the old clock on the mantel. "We need to leave and head over for the rendezvous."

"You know I have to kill."

His words fell heavily into the room.

"The phoenix in those woods—the man you called Jon Abrams—he won't stop until *I* stop him." The floor creaked as Dante walked toward her. Then his hand was on her shoulder.

Cassie forced herself to glance back at him.

"You can say the world is about sacrifice, but I won't let him keep threatening you. And I won't let the bastard hunt me. Running isn't my way."

No, not his.

"So I'll go with you to meet your friends. And when you're safe"—Dante gave a grim nod—"I will end Jon."

The house sat, with its lights shining, at the end of Hollow Way. They hadn't come to the home of Keith Adams in their loud, grinding truck.

A backup ride had waited for them at Cassie's safe house. "Do you think they're inside?" Cassie whispered.

She wouldn't look at Dante—not for long, anyway. Her gaze kept darting from him. He'd upset her back at the safe house.

He knew that he had.

Would you cry for me, Dante?

It would have been easy to lie and say yes, but he didn't want to lie to her. She deserved his honesty.

He hadn't cried for anyone in hundreds of years. He'd cried after his brother was gone, but . . .

That hadn't done much good.

"Let's go around to the back," Cassie said, her voice low.

They slid through the shadows, easing up the back

porch. Cassie crept toward the door and rapped lightly against its surface.

Dante inhaled, pulling all of the scents into his lungs. *Wolf.* Werewolves often had that slightly woodsy odor. "Your werewolf . . . was here." *Is he still?*

Dante pulled in more scents. "Ash . . ."

"Cain?" she whispered, glancing at him from the corner of her eyes.

Dante wasn't sure.

The door creaked open. A man stood there. His hair was gray on the sides and deep lines were etched across his forehead. "They said you'd be comin', Cass," he whispered and opened the door. His eyes narrowed when he caught sight of Dante. "Who's this?"

"A friend," Cassie quickly told him. "Dante's a friend of mine."

Dante frowned at her. He was a whole lot more than just a friend.

The man's gaze assessed him. "You vouching for him?"

"Yes."

After a small hesitation, the guy waved them inside.

Dante crossed the threshold.

Cassie followed the man through the kitchen and down the hallway.

The scent of ash and that wild, woodsy scent grew stronger. He'd thought the werewolf was close but—

Is that Trace?

The scent actually seemed to be blending with the ash as they were nearing the living room.

Cassie reached out, as if unable to help herself, and caught the man's arm. "Keith, I'm so sorry . . ."

Dante heard the restrained emotion in her voice. The whisper of pain and sorrow. "But there's something I have to tell you. It's Vaughn . . ."

Keith's face hardened.

"He's dead."

Dante thought the man would break down, but Keith shook his head. "No, he's not."

"He is," Cassie said, the words soft but certain. "I saw him. He was staked and—"

"He's still alive, and that's why"—Keith lunged toward Cassie and shoved a needle into her neck—"I have to do this."

Dante roared. He grabbed Cassie, snatching her from the man's hold even as he threw the human back. Keith's body slammed into the wall with a thud.

"Cassie?"

Her breath heaved out. Her lashes began to fall.

"I had to!" Keith shouted as he rose. "He has my son!"

Carefully, so carefully, Dante put Cassie on the floor. Then he looked up at Keith Adams. "You're a dead man."

A door opened behind him. The scent of ash and woods—that damn scent—was stronger.

"No, Dante, he's not dead."

Dante knew that voice and spun around.

Jon Abrams was staring at him. The man's body was covered with burns.

"*You* are," Jon said. He raised his hand and fired the gun he gripped in his fist. The bullet tore right into Dante's chest.

He fell back, ramming into the floor, his body landing just inches from Cassie's. As death claimed him, she was the last sight he had.

Cassie . . . so still. So pale.

Would you cry for me, Dante?

"I'm sorry." Keith's broken voice.

No, the bastard wasn't sorry, but he would be. Dante would make sure of it.

* * *

The rest of Jon's team slowly swarmed the house. They'd stayed back because Jon had worried that the human might slip up and give away his plan.

Humans could be such screw-ups.

Dante lay sprawled in the hallway, blood pooling beneath him.

Keith crouched over Dante, with his hands drenched in the phoenix's blood. Was the fool actually trying to save him? It sure looked like he was attempting to stop the blood flow.

Humans. *Screw-ups*. Jon was so glad he wasn't one of them any longer.

I'm so much better.

"You never said you were killing him!" Keith yelled as he looked up at Jon. "You said you were taking them into custody! That you wanted them alive!"

"Relax." Jon motioned to two guards. They needed to get Cassie out of there before Dante started to burn. "It's not like he'll stay dead."

Keith jerked his hands away from Dante. "Vampire?"

"Guess again." Jon winced when the burns on his shoulder brushed against the wall. He hadn't summoned any more fire in the last six hours because when he conjured the fire, it *hurt*.

As much as he would like to kill Dante when the phoenix started to rise, he couldn't.

I need him.

Jon knew that his body wasn't holding the phoenix transformation. His cells weren't strong enough. Not yet. A few more dosages of the serum, and maybe those cells would be strong enough.

I need his tears.

As Jon's men carried Cassie out of the house, he knew that he had the perfect means of getting those precious tears.

"We have to transport him ASAP," Jon ordered the guards in the fireproof suits who had just arrived.

How long would those suits last once Dante's fire lit? They sure hadn't lasted long before.

"If he rises during transport, put a knife to Cassie's throat. That'll keep him calm." Jon winced. His burns *hurt.* "When he's calm, kill him. Just keep killing him until we get back to the lab."

The lab *he'd* taken over as soon as he got to New Orleans. Genesis had tentacles everywhere, and the closed-down lab a few miles away from the Tulane campus had been easy enough to acquire. It had all the equipment that he needed.

And he had the phoenix that he needed, too.

All nice and neat.

Time for the tears. Jon wasn't going to lose his power. He wouldn't go from being a god to being a rotting husk of flesh. He'd do anything necessary, but the phoenix *would* cry.

It was all a matter of motivation.

You'll feel plenty motivated when Cassie screams for you.

CHAPTER SEVENTEEN

When Cassie opened her eyes, she was in—*a truck*? Some big, jostling vehicle, it almost looked like a moving van, and a man with a knife was sitting beside her, pretty much holding her upright.

She smelled smoke.

Her gaze flew to the left. Dante. He was lying on his back, and there was smoke rising from him. Men in those familiar white, flame retardant suits were all around him.

Keith sold us out.

She didn't see Keith anywhere. If he'd tried to deal with Jon—*if? yeah, right*—the guy could already be dead.

"He's rising," Cassie whispered as her gaze slid back to Dante.

The guy with the knife jerked. He needed to be more careful with that jerking. He'd almost cut her skin.

She warned him. "This is the time when you need to run like hell. Those flames are going to be white-hot, and they'll kill us all if we don't get out of here."

The man was sweating. He lifted the knife and pressed the blade to her throat. "The lieutenant colonel said he won't attack, ma'am, as long as we've got you."

"In case you haven't noticed . . ." *How could the guy miss it?* "Your lieutenant colonel is crazy. When Dante rises, he won't even know who I am. You could shove your knife all the way through my throat, and it wouldn't matter to him." Cold, brutal words. True words. "He'll still burn this whole ride down around us."

The blade trembled and definitely nicked her skin.

Since she had the guard's attention, she kept pressing. "When he rises, he's all animal instinct, and his main instinct is to kill." Her gaze swept the back of that truck. The flames were starting to crackle. They did *not* have much time. "Why do you think that Jon isn't back here with us? He knows we'll all die here."

"No, no, ma'am. He said—he said as long as we had you—"

The guy needs to listen! "Dante won't know me! He'll *kill me*!"

The man's eyes got glassy.

Cassie's heartbeat froze. Wait. She pitched her voice low, trying to use that soothing tone that had worked with Trace. *A siren's power?* Hell, it was worth a shot. *"Put down your knife."*

Dante had said that she made him remember his past, that she'd soothed Trace. Maybe she was getting better at channeling her power.

She was definitely feeling stressed, so if she could use a siren's suggestion on him . . .

"Put down the knife."

He lowered the knife.

Her breath rushed out. And she counted—four guards. There were four other guards with them.

"Go to the back of the truck and open the door," Cassie ordered the guy.

The man stood up immediately. Headed to the back of the jostling truck.

It's working. She sucked in a couple more of those deep breaths. The breaths were starting to taste of smoke.

And the guy was trying to open the back door. It was insane. It was *working.*

Dante had been right about her.

Now, if she could just save *them.*

But as the guy hurried to obey her instructions, the others all whirled to face her. *Crap.* Could she control so many at once?

Cassie had no clue. *Let's find out.*

"Pick him up." She fought to keep her voice low and soothing when she wanted to shout.

At first, no one moved.

Then the guy shoved open the back doors, just as flames licked around Dante's legs.

"Pick him up."

If his fire started in the truck—with the gasoline in the vehicle's tank, hell, they could all explode.

The remaining guards moved as one and picked up Dante. Cassie hurried toward the open doors. The dark road stretched behind them. The fire burned hotter. The men—even in their suits—wouldn't be able to hold him for long.

She hated to do it, but there wasn't a lot of choice. *"Throw him out."*

Dante would recover.

He would—

They threw him.

She saw the flames when he hit the road.

Then she braced herself because she had to jump, too. There was no way she could stay in that death truck and let Jon take her wherever the hell he wanted.

She knew it was Jon taking her. Even as she'd fallen to the floor, her body heavy with numbness, she'd heard his voice.

Dante was right about him. It looked like the only way to stop him was to kill him.

Her fingers curled around the edge of the vehicle.

The only way to stop him . . .

If she jumped, Jon would come and find her.

He'd keep searching for her *and* Dante.

Maybe it was time to end all the hunting. Cassie knew Jon had forced Keith to help him. She remembered what Keith had said. *He has my son*!

Was that true? Was it even possible that Vaughn was still alive?

If she stayed in that rig, she'd find out, and possibly get to Vaughn. She'd definitely get an up close and personal audience with Jon.

Then I'll see just how well my voice works on him. She had a weapon that Jon didn't know about. One that he couldn't fight.

Finally, the advantage would be hers.

Behind that truck, the flames were growing brighter in the darkness.

"Good-bye, Dante," she whispered. When this was over, when she'd finished *her* battle, and stopped the experiments, she'd go to him.

But Genesis—her father—had made one more monster that she had to slay first.

I hope you're ready for me, Jon. Because she was ready for him.

"Close the doors," Cassie said.

The fire burned. Consumed. Dante's hands pushed against pavement—rough, hard—and he climbed to his feet.

The darkness was around him.

Her scent . . . faint, fading . . . drifted in the wind.

The fire kept burning.

Her.

He could see a ghost of her image in his mind, but he couldn't call up her name.

Her scent was so faint.

He took a step forward. She smelled of sin and sweetness. Not fire. He was tired of the smell of ash.

He wanted sin.

Sweetness.

Another step.

She'd left him.

He'd find her.

Another step. Another.

Then he was running. Rushing as fast as he could. After her.

The truck rumbled to a stop. Cassie glanced at the men near her. They looked dazed, and that was the way they should look. She'd told them to forget everything that had happened in the back of that truck.

So far, her command seemed to be working.

She heard voices. Footsteps. Then the doors were being opened once more.

Cassie stood in the middle of the truck. The men were against the back wall.

Jon frowned up at her. "What the hell? Where's the phoenix?"

She smiled. "Next time, instead of leading your prisoners, maybe you should follow behind them," she advised him. "That way, you might actually notice when someone escapes."

He leaped into the truck.

She saw his face—her breath sucked in. "Dante burned you." She didn't remember the fire at Keith's house.

Jon shook his head. "Where the hell is he?"

"He ditched the ride a while back." Her chin lifted. "And now you're left with me." This was it. The moment she'd waited for. *"Take me to Vaughn."*

Jon blinked at her.

"Take me to Vaughn." Her heart was a drumbeat in her ears.

Jon took her hand. Led her to the back of the truck. They jumped down.

And headed toward the long, flat building on the right. Two armed men blocked the door, but Jon waved them aside.

The interior of the building smelled of . . . blood.

"Do your superiors know what you're doing?" Cassie asked. Just how far-reaching was his madness?

"I don't have superiors. I do what the hell I want."

"Do they know that?" Cassie asked, glancing back to the guards. "Or did you tell them all that you're still working for the government?"

He stopped. Frowned at her. "Where are we?"

Crap. "Vaughn. Take me to Vaughn."

A woman rushed up to them. Cassie recognized her. The blonde—Dr. Shaw—who'd taken all of those samples from her at the ranch. It was hard to forget someone who'd made her bleed.

"The vampire," Jon blasted at her. "We need him."

Dr. Shaw's eyes widened, but she turned on her heels. Jon kept his hold on Cassie and pulled her down the hallway, following the other woman.

The scent of blood grew stronger.

"Where's Keith?" Cassie asked nervously.

"I have a guard at his house . . . in case any of your other friends show up."

And they would. Jamie. Charles. Eve. Cain. It was just a matter of time until they all walked into the trap.

They'd be taken to Jon, too.

I'll stop him.

One step at a time. She would do this.

Dr. Shaw pushed open a heavy metal door. An operating room waited inside. Vaughn was . . . oh, jeez, Vaughn was on the table, and it looked like someone had tried to carve out his heart.

"Vaughn!" Cassie ran toward him.

His eyes opened. "Shouldn't . . . be here . . . Go . . ."

"You shouldn't be here, either." The fact that he was still alive with that kind of injury . . . *he hadn't returned to a human state.* She could see the sharp points of his canines. Fangs.

He was strapped down to that table. She saw the switch for the release button on the straps, and lunged toward it.

Only to find her way blocked by Dr. Shaw. "What do you think you're doing?" the other woman demanded.

It should be obvious. "I'm getting him out of here."

"Jon!" Dr. Shaw screamed. "What's happening?"

Jon shook his head, but didn't advance.

"Get out of my way," Cassie said, pitching her voice low. *"Just step to the side and get—"*

Dr. Shaw started to laugh.

That laughter chilled Cassie.

The chill got even worse when Dr. Shaw said, "Really, half-breed? You think you have enough power to tell *me* what to do?" Then Shaw's gaze turned to Jon. "Grab her and *hold her.*"

Even Cassie could feel the power in the woman's voice.

Jon immediately grabbed Cassie.

She stared at Dr. Shaw in shock.

"What?" Shaw's perfectly arched blond brows rose. "Did you seriously think you were the only siren around? How do you think I convinced that crazy bastard"—she pointed at Jon—"to keep me alive?"

Before Cassie could think of a reply, Dr. Shaw leaped forward and shoved a gag into Cassie's mouth. Cassie tried to fight her, but Jon was holding her too tightly.

Shaw secured the gag then pointed to the second operating table on the right. "Now strap her down."

Jon followed Dr. Shaw's instructions with that dazed look in his eyes.

"If you can't talk, then you don't have any power." Dr. Shaw smiled at her. "And I don't want you to have any power at all."

Jon had strapped her down, controlling her struggles like they were nothing.

"You let the phoenix go, didn't you?" Dr. Shaw asked her with narrowed eyes.

Cassie glared at her.

"Love—it makes women do some damn stupid things. But no worries." Dr. Shaw pulled out a syringe. "I'm sure he'll follow you here. From what I could tell, he's mated to you, and he'll follow his mate anywhere." She drove that needle into Cassie's flesh.

Fire burned through her blood.

"Does this feel familiar?" Dr. Shaw's voice was mild. "It's similar to the dosage your father gave you when you were a child, after the first time he accidentally killed you." She shrugged. "Or maybe it wasn't so accidental. Who knows?"

The burn . . .

"Because of your siren blood, the guy actually stumbled onto a serum that would make you nearly immortal. You could heal from any injury. Amazing." Dr. Shaw actually sounded like she meant that. "Of course, I didn't exactly know what was happening until I took all of those wonderful samples from you at the ranch. Then I saw just what you could do."

When I get loose . . .

"The drug I just gave you? I'm afraid it's going to have the reverse effect on you. No more super healing for you."

It seemed as if Cassie's heartbeat was slowing down.

"It's nothing personal. Well, maybe it is." Dr. Shaw tapped her chin with a white-gloved finger. "You see, I need to hurt Dante because he hurt me. He took something incredibly precious from me a long time ago."

Cassie's gaze narrowed.

Jon was standing stock-still.

Vaughn groaned.

"Once upon a time, I loved a man very much. I loved him so much that I wanted to make sure that no one would *ever* be able to take him from me," Dr. Shaw said.

There were *tears* in her eyes.

"So I took steps to protect my Wren. Only . . . Dante didn't do what he *should* have done. Instead of dying, he took my Wren's life."

Wren. Dante's brother.

"The way to break a phoenix isn't just by going through the fire. It's by taking their hearts. I'm going to kill you, Cassie, and Dante will lose his heart. Then Jon"—she waved her hand toward the still man—"will finish Dante, and maybe then . . . *maybe then,* I will sleep for the first time in centuries without hearing the echo of Wren's last cry—without hearing him scream my name before Dante killed him."

Oh, shit.

They were so screwed.

He knocked out a guard, and, since he didn't feel like rushing into the building naked, he grabbed the guy's clothes.

A little tight, but they'd do.

He inhaled. She was in there.

Waiting for him. Once he had her safe in his arms, he would burn the whole place down.

He didn't worry about being subtle. He just rushed toward the main entrance. When another guard turned on him with a gun, he melted the gun.

The guard ran.

Dante went inside.

I am Dante. Dante.

The name had come to him because he remembered her whispering it. *Good-bye, Dante.* The faint words had seemed to drift in the wind.

It wasn't good-bye. It would never be, for them.

Inside, more guards came at him. He lifted his hand. His fire made them flee, too.

Too easy. Humans were no challenge for him.

They never had been.

He followed her scent. Saw the metal door. She waited behind it. He was so close to her.

So very close.

His fire sent the door crashing in. He surged inside. Found her instantly. On the table. With her head turned toward him, her eyes wild and afraid.

And a . . . gag in her mouth?

He stepped toward her.

"Stop, Dante."

The voice seemed to slide inside him, freezing him.

She walked from the shadows. Her blond hair brushed her shoulders. Her face—beautiful, cold—seemed familiar.

"Remember me. Remember everything."

He went to his knees as the images flooded through his mind. Images. Voices. Death.

"What would be the point of all this if you didn't remember?" she asked. *"You have to remember so that you can suffer."*

Her voice . . .

I love him, and we will be together. Nothing will ever take me from Wren. Her eyes, that icy blue, had found his. *You will die. All of the phoenixes will fight until death, and then only my Wren will remain.*

Zura.

Dante saw her in a field stained black by ash—the ash that had come from the dying phoenixes. So many dead.

She was screaming.

Wren was dying.

Dante frowned. "You're . . . dead . . ."

"No, I'm not. It took me a good century to heal from my burns and to look *normal* again, but I'm very much not dead." She smiled at him. "You won't be able to say the same soon." Zura pointed to him. *"Don't move a single muscle."*

His body locked down.

"Did you know . . . much like a vampire and a phoenix, a siren's power only increases with age? A mere whisper from me"—she walked next to Jon and whispered in his ear—"can compel even the strongest of paranormal beings."

Jon crossed to the nearby table and picked up the gleaming knife that waited there.

"You should know, Dante, that, before you arrived, I gave Cassie a little injection." Zura smiled. "I'm a pretty good doctor, too, you know. When you can live forever, you have the chance to pick up so many skills."

She shouldn't be living. She'd been dead.

But . . . he remembered . . . Wren had been over her. Clinging to her.

Had his brother cried for her?

He must have.

"Once I found the original formula that helped to make your Cassie so indestructible, well, it was easy enough to find a way to undo that little process."

Jon had taken his knife and was stalking toward Cassie.

Cassie shook her head and desperately tried to speak behind the gag. Her eyes were on Dante.

"She won't be so quick to heal this time," Zura promised.

Jon was over Cassie. Staring down at her.

His body shuddered, but he lifted the knife. "S-sorry . . ." he gasped.

"Don't be sorry," Zura ordered. *"Kill her."*

Dante couldn't even speak. Couldn't move even a finger to help her.

Cassie was less than ten feet away from him, and he could do nothing.

Jon drove the knife into Cassie's chest.

No!

"Oh, wait. It gets better." Zura was nearly purring. "You see . . . she won't come back. She won't heal. She'll just rot." Zura smiled at him. "Told you . . . *better.*"

Jon stared down at Cassie. Then he pulled out the bloody knife. The sound that it made . . .

Cassie's eyes were closed.

"Do you feel like the knife just went in you? Do you feel like you're the one who died, Dante?" Zura demanded.

He couldn't speak.

"Respond!" she screamed, freeing him from her spell.

Oh, he'd fucking respond all right.

He sent a blast of fire rolling right toward her. *You should have been more careful with your damn words, Zura.* A siren had to be very, very careful what she said.

The fire rolled over her. The scream she gave was full of pain.

He grabbed out with his hand. Caught the instrument tray. Picked up one scalpel.

Jabbed it into his right ear.

Then the left ear.

And he couldn't hear her screams anymore.

He couldn't hear anything. Blood poured from his ears, but he didn't care.

Cassie was all that mattered.

He ran to her, even as Jon pushed Zura to the ground and began to pound out the flames on her body.

Dante yanked the gag from Cassie's mouth. Broke the straps that held her down.

"Cassie?" He couldn't hear his own voice, but his throat vibrated.

She didn't stir.

He stared down at her chest. So much blood. Zura had told Jon to kill her, and it looked like the bastard had tried his best to carry out her order.

Would you cry for me, Dante?

"I won't let you go." He would cry, he would—

Jon tackled him. They hit the table that Cassie was on, and she fell to the floor. They all fell, tumbling across the hard tile.

Dante grabbed Jon. Punched him. Again and again and again.

He was the man who'd hurt Cassie. Who'd stabbed her. Killed her?

Not gone yet. I won't let her be gone. I can save her.

He just had to get to her.

The bloody knife was inches from his hand. He grabbed it—and drove the blade deep into Jon's heart.

Payback.

Jon stared up at him, eyes wide and lost.

"When you rise," Dante rasped out, "I will be here. And I will destroy you. You won't come back ever again."

The life drained from Jon's eyes.

Dante grabbed for Cassie. His eyes were burning, but not from the fire. From tears that were coming—coming up from the phoenix who would not let his mate vanish. He would not—

A gunshot blasted.

He felt the bullet tunnel through his back, then it ripped from his chest.

Cassie hadn't opened her eyes.

He was falling . . . dropping down on top of her because Zura had shot him. Killed him, before he could save

Cassie. If he didn't heal her before he rose, his fire would take her.

And there would be nothing left.

His own eyes closed, and he thought, hoped—fucking prayed—that the tear drop would fall before he died.

Then he felt arms yanking on him, pulling him away from Cassie.

No.

His hands clamped around her, and his face brushed against hers.

She loved him. Screwed up, twisted monster that he was, Cassie loved him.

He wasn't going to give up on her. Never.

He kicked out, his foot slamming into something soft.

I would cry for you, Cassie. I would bleed, beg, kill, and damn well die for you.

The secret he'd held so long, the one he'd been afraid to reveal—when he feared nothing else—was that he didn't remember her each time just because they were mates.

It wasn't about biology. About her being a siren and him being a phoenix.

It was about a man and a woman.

About love.

He'd loved her for years, and the memory of love—that was the only thing that could always get through the fire.

They were both dead.

Cassie. And the big, tough-looking bastard who'd tried to save her.

Dead.

Vaughn craned his neck, trying to see them. They were on the floor. It looked like the one Shaw had called Dante was holding Cassie, even in death.

Shaw was trying to pull Dante's body off Cassie's.

Not working. The woman wasn't physically strong, no matter what crazy mojo she could do with her voice.

Dante made sure he couldn't hear her. When he couldn't hear her, she couldn't control him. That bastard had played hard when he'd driven the scalpel into his own ears.

Smoke began to rise.

Shaw was standing above Vaughn, and she looked . . . scared.

Why? Everyone else was dead. What did she have to fear? Vaughn was strapped. Weak from blood loss, and, unless he missed his guess, about to join all of the others in death.

"When I free you, do exactly as I order. You don't attack me."

He hated her voice, even as it seemed to wrap around him like a dark temptation.

She disengaged the straps. Blisters were on her arms. *"Drag Dante away from Cassie. If that fool actually cried for her . . . No—no, he wouldn't. He wouldn't."*

It looked like the guy had died for her.

Vaughn rolled off the table. Hit the floor. His blood splattered everywhere. But he was helpless to refuse her orders.

When she spoke, she controlled.

So I have to stop her from speaking.

He caught Dante's leg. Pulled him.

Cassie's eyes were closed. Her chest didn't rise.

And the smoke wasn't coming from Dante. The smoke was coming from the other guy. Jon. Great.

He dropped Dante.

"Now pick up that stake, and stab it in your heart," Shaw ordered.

He turned toward the stake, the one the bitch had oh, so conveniently left on the table. The lady had planned well, he'd give her that, but from the sound of things, she'd been planning revenge for one very long time.

His gaze slid to Cassie. Had her chest just moved? It looked like her lips had parted, but maybe he'd imagined that.

Then he heard voices. Shouting.

Coming from outside in the hallway.

"I want my son!"

His father's voice. Breaking with emotion. It had been so long since Vaughn had seen his father.

His last memory of him, the last clear memory was from the night he'd been bitten.

I think I tried to kill him.

"Damn humans," Shaw muttered. "Time to kill them all. Vampire, let's have some fun."

He knew he wasn't going to like her idea of fun.

"Come with me."

He turned away from the stake. The room's doors had been blown away by Dante, and he followed her outside like a damn sheep to the slaughter.

And there was his father. A guard had a gun shoved into his dad's back. A boy—maybe around fourteen—stood beside him, and there was another man, with thin blond hair, a guy who was trying to shield the boy.

"Don't come at him again!" the blond man screamed when he saw Vaughn.

Again?

Shame slid through Vaughn even as his gaze swept over the boy. He was familiar.

I'm sorry.

Vaughn knew he'd hurt the boy. Hurt so many.

His gaze turned to his father. His dad looked as if he'd aged twenty years since the night of Vaughn's attack.

"V-Vaughn?" his father whispered. "Are you really back?"

Vaughn nodded.

"Now for the fun," Shaw murmured. *"Vaughn, go rip out their throats, starting with your father."*

Keith's eyes widened. "No, son. *No!*"

"Sorry, but he's not taking orders from you now," Shaw said. "It's my voice that he follows. *Mine.*"

Helpless, Vaughn started to walk toward his father. "Get away, Dad," he whispered. "Get the guard's gun. Shoot me. Get out of here!"

But his dad seemed frozen. Broken.

"I missed you, Vaughn," Keith said softly. "Your mother . . . had a heart attack a few months back. I lost her. I didn't want to lose you . . ."

And Vaughn didn't want to kill his father.

The boy—lunged forward and caught the guard unaware. The kid grabbed the gun and aimed it at Vaughn. "No more!" the kid screamed.

"Drop the gun," Shaw said, her voice cracking with power.

The gun immediately fell from his hands.

The blond man pushed the boy back behind him.

Vaughn was almost in front of his father. Nearly close enough to kill.

"Make them suffer," Shaw shouted, her voice feverish and wild. *"Make them—ahhh!"*

Vaughn's head jerked around as her words ended. She was . . . gurgling—

Choking.

On her own blood.

Cassie *had* been breathing. She stood there, covered in blood, and her hand was still around the scalpel that she'd shoved into Shaw's throat.

"I think you've done enough talking," Cassie whispered. "Now, you can just die."

CHAPTER EIGHTEEN

Every part of Cassie's body *hurt,* but she was alive, on her feet, and that crazy bitch who'd tried to kill her was going down.

She yanked the scalpel to the left. "The power's in the voice, right? Try talking now." An impossible task since she'd just taken Dr. Shaw's voice box.

Then, because it wasn't about someone suffering, but because she just wanted to *end* it, she pulled the scalpel back and prepared to send Zura to whatever world waited for her next. *Hope it's a fiery one.*

But . . . there was already fire. Burning so bright and hot behind Zura. A man—surrounded by flames.

He reached for Zura even as Cassie scrambled back.

Zura tried to scream, but she couldn't.

She was burning.

The smell was horrible and Cassie turned away—only to see Charles blocking Jamie's view of that terrible scene. "Charles, get Jamie out of here!" He already had enough nightmares.

Charles grabbed him and they ran. The guards were all running, too, fleeing from the beast that was attacking.

Or maybe . . . with Shaw gone the guards were finally free.

"Dad?" Vaughn's rough voice.

He was hugging his dad.

It wasn't the time for hugging. "Vaughn, get him out of here!"

That wasn't Dante in the middle of the fire. She still had a chance of reaching him. Controlling him.

He hadn't risen.

When her eyes had opened, he'd been near her. Dead.

The fire was coming from Jon. He was the one who'd risen first. The one who'd just burned Dr. Shaw.

Vaughn held tight to his dad and they ran.

Cassie took a few careful steps away from Jon. Zura was—just gone. Only ashes drifted in the air.

Jon stared at her through the flames. His eyes were burning as bright as the fire. The flames began to roll away from him, toward her.

"Jon, stop."

The flames flickered, then died away. Jon stood there, and—she sucked in a sharp breath—burns covered him. "You—" She could barely make herself speak. "Something is wrong. The fire is—"

"Killing me," he finished, voice rasping. "Because I still have . . . human in me. I need *more* of . . . the tears. More of the serum."

He'd lost her. "What serum?"

"The female . . . Sabine . . . we got her tears." He smiled, and the sight was horrific on his damaged face. "Killed her, broke her, made her . . . cry again and again before Ryder . . . changed her."

Cassie finally understood. "You used her tears." Used them to try and become a phoenix. Just as the previous experiments at Genesis had made him become a wolf shifter.

"Wolf shifter DNA made me stronger . . . just not strong enough."

He'd wanted to be like the phoenix.

"No death . . . just fire." He glanced behind him. At

Dante's prone body. "You're alive, so . . . that means he cried for you."

Yes, he had.

She couldn't even think about what that meant. *One monster at a time.*

"I need more . . . tears . . . to be stronger."

Cassie shook her head. "It's not about the tears. Your body just can't keep regenerating—the fire is too strong for you to handle!" He had to see that.

"I *will* be stronger!" he roared and lunged toward her.

"Stop!"

He froze.

"Let me help you," she pushed as much of that soothing power as she could into her voice. *"This isn't what you want. When we first met, you wanted to change the world."* What had happened to that man?

"No, I wanted to change *me* . . . and *own* the world." Fire crackled above his damaged fingers. "I won't go back to being human."

There wasn't a choice for him.

"You won't survive more risings." She could see that. *Anyone* could see that.

His human side wouldn't be able to do it. It looked as if his skin were melting away, until all that remained was the fire he'd foolishly tried to harness inside himself.

"I just need the tears!"

She shook her head. "They won't help you. They won't—"

He bent and picked up the scalpel that had fallen on the floor. "Have to stop . . . your voice."

Her heart was racing. She backed up.

"If you can't talk, you can't control me."

"S-sto—"

He grabbed for her. Cassie screamed when his fire licked

across her arm. His touch was scorching, burning her right to the bone. And his weapon was coming up to her throat.

Fire was all she could see. Fire and death, coming for her.

"Cas . . . sandra . . ."

That deep, dark voice rose over the flames.

"My Cassandra . . ."

Dante had risen, and Jon had been so busy with her that he hadn't even noticed the phoenix—a pureblood phoenix—stalking him.

Jon stiffened at Dante's voice and he froze with that scalpel inches from her throat.

Cassie smiled at him.

She'd kept him distracted, been willing to suffer, so Dante could rise.

As she'd told her lover, it wasn't always about killing. Sometimes, it was about sacrificing in order to protect the one you loved.

Dante spun Jon to face him.

"How do you remember her?" Jon shouted. "You should have nothing! Know nothing."

"I know her."

"How?"

"Because he loves me," Cassie whispered, certain. It wasn't just about lust and mating. It was about a phoenix who had shed healing tears for the woman he loved.

"No!" Jon yelled. "He can't love! He can't! He burns, he kills, he—"

"I do kill," Dante agreed. The flames crackled around him "You will not hurt her ever again."

"I will!" Jon swore right back. "You think you get to keep Cassie? I was the one who asked her for marriage! I was the one who stayed in that facility for her, I was the one—"

"I was the one who couldn't live without her. And I was the one who went back to hell, again and again, for her." Dante put his hands on Jon's chest. "It's time for your visit now."

Fire wasn't supposed to hurt another phoenix. But, Jon wasn't really another phoenix.

Not completely. The serum he'd had must have been far too unstable when combined with his own already altered DNA.

"I'll show you fire!" Jon snapped back as he pulled away from Dante. "I'll show everyone!" He raised his hands. Fire leaped from his fingertips.

Seemed to burn from *within* him.

Dante caught Cassie's hand. "Go outside. Wait for me."

She shook her head. "I'm not leaving you!"

"The fire only makes me stronger." He pressed his lips to hers even as she felt the heat build. "Get the others out. Go!"

She stumbled away from him. Jon was sending fire everywhere, and he seemed to be consumed by the very flames that he made.

Cassie could hear voices crying out. Terrified screams. She cast one last look at Dante. "You'd better find me," she whispered then turned and ran for the others.

The flames seemed to chase her as she ran.

"You won't have Cassie! You won't!" Jon was snarling.

Cassandra was gone.

Dante couldn't remember everything, but he knew . . . the man was a threat that had to be stopped. A phoenix, but one who burned too hot and too bright.

A phoenix could only die when he rose.

Yet the man was burning himself from the inside out.

Jon grabbed him. "I *won't* let you go to her!" He shook his head and said, "Her voice, she tempts me, always tempts . . . calls to me. Shaw said . . . Cassie had to be mine. That she could never get away."

"Cassie isn't yours."

The flames rolled across the ceiling.

Jon's head kept frantically shaking. "I won't let her belong to you!"

"And I won't let you live."

Growling, Jon lunged at him.

Dante lifted the gun that he'd found lying so conveniently near his body when he'd risen. He'd deliberately kept his flames low because he hadn't wanted to melt the weapon. Not when he had plans for it.

For Jon.

He fired at the man, a shot that took him down.

The flames kept burning.

Dante didn't leave, even as the ceiling began to groan. The walls to collapse.

He didn't leave.

There was a job to do.

The only way to truly kill a phoenix . . .

The fire was raging out of control. Alarms were shrieking. Smoke thickening the air.

Another part of the ceiling gave way and slammed into the floor.

Dante still didn't leave. He couldn't.

Not until Jon came back.

The only way to truly kill a phoenix . . . is when he rises.

Flames consumed the building. Cassie stood back, watching the fire as it raged higher. Glass exploded as the windows blew out, and the roof sunk in.

Dante hadn't come out yet.

The fire won't hurt him.

She just . . . needed to see him.

"Cassie!"

Her head jerked to the left. Cain and Eve were running toward her. It figured that a phoenix had been able to sniff out the flames.

"Where's Dante?" Cain demanded.

She glanced toward the flames.

Cain swore and ran for the fire.

She wanted to run with him.

Eve caught Cassie's hand. "What happened?"

So much. A revenge-crazed siren who'd wanted death for them all. A phoenix gone mad. A healed vampire. "Dante is making sure that we aren't hunted."

Another section of the roof fell away. Cassie saw the sparks fly high into the air.

Please, Dante, come back to me.

A growl sounded behind her.

The guards had run—fled as quickly as they could. Charles, Jamie, Vaughn, and Keith had gotten away. She'd sent them back to Keith's house. But someone else was there.

Someone, something.

Another growl.

Trace.

"He hasn't attacked anyone," Eve said quickly. "He caught up with us outside of Belle, and I've been keeping him near me. But I think . . . his beast is close."

Cassie could see it. He still hadn't returned to a normal size—normal for him, anyway, and Trace's claws were out even as his eye blazed with the hunger of the beast.

She slipped away from Eve and headed toward him.

Another growl came from him.

"Maybe it's not about a cure," Cassie whispered. Not this time. Maybe it was all about soothing the beast. She pulled in another deep breath. *"Trace, control the beast."* The more she used her power, the more she focused, the easier it seemed to be for her.

His eyes flickered, shifting from that glow to a man's stare. Once. Twice.

Then the beast was back.

"Trace, control him." She pushed harder with the power that had been locked inside her for too long.

"Uh, yeah," Eve muttered, sounding nervous. "I think it might be harder than—"

The glow faded from his eyes. His claws . . . retracted. His thick muscles didn't vanish, but he sucked in a deep breath and said, "Cassie."

She felt the ripple of shock slide over Eve.

"Yes, Trace." Yes! "And it's okay. Everything is going to be—"

A loud boom shook the night. Cassie's gaze flew back to the building.

There was nothing there. Just fire.

"Cain!" Eve screamed and she ran for the flames.

Cassie raced right behind her.

She saw them. Cain. Dante. Striding right through the twisting fire. Coming out of the flames.

Eve rushed forward and grabbed tight to Cain. "You said you would *never* scare me like that again!"

He didn't answer. His mouth just crashed down on hers.

Cassie stumbled toward Dante. "Dante!"

Wait. He knew her, right? He'd said her name inside and—

Hell, just to be sure, she was going to use her siren card from now on. *"Remember me."*

He grabbed her, pulled her close. Held her in a grip of molten steel that didn't burn at all. "I already do. Always will." His mouth took hers. Hot. Hard. Consuming.

Her phoenix.

She held onto him as tightly as she could. Her body was shaking. She was covered in blood and grime and ash, and she didn't care.

Her phoenix had just walked out of the fire.

And he loved her.

Dante's mouth pulled from hers. "He won't ever come after you again. Jon's gone."

She knew why Dante had stayed inside so long to face the fire. The rising. He'd waited to make sure Jon wouldn't come after them again.

"You're free."

She had a cure for the primals. Though she could use her voice to keep Trace controlled and more man than beast, he wasn't out of the woods yet. She'd keep working until he was completely back to normal again.

But she didn't want to do that work alone.

What happened to a phoenix once the fire cooled?

"I don't want to be free of you." Her confession.

"And I will *never* be free of you. You're in my heart, my Cassandra, in the soul that I'd thought burned so long ago."

He was about to make *her* cry.

Her tears would do nothing but make her look like more of a wreck. Cassie was sure she appeared pretty night-marish.

She sniffed, trying to hold the tears back. Failing. "I've loved you for so long," she confessed.

"And I've loved you—only you."

"Why didn't you say something? Why—"

He smiled at her. Her naked phoenix covered in ash smiled, and it was the sexiest thing she'd ever seen. "I don't remember you mentioning love until a few hours ago."

"I-I was scared." Scared that he wouldn't feel the same. That he'd . . . pity her.

"I'm a monster. I'll always be." His voice roughened. "I didn't think you could ever truly—"

She pushed up onto her toes and kissed him again. "You're no monster. You're the man I love." The man she'd gladly spend an eternity with.

Sirens wailed in the distance. Firefighters, probably. Even

the humans out there wouldn't be able to overlook this blaze.

It was time to leave. Explanations about a vengeful siren and a phoenix gone mad wouldn't exactly go over well.

They'd slip away. Vanish. Rumors would cover the blaze. Rumors covered everything in that city.

She caught Dante's hand and pulled him toward the SUVs that were waiting. Vaughn had flashed some fang to make sure they had two rides waiting for them. The humans hadn't been in the mood to fight him.

Dante was strong and solid beside her. Trace wasn't killing anyone.

And the flames were dying away.

It was time for a fresh start. With no one hunting them. No one looking to destroy a phoenix, a vampire, a werewolf, or even a siren.

They could start fresh.

And they could just *live.*

A life with love . . . and plenty of fire.

EPILOGUE

"Dad!" The bellow echoed through the house.

Cassie glanced up, her mind still on the sample beneath her microscope. Jamie came barreling into her lab.

Not a scared, shaken fourteen-year-old any longer. Her "son" was bigger, tougher, and at sixteen, he thought he was ready to take on the world.

"Where's Dad?" Jamie asked. It had been a full year before he started to call Dante *Dad*. The first time he'd done it, Cassie wasn't sure who'd been more shocked.

Probably Dante.

But he and Jamie had grown close, so close. The wall that Dante had used to keep everyone out was gone. Burned away. Heck, he even went out with Cain every now and then to, uh, literally light up the town.

"He said I could get my driver's license today." Jamie's smile was huge. "He and Uncle Vaughn are supposed to take me."

She used to be afraid of power-mad phoenixes. Now she trembled at the idea of Jamie behind the wheel. "Well . . ."

"Let's go!" Dante said, coming into the room. A wide grin lifted his lips. "Vaughn's got the ride ready."

Jamie whooped and rushed back up the stairs.

So carefree and happy . . . but that, too, hadn't been easy. They'd all had to struggle to get where they were.

But we're happy. And no one will take that from us.

Dante didn't follow Jamie up the stairs. Her phoenix filled the doorway, and his gaze focused on her.

There was love in his eyes. Always now, love.

Maybe it had always been there, just buried beneath the fire.

"You okay?" he asked her.

She gave him a little nod.

He crossed the threshold and went to her. Pressed a kiss to her lips, and then his hand went to the curve of her stomach—and to the little life that was growing there. "And how's my princess?"

His whole face softened as he felt the kick against his hand. A very powerful kick. A princess ninja?

He looked back up at Cassie. "I'll protect her. I swear I'll keep her safe."

Her hand covered his. "I know you will."

"I . . . love her already. Because she's part of you." His lips brushed hers.

Damn the phoenix. He kept making her want to tear up.

"Do you think . . . she'll be more like me?" Dante whispered against her lips.

A girl who could toss fire when she was angry.

"Or more like you?" Another kiss.

A girl who could control all those near her with just a whisper.

"I—"

"Dad!" Jamie's bellow.

"See you tonight," Dante told her, giving her the smile that always made her heart race a little faster.

Then he was gone. Rushing up the stairs.

Her hand stayed over her stomach. She already knew just what her little girl would be like. She'd tell Dante soon enough.

Daddy's little princess was going to be . . .

Fire—a phoenix.
Control—a siren.
A deadly combination.
The world wouldn't know what hit it.

Keep reading for excerpts
from the first two books in
The Phoenix Fire Series

BURN FOR ME

and

ONCE BITTEN, TWICE BURNED

Available now.

from **BURN FOR ME**

The first time Eve Bradley saw Subject Thirteen, he was in chains.

She froze in front of the glass wall that separated her from him—a wall that, to Subject Thirteen, would look just like a mirror. The two-way mirror let the doctors and observers watch his every move. Not that the guy could do much moving when he was chained to the wall.

"I-I thought . . ." Eve tried to fight the tremble in her voice. She was supposed to look like she belonged here. Like she fit in with all the other researchers who were so eager to experiment on the test subjects. "I thought everyone was here voluntarily."

Dr. Richard Wyatt turned to face her, his white lab coat brushing against her. "The chains are for his safety." His tone implied she should have realized that obvious fact.

Yeah, right.

Was she really supposed to buy that line? Being chained up—that equaled safety in what mixed-up world?

"Dr. Bradley . . ." Wyatt's dark eyebrows lifted as he studied her with an assessing gaze. "You do realize that all the subjects here are far, far from human, correct?"

She knew the spiel. "Yes, of course I do. They're supernaturals. Here to take part in experiments that will help the U.S. military." So all the fancy guys in suits had told the media when the Genesis group started their recruitment program last fall.

Not that she believed their story. It had taken her months, *months,* to set up this cover and get inside the research facility.

If she'd been on her own, she never would have passed clearance. But, luckily, Eve had managed to make a few powerful friends over the years.

Friends who wanted to know the truth about this place as much as she did. They all had an interest in Genesis.

Some reporters really could smell a story. Right now, Eve's nose was twitching.

She glanced back at Subject Thirteen. Everyone knew paranormals were out there, living in the midst of humans. About ten years ago, the first supernaturals had made themselves known. They'd come out of their paranormal closets. And why not? Why should they have been forced to keep hiding? Always hiding in the shadows had to suck. Maybe they'd just gotten tired of living a lie and decided to force the humans to see what was right in front of them—or what was living right beside them.

Since the big revelation, things had changed for the paranormals. Some were hunted. Some turned into instant celebrities. The reaction from the humans, well, that was mixed, too.

Some humans hated the supernaturals. Some feared them. Some really enjoyed fucking them.

Eve didn't necessarily fall into any of those categories.

Subject Thirteen was staring right at her. A small shiver slid over Eve's body.

His eyes were dark. They looked almost black—as black as the thick hair that hung a little too long as it brushed over his broad shoulders. Thirteen was a handsome man, strong, muscled—*definitely muscled*—and with the sculpted bone structure that had probably caught plenty of attention from the ladies.

High cheeks. Square jaw. Lips that were hard, a little thin, but still sexy . . . though she could have sworn that mouth held a cruel curve.

Her heartbeat began to pound faster. Thirteen's eyes were sweeping over her body. A slow, deliberate glance. "Can he—can he see through the mirror?" His gaze felt like a hot touch on her skin.

"Of course not" was Dr. Wyatt's instant response. The doc sounded annoyed with her.

Her shoulders relaxed.

Subject Thirteen smiled.

Damn. Her shoulders tensed right back up again.

Wyatt checked his notes and then told her, "Go check his vitals before we begin the procedure for today."

Right. Vitals check. Her job. Eve nodded. She'd done two years of med school before realizing the gig wasn't for her, so she could pass muster with these guys, no problem. Only part of her résumé was fake.

The good part.

Eve walked slowly toward the metal door that was the only entrance and exit to Thirteen's holding room. A guard opened the door for her. An *armed* guard—which brought up the next question. *Why did volunteers have to be guarded?*

Oh, jeez, but this place was creeping her out. *Volunteers, my ass.*

Sure, she'd seen a couple other subjects during her time at the Genesis facility. Not many, though. Her clearance wasn't high enough to get her past level one. Or it hadn't been . . . until today.

Until she'd been told that Dr. Wyatt needed her services for his latest experiment. Dr. Richard Wyatt *was* Genesis.

A former kid genius, the guy had a couple fists full of degrees, and currently was the leading expert in the field of paranormal genetics.

He was also a hard-ass who gave her the creeps when his cold green eyes locked on her. Maybe he was a fairly attractive guy, but something about him made her blood ice.

The guard waved his hand, indicating that it was clear for Eve to proceed. When she walked into Thirteen's holding room, Eve saw the slight flare of the man's nostrils. Then his head turned toward her slowly, the move almost like a snake's as he sized her up.

He didn't speak, but his powerful hands clenched.

Eve opened her small black bag. "Hello." Her voice came out too high-pitched. She drew in a steadying breath. The guy was chained. It wasn't like anything could happen to her. She needed to get a grip and do her job. "I'm just here to run a few quick checks on you." No machines were hooked up to him. No monitors. Wyatt wanted these checks done the old-fashioned way—hell if she knew why. Eve pulled out her stethoscope and stopped a foot away from Thirteen. "I-I'll need to listen to your heartbeat."

Still nothing. Okay. Eve swallowed and offered a weak smile. Obviously, she wasn't dealing with a chatty fellow.

Eve slid closer to him. Her gaze darted to the chains. They held his arms trapped at his sides. Even if he'd wanted to grab her—*don't grab me, don't!*—he couldn't move.

What if Wyatt was setting her up? The guy was chained and that had to mean he was dangerous, right? Those were some seriously thick chains. They looked like something right out of a medieval torture chamber.

"I won't hurt you."

She jumped at the sound of his voice; and what a dark, rumbling voice it was. When the big, bad wolf from that old fairy tale talked, Eve bet the beast had sounded just like Subject Thirteen.

She exhaled and hoped she didn't look rattled. "I didn't think you would."

His lips twisted in the faintest of smiles—one that called her a liar.

Eve put the stethoscope over his heart. She adjusted the equipment, listened, and glanced up at him in surprise. "Is your heartbeat always this fast?" Grabbing his chart, she scanned through the notes. Fast, but not *this* fast. His heart was galloping like a racehorse.

Eve put her hand against his forehead and hissed out a breath. The guy was hot. Not warm, not feverish, *hot*.

And she was so close to him that her breasts brushed his arm.

Subject Thirteen's heartbeat grew even faster.

Oh . . . just . . . *oh*. Hell. She hurried backward a bit.

"I need to draw a sample of your blood." She also wanted to take his temperature because the guy had to be scorching. Just what was he? Not a vampire, those guys could never heat up this much. A shifter? Maybe. She'd seen one of those subjects on her first day. But the shifter had been in a cozy dorm-type room.

He hadn't been shackled.

Eve put up the stethoscope and reached for a needle. She eased closer to Thirteen once more and rose onto her toes. The guy was big, at least six three, maybe six four, so she couldn't quite reach his ear as she whispered, "Are you here willingly?"

Eve began to draw his blood. Thirteen didn't even flinch as the needle slid into his arm.

But he did give a small, negative shake of his head.

Shit. She eased back down and tried to figure out just how she could help him.

"I'm Eve." She licked her lips. His gaze followed the movement. The darkness in his stare seemed to heat. Everything about the guy was hot. "I-I can help you."

He laughed then, and the sound chilled her. "No," he said in that deep rumble of a voice, "you can't."

Eve realized she was standing between his legs. His unsecured legs. His thighs brushed against hers, and she flinched.

The smile on his face was as cold as his laughter. She'd been correct when she thought she saw a cruel edge to his lips. She could see that hardness right then. "You should be afraid," he told her.

Yes, she was definitely getting that clue.

Eve pulled out the needle. Swabbed some alcohol over a wound she couldn't even see. Then she stepped back, as quickly as she could.

"Don't come back in here," he told her, eyes narrowing. A warning.

Or a threat?

Eve turned away.

"You smell like fucking candy . . ."

She stilled. Now her heartbeat was the one racing too fast.

"You make me . . ." His voice dropped, but she caught the ragged growl of "hungry."

from ONCE BITTEN, TWICE BURNED

His mouth was desert dry. His fangs fully extended and aching. He could already taste her.

I just want her.

His tongue swept over her neck. Sampled, then he sank his teeth into her throat.

The woman—Sabine—gasped against him. Her body arched into his as the first tender drops of her blood spilled onto his tongue.

"Make sure the recording is operational." Wyatt's voice seemed to come from far away. "I want to get every bit of this."

But Wyatt and what he wanted didn't matter. Sabine's blood was on Ryder's tongue, and her blood was like nothing he'd ever tasted in all of his years of existence. Not just warm—the blood was hot. Spicy. Rich with flavor. He wanted to lap it up, to savor it.

To gorge on it.

His hands hardened on her. He'd meant to take just a few drops.

He wanted to lift his head away. Wanted to so badly, but *her blood was too good.*

He drank more, greedy now. Desperate. Her blood flowed through him, heating his body from the inside out and sending tendrils of power pulsing through him. Some humans tasted of wine. Some of the euphoria that came from drugs.

No one had ever tasted like her. Life. Sex. Pleasure. Everything he wanted was right there, in her blood.

He drank deeper.

"S-stop." Her voice was weaker than before.

He didn't want to stop. He'd looked for this—he'd always wanted this taste. Craved it, when he hadn't even known what he was missing. His body seemed to be growing stronger, the muscles tensing, with every drop of her blood that he took.

She sagged against him, and Ryder scooped her into his arms, holding her even when her head fell to the side and her breath rattled in her chest.

More.

More.

At first, he thought the urging was just inside of himself, but then he realized that bastard Wyatt was the one urging him on.

And the woman . . . Sabine wasn't fighting him any longer. She barely seemed to be breathing.

He jerked his head away. Stared down at her in disbelief. He hadn't taken that much, had he?

But he couldn't remember how long he'd been drinking. He only knew—

I still want more.

He lifted her higher against his chest. Held her cradled in his arms. There was no more weakness for him. Only strength. But she . . .

Her lashes were closed.

A fear unlike any he'd known before had his whole body tensing. He'd just found her. Ryder knew he couldn't lose her this soon. *Not. Now.*

And sure as hell not by his own hand. Or teeth.

He brought his wrist to his mouth. Slashed open the

flesh. He knew what she needed. "Drink for me." She'd be all right once she drank his blood.

"No!" Wyatt's voice thundered out. "Stop! Put Sabine down and back away."

"Fuck off." He lowered them both to the floor so he could better tend to her. But he kept her close as he put his wrist to her mouth. "Drink." She'd just need a little of his blood, and she'd heal.

If she'd just drink . . .

An alarm began to sound. Voices shouted over the intercom. Then footsteps rushed outside of his door. The guards were finally coming in to face him.

Now was the perfect time to kill them. But if he moved away from Sabine, she'd die. She needed more of his blood. She needed him to survive.

His eyes narrowed on her face. *What are you?* She'd been afraid, but she'd still fought him. She'd stared at a monster and asked to go home.

Now she was almost at death's broken door.

"Get away from her!" Wyatt was shrieking now.

She wasn't drinking. He pried open her mouth. Forced drops of blood onto her tongue and then massaged her neck, trying to make Sabine swallow. *Live.*

The guards grabbed him, trying to yank him away from her. *Hell, no.* He threw them back. Heard thuds when they hit the walls.

"You have to swallow the blood," he told her, voice dark and rumbling with command. "Come on!" *I didn't mean to do this.* She'd been so afraid. He'd told her that he'd hold on to his control.

But the beast that he was hadn't been able to hold on. The beast . . . Ryder . . . he destroyed. That was his life. All he knew. And he'd destroyed her, too.

His vision seemed to blacken. She was the only thing he could see in that growing darkness. Beautiful, so still.

His head sagged over her. *"Please."* Now he was the one to beg. He'd tasted heaven, and he'd tossed her to hell, all in one instant of time.

"Get away from her!" Wyatt's voice wasn't on the loudspeaker any longer. It was right there. In the room with him.

Kill him.

Ryder's head jerked up. He bared his fangs.

And . . . and felt her mouth move lightly against his wrist. She was trying to drink, to take his blood.

Sabine was fighting to live. *Yes.*

His gaze snapped back to her. "That's it! Come on, just drink some—"

Gunshots blasted. Bullets drove into his chest. One. Two. Three. The force of the hits had him falling back even as his blood sprayed the wall behind him.

"I *told* you," Wyatt raged as he lifted his weapon. *Wyatt had fired?* "Back away from the female subject!"

Ryder ignored the pain and reached for her again.

"Stop him," Wyatt ordered. Ryder realized the guards were back on their feet. "Shoot him until he stops moving. The bullets won't kill him, but they can put him down for a time."

Then the bullets exploded, popping like firecrackers over and over again as they sank into Ryder's body. His chest. His arms.

He hit the floor. Blood seeped from his wounds. Pooled around him on the stone floor.

"Enough!" Wyatt lifted his hand. His eyes went from Ryder to Sabine.

Her head had turned and her eyes—wide open, still alive—were on Ryder. He could see the life in her gaze. She was trying to come back to him. *Trying.* She just needed more of his blood.

Her hand had lifted. Was she reaching for him? Ryder

gathered every single ounce of strength that he had. "My . . . blood . . ." Only a little more, and she'd be fine. He could save her. Her death—unlike all the others—wouldn't be on him. He started crawling to her through the blood.

"She's gonna live," one of the guards muttered. "I thought he was supposed to kill her."

He could be more than a killer. She could be more than a victim. Blood soaked his clothes. The power he'd gotten from her rich blood was gone, stolen away by a hail of bullets.

"He did kill her." Wyatt's voice was flat. "We just have to wait for her to die."

No! "Can . . . help . . ." He was almost to her side.

"Chain him," Wyatt ordered. "He's too weak to fight you. Chain the vampire and let him watch."

Their arms grabbed him. Jerked him away from her. But he wasn't as weak as they thought, not even with the bullets lodged in his organs. Ryder fought them, clawing and snapping with his fangs. Half a dozen guards had to jump on him and yank him back to the far wall. Then they locked thick chains around his wrists, trapping him. The guards hurried back as soon as those locks snapped in place. They were bloody now, too—from the wounds he'd given them.

When they moved away, he saw her again. Her chest was struggling to rise. Her eyes were still open.

"Don't . . . do this," he growled as he strained to break free.

Wyatt walked around her, staring down at Sabine as she sprawled on the floor. "Why do you even care? Shouldn't she just be food to you?"

Ryder didn't speak. He wouldn't tell this bastard anything about himself.

"I think one of the bullets must have ripped into your

heart"—Wyatt didn't sound particularly concerned—"you're bleeding far too much. Hmmm . . . I should have considered . . . will that wound to the heart kill you?"

No. It wouldn't. He was healing already.

"I didn't intend for them to shoot you in the heart." Wyatt frowned at the guards. "Errors like that cannot be tolerated here."

The guy was psychotic.

A bullet to the heart wasn't normally an error. It was murder.

"You're just . . . gonna watch . . . her die?" Ryder yanked at the chains and didn't care when they cut into his wrists. He'd heal. He always healed.

She won't.

"Yes." Wyatt nodded and offered an almost-absent smile. "Yes, yes, I am."

Her eyes were on Ryder—her eyes . . .

He saw the life leave them. Actually saw a veil of nothing sweep into her stare. *"No!"* He yanked at the chains, twisting his hands, breaking his wrists as he fought to get free. He smashed his fingers as he tried to jerk his hand through the ring that bound his wrist. He didn't feel the pain as he struggled.

Dead.

"Exit," Wyatt snapped, *"now."*

The guards started hauling ass. They were leaving her like that? Just sprawled on the floor like a broken doll?

Maybe there was still time. His right wrist shattered. *Maybe.*

"If I were you, I wouldn't move," Wyatt advised Ryder with a quick frown as he paused by the door. "This is her first change. I have no idea how powerful it will be."

Ryder didn't understand the bastard. He was moving, all right. *Won't give up. Won't—*

The door slammed shut behind Wyatt and his men. And . . . the scent of smoke teased Ryder's nose.

What the hell?

His gaze snapped back to Sabine. Her eyes were still open, only her eyes weren't dark brown any longer. The brown was changing, turning to a gold, then seeming to burn red.

Red like fire.

The scent of smoke deepened around him. Ryder pulled his broken right hand free. Now the other—

Her body began to burn.

He yelled then, roaring her name, but the fire didn't stop. It blazed hotter, higher, and swept over Sabine's slender form. The white-hot heat from the blaze rushed over his skin, almost singeing him. Sprinklers erupted with a powerful spray from overhead, and the water drenched him but did nothing to stop the blaze that consumed Sabine.

His breath rasped out. Ryder stopped fighting for his freedom. There was nothing to be done now. No one could come back from those flames.

So there was nothing for him to do in the end but watch the fire burn, to hate himself for the monster that he was, and to wish that Sabine Acadia had never had the misfortune to walk into his prison.

But then something began to move within those flames. *She* moved, and Ryder realized that Wyatt's experiments were just getting started.

Because even though she'd just died right in front of him, even though Sabine was burning, it sure looked like she was trying to rise from the fire.